D0065367

BAD
LUCK

Also by Anthony Bruno

BAD GUYS
BAD BLOOD

ANTHONY BRUNO

BAD LUCK

Delacorte
Press

Published by
Delacorte Press
Bantam Doubleday Dell Publishing Group, Inc.
666 Fifth Avenue
New York, New York 10103

Library of Congress Cataloging in Publication Data

Bruno, Anthony.
Bad luck / Anthony Bruno.
p. cm.
ISBN 0-385-29967-2
I. Title.
PS3552.R82B36 1990
813'.54—dc20 89-71343
CIP

Manufactured in the United States of America
Published simultaneously in Canada

July 1990
10 9 8 7 6 5 4 3 2 1
BVG

For Barbara

• 1 •

The steel I-beam sailed through the clear blue sky, so nice, like a bird. Sal Immordino stood there facing the yellow-beige aluminum wall of the trailer, looking straight up at the towering crane and the rust-colored I-beam on the end of its cable, pleased to see that something so big and heavy could be so graceful. He followed the long metal beam's flight high over the construction site, grinning a little as he pulled down his zipper and fished around in his underwear.

"Hey! Whattaya doing over there?"

"Leave him alone, Mike."

Aaaahhhhh . . . A dark blot spread through the sand on the ground. It made a nice sound, Sal thought, the steady stream hitting the sand. Sorta plopped when you poured it. He stared up at the sky, smelled the salt air on the breeze, and ignored the two stupid bodyguards standing over by the trailer door.

"Go use the Porta Pottie, for chrissake."

"Shut up, Mike."

"Whattaya mean, shut up? He's out in the open, peeing against the wall, for crying out loud. That's not right."

"Just shut up, Mike."

"What? You think he understands me? Lemme tell you. That guy's not right in the head. He's a friggin' dummy. He doesn't understand what you say. That's why he's standing there with his thing hanging out, doing it like nobody can see him."

"Mike, *shut up.*"

"Hey, what's he gonna do, beat me up?"

"Shut up, will ya? He's gonna hear you."

"I'm supposed to be afraid of him because he's big, because he used to be a pro boxer, a heavyweight? I don't give a shit. Look at him. He's all fat. He must weigh two sixty, two seventy. At least."

Two fifty-five, Sal thought, shaking himself off. Two fifty-five and six foot four, asshole.

"I don't get it. What the hell could Mr. Nashe want with this big jerk? I mean, look at the way he's dressed. Mr. Nashe doesn't even let the janitors at the hotel go around looking like that."

"Mike, will you just shut the fuck up?"

Yeah, shut the fuck up, Mike.

Sal zipped his pants and headed back inside, deliberately dragging his feet in the dirt. As he came up to the steps leading to the trailer door, he got a good look at this Mike character. Sal didn't like his looks. Tall, built like a light heavyweight, the type who thinks he's good-looking. Straight dark hair falling over his forehead, deep-set eyes. Probably thinks he looks like Tom Cruise or something. Suspicious eyes. A real wiseass. Sal didn't like his looks at all. He looked like a fucking cop. Prick.

As Sal lumbered by he deliberately bumped into the guy's shoulder, hard. He stared the asshole in the eye. "You my brother? You Joseph? You ain't Joseph. No . . . Where's my brother Joseph?"

The guy shook his head and stared right back at him. "In

there, genius," and he jerked his thumb at the door. Real arrogant little prick. Typical bodyguard, all balls and no brains.

Sal climbed the steps and opened the metal door. It was like a piece of cardboard in his hand. He shut the door behind him and turned the bolt, glanced at Joseph and the Golden Boy, then went back to his chair, the metal folding chair. He didn't like the other ones in here. They all had arms. He usually didn't fit into chairs that had arms.

"Sal, why don't you take one of these chairs? They're more comfortable," the Golden Boy said.

Sal looked at the floor and shook his head. He never risked getting stuck in a chair with goddamn arms when someone was watching.

"Okay. Whatever makes you happy, Sal. So where were we?"

Sal reached into the pocket of his warm-up jacket and pulled out a black rubber ball. As he started to squeeze it, he stared at Nashe, the Golden Boy, standing behind that drafting table.

Russell fucking Nashe. Mr. Cash. He better be. Jesus, please, he better be.

Sal pulled a pack of Dentyne out of his other pocket. He stopped squeezing the ball long enough to unwrap two pieces and stick them in his mouth. He looked at Nashe blankly as he rocked back and forth in his seat, chewing his gum and squeezing the rubber ball, giving the man a good show. Nashe was smiling at him, leaning over the drafting table in his two-thousand-dollar banker's suit, his knuckles on the blueprints, smiling with his eyebrows, like he was posing for the cover of *Time* magazine. Sal kept rocking back and forth. Russell fucking Nashe. Bright blue eyes—probably bright blue contacts. Wavy dark hair slicked back with that mousse crap they use now. A skinny guy but with a big head—too big for the rest of him. Chubby cheeks, like he always had something stuffed up his mouth. And those stupid buckteeth. Sal switched the ball to his other hand. Billionaire, huh? Nashe looks like a goddamn rabbit. He looks like Bugs Bunny. How can you trust a guy who looks like Bugs Bunny?

Nashe crossed his arms, rubbed his chin, shifted his smile over to Sal's older brother Joseph, who was sitting in one of the good chairs, the chairs with the arms. "Twenty-nine million . . . That's a lot of money. I can't just write you a check, just like that. What do I look like? Donald Trump?" Nashe flashed that wiseass smirk of his with the rabbit teeth sticking out.

No, not this time, you fucking jerk. Don't wanna hear the song and dance anymore. Time's up. For both of us.

Sal looked at his brother, waiting for him to say something, but Joseph just sat there, stroking his silver-gray pencil-thin mustache, glaring up at Nashe. Another fucking jerk. Joseph thought he was tough. He thought he looked like Burt Reynolds too. Maybe Burt Reynolds with a potbelly and without the wig. Maybe. Joseph thought he was being real cool now, but his red face gave him away. He was pissed as shit, ready to explode. He wasn't saying anything now because he knew he'd start screaming like some kind of cuckoo bird if he opened his mouth. Burt Reynolds, huh? How about Elmer Fudd? These two were a fucking pair. They deserved each other.

Sal turned away and looked out the window, biting his bottom lip. He scanned the muddy construction site outside—the big hole they'd dug last November, the cement trucks revving their motors and spinning their drums, the construction guys yelling at each other, telling each other what to do, the big sign down by the boardwalk with the twelve-foot redhead in a Hawaiian-print sarong: "The BIGGEST name in Atlantic City is building the BIGGEST casino hotel in the world. NASHE PARADISE. Coming Soon." Sal lowered his head so he could see the giant silver letters on top of Bugs Bunny's other casino down the other end of the boardwalk. He wanted to see if Nashe was using the same typeface for the new casino. The letters were blinding in the sun, so it was hard to tell. C'mon, Joseph, say something, for chrissake.

"Twenty-nine million, four hundred thousand," Joseph finally said, struggling to hold his temper. *"Today."*

Nashe was grinning at him. "I made my original deal with Seaview Properties, Joseph. I think it's only proper that I continue with them."

Joseph kept stroking his mustache. "We *represent* Seaview Properties. Two weeks ago you could've dealt with them. Now you're late, so you deal with us." Joseph sucked on his teeth. Must've seen that one in an old gangster movie. Cagney, maybe. What a jerk.

Nashe shook his head, still grinning. "You know, Joseph, you come here to the construction site to find me, no appointment, no warning, nothing. This isn't my office. I've got no papers with me, no files. You expect me to just give you a check right here? Is that what you think? Be real. I have to review the contract. I don't have the exact terms of the contract in my head."

Joseph straightened his tie. Now he was gonna be Rodney Dangerfield. "You don't remember the terms, huh? Well, I'll remind you. Down the other end of the boardwalk you happen to have a casino—you remember that one? Nashe Plaza? Well, under that big casino of yours, there's land. And that land under your casino was leased to you five years ago by Seaview Properties. Is it coming back to you now? The terms of that deal were that you'd put down five mil—which you did—pay two million a year for the first five years—which you also did—then in the fifth year, you'd make up the balance in a balloon payment, which you *haven't* done yet and which is now two weeks overdue. *That* was the deal. Okay, now? Anyway, you should know the terms, because you were the one who came up with this balloon-payment idea in the first place."

Sal chewed the cinnamon-flavored gum with his front teeth and squeezed the ball harder. Bugs Bunny knows all this, Joseph. He's just jerking you around, for chrissake. Stop playing around and just put it to him.

Nashe rolled up the blueprints on the table and crossed his arms with the roll in his hand, like some fucking king.

"Of course, I remember *that,* Joseph, but there are details in the contract that have to be checked."

"I don't want to hear this crap, Nashe. Just get the money up."

Nashe tapped the back of his head with the blueprints and stared at the floor for a minute. Then he started pacing.

Sal dug his fingers into the rubber ball. He could feel his heart thumping. Now what, you son of a bitch? What's the excuse gonna be now?

Nashe puckered his lips and nodded before he spoke. "Joseph, let me say from the outset that you *will* get your money. That isn't even an issue here. The issue is commitment, and that's what I don't think you and your brother understand. We are all in the business of making money—that goes without saying. But you have to recognize that there are different *styles* of making money. Some people stick their money in the bank and they're happy getting that nice little five-percent interest. It's safe, it's what they want. Other people are a little more adventurous with their investments. They're willing to accept a certain degree of risk for a better return. But when you're talking about making *big* money, you're talking about *major* projects, and for that you've got to really commit your money. And that means tying it up."

Joseph waved his hand at Nashe. "Hey, hey, I don't want to hear this shit. All I know is—"

"No, Joseph, just hear me out for a minute. Where I am standing right now will be the biggest casino in the world, *in the world.* Nothing else will even come close. Thirty-two hundred slots, one hundred seventy-five blackjack tables, fifty craps tables, fifty roulettes, twelve big sixes, fifteen baccarat tables. We're gonna have *two* showrooms. Big names playing all the time and *at the same time.* Just try to imagine this. We'll have, say, Liza in one room and Sammy in the other. They'll do walk-ons on each other's shows. People won't believe it. It'll look totally spontaneous. Can you imagine this? You're sitting there listening to

Liza singing 'New York, New York,' say, and all of a sudden Sammy walks out onstage. *That's* entertainment, my friend. *That's* what brings people in. And *that's* what the Paradise will be known for. But you can't wait till the place is built to start lining up talent like that. No, no, no, no, no. To get big talent like that you've got to line them up long in advance. And that's what we're doing right now. But that takes capital, Joseph."

Joseph straightened his tie again. "I don't give a shit about your two rooms. All I want is—"

"Hey, take a look out that window." Nashe pointed with the rolled-up blueprints. "See all those guys working out there? If I gave you your twenty-nine million today, how many of those guys would be there tomorrow? None. That's how many. And what about all the people who're waiting for jobs here? I'm talking about *thousands* of jobs, jobs that I promised the governor I'd give to Atlantic City residents first. Why? Because I'm the only casino owner in this whole town who gives a damn about this community. It's time the casinos stop taking and start giving a little. This city is a disgrace. This town is *built* on money. There shouldn't be slums here. There shouldn't be poor people here. These people should have jobs, and if I have to do it alone, I will make sure the people of Atlantic City get good jobs and are treated right so they take pride in this place."

Sal squeezed the ball in half. Gas pains were piercing his gut.

Joseph sat forward with his elbows on his knees. "I don't give a good goddamn about these jigaboos down here. I got my own charities to worry about."

Sal rocked and nodded. Yeah, that's right. Cil's place. Sal looked at Nashe, wondering what other bullshit excuses the rabbit was gonna pull out of his hat.

"Joseph, if the Paradise was the only project I had going right now, you wouldn't have to be here. You would've had your money by now. But I'm also in the middle of promoting this fight." Nashe pointed with the rolled-up blueprints to the poster taped to the wall. "Two weeks from this

Saturday. The biggest fight in the history of professional boxing, with the biggest cash purse in the history of professional boxing. Forget the Rumble in the Jungle. Forget the Thrilla in Manila. This is the ultimate, *the War Down the Shore.*"

Nashe was grinning again, pleased with himself. Joseph was glaring at him, ready to jump out of his skin. Poor Joseph didn't know what the hell to do next. Sal squeezed the rubber ball and rocked. Joseph don't get no respect. That's 'cause he doesn't demand it. You gotta *demand* it, Joseph. C'mon! We gotta get the money!

"Look, Joseph," Nashe said, waving the blueprints around, "I know you don't want to hear any of this, but I want you to understand where I'm coming from. Originally I had no intention of getting involved with this fight to the extent that I have. What the hell did I know about promoting a fight? But the opportunity came my way and I grabbed it. Why? Because there was big money to be made with this fight. But once again, to make big money you've got to *commit* big money."

Sal's gum was beginning to lose its flavor. He tuned out Nashe's bullshit, tired of hearing it, and stared at the two fighters on that poster on the wall, two heavyweights facing off, arms bulging, faces mean, skin oiled and shining. Sal didn't like the reigning champ, Dwayne "Pain" Walker. He was a street punk, the kind who'd rape your grandmother. Sal liked the challenger, Charles Epps. He was bigger and had a longer reach. Unfortunately he was also a lot slower and a lot older than Walker. Christ, Epps had fought Ali—that's how long he'd been around. Still, Sal liked Epps because he reminded Sal of himself when he was fighting. Same kind of body, same style. No footwork to speak of, but a killer right. When Sal fought he never fooled around working on the body. He went right for the head, looking for the knockout. Epps used to fight the same way, but his time had passed. They were just rolling him out now to face Walker because he used to be a big name and had held the title for about ten minutes in the late seventies. Epps wouldn't go more than four rounds, no way. Sure, Sal liked the guy, but he wouldn't put any money on him.

Joseph was raising his voice now. He sounded like Grandma. "I'm getting tired of the crap, Nashe. I want to know what the hell you're gonna do here." Joseph was begging now. Bad, very bad.

Nashe threw Joseph a patronizing smile as he moved a stool around the drafting table and sat down in front of Sal. He was through talking to the dummy—he wanted to deal directly with the ventriloquist now. "Sal, as I said, you're going to get your money. With interest, of course." Nashe toned down the snake-oil pitch, but he was still flashing the Bugs Bunny grin.

Joseph's eyebrows started twitching. "What the hell you talking to him for? Leave my brother alone. You don't talk to him. You talk to me."

Nashe nodded to Joseph but kept talking to Sal. He knew who the boss was. "Sal, I know you understand what I'm talking about. A good opportunity cannot be overlooked. So you have to steal from Peter to pay Paul. So what? You make it up to Peter later and you do right by him. As God is my witness, I genuinely wish I didn't have so much tied up with the Paradise and the fight right now, I really do. I *want* to pay you. Just ninety days. That's all it'll take. Ninety days at ten percent. Does that sound fair?"

Sal looked out the window at the cement trucks and started to shake his head, laughing to himself. Ninety days? That must be a joke, right? Mr. Mistretta gets out of prison in a couple of weeks. He doesn't want to know nothing about no ninety days. Mistretta wouldn't give you nine minutes, you fucking clown. He won't give *me* nine minutes. He wants that money waiting for him when he gets out. And if it's not there . . . Sal started rocking again. He didn't even want to think about it.

Nashe leaned closer. "Talk to me, Sal. Say something. Everything is negotiable. What don't you like? Tell me."

Sal almost spit out a bitter laugh. He didn't like much of

anything lately. He stared at the rolling drums on the concrete trucks and squeezed the black rubber ball a few times. He'd been acting boss of the Mistretta family for almost four years now, and nothing had worked out the way he'd wanted it to. He had big plans when Mr. Mistretta left him in charge just before he went to prison. It wasn't like Sal wanted to take over or anything. That wasn't his intention.

What Sal wanted to do was bring the family up-to-date a little, get more into legitimate businesses the way the other families were doing. Why reinvest gambling money back into gambling and whore money back into whores? Drugs aren't even worth the risk anymore, not with the fucking Colombians controlling all the coke and the Chinks bringing in heroin. And crack—forget about that. You gotta be crazy to deal with those fucking nuts. Mistretta doesn't like to hear it, but the smart thing to do is go legit with your profits. And that's what Sal had wanted to do. He even had the businesses he wanted to buy all picked out and everything. Three concrete plants, one on Staten Island and two here in Jersey. They could've consolidated them and had a nice little monopoly for themselves in that area. Sal had it all planned out. He even promised Joseph he'd set him up as president of the company. You clean him up a little, shave off that stupid mustache, get him some nice conservative clothes, and he could almost be one of those Knights of Columbus types, very respectable. But things just didn't work out that way.

Sal shook his head, staring at one of the concrete trucks, the drum spinning round and round, red and yellow stripes spiraling. Mistretta, that clever bastard, left him in charge, yeah, but he squirreled away most of the family's money where Sal couldn't get at it. So any major purchases Sal wanted to make had to be made with money he made himself. In the beginning Sal still thought he could pull it off—they were making good money with gambling and girls, and they were doing all right with the garbage trucks too—but then one thing after another happened. One guy needed money for this, another guy needed money for that, Mistretta's daughter wants a new house, his wife wants a condo in Florida, then his nephew wants to buy into an auto mall, then the bail money for everybody and his uncle, and the next thing you know, there's no money for what Sal wants. The three concrete plants are still up for grabs, but all he's got is about thirty mil to work with. Personally he could come up with another two himself, but what the hell's that? Nothing. Enough for one of the concrete plants maybe. But you've gotta have all three or it's no good. You won't have the control otherwise. Well, fuck it. Mistretta gets out at the end of the month and then it's his problem, thank God. Better to go back to running the crew again. Just be a captain, worry about your own guys. The concrete thing would've been nice, but it's too late now. Just get Mistretta his goddamn money and keep him happy. That's all that's important now.

Sal glanced up at Nashe who was waiting for an answer like a dog waiting for dinner. Fucking jerk. Yeah, he could smile. Joseph too. They weren't gonna be the ones to tell Mistretta that he didn't have the money yet. No, that wasn't gonna be their job. Even if he broke both of Nashe's legs right now, he'd be getting off easy by comparison. Mistretta did not like to be disappointed. Sal remembered what Mistretta did to Tommy Ricks, and a pain shot through his gut so bad he nearly doubled over.

Nashe suddenly put his hands up as if he were being robbed, except he was still grinning with those big stupid teeth of his. "Sal, I give up. Just tell me what you want. I can accommodate you. We can work something out. Just *talk* to me."

Joseph stood up, mustache twitching, eyebrows squiggling all over his forehead. "Hey, I already told you. You don't talk to my brother. He's a very sick man. He doesn't know what the hell you're talking about. *I'm* the one you talk to—"

Sal stopped rocking then, raising the hand with the rubber ball and waving his brother off. Enough! They had to have that money and they had to have it soon. Joseph wasn't gonna get it out of Nashe. It was time for Sal to speak for himself. No sense playing dumb with Nashe. Bugs Bunny knows the score.

"Listen to me, Russ," Sal started, then cleared his throat.

"Sal! Whattaya doin'?"

"Don't worry about it, Joseph." Sal pointed his finger at Nashe as he turned back to him. "Let me tell you something, Russ. When I want something I pay for it. I just pay for it. No credit cards, no leveraging, no junk bonds, no fancy mortgage arrangements. I pay *cash.* That's all there is to it. Now, five years ago you wanted something from us, the land on the boardwalk, and so we leased it to you. *You* drew up the conditions, we didn't. Now, according to those conditions, it's time to pay. So naturally we expect you to live up to your promise and pay up. That's not unreasonable, is it?"

"No, of course not, Sal. But by the same token you're not appreciating my point of view here." Nashe was on the edge of the stool, hovering over him, still grinning that stupid rabbit grin.

Sal looked at the floor and shook his head as he switched the rubber ball to his left hand and made a fist with his right. He had to make Nashe "appreciate" *his* point of view.

"You see, Sal, I can make it worth your while if you—"

Sal's fist shot up like an erupting volcano, a solid uppercut to the middle of Nashe's chest that knocked the Golden Boy off his stool and back over the drafting table. He crashed to the floor on his shoulder, the blueprints crushed underneath him. Bugs wasn't grinning now. Sal was.

"Mr. Nashe. Mr. Nashe!"

Sal glared at the voice coming from the other side of the trailer door. It was that wiseass bodyguard, Mr. Mike.

"Are you okay, Mr. Nashe? Mr. Nashe?" The asshole was pounding on that flimsy aluminum door like he was gonna break it in.

Joseph looked jumpy. "Who the hell's that?"

"One of my bodyguards," Nashe rasped, holding on to his chest.

Sal watched Nashe crawl to his knees. The Golden Boy was rubbing his chest, sitting on his heels, staring up at the poster on the wall with fear in his eyes, like he was praying to it for mercy or something. Sal looked at the poster, the challenger and the champ eyeballing each other, nose to nose, muscles rippling, legs like tree trunks. When he looked at Nashe again, the Golden Boy was nodding at the poster. His Bugs Bunny teeth were sticking out, but he wasn't smiling. Good. Maybe he was ready to get serious now.

"You know, Sal, I may have an idea for you."

Mr. Mike was still pounding on the door, going crazy out there.

Sal nodded toward the door. "Take care of your man first."

Nashe nodded. "It's okay, Mike," he called out as he got off his knees and brushed himself off. He unlocked the door and opened it. "What's the problem, Mike?"

The asshole bodyguard stood in the doorway, glaring in at Sal and Joseph. Real tough guy. "I heard a big noise, Mr. Nashe."

"It was nothing, Mike. I knocked over a stool. That's all."

Mr. Mike looked very suspicious. He was staring at the crushed blueprints on the floor. "You sure you're okay, Mr. Nashe?" He was eyeballing Sal.

Nashe clapped him on the shoulder and came up with a confident bunny smile. "You're doing a good job, Mike. Believe me, everything's okay. I'll let you know when I need you. I promise. Okay?"

Sal stared right back at the guy, right in the eye, but the asshole didn't flinch. Sal didn't like this guy at all.

Mr. Mike looked around the trailer one more time, then finally left. Nashe closed the door and locked it.

"What's his problem?" Sal asked.

"Yeah, what the hell's his problem?" Joseph chimed in.

Nashe bent over to pick up the stool, squinting a little as

he felt his chest with the other hand. "Mike? Mike's a good guy. Don't worry about him. He's new, that's all. Eager to please." Nashe set the stool down behind the drafting table and sat down. "One of your *paesans,* by the way. Tomasso's his name. Mike Tomasso."

Sal shrugged, unimpressed. He didn't need any more *paesans.* He needed the money. "So what's your idea?"

Nashe looked up at the fight poster again and flashed his nervous-rabbit grin at Sal. "I think you're gonna like this, Sal," Bugs said. "I think you're gonna *love* it."

Sal glanced at the two fighters on the poster, then tilted his head back and looked at Mr. Bunny. "Oh, yeah? Tell me what I'm gonna love."

Bugs showed more teeth. "It's gonna be a big fight. The biggest there ever was. Two weeks from this Saturday."

"So?"

"You a betting man, Sal?"

He tilted his head to the side, staring at the big rabbit with the chubby cheeks in the expensive suit, and started squeezing the black rubber ball again. "Keep talking."

• 2 •

FBI Special Agent Cuthbert Gibbons looked at his boss sitting behind his big mahogany desk, his upper body framed by the high-backed oxblood leather executive chair, one of the towers of the World Trade Center rising behind him out the window. At the edge of the desk, there was a new brass nameplate with the new title: "Assistant Director Brant Ivers." Something new—special agent in charge of the Manhattan field office is now automatically an assistant director too. Ivers looked the part. He seemed a little grayer at the temples all of a sudden, a little craggier around the eyes, the chin dimple a little deeper now. Over Ivers's head, windows in the World Trade Center sparkled against a clear blue sky. It was an inspiring sight, a portrait of a modern American lawman. Assistant Director *and* Special Agent in Charge Brant Ivers. Gibbons took a deep breath and let it out slow. Shit is still shit, no matter what you call it.

Gibbons had noticed the portable tape recorder on

Ivers's blotter when he first came in. Ivers was glancing down at it now, staring at it actually. Gibbons assumed it had something to do with why he'd been called in here.

"So, Bert," Ivers started, leaning forward and lacing his fingers on top of the desk, "is everything all set for the big event?"

Gibbons squinted at him. "What big event?"

Ivers chuckled softly. "Come on, Bert. The wedding, of course."

Gibbons looked down at the dark red Bokhara rug and scratched his scalp through his thin steel-gray hair. He hated it when people called him Bert, hated it almost as much as he hated his given name, Cuthbert. Anyone who knew him at all knew it was Gibbons, just Gibbons. But what he hated even more was being asked about his personal life. The wedding was none of Ivers's goddamn business. Asshole.

"It's coming along just dandy," he said, his upper lip curling back like a Doberman's.

"That's great. I'm glad to hear it, Bert. It's not often that we get to celebrate weddings around here. Agents are usually pretty settled by the time they get to this field office. And very often marriage isn't a viable option for a man when he reaches a certain age."

Gibbons lifted his chin to tighten up the flesh under his chin. "And what age is that?"

Ivers smiled and crinkled his eyes. "Well, face it, Bert, we're not spring chickens anymore, neither of us. And you —well, you are past retirement age."

"*Bureau* retirement age," Gibbons reminded him. "Retirement is sixty-five for the rest of the country."

"No insult intended, Bert. You're an exceptional agent. That's why we made an exception in your case and let you stay on."

Gibbons raised an eyebrow. He loved this royal *we* shit.

"Anyway," Ivers continued, "what I'm trying to say is that the Bureau wishes you and Lorraine all the best. You both deserve it."

"Thank you." Asshole.

"I'll bet Lorraine is relieved that you're working here in the office and off the streets now." Ivers pushed the small tape recorder to the middle of his desk.

"Oh, yeah." Deskwork is a real gas, Brant. I just don't know how to thank you.

"It may be a cliché, but in your case it's true. You're a very lucky man, Bert. Lorraine is a . . . an exceptional woman."

Gibbons's upper lip curled back again. "Thanks for saying so." Lorraine *used* to be exceptional. Now she's just exceptionally loony. The old Lorraine was a good woman. She was the one he wanted to marry. She had goddamn sense. But the one he's got now is fucking out of her mind, and she's driving him batty too. It's all this wedding shit. It's affected her brain. It's all she worries about—the flowers, the dress, the caterer, the church, the this, the that . . . The wedding arrangements and curtains. She's got this thing about curtains all of a sudden. Stupid-looking frilly curtains that block out all the light. There isn't a window that's safe when she's around. The worst thing, though, is that she won't even fight with him anymore. Whatever he says, she goes along with it right away. She bends over backward to make things nice for him. Too nice. He knows why, though. She's afraid he'll get cold feet and back out of the wedding. That's why she's acting so gooney. He has a good mind to call the whole thing off and show her. Yeah, call it off until the loony bird flies south and the old Lorraine comes back.

"Tell me, Bert," Ivers said. "Is Tozzi going to take part in the ceremony?"

Gibbons frowned. Ivers was getting cute now. "Tozzi? I haven't seen Tozzi since you separated us. Tozzi's been on an undercover for the past two months, and I've been chained to my desk. You know that."

"Well, I only ask because Tozzi was your old partner and he is Lorraine's cousin, isn't he? I just assumed that he'd be part of the wedding. Maybe your best man, I don't know."

Ivers was staring down at the tape recorder, running his finger along the buttons.

Gibbons crossed his arms and stared at Ivers until the man looked up at him again. "How about we drop the small talk and cut to the chase, okay?"

The SAC peered up from under his brows and grunted a cough. He didn't look so bullshit friendly now. Good.

"Have you seen Tozzi recently?" Ivers asked grimly.

"I told you. I haven't seen him in two, two and a half months. Why? Is something wrong?"

Ivers looked down at the tape recorder again. "Do you know anything about his current assignment?"

Gibbons was getting pissed. "Undercovers are classified information. I have nothing to do with that investigation, whatever it is. I'm not supposed to know anything about it." He'd heard some rumors from other agents, but not much.

"Tozzi is based in Atlantic City, using the alias Mike Tomasso. He's working as a bodyguard for Russell Nashe. Are you familiar with him?"

"The real estate tycoon? Sure. Who isn't? You see his face everywhere these days."

"We have reason to believe that Nashe is involved with the mob, specifically the Mistretta family."

What a big surprise. Gibbons crossed his legs and laced his thick fingers over his knee. "Based on what?"

"A former Mistretta family associate named Donny Scopetta, who is currently living under federal-witness protection, unexpectedly found himself in a rather tight spot. Originally, in exchange for immunity from prosecution, he had cooperated with the United States Attorney's office on several cases involving illegal dumping of toxic waste. He and his family were relocated, given new identities and so on, and apparently he thought he was home free. But then his name came up in a kidnapping-murder case that the Albany office had been working on for some time. Apparently Scopetta was the one who had driven the victim, a Mr. Barry Grunning, over the border into New

York in the trunk of a rented car. Mr. Grunning was a loan officer at a bank in Passaic who got religion one day and suddenly decided he wasn't going to do business with the loan shark he'd been bankrolling for nearly ten years. Scopetta apparently did not participate in the actual killing—he just delivered the victim."

"He's still an accessory."

"Of course. And the prosecutors up in Albany were prepared to try him, but then Scopetta's attorney offered them a deal. He said his client had more good information to offer in exchange for reduced charges. Scopetta, it turns out, had some very interesting things to say about a lot of people, one of them being Russell Nashe. Scopetta claims that Nashe had a long-standing relationship with the Mistretta family. He claims to have overheard conversations in which people high up in the family discussed dealings with Nashe. What he said about Nashe amounts to hearsay, really—essentially useless to the prosecutors. But they passed on a copy of the transcripts to our office, and I thought it was worthy of a follow-up. That's why I sent Tozzi down to Atlantic City."

Gibbons was getting impatient. "Yeah? So what's the problem?"

Ivers picked up a pencil and started tapping the tape recorder. "I'm not even sure there is a problem. It's just a suspicion right now. But a very strong suspicion."

Gibbons shifted in his seat. "So are you gonna tell me, or is this gonna be a Hitchcock movie?"

Ivers frowned. "I want you to hear something," he said. The SAC stood the small tape recorder up on one end and pressed the Play button.

Gibbons heard the hiss of interference, then a phone ringing twice. Someone picked up. *"Yeah?"*

"Hello, Mamma? This is your favorite son, Mike." Gibbons recognized Tozzi's voice. *"The ravioli wasn't very good this week. No taste at all."*

"That's too bad. Keep in touch, Mike," Tozzi's contact responded. Someone hung up, then a dial tone.

Gibbons grinned to himself, recalling Tozzi's favorite undercover call-in method. He reported on his progress as if he were critiquing Italian food. When the food wasn't good, that meant he had nothing to report. When the food was good, that meant he was on to something. When it was out of this world, he'd hit the jackpot.

Ivers unbuttoned his suit jacket and Gibbons spotted his pale yellow suspenders. Very fashionable, Brant. Gibbons brushed a speck of lint off his charcoal-gray suit pants as the dial tone ended and the tape rolled silently. He'd bought this suit in 1974, on sale. It was August. He remembered because it was one week before Nixon had resigned. It came with two pairs of pants and cost sixty-nine ninety-five. Whenever he wore it, he couldn't help thinking of Nixon waving to his staff as he got into the helicopter on the White House lawn like some banana-republic dictator making a run for it. It was a good suit.

The phone on the tape started ringing again. The gruff man's voice answered again, Tozzi's contact. *"Yeah?"*

"Yeah, Mamma, this is your boy, Mikey," Tozzi said. Even with the pay-phone static, Gibbons could detect a wiseguy edge in Tozzi's voice. Maybe someone was listening and he had to stay in character.

"Where've you been, sonny boy? You forget about your mamma? It's been almost two weeks. Pappa's been worried about you." The contact made no attempt to hide his annoyance. Gibbons looked up at Ivers. Pappa.

"The ravioli, Mamma. It still stinks."

"That's all?"

"What do you want from me? I'll let you know if it gets better."

"Be sure you do."

"Don't worry about it."

They hung up.

Ivers picked up the recorder and fast-forwarded the tape. "The next call-in is essentially the same." Ivers hit the Play button and set the recorder back down on the desk.

Two rings. *"Yeah?"*

"Mamma, Mamma, this is your Mikey-boy."

"Where the hell have you—?"

"Listen. The ravioli is getting better. Very tasty, but so far I've only gotten a taste, if you know what I mean."

"Explain."

Tozzi lowered his voice. *"Our friend had a meeting this morning with a couple of meatballs . . . two brothers."*

"Who?"

"Sal and Joseph Immordino."

"What was discussed?"

"I dunno. Nashe made me wait outside."

"Any guesses?"

"Not yet, Mamma."

Gibbons didn't like the tone of Tozzi's voice, and from the sound of it, neither did his contact. It was *too* smartass.

"I want to hear from you by the weekend, sonny-boy. Pappa is very concerned about you."

"Yeah, yeah, yeah."

"That's a direct order from Pap—"

Tozzi hung up on him.

Ivers shut off the recorder and leaned back in his chair. "That was two weeks ago. He called in twice more since then with nothing new to report." Ivers rebuttoned his jacket. "Same attitude."

"So what's your suspicion?"

Ivers raised his eyebrows and shrugged. "It's not unheard of for a man undercover to forget who he is and choose to become his alias."

Gibbons shook his head. "Not Tozzi."

"Russell Nashe's world is very seductive. Money, fancy cars, available women, high-stakes gambling. Everything is always the best with Nashe. It's a tempting life-style. Hard to resist when you're right in the middle of it, I imagine." Ivers was doing more than just speculating.

"Tozzi gets into that glitzy, wiseguy crap. It's in his guinea blood. But he'd never turn. I know him. He was my partner."

"People change."

"Some do." Gibbons considered the possibility. Tozzi did have an overactive imagination, and the last time Gibbons talked to him he hadn't been very happy with life. The usual I-ain't-got-no-woman blues. It's possible that the excitement of living as someone else had gotten to Tozzi, but with Tozzi *anything* was possible. Tozzi's crazy. Still, Gibbons wasn't going to say anything to Ivers. "What about the Immordino brothers?" he asked, to change the subject. "What do we have on them?"

Ivers swiveled around in his chair and picked up a file lying next to his computer. He opened the folder on his desk and referred to it as he spoke. "Salvatore 'Clyde' Immordino, age forty-two, a *capo* in the Mistretta crime family, alleged acting boss of the family in Sabatini Mistretta's absence. Mistretta is currently serving time at Lewisburg for tax evasion."

Gibbons covered his mouth with his finger and nodded, imagining that big lummox Immordino. He remembered Sal from his boxing days in the early seventies. It was around the time he'd bought the suit, come to think of it. Hard puncher but no style at all, no moves. People went to his fights just to see him, though. He was a big guy—not just tall, BIG. A freaking monster. He'd gotten the nickname Clyde from a sportswriter with the *Daily News* who compared him to a Clydesdale. The writer was being kind.

Ivers put on his half glasses and scanned the file. "In 1985 Immordino was tried with three other Mistretta family members on a variety of racketeering and murder charges, but his lawyer pleaded mental incompetence and got him separated from the trial. Their claim was that Immordino had suffered permanent brain damage in his boxing career and that he was incapable of knowingly committing any crime. The defense produced a very convincing witness"—Ivers had his finger on the page—"a Dr. Stephen Goode who was treating Immordino at Our Lady of Mercy Hospital in Reading, Pennsylvania. The doctor made it all very clinical and referred to Immordino's condition as 'Pugilistic Brain syndrome.' He compared Immordino's symptoms to Muhammad Ali's, which apparently gained a lot of sympathy for the defense. The doctor had a very smooth bedside manner on the witness stand, and the jury bought his testimony. To this day Immordino reinforces that diagnosis by appearing to be a harmless, punch-drunk ex-palooka, though we have no doubts that this is an act. From time to time he reinforces this charade by doing things like walking around town without his shoes, talking to his hands, singing at the top of his lungs, crying . . . that sort of thing.

"His older brother Joseph, age forty-seven, is his constant companion. Joseph Immordino apparently acts as his brother's mouthpiece in most instances. Before 1985 Joseph Immordino had no known history with the Mistretta family and to this date has no criminal record. Prior to 1985 he was the sole proprietor of Immordino's Quality Meats, a butcher shop in Sea Girt, New Jersey."

Gibbons nodded. He knew about Joseph Immordino too. A momo, a hanger-on. A prop in Sal's act.

"Under Sal's leadership the Mistretta family has been unusually quiet. Some sources say that his palooka act is a hindrance. People supposedly don't like dealing with him through Joseph. According to other sources, though, that isn't the problem at all, since those people he does deal with know that there's nothing wrong with him mentally, and that Joseph is only there for show. Most sources do agree that although Sabatini Mistretta gave Immordino the position of acting boss, he put him on a very short leash." Ivers looked over his glasses. "We know from past investigations that Mistretta does not like to delegate power."

Gibbons snorted a laugh. "That's putting it nicely. Didn't he break his wife's arm once because she signed his name to a check to pay an overdue water bill when he was out of town?"

Ivers peered over his glasses again. "I never heard about that. You mean he wouldn't let his wife have her own checking account?"

"Are you kidding? This guy's from the old country. She's lucky he let her in the house."

Ivers shook his head and closed the folder. "Well, be that as it may, whatever Sal Immordino and Russell Nashe discussed in their meeting, we can probably assume it was old business. Immordino doesn't seem to be empowered to make any initiatives for the family."

Gibbons shrugged. "Who knows? Immordino's no slouch. When he was running his own crew, before Mistretta was put away, it seemed like he was running everything over in Jersey City. I wouldn't rule out anything with him. You want me to do some checking on his recent interests?" Please. Anything to get out of this office and back on the street. A few all-night plants would be so nice, give me a break from Lorraine and her curtain catalogs and her goddamn back issues of *Bride* magazine. Come on. Be a guy.

"No."

Shit. Asshole.

"Bert, I want you to go down to Atlantic City and check up on Tozzi. Get as close as you can without compromising his cover and find out if he's okay."

"Right." I take it back. You're not an asshole. Not this time. "Anything else?"

"Just get yourself there and in place by noon on Monday. If Tozzi has flipped, I want to know as soon as possible."

Gibbons was already up, backing toward the door. "Anything else?" Come on, come on, let's go.

"Yes." Ivers took off his glasses and set them down. "One more thing."

Now what?

"I want you to give my best to Lorraine."

"Yeah, sure. I will." Gibbons reached for the doorknob, waiting for him to say something else, but instead Ivers swiveled to his computer and punched something up.

Gibbons paused and stared at him. What does he mean,

give his best to Lorraine? That's my job. Who the hell wants *your* goddamn best? Asshole.

Gibbons kept staring at Ivers as he opened the door and left.

3

". . . And this will be, without a doubt, the biggest fight in the history of professional boxing. The biggest purse, the biggest crowd, the biggest worldwide television audience . . ."

Tozzi was bored. He pushed the sunglasses up his nose and stifled a yawn as he watched Russell Nashe's back. Nashe was at the mike, blowing his own horn again. So what else was new?

He snuck a glance at his watch. He'd been standing there behind the rostrum for the past half hour, a row of backs sitting at the long tables on each side, facing a restless mob of reporters and cameramen, lights shining in his face, trying his absolute best to tune Nashe out. Thank God for the back of Sydney Nashe's head. It was much more interesting. Tozzi wondered how she got her hair that way, a long pageboy that just touched her shoulders and rested so nicely on her collarbone, not a hair out of place. And that white-blond color—it was hard not to stare at her. He could make out the contours of her back through the sheer lavender silk blouse, the delicate bones, the slight, little twisting movements she made with her body as she sat there. He could picture her small turned-up breasts. Irish-nose tits. Tozzi suppressed a grin. She didn't like it when he'd called them that. He stuck his hand in his pants pocket, fingered the foil condom pack, and sighed. Unbelievable.

Tozzi still couldn't get over the fact that a woman like Sydney had actually pursued a guy like him. For him, Sydney was like a hot little sports car, a lipstick-red convertible—the kind of car you look at and imagine yourself driving, even though you know it's totally impractical, too rich for your blood, out of the question for a guy like you. But then you look inside at the genuine leather upholstery and you see a note with your name on it taped to the woodgrain steering wheel that says, "Come on. Take a spin. I *want* you to." Very hard to resist. How often does the average guy get a ride like this? Unbelievable. Tozzi ran his finger round and round over the foil-wrapped condom in his pocket, staring at her hair, getting off on the whole incredible situation.

"Hey, Tomasso! Stop checking out the boss's wife. That's not what you're paid for."

Tozzi looked straight ahead. He knew the voice all too well—friggin' Lenny. "I gotta look at her to protect her," he said in a loud whisper.

Just then Sydney looked over her shoulder, smoothed the pageboy away from her profile, and stared at him for a long second. Green eyes, green like Sucrets. Plum-colored nails on that white-blond hair. She lowered her lashes then and turned back.

Oh, man . . .

"See? Now you're in trouble." Lenny Mokowski, the head bodyguard, had Tozzi by the elbow now. A retired cop from The Bronx, Lenny was a tough little bastard, built like a bowling ball, with arms like Popeye. Tozzi could usually smell him coming from the hair oil he used to build up the Ronald Reagan pompadour in his two-tone gray hair. "Just do your effin' job and stay out of trouble, Tomasso," Lenny said under his breath. Lenny never used the f word. He was proud to tell you that he was a good Catholic.

Tozzi took his hand out of his pocket. "I'm doing my job."

"Don't give me any lip," Lenny spat in his ear. "Just listen to me now. This is a news conference, you understand that? So there may be a little action up here. People are gonna yell at each other, start making threats. The fighters may even try to take a poke at each other maybe. But that's all for the cameras, you understand? So don't overreact. This is all part of this fight thing here. It's just publicity. It's just a big act." Lenny pointed with his pompadour at the champ, Dwayne "Pain" Walker, who was sitting on one side of the podium, and the challenger, Charles Epps, who was sitting on the other. "Don't get nervous, okay? These two guys know what they're doing."

Tozzi nodded at the champ. "Even him?"

"Yeah, yeah, even him. So don't make a move unless Mr. or Mrs. Nashe are directly threatened. You got it?"

"I got it, Lenny. Don't worry, be happy."

Lenny gave him the Popeye squint as he rolled off to Frank, the other bodyguard on duty, who was standing on the other side of the stage behind the Epps camp. As Nashe kept going on and on about himself, Tozzi studied the challenger. Charles Epps was a big, fleshy, light-skinned guy with an expensive, confident attitude that seemed to take up two seats. Sort of a black Babe Ruth. With his shaved head and his elbow resting casually on the back of the next chair, he surveyed the scene like a sultan. He was an old man—by boxing standards—thirty-nine years old, and this fight marked his third comeback. But boxers never stay retired. They keep coming back, hoping for miracles, begging for humiliation.

Couldn't blame Epps for coming back this time though. Eight and a half million balloons, guaranteed, just to get into the ring with Walker is nothing to sneeze at. Hey, so what's a little brain damage? Epps had fought all the top heavyweights back in the seventies—Ali, Holmes, Norton, Frazier, Foreman—and here he was again. Unbelievable. No one thought Epps had a prayer, but there was something about him, something about the way he sat there that made Tozzi believe the guy might still have something. Everything he did—the way he wiped his face with the palm of his big hand, the way he rotated his shiny head like a gun turret to scan the crowd, the way that sly grin stretched across his face and just kept on going—seemed deliberately slow and ominous. The man looked like a Tyrannosaurus rex waking up for a meal.

Tozzi looked over at Walker on the other side of the podium. He looked like the kind of guy you'd find locked up on Rikers Island, the kind of guy who mumbled and brooded and called everyone "motherfucker," a bad kid with a lot of attitude and empty eyes. If he had a good side, Walker made sure no one ever saw it. He was twenty-six years old with a twenty-five and oh record, all knockouts but one. A real nasty temper. He made you believe he actually despised every man he'd ever fought and that he genuinely wanted to kill the guy in the ring. The boxing commissions were constantly reprimanding him for the shit he pulled outside the ring—punching out reporters, trashing camera equipment, causing scenes in restaurants, hassling women in bars, shit like that—and the purists had made it plain a long time ago that they'd love to see someone beat the shit out of him and drive him from the ranks. The champ was good with the gloves, though. You couldn't deny that. He was tough and efficient. He could take a punch and he had a talent for finding the openings. Tozzi zeroed in on the back of Walker's head where he'd had his nickname shaved into his close-cropped scalp: PAIN.

Sitting next to Walker was his trainer, Henry Gonsalves. He was the animal trainer, there to keep Walker from going berserk. Gonsalves was an ex-pug himself, and he looked it—flat nose like a glob of Silly Putty pressed to his face, eyes slightly out of line like an iguana's, lumpy head, crouched posture, even when he was sitting. But the man had been training fighters for years, and his efforts finally paid off with Walker. Gonsalves was supposedly the only one who had any influence over the champ—some said he had a *lot* of influence over the champ—and Walker supposedly always called him "the father I never had," but Walker mumbled and spoke hard-core "ghetto," so no one was ever sure what the hell he was saying. But on top of being the champ's trainer and surrogate father, Gonsalves's other job—some say his primary job—was apologist. He was constantly making excuses for his man, and he had a rap that Tozzi must've heard at least a dozen times on TV about how Walker had been abused and confused as a child, how he'd been brought up by the state, how the media have misconstrued him, how he's basically a good kid trying to work things out for himself, yada-yada-yada . . . Every time Walker fucked up, Henry would get up in front of the cameras and deliver the rap, and most of the time people bought it. People wanted to. Walker was a son of a bitch but he made headlines, and people love to see celebrities self-destruct in public. It makes them feel superior, the way Tozzi figured. That's what made Walker big box office. If it weren't for Gonsalves, though, Walker would fade away like a phony-looking, rubber-suit monster in a low-budget horror movie. No one cares about an asshole. But Gonsalves made Walker human and that's why people stayed curious. Whatever Walker was paying his trainer, it wasn't enough.

As the reporters started yelling out questions for Nashe, Tozzi went back to staring at the back of Sydney's head. She was so fine, with that hair of hers, the kind of classy woman most guys don't even consider, because they know they wouldn't stand a chance. Tozzi grinned to himself. Nothing at all like Valerie. His grin widened. Oh, what a naughty boy.

"Mr. Nashe! Mr. Nashe! Tell us the truth." One reporter overrode the shouts of his brethren. "We aren't supposed to take this matchup seriously, are we? This is a Nashe event, a patented Nashe extravaGANza." The reporter mimicked the billionaire's ringmaster delivery. His brethren snickered behind their notepads. "You don't *really* expect us to take this matchup seriously, do you?"

Nashe started to answer, but Epps stood up and leaned into his microphone to interrupt. "*I* don't take it seriously. That joke sitting over there has never had a real fight in his entire life. He's the only one who should take this seriously, because he's gonna be in *serious condition* after he meets me."

Walker stood up in a shot. He shouted over Nashe's head. "Suck my dick, cocksucker!"

Gonsalves pulled on Walker's sleeve. "Sit down, Dwayne. Come on, sit down and be good."

Epps turned his head slowly, looked the champ in the eye with a mocking little grin on his face. He moved up right next to Nashe. Camera flashes strobed the room. Everyone wanted to get this shot: Billionaire extraordinaire Russell Nashe sandwiched between the champ and the challenger.

Epps wrapped his big hand over the mike. "Pull down your pants, son, and I'll *bite* it off. If I can find it."

Walker's face bulged and contorted in fury, like his brain was bouncing around in his head, trying to break out. He lunged, swung wild with his right, and caught the back of Nashe's head in the crook of his elbow. Nashe's forehead bashed into the mike as he was thrust forward. Tozzi jumped, rushing to grab Walker from behind before he could throw another punch. In the meantime Nashe slid down the podium and scuttled out of the fray.

"Lemme go, mothahfuckah," Walker growled at Tozzi, swinging his shoulders to get free. "Lemme go!"

Tozzi tightened his bear hug on the champ, and Walker glared at him out of the corner of his eye like a wild horse. Tozzi strained to keep his grip on those massive arms, but it was like trying to hold down Lon Chaney as the full moon came out. Walker started ramming his head back, trying to butt Tozzi in the face. Tozzi arched his head back out of the way, but Walker still caught him on the chin. The shaved scalp scraped Tozzi's skin like heavy-duty sandpaper. Tozzi made a face. Sharkskin is supposed to feel like that.

"Let the chump go," Epps bellowed. "He ain't gonna do *nothin'.*" He came around the podium and stuck his face in Walker's.

Tozzi frowned. Thanks a lot, Charles. I need this aggravation.

Walker was going crazy, hopping up and down, trying to shake Tozzi off. Tozzi didn't dare let him go now, afraid of what this mental case might do. He glanced over his shoulder. Why the hell wasn't anybody helping him? Where the hell was Frank? Where was Lenny?

"Let him go!" Lenny was suddenly yanking on his arm, trying to break his grip. "Let him go, Tomasso."

"What're you, crazy, Lenny?"

But Lenny wasn't about to discuss it. He slapped his hand over Tozzi's face, thumb under the earlobe, fingers pressed over the nose. Tozzi knew what was coming, an old police move for subduing uncooperative suspects. Shit. Before Tozzi could react Lenny dug his thumb into the pressure point where the jawbone met the ear. The pain zinged through Tozzi's molars and he was instantly nauseated. Unconsciously he loosened his grip and the werewolf broke free. Lenny grabbed Tozzi's elbow and pulled him away.

"Tomasso! What the hell did I tell you? I told you not to do nothin' unless you absolutely had to. Isn't that what I said? What the eff is wrong with you?"

Tozzi was rubbing his jawbone. "What're you, blind? Walker took a swing at Mr. Nashe."

"I don't want to hear about it. I told you these guys know what they're doing." Lenny pointed with his greasy pompadour at the fighters standing toe-to-toe. They were barking at each other, but they weren't throwing punches. Gonsalves was shouldering his way in front of Walker, and

Epps's manager was trying to do the same. It definitely wasn't enough interference to keep them from slugging it out if they really wanted to. Lenny was right. This was all for the cameras.

"You know, Tomasso, you're more trouble than you're worth. I'm gonna have to have a little talk with Mr. Nashe—"

"About what, Lenny?" Russell Nashe was suddenly standing over Lenny's shoulder, grinning around his big buckteeth at Tozzi. Sydney was standing next to him, a head shorter, even in heels. She was grinning at him too.

"He messed up, Mr. Nashe. I'm sorry. I told him to stay put and let the fighters do their thing for the press, but no, he had to jump right in there. This guy's got a hard head, Mr. Nashe."

Nashe nodded, still grinning. "Hard head or not, I have to thank this man. Dwayne wasn't supposed to throw any punches—he knew that. Christ, my face would've had a big hole in it if he'd had a chance to follow up on that right with a left hook. You did the right thing, Mike. Good work."

Tozzi looked down at the tough little bowling ball who just stood there steaming, saying nothing. He was the gutter ball now.

"Of course, if he *had* hit you," Sydney said, "the story would've moved out of the sports section and onto the front page. That's the kind of publicity money can't buy. Too bad."

Nashe stopped grinning for a moment. "You've got a point. A punch in the nose could've increased the pay-per-view subscriptions by at least ten percent. Jesus, Mike, you just lost me a couple of mil." Nashe stared at him as if he were serious. Then the stupid grin came back. "Just kidding, Mike, just kidding."

"I'll bet." Sydney rolled her eyes and laughed that high-pitched titter of hers. There was just a hint of sarcasm in her laugh, just enough to let her husband know that she might've enjoyed seeing "Pain" Walker knock his famous front teeth down his throat.

The confrontation at the podium was degenerating into jeers and catcalls from the supporting players. Walker and Epps had been separated, and now they were just glaring at each other as their managers leaned into the microphones set up on their respective tables and shouted at each other. Each time Epps's manager made a typically outlandish claim concerning his man's physical superiority and divine calling, Walker's manager overrode him with the champ's signature line: "When 'Pain' Walker talk, people better be list'nin'."

When Tozzi turned back, Sydney was whispering something into her husband's ear.

"Okay," Nashe said, "no problem. Lenny and Frank can take care of things here. Mike, you go with my wife. She's got an appointment upstairs with some new decorator or something."

Tozzi nodded. Sydney was grinning at him like a cat. He suddenly became very aware of the condom in his pants pocket, sort of radiating in there like uranium.

She looked up at her husband. "I'll see you later?"

"I don't know. I'll give you a call." His attention was on the crowd of reporters now. They weren't asking questions. They were getting bored with the show. Nashe couldn't afford to let them get bored and lose interest.

Sydney caught Tozzi's eye and shrugged, then turned to leave. Tozzi followed her off the stage, staying just far enough behind to watch her shoulders work under that sheer silk blouse. Now and then, as they walked backstage to the long corridor that led to the lobby, Sydney would delicately draw back the curtain of her perfect blond hair ever so slightly so she could take a sly look at her bodyguard out of the corner of her eye. By the time Tozzi pushed the crash bar on the door that opened onto the plush, green-carpeted lobby, he had an incredible hard-on.

As they passed through the lobby Tozzi's eye automatically went to the bar tucked under the grand escalator.

Valerie usually worked this bar, but she wasn't on right now. Tozzi was glad. It wasn't that Valerie suspected anything—it would just make him feel awkward if she saw him walking alone with Sydney like this. Even though Sydney had the tight little bod and the perfect face and all, she was basically a lightweight, a grown-up cocktease, and her main interest seemed to be playing mind games. Valerie had substance and she didn't play games. She was real. Seeing the place where Valerie tended bar, where he liked to hang out when she was on duty, he suddenly felt a little guilty. But he still had a hard-on.

Sydney stepped across the green carpeting, her legs moving in a sublime calypso rhythm that only Tozzi could hear. As they passed the reservations desk the clerks nodded and greeted the boss's wife. She smiled and waved with her tapered, plum-colored nails. She walked on to the bank of elevators and stopped in front of one of the private cars, the ones that go straight to the VIP suites on the upper floors. Tozzi pressed the Up button and nodded to the doughy-looking security guard whose only job was to make sure only VIPs used the VIP elevators. The guard nodded to Tozzi, no expression on his face, his eyes hidden behind thick, dark glasses. Roy Orbison in a green uniform blazer and tie.

As they waited for the elevator Tozzi scanned the soaring lobby. It was done in gold and two shades of green. Sydney had picked the colors. They weren't the color of money, but the difference between the shades was the same as that of the two greens on a dollar bill, she said. These greens were more aesthetic, she said, but psychologically it had the same effect. It made you feel like you were swimming in money. That's what she said.

The elevator arrived and he followed her in. The interior was wood paneled with polished brass railings. Mr. Orbison, the security guard, made sure no one else got on with the boss's wife. Tozzi hit the button for the top floor where the Nashes' suite was. As the doors started to close Sydney reached over and pressed the button for the seventeenth floor. That's where Sydney kept a private suite for her own use. Tozzi suppressed a grin. Oh, pretty woman.

The elevator started to ascend. Sydney faced Tozzi and slid her hands under his jacket, scratching his back with the tops of her plum-colored nails. When she got to his shoulder blades, she pulled him down to her level and kissed him, mouth open, making little hungry noises. Tozzi linked his fingers around the small of her back. She was a lot easier to hold than "Pain" Walker. He lifted her up a bit and brought her closer to his level. She ground her lips into his with no sign of wanting to come up for air. Tozzi grinned through the kiss. She was like that one unattainable girl from everybody's high school—the one with the looks and the personality and the friends and the boyfriend away at college. And for the moment she was all his.

A moment later she disengaged reluctantly, pecking for more as they parted. Then she paused and just looked into his eyes. "So, Mr. Tomasso, what's new?"

He lowered her back down. "Nothing much." He couldn't hold back the smile as he wiped her lipstick off his mouth with his fingers. Here we go.

"Nothing?" she said.

He shrugged.

She shrugged back.

Tozzi raised his eyebrows.

She did the same.

It always started this way, the little game she liked to play with him, the Information Game, her version of Trivial Pursuit. Or better yet, What's Russell Up To? She claimed that her husband kept her in the dark about everything he was doing, but Sydney wasn't the type to be left out of anything, so apparently she'd cultivated her own little network of informers among the employees. Tozzi didn't actually know of any others—he just assumed he wasn't the only one. It wasn't clear why Nashe didn't tell her anything about his business, but Sydney certainly seemed to enjoy the intrigue of finding out for herself. Tozzi had asked her once why she bothered to spy on her husband. Did it really matter to her how he made his money? She said she did it to keep Russell on his toes—whatever that meant.

As he looked into those sly green eyes of hers, Tozzi wondered just how extensive her network of informers was. He hoped he was the only one of her operatives whose method of remuneration was goods for services. Tozzi gave her the goods on Nashe and she allowed him to service her. Not a bad deal. But his main interest in Sydney, he kept telling himself, was the tidbits he picked up at their little meetings. In the past couple weeks since he'd joined the spy trade, she'd given him some good insights into the billionaire tycoon's life-style. Nothing earth-shattering, but he had high hopes that sooner or later some hard information might slip out between the sheets.

"So there's *nothing* new?" she purred in his ear.

"Nothing much." He smoothed the material of her skirt over her ass as he decided how he should offer the bait. "Just a couple of bigshot visitors who've been hanging around lately."

"A couple. Hmmm . . . George and Barbara? Ron and Nancy maybe?"

"Not that big. Two brothers."

"Really." Her voice was bored, but her eyes were sparkling, eager to know. "You'll have to tell me all about it."

Tozzi grinned. "Maybe."

Sydney lowered her lashes and looked away, then she started to scat sing, the theme song from *The Patty Duke Show.* "Daaa, dum, da-dum, dum, dum, dum, dum, dum. Da-dum, dum, dum, to Berkeley Square . . ." Sydney always seemed to have a theme song from some old TV show on her mind. Tozzi still found it hard to believe that a classy bitch like Sydney would be so into old television shows. Maybe her husband owned them all.

She stopped singing and looked up at him again. "Well, Mike, if you want to keep secrets . . ." She pulled him down for another grinding kiss.

Jesus. He was horny as hell now. No wonder Mata Hari

was so effective. He kneaded her ass, pulling her up, wanting more. Christ, whatever you want to know, Syd. Anything you want—

The elevator pulled to an abrupt stop and Tozzi felt the rush in his gut. He glanced up at the lighted numbers over the doors and saw that they were on seventeen. The bell dinged and the doors started to open. Immediately she disengaged and put a discreet distance between them, the cool, aristocratic expression returning to her face. The doors parted and Tozzi noticed her face suddenly change again—a not-so-pleasantly-surprised face. A large, looming figure was waiting outside the elevator. Instinctively Tozzi stepped in front of her. It was Sal Immordino. What the hell was he doing up here?

Sal looked at Tozzi, then looked at Sydney. "Gotta talk to you," he said to her.

She didn't say a word, just held that look of mildly annoyed surprise, lips flat, brows raised. Sal didn't ask again. He reached past Tozzi and grabbed her wrist.

Tozzi grabbed the big man's arm. "Hold on there, Mr. Immordino."

Sal shot him an evil look, worse than "Pain" Walker's when he had the champ in a bear hug.

"Mrs. Nashe, do you want me to—?"

Immordino's open palm shot into Tozzi's Adam's apple like a piece of flying shrapnel and drove him back into the elevator until his head slammed against the paneled wall. It took a moment for the pain of the impact to register, then it started to hurt, first at the back of the head, then at the temples, blurring his vision for a few seconds.

Immordino kept his hand on Tozzi's throat, leaning on it with all his weight. Two hundred and seventy-odd pounds of wiseguy scum right on his windpipe, cutting off his air supply. Tozzi kept blinking his eyes to make them focus. He had to get this ape off him, fast. Slap the sides of his head like cymbals. Force air into his ears so hard and fast it'll burst his eardrums. Break his grip. Get him off—

"It's okay, Mike." Sydney's cool, officious voice. The

white-blond head came into Tozzi's view. She had her finger on the open button. "There's no problem. You can go now."

"But—"

"You can go now," she repeated. The boss's wife. The pretty, unattainable bitch with the boyfriend in college.

Sal dropped his hand. Sydney took him by the arm and led him out into the hallway. The bell dinged again and the doors started to close, but before they did, Sal turned and stared Tozzi in the eye.

Catching his breath, Tozzi loosened his tie and unbuttoned his collar. The elevator started to descend. He leaned against the brass rail and rotated his neck. Jesus Christ. Why the hell is Immordino so anxious to see Sydney? They seemed to know each other—better than they should. Tozzi rubbed the back of his head and remembered the way Immordino had looked at him that day in the trailer on the construction site. Immordino seemed to recognize him just now. Maybe he knows who all of Nashe's bodyguards are, all ten of us. Maybe not though. Why would a mob boss worry about somebody's stupid piddly bodyguards? Maybe he just knows me, Tozzi thought. He seems to. Then Tozzi felt his gut sink and a bad taste crept into his mouth.

Maybe Sal Immordino knows me because he knows I'm a fed.

Jesus, no. . . .

4

Gibbons stood there with his shoes untied, pant legs bunched up around his ankles, wondering what the hell he was doing here in a Macy's in a goddamn suburban mall on a Saturday morning, trying on suits. What is it, a law? You *have* to have a new suit to get married? Shit.

He glanced over at his intended, Lorraine Bernstein, formerly a wonderful person, currently a matrimonial yo-yo. She was looking him up and down, squeezing her chin, inspecting him as if he were a horse on the auction block. Gibbons frowned. She had that school-marm look he hated. They'd been together sixteen years and in all that time she'd never, ever, looked like a Princeton professor of medieval history, not on the weekends. Not until now. He hated her hair tied back like that. He liked it loose, dark, silver-threaded, hanging below her shoulders. He liked her in jeans and sweaters too. But now she was beginning to look like all the other married women in this goddamn mall. Frumpy blouse, clodhopper shoes . . . shit. This isn't the Lorraine he's been with all these years, this isn't the woman he thought he was marrying. He should never have agreed to this. Too late to back out now, though. She's too hopped up on this whole wedding thing. If he suggested that they forget about it and just keep things the way they are, that would be it, *finito,* the end. And he didn't want that. He loved her, for chrissake. When she wasn't acting like a nut case, that is.

"I like this one," she said. "It looks good on you."

"I don't like it."

"Why?"

He held the sleeve out. "The color. It's too light."

"All your suits are dark. You don't have anything like this. I think it looks very good on you."

"I don't." He started to take the jacket off. "I don't need a new suit. I can wear my blue suit."

She motioned for him to be still. "Leave it on. Button the jacket."

He could feel the muscles in his jaw contracting. "I never button my jacket. I always wear it open."

"Just button it."

She reached out to do it herself. Like a bossy mother buying her kid a Communion suit. He buttoned it himself before she could. Christ Almighty!

She smiled and nodded, satisfied with what she saw. "It's a very good cut. It looks good on you."

He blew air out his nose. "But I don't like the color. It's too light."

"It's a June wedding. You can't wear navy-blue in June. It's too somber. We have to look more . . . more spring-y."

Spring-y? A Ph.D. with twenty-plus years of teaching experience at an Ivy League university, author of three scholarly books and God knows how many articles, and she wants to look *spring-y*? She's snapped. She's a fucking wack. She should be committed.

Lorraine sighed and crossed her arms over her chest. She looked disgusted. "All right, all right, take it off. You didn't want to come here in the first place. Wear what you want."

She turned away and put on the pout. Gibbons looked at the ceiling. Here we go. This was getting to be an old routine. It started with the pout. The unspoken, married-people's compromise.

"You really think it looks okay?" He made like he was inspecting the tags on the sleeve while he watched her.

"I told you what I thought." Indignation in her voice now. Gibbons stared down at the pant legs bunched up around his ankles and nodded in thought. The color wasn't that bad. May as well buy the goddamn thing. If he didn't do it today, she'd drag him out to more stores next week, and he definitely didn't want to waste another day in another goddamn mall. Just buy it and be done with it. By tomorrow he'd be down in Atlantic City, out in the field and on the job. He couldn't wait. He hadn't told Lorraine about his new assignment yet. She wasn't going to be happy. She didn't like him working the streets. Well, too bad. He had to get away from her precious wedding arrangements before she drove him nuts. Just get the suit and make her happy so that when he tells her that he's gonna be gone for a while on assignment, she won't be able to say anything. That was how the deal worked, the unspoken, married-people's compromise.

"Yeah, you may be right, after all," he said. "I guess it is better to wear something light in June. Dark colors absorb sunrays or something like that, make you hot. It's not a bad suit, really. I think I'll take it."

"Thank God," she said, rolling her eyes. "Stay here. I'll get someone to take a fitting." She steered around a rack of herringbone-tweed sport coats to look for a salesman.

Gibbons scratched his ear and watched her go. This was depressing. He never used to scheme and negotiate like this with Lorraine. Why was it so different now? Just because he finally agreed to make it official? They weren't even married yet, and he was already beginning to miss the way things used to be. Tozzi was a lucky bastard. He was single and he was working undercover. What more could you want? Lucky bastard.

Gibbons scanned a row of suits hanging against the wall, slick-looking European-cut suits. Giorgio Porgio, Tozzi's kind of thing. A black one with faint blue pinstripes caught his eye, and he picked up the sleeve to check the tag. He saw the price and nearly shit his pants. Eight hundred and ninety-five bucks? For a suit? In Macy's? You gotta be kidding.

He parted the suits on the rack to get a better look at this thing. It was definitely Tozzi. Tozzi liked guinea clothes like this. He'd spend nine hundred dollars on a suit like this if he could afford it. He had champagne tastes about a lot of things, come to think of it, but he was in the wrong line of work for the high life. A special agent's salary just didn't stretch that far . . .

Gibbons thought about that call-in tape that Ivers had played for him, Tozzi's wiseguy attitude. Champagne tastes. Must be a lot of perks working for someone like Russell Nashe. A lot of temptations too. A personal bodyguard must see all the good stuff—the cars, the women, everything money can buy. Everything Tozzi could never afford. Maybe Ivers's suspicions aren't that farfetched. Maybe Tozzi likes being Mike Tomasso. Maybe it's more fun than being Mike Tozzi.

Of course, Tozzi isn't the type to be satisfied working as someone else's body slave. Tozzi's too much of a hot dog. He never goes for the first down, not when he can grandstand it and throw the bomb. Gibbons looked at the black suit on the rack. Tozzi is in a good position if he decided to go bad. Offer Nashe a deal, offer to string out the investigation, make it look like he's digging hard, then in the end tell the Bureau he's come up empty, that Nashe is as clean as they come. In exchange for the good report card Nashe pays him off nicely. And then there's Sal Immordino. Mafia guy like him would love to have an FBI agent in his pocket, especially one from the Manhattan field office. Lot of potential there if Tozzi wanted to turn bad.

Doubtful though. Not Tozzi. He can be an asshole, but he's not a rat. Gibbons puckered his lips and looked at the nine-hundred-dollar suit, imagined Tozzi in it, behind the wheel of a black Mercedes or a Corvette maybe, Ray-Bans, hot-looking babe next to him. Gibbons dropped the sleeve with the price tag and buried the suit back in with the others. He didn't want to think about it.

"Is this the lucky groom?" a swishy voice crooned behind him.

"That's him."

Lorraine was standing behind the swish, that gooney wedding-smile on her face. The guy had the same gooney smile curling under his big beak. *The lucky groom?* What the hell was she doing, telling this guy their personal business? For chrissake. A potbellied old queer with dyed red hair and a face like a cockatoo. Gibbons spotted the yellow tape measure hanging around the queer's neck. He looked at Lorraine and groaned. Shit, this *must* be love. Why else would anyone put up with this crap?

"If you'll come this way, sir, we can get your measurements and you'll be all set."

Gibbons didn't say a word. He picked up his pant legs and padded off behind the cockatoo toward the fitting room, Lorraine bringing up the rear. In the fitting room the cockatoo bowed his head and gestured like a coachman for him to stand up on the carpeted blocks in front of the three-way mirror. Gibbons stepped up and looked at his three reflections in the three mirrors. Three guys with thin gray hair and too much forehead in baggy pants and untied shoes about to buy a suit he didn't even like. Three fucking married men. He sneered into the mirror just to show himself that he was still the same guy.

"Now we'll just button this up." The cockatoo reached around Gibbons's waist from behind. Instinctively Gibbons clenched his wrists.

"I can do it," he said.

"As you wish." The cockatoo seemed unperturbed.

Probably likes being manhandled, Gibbons thought. His kind do.

The cockatoo pulled down on the hem of the jacket, then smoothed the material over his back. He kept running his hands over Gibbons's back, pulling and tugging here and there, making little frustrated grunts and mumbles with each yank on the material. Gibbons glared over his shoulder, wondering what the hell he was doing.

"You got a problem back there?"

"Well . . . yes. I do." The cockatoo kept fussing with the jacket. "Are you standing up straight, sir? This jacket just isn't hanging right on you."

Gibbons grinned and caught Lorraine's eye in the mirror. The cockatoo kept pulling on the jacket, trying to figure out where the problem was. Then he found it, under the left armpit. Gibbons unbuttoned the jacket and reached in where his gun rested snugly in its holster. Excalibur, the .38 Colt Cobra Gibbons had used his entire career as an FBI agent. The cockatoo stared at the revolver in the mirror. He looked pretty pale all of a sudden.

"You can let it out a little on this side, can't you?" Gibbons was trying not to smirk.

The cockatoo coughed. "As you wish, sir."

"I wish," Gibbons said.

"I don't," Lorraine said. She looked pissed as she stepped over and hissed in his ear. "Did you have to bring that?"

"I always bring Excalibur when I get a new suit. Otherwise it ends up being too tight."

"This suit is for our wedding, for God's sake. You don't need a gun to get married."

"Well, I'm not gonna wear it just once. After the wedding I can wear it to work. What the hell did you think?"

She didn't answer. He knew what she wanted to say, but she didn't say it. Another one of the symptoms of this wedding disease she had. No arguments. Extremely non-confrontational. She was probably afraid he'd back out if she got him too riled up. Of all the crazy things she was doing now, this was the worst.

She pursed her lips and nodded. "Of course. You're right." Then she went back to her place.

Goddammit! He hated when she did this. These days she just swallowed whatever he said and made like everything was fine and dandy. He knew she didn't like his carrying a gun and working the streets, but she hadn't said boo about his work in the past two months. Anything not to rock the boat. Jesus!

"Sir, I'm sure we can accommodate your . . . your—"

"Gun."

"Yes, I'm sure our tailor can take the jacket out as you wish." The cockatoo looked very jumpy.

"Good. You do that."

The cockatoo nodded and went back to work with his tape measure, chalk marker, and pin cushion. Quietly, this time.

Gibbons tried to catch Lorraine's eye in the mirror again, but she wouldn't look at him. This was the suffer-in-silence phase.

"What do you hear from Tozzi these days?" he asked. She loved her cousin, used to baby-sit him when he was a kid. Gibbons knew this would bring her out.

She lifted her eyes and shrugged. "Not much. Aunt Concetta told me he dropped by to see her a few weeks ago. She said he didn't look happy, but he wouldn't talk about it. She said he got very moody when she asked him if there was anything wrong. She called and asked me if I knew what was wrong with him. She was certain there was something wrong."

"Your relatives always think there's something wrong," Gibbons said. "It's in the blood." Goddamn suspicious Italians. Never met one who wasn't.

Lorraine shrugged again. "Maybe so, but Aunt Concetta is pretty sharp, even at her age. She was right about Daniel."

"Who?"

"Daniel. My ex. The guy who ran out on me."

"Oh yeah. Mr. Bernstein." Another queer.

"Aunt Concetta thought there was something wrong with him the first time she met him. She was right. The bastard had another wife in Missouri and a fiancée in Toronto."

"And he was a homo too, wasn't he?" Gibbons glanced in the mirror at the cockatoo for a reaction. The bird kept his head down and concentrated on sticking pins in the pants. Probably afraid he'd get shot if he said anything.

"Bisexual. And that was just a rumor. We never found out for sure."

Lorraine's face changed. The dopey smile was gone and that handsome, ageless beauty was back. She could look like a great painting sometimes. A face you could study for years and never pin down in your mind. This was the Lorraine Gibbons wanted to marry.

"Bastard," she said in a whisper.

"Excuse me, sir," the cockatoo whispered, afraid to interrupt. "Do you want cuffs on the trousers?"

Gibbons looked down at the cockatoo on his knees. "No cuffs." The guy seemed to be shaking a bit, afraid he'd stick Gibbons with a pin. Gibbons shook his head. Pathetic. "What about that girl Tozzi had been seeing? The redhead. She still around?"

"Roxanne?" Lorraine shook her head. "That's all over with. I don't think her nerves could take it. Last time I talked to Michael—"

"When was that?"

"Oh, at least five or six weeks ago."

"Yeah, what did he say?"

"He just mentioned something about Roxanne leaving a message on his machine after he hadn't seen her in months, but he decided not to return her call. It wasn't worth it, he said. They really didn't have that much in common, he claimed."

Gibbons didn't like the sound of this. Shitcanning the old girlfriend when she's making an attempt to reconcile. Could be a bad sign, burning his bridges behind him. Was Tozzi trying to erase his old life to make room for a new one? Maybe he really is going bats. "Did he happen to say anything else when you talked to him? I mean, about how he is, what he's doing? You know."

"Are you kidding? When do you guys ever say anything about what you're doing. G-men don't make chitchat."

The cockatoo had moved on to Gibbons's sleeves, pulling them down snugly to mark the length. "Will you be wearing French cuffs with this suit, sir?"

Gibbons gave him a hard stare. "What do *you* think?"

The cockatoo cleared his throat. "I didn't think so," he mumbled. His hand was definitely shaking as he marked the sleeve, but he managed to make a reasonably straight line. Grace under pressure.

"You know, I was thinking," Lorraine said.

Gibbons looked at her in the mirror. The handsome beauty had disappeared from her face. She had the gooney look again.

She wrinkled her nose. "The food we picked for the reception? Chicken parmigian' and baked ziti seems awfully mundane. Maybe we should have something a little more unusual."

"Your relatives don't eat unusual. If there's no macaroni, they won't come."

Lorraine scowled. "They're not that bad. Not all of them."

"Ma'am, if I may offer a suggestion?" The cockatoo was on his knees again. He looked up warily at Gibbons before he continued. "I attended a wedding last fall out in the Hamptons that was very special. They served *Indian* food for the reception, and it went over very well with all the guests."

"Really." Lorraine looked intrigued. Gibbons rolled his eyes. You gotta be kidding.

The cockatoo was more at ease with her, and he launched into a detailed description of this Indian affair. Lorraine seemed to know what he was talking about, but Gibbons had no interest in finding out what *pappadum, pakoras,* and *samosas* were.

Gibbons could tell from Lorraine's face that she was enthralled. Anything about weddings enthralled her these days—she enthralled easy—and she kept egging the guy on.

When the faggot got to the main course—some kind of curried lamb with a yogurt sauce—Gibbons's stomach grumbled. He tried to tune out the cockatoo and the gooney bird, but they were working themselves up into a frenzy, the two of them, squawking and tittering and going on and on about this Indian wedding shit. Just what Lorraine needed, more stupid ideas. Shit. Standing there with more pins in him than a voodoo doll, Gibbons stared at himself in the mirrors and suddenly he began to understand why some men got the uncontrollable urge to run away and become someone else. Like Mr. Bernstein. Like Tozzi maybe.

5

Sister Cecilia Immordino turned the corner at Forty-third and Ninth Avenue, holding both the veil and the skirt of her black habit against the strong breeze, squinting through her big glasses. She glanced up at the majestic clouds in a clear blue sky and allowed a small smile to grace her lips. The sun was bright and spring was in the air. It was the perfect kind of day for prayers to be answered. Sister Cil was hoping. Today, dear God. At long last please let it be today.

Sabatini Mistretta, her brother Sal's boss, trudged along the sidewalk, scowling at the stiff wind whipping down the avenue. He was short and round and somewhat gruff, and Sal, in moments of unkindness, would say he resembled a frog. Sister Cil saw his point, but such characterizations were uncalled for, no matter how truthful they were. It was obviously God's will that Mr. Mistretta was the boss, and for that reason alone he should be respected. Even if he did look like a frog.

As they walked up Ninth Avenue she took note of every poor soul they passed—bums in doorways, lustful young women selling their bodies, wild-eyed drug addicts ignorant of their own spiritual and bodily needs, living mindless lives like base creatures, craving only the temporary relief they could get from their drug. It was remarkable, she thought, how God in His infinite wisdom had provided such an array of human degradation so that the rest of humanity would be shown the way not to go. Unfortunately some people do not pay attention to these examples, and that's why others must dedicate their lives to saving those who stray, others such as herself.

Waiting for the traffic light to change at Forty-fourth Street, she was careful to step down off the curb and maintain an arm's length between herself and Mr. Mistretta so as not to accentuate the difference in their heights. She did not want to upset him in any way, not at this most crucial time when his approval was the final thing they needed to make her long-anticipated dream a reality. Finally she would not have to turn girls away for lack of space, girls who stood a good chance of ending up here on the street with the legions of lost Jezebels. No, Sal would make sure of that. He had made her a promise years ago, and he assured her that he would follow through on it as soon as it was economically feasible. And her brother Sal was a man of his word. They'd been brought up right, after all.

And now, after all these years of planning and praying, he would finally be able to earn the money to make the huge donation she needed to start construction on the new facility for the Mary Magdalen Center, the home for unwed mothers she ran in Jersey City. All they needed now was Mr. Mistretta's okay on Sal's new venture, that's all, and she was confident that Mr. Mistretta would not disappoint her girls. She'd said a novena to the Blessed Virgin Mary, who knew how to intervene in these matters.

The traffic light changed and they started to cross the street. Mistretta turned and looked over his shoulder. "You see that tall guy with the curly hair back there, Cil? The one in the brown jacket?"

Sister Cil held on to her veil and turned around. "Yes."

"Parole officer. He follows me around every day." Mistretta spoke in a hoarse whisper. "Every day since they transferred me to this halfway house here, this guy's been on my tail. Why didn't they just leave me at Allenwood for my last month? No, they said I gotta come here to ease me back into the community. Baloney. They don't fool me. This is one of their little scams. They give me a little freedom, let me walk around town during the day, and they figure they can catch me doing something. But I got them all figured out, these guys. Bunch of stupids."

Sister Cil nodded. Mr. Mistretta has always been a very cautious man. That whole time he was at Allenwood Penitentiary, he wouldn't allow any visitors except his wife and her. Once a month one of Sal's men would drive her all the way out to Pennsylvania to pray with him in the visiting room, holding their rosaries across the long bingo table, with the guards standing there watching them. Sal said Mr. Mistretta was paranoid, but he's just very cautious. He could arrange to meet with Sal now that he's in the Bureau of Prisons Community Treatment Center. His days are free, he only has to check back in at night. But Mr. Mistretta didn't want to see anyone until he was released and *completely* free. She could understand that. After all, the court had come down awfully hard on him, and just for tax evasion. It was a terrible way to treat a businessman simply for being entrepreneurial.

"Look at that," he said, with disgust in his voice.

"What?"

"Up on the roof. Across the street. See? They think they're so clever."

It took her a minute to see what he was talking about—three men in grimy work clothes tarring the roof of an old tenement building. One man hauled buckets of hot tar up a pulley while the other two appeared to be spreading it out with rollers. On the sidewalk below them a fourth man stood by a noisy, smelly machine of some kind that kept the tar hot. There was a dirty, smudged sign on the machine that said "Stuyvesant Roofing, Inc."

Mistretta shook his head and tried to grin. His grins never looked like grins, poor man. Sister Cil blushed as she remembered something else Sal had said. It was true, though. A Mistretta grin seemed more like a reaction to gas pains.

"They're so obvious, I can't believe it," he whispered. "The stupids. Those aren't rollers they're holding. Those're those special things they got. Like rifles. You know what I'm talking about? To listen in on us. They point those things at the store windows over here and pick up the vibrations of what we're saying off the glass. A guy told me all about it in prison. The stupids." He shook his head and tried to grin again. "Listen to me. Don't say anything else until we get there, okay? Don't give them the satisfaction."

Sister Cil nodded. He was a very cautious man. She just assumed those men on the roof were simply fixing the roof. She held her veil in place and squinted up at the "roofers." How did he know such things? Remarkable. It just went to show why he was the boss.

They walked in silence up the next block. At the corner of Forty-fifth Street she turned around and saw that tall man with the curly hair again. He wasn't ten feet away now and *he was looking right at her.* Lord God in heaven, he was close enough to eavesdrop on them! How could she ask Mr. Mistretta for his permission with this man hovering over them? Her brows furrowed behind her glasses.

They crossed the street and passed a liquor store on the corner, where the owner was trying to keep a persistent bum out of his store. She watched to see whether the tall man following them would stop and assist the poor, overweight liquor-store owner before he had a heart attack, but the tall man just kept walking. Sister Cil frowned, outraged at the man's lack of concern. It just goes to show what these people's concept of the law is all about. Better to harass a poor businessman who's already paid his debt to society than help someone being tortured by an obviously sinful individual. Lord God, have mercy on their souls. They were worse than stupid.

At the next corner they waited for the light and crossed Ninth Avenue. From the crosswalk Sister Cil could see the narrow redbrick church wedged between the tenements on the side street, a single slate-roofed steeple standing tall over the surrounding squalor. Sister Cil smiled when she spotted the name of the church in the glass case bolted to the brick front. Our Lady of Mercy Roman Catholic Church. Same as the hospital where they had done so much good for Sal when he was so sick. Cil brushed a tear of hope from the corner of her eye. It was a sign, a good sign. Mr. Mistretta wouldn't disappoint the girls, she knew it.

They climbed the stone steps and Mr. Mistretta pushed through the heavy oak doors. The vestibule was dim, of course, filled with the smell of burning candle wax and the lingering scent of incense from past funeral services. They dipped their fingers in the white marble holy-water font and crossed themselves, then went into the nave and took a pew near the front. The church was empty. Sister Cil noticed that the floor was old, cracked, marble-patterned linoleum and that there was no Jesus on the cross over the altar. It was just a simple wooden cross with a little carving on the top. A poor parish.

She was just detaching her rosary beads from the sash of her habit when a column of light suddenly appeared in the center aisle, beaming in from the vestibule. She heard the front doors close with a wooden bump, and the light was gone. Then she heard the footsteps coming down the aisle. Out of the corner of her eye she saw the tall man with the curly hair, the parole officer. Oh, God, no!

The man's step had a proud, careless rhythm as he walked up to the pew behind theirs. He stepped in sideways and took a seat right behind them. She blinked behind her glasses and pressed her forearm against her nervous stomach. She could feel his eyes on her back. He just sat there, watching them, didn't even have the courtesy to *pretend* to be here for prayer. Bad enough that he was sent by the devil to thwart her plan, he was rude and disrespectful as well. The product of a public-school education no doubt. Disgraceful. Incensed, Sister Cil turned around in her seat and looked him in the eye.

She held up her rosary and let the cross dangle in front of the awful man's face. "You're welcome to join us, young man," she said primly, "if you're here to pray."

Mistretta turned around. "Yeah, come on, Saperstein." He held up his own black rosary. "Here, you can use my beads."

Saperstein looked from one to the other, his mouth set. "No thanks," he muttered, then left the pew and moved back to the vestibule to watch them from the doorway.

They settled in then, kneeling down on the padded kneelers, elbows on the pew back in front of them, rosaries dangling, and started to pray. *"Hail Mary, full of grace, the Lord is with thee, blessed art thou amongst women . . ."* Mistretta's voice was low and grumbly, hers was a clear mezzo. They prayed together just as they had at the prison.

They finished the first Hail Mary and simultaneously swallowed one bead between their thumbs and index fingers. Mr. Mistretta started the next Hail Mary by himself.

"Sal has a very interesting proposal before him right now," she said in a droning, singsong rhythm that mimicked his Hail Mary. "He wants your permission to go ahead with it." She turned and faced him slightly so he could hear. This was how she had delivered messages to him at Allenwood. It had been his idea. He said his gravelly voice would cover her higher pitch if they were ever bugged. Mr. Mistretta was a very cautious man.

"Russell Nashe suggested it to him."

Mistretta looked up at her. His eyes bulged a bit. She inhaled sharply, a sudden pain piercing her side. Should've had a little something to eat before she came, but she was too nervous to eat this morning and Mr. Mistretta wasn't making her feel any better now. He looked suspicious already. Just listen to the rest. Please.

"Sal told me to tell you that Mr. Nashe did not make his payment to Seaview Properties, but that he offered this counterproposal in lieu of making that payment he was supposed to make. Twenty-nine—"

". . . and blessed is the fruit of thy womb, Jesus." Mistretta overrode her and nodded once. He knew how much Nashe owed.

Sister Cil cleared her throat and adjusted her glasses. She knew she'd have to present this to him just right, make him see the benefits, make him understand. If he said no, the Mary Magdalen Center would have to go on in that cramped, drafty old brownstone they had now, and more girls would have to be turned away. Like the Blessed Mother being turned away from the inn on Christmas Eve. No, that was unacceptable. She couldn't let him say no. It was up to her now.

"You may have read in the papers about the boxing match Mr. Nashe is sponsoring at his casino in Atlantic City," she said, straining to keep her voice under control. She paused to mark off another bead as he was finishing another Hail Mary. "Mr. Walker versus Mr. Epps?"

Mistretta nodded once. *". . . the Lord is with thee . . ."*

"If Mr. Walker wins the fight—as he's expected to, because he's the champ—he will make a little over seventeen million dollars. But if Mr. Epps wins, he only gets eight and a half million." This didn't seem fair to her, but she continued with her presentation, just as she and Sal had rehearsed it. Sal assured her that a clear, businesslike presentation was the best way to approach Mr. Mistretta. "Mr. Nashe would like Sal to convince the champ that he should throw the fight."

Mistretta gave her the bug-eyed-frog look again. Her heart leapt. Her eye suddenly caught a painted statue in a corner by the confessionals and her heart leapt again. St.

Jude with a burning heart in his hand. The patron saint of lost causes.

She cleared her throat. "If you let Sal go ahead with this, Mr. Nashe will pay the champ three million dollars off the books through an offshore account in the Cayman Islands." She felt a bit shameful using terms like "off the books" here in church, but Sal said this was how she should say it in order to convince him. She just kept telling herself that she was doing this for the girls, the poor girls. "This three million dollars will actually be more than twice what Mr. Walker would net if he won, after his manager, the promoters, and the IRS take their share. Obviously Mr. Nashe would rather have Mr. Epps win so that he won't have to pay out so much in winnings. So if Sal can make sure Epps wins, Mr. Nashe promises to put five million dollars of the money he saves on the fight toward his outstanding debt on the land under—"

"Hail Mary, full of grace . . ." Mistretta overrode her again. He knew what land Mr. Nashe owed the money on. Of course, of course. . . .

Sister Cil coughed into her fist. Maintaining this monotonous pitch was a strain on her voice, but she had to go on. "But the best part of this plan, as Mr. Nashe pointed out to Sal, is that the family can place as many bets—" She coughed again, glanced at the empty cross, and lowered her eyes. "You can place as many bets on the fight as you'd like, with the prior knowledge that Epps is going to win." Her face was hot. She stared at the wood grain on the next pew, avoiding the dangling crucifixes on their rosaries. She kept thinking of the girls. Keep talking. "Sal suggests that you let him wager the entire thirty million dollars you left him in charge of. Depending on the odds at fighttime"—her heart was pounding—"he says we can make between one hundred twenty and one hundred fifty million dollars."

She looked for a reaction, a sign of consent, but he was staring straight ahead at the altar, rumbling through his Hail Mary. She glanced back at Mr. Saperstein standing in the doorway, then looked to the cross over the altar. Holy Mary, Mother of God, give me the strength to go on!

She pressed her aching stomach against the pew in front of her and continued, just as she and Sal had rehearsed it. "Sal says there are many benefits to be gained from this venture. First of all, you will be in very good financial shape for any future projects you want to undertake. Also, if you let Sal do this, Mr. Nashe promises to pay the balance of the money he owes on the land in six-month installments over the next five years. In exchange for his contribution to this venture, all Mr. Nashe wants is that half of his debt be considered satisfied once the challenger is officially declared the winner."

She swallowed and waited for a reaction. Sal said he wasn't going to like this part. Mistretta just kept praying. "So in effect," she went on, "it would cost us a little less than fifteen million to make up to ten times as much."

Her scalp suddenly felt hot under her veil. She felt as if she were burning. Out of the corner of her eye she spotted another statue, St. Michael, the archangel, on a side altar, sword held aloft, feathered wings on his back, the flames of hell licking his sandaled feet as he stood on a serpent's head. Mr. Mistretta was still grumbling his Hail Marys, not even looking at her, acting as if he hadn't heard any of this. Blessed Mother, please!

She drew a shallow breath. Sal had warned her not to mention the new facility for the center. He said it definitely would not help their cause. Sal said Mr. Mistretta had this thing about his men having their money spent before they'd made it. It was the kind of thing that made him very angry.

But Mr. Mistretta was a very religious man, she reasoned. Look how fervently he prays. Sal's wrong about this. This *will* convince him. Once he understands that there are so many pregnant teenage girls with no place to turn that she actually has to turn some away because she just doesn't have the room, he'll agree that Mr. Nashe's proposal is a worthwhile endeavor. If for no other reason than to have a new, modern, spacious building for the Mary Magdalen Center. He couldn't refuse that. Not a good Catholic like Mr. Mistretta.

"And one more thing," she started again. "Sal has promised to use his own profits to make that big donation to the archdiocese we've always talked about so that we can finally break ground on a new facility for the home for unwed mothers. The one that I administer? In Jersey City?" Her heart was glowing with hope. She was certain she had done the right thing. *This* would convince him.

He finished his Hail Mary before he responded. He glanced up at her, looked her in the eye. "Tell your brother I said no."

She blinked behind her thick glasses, kept blinking, couldn't stop. What?

"No new business until I'm released. You tell him that."

"But Sal says this is a sure thing—"

"There's no such thing as a sure thing. And you never bet the rent on a prizefight. Your brother oughta know better."

"But—"

"I said no and that's it. You tell him." He started an Our Father then.

Sister Cil swallowed back the tears and forced herself to join him in the Our Father. She stared hard at the Christless cross over the altar, bitterly wondering why her poor girls always had to get short shrift, why Mr. Mistretta couldn't listen to sound business advice and do the right thing. All that money, millions of dollars, and he won't let Sal make it. It's a shame. It isn't fair to the girls. It's terrible. Shameful. Unfair!

She looked over her glasses at Mr. Mistretta as they finished the prayer. "*. . . Thy kingdom come, Thy will be done. Amen.*"

She let out a long sigh. She felt totally empty all of a sudden.

"Anything else?" Mistretta muttered. "From Sal?"

She looked at him, at his flabby frog-face and wondered

whether this was a trial, a trial from God, a test of her faith, a test to see just how dedicated she was to her girls.

Totally dedicated—that's how dedicated.

"Exactly when is it that you're going to be released?" she asked. "Sal wants to know."

He rolled his froggy eyes up at her. "Two weeks from yesterday."

Sister Cil nodded once and swallowed a bead on her rosary. She was trying to remember exactly what day Sal said the fight was going to be. She nodded again, to herself.

Gibbons shifted in his seat, careful not to spill the coffee in his hand. He sipped from the blue plastic Thermos cup and watched Dougherty fiddling with the video equipment. It was cramped inside the van but not uncomfortable. Not the way these things used to be. Gibbons remembered what it used to be like being cooped up in a surveillance van loaded with low-tech still cameras and reel-to-reel tape recorders, squatting on a hard wooden milking stool for hours on end, sweating through your clothes, sticking your face in the roof vent every chance you got so you wouldn't pass out. Shit, this rig was a fucking luxury liner by comparison. He looked at Dougherty sitting at the controls. These young guys don't know how easy they have it.

Dougherty was wearing tan PSE&G coveralls in case someone came by and wanted to know why there was a Public Service Electric and Gas van parked on this narrow, wooded road in this got-rocks section of Alpine, New

Jersey, on a Sunday afternoon. Dougherty had even hung some loose wires and rope from the nearest pole to make it look like he was fixing something. Dougherty supposedly knew what he was doing. Best surveillance man in the field office, according to Ivers. No, best *technician.* That's what they call these guys now. In the old days the street agents took care of surveillance, all part of the job. Now agents get teamed up with technicians on plants like this. Gibbons stared at the mess of electronic equipment packed in tight against one wall of the box. Just as well. Who the hell wants to learn how to use all this shit?

Dougherty swiveled around in his seat, one hand poised on his headphones, the other turning a dial on the board. Looking at him now, Gibbons finally figured out how he got that weird balding pattern, a hairless strip running from ear to ear over the crown of his head with a wispy dirty-blond patch standing on end in front. The bald strip was where the headphones rubbed. Must be a dedicated bastard.

Dougherty gazed up at the roof of the van, looking at nothing, just listening, slowly moving the dial with that perpetual open-mouthed smile on his face. Dougherty smiled at everything, no matter what. He couldn't be more than thirty-two, thirty-three, Gibbons figured, and he even smiled when he talked about losing his hair. He wasn't stupid or anything, just relentlessly pleasant. Who knows? Maybe life was a carnival for this guy. But Gibbons had *never* met an Irishman this happy. Not a sober one. Maybe Dougherty's mother was Polish or something.

All of a sudden the smile grew wider and those Irish eyes twinkled as he stopped fooling with the dial. Dougherty looked at Gibbons. "I think we're in business." He swiveled back to the controls and threw a few switches. One of the three monitors mounted on the front wall came to life, switching from silent static to a shadowy black-and-white picture of a woman in a floral-print dress mixing salad at a long dining room table set for a big meal. Because of the camera angle a gaudy chandelier was obscuring her face.

Dougherty pointed to a second set of headphones hanging on the wall. Gibbons took them down and held one cup to his ear. He could distinctly hear the sound of the wooden utensils clacking against the wooden bowl.

"Where are the cameras?" Gibbons asked.

Dougherty slid the headphones off one ear. "I put 'em in the trees. I got five out there, but one's screwed up, the living room one. The others are working fine, though. We got the dining room, the kitchen, Sal's bedroom, and his bathroom. Nice picture for shooting through a window, huh?"

Gibbons nodded and smiled like a crocodile. If Sal Immordino knew that his million-dollar mansion set way the hell back there on twenty wooded acres was under surveillance, he'd really go nuts.

On the monitor Sal's brother Joseph entered the dining room then. He circled the table, checking out the spread before he said anything to the woman. *"Whad'ja make? Chicken again?"*

"Eggplant and veal," the woman answered.

The sound quality was very good, as clear as anything Gibbons had ever heard on a surveillance tape. "You got rifle mikes up in the trees?"

Dougherty's Irish eyes twinkled devilishly. He just shook his head.

"You got into the house?"

Dougherty kept smiling and shook his head again.

Gibbons listened to Joseph interrogating the woman on how much the veal had cost them, asking her why the hell she spent so much money on "those guys." Joseph was a jerk and always had been, as far as Gibbons could tell. An aging greaseball in a shiny suit and diamond cuff links, forty years behind the times. He kind of reminded Gibbons of that other greaseball, the one from the movies, Cesar Romero, but minus the Latino charm.

The woman finished with the salad and moved around the table. They could see her face now. She was as tall as Joseph with short, dark, nothing hair. A pair of impenetrable oversized eyeglasses dominated a typically severe, middle-aged Italian female face. Gibbons knew it well. A lot of his future in-laws had that same look.

"Who's the woman?" Gibbons asked.

"That's Cecilia Immordino, their sister, the nun."

"*That's* Sister Cil? Dressed like that?"

Dougherty nodded. "She doesn't wear her habit when she goes home."

"Why not?"

Dougherty glanced back at Gibbons and shrugged. "It's not that unusual. Nuns don't have to wear their habits all the time anymore. They can go human once in a while. It's not like it used to be when I went to Catholic school."

Gibbons took his word for it. John Joseph Dougherty ought to know.

Gibbons stared up at the monitor and saw Sal Immordino coming into the dining room with a pack of his heavy hitters. He counted nine wiseguys in all and recognized most of them as captains in the Mistretta family. Two guys skulked into the room behind the pack, hugging the walls and keeping to themselves. They were too young to be *capos.* Probably Sal's gofers, his protection. Lean and hungry men.

Gibbons followed a skinny, pinkie-ringed greaseball as he moved around the table, walked right up to the nun as if they were old friends, kissed her on the cheek, and started up a conversation. She smiled and nodded as they talked—real pleasant—then she showed the guy the gold cross hanging around her neck, a big showy thing, at least four inches long. She was telling the guy that it was a gift from Sal. The guy held the cross delicately in his fingers and inspected it with great appreciation, complimenting Sal on his generosity and good taste. Gibbons couldn't believe it. This was "Juicy" Vacarini, the biggest whoremeister in north Jersey.

Gibbons noticed that most of the wiseguys tripped over themselves to get in a good word with Cecilia Immordino, while a few of them just said hello and moved on, not too friendly. "So what's the story with Sister Cil? Is she a real nun or what?"

"Oh, yeah, she's real," Dougherty said. "She checks out with the archdiocese and everything. She's hard to peg, though, as far as her relationship with her brother Sal goes."

"Whattaya mean?"

"Some of these guys don't like her at all. We've got a couple of them on tape complaining that she has too much influence over Sal. But we've also got other guys on tape saying just the opposite. What we do know is that Sal likes to have her around, especially in public every once in a while. She always wears her habit when they go out together, by the way. He probably thinks it enhances the image. You know, helpless mental retard being led around by a nun. Makes him look like a victim."

"So what do you think she's all about?"

Dougherty stared at the monitor and shook his head slowly. "I've been watching the Immordinos since last Thanksgiving, and I still can't quite figure her out. She's not stupid, she knows what's going on but only up to a point, it seems. She knows that he's into gambling and loan-sharking and racketeering and all that, but she also firmly believes that he never has and never would hurt or —God forbid—kill anyone."

Gibbons studied her face on the monitor. "Bullshit."

"I've got it on tape. From her and from other people. Funny thing is, she seems to approve of the criminal activities he admits to. The exorbitant profits the family makes on loan-sharking and prostitution are, in reality, the righteous punishment that sinful men must suffer for seeking out these vices. That's almost her exact words. I got it on tape. Can you believe it?"

Gibbons sipped his coffee. "Nope."

Dougherty paused and fiddled with his dials for a moment. "My feeling is that she's deliberately put the blinders on. Sal makes big donations to the church, and she doesn't want that to dry up. She's got a real bug about putting up a new building for the place she runs, a home or something for pregnant teenagers. She talks about it all the time. Christ, I've got hours of tape with her going on and on and on about it. My opinion is that she's willing to look the other way if it'll lead to a good donation. You know what I'm saying? Like, what's a little venial sin among friends?"

Gibbons took another sip of his coffee. Going to Confession must come in handy for this bunch.

On the monitor the men were all seated at the table now, Sister Cil standing at one end, dishing out her veal and eggplant, telling them to pass the plates. They rubbed their hands and sniffed the food, told the nun it sure smelled good, waiting for everyone to be served. It was a real homey scene, with big Sal at the head of the table at the top of the screen. A Mafia "Last Supper."

Sal tore off a hunk of bread from a long loaf and passed it on. *"So you understand how we have to do this now, right? We use only people we know we can trust out there. None of this friends-of-friends-of-friends shit. Only people we can vouch for."*

Juicy Vacarini sloshed red wine into his glass. *"Don't worry about it, Sal. I got some good people out in Vegas. They know how to keep quiet."*

"Yeah, but I want a lot of good people," Sal said, heaping salad into a bowl. *"I don't want any one person making bets over fifty grand. That's the limit. That's why we need a lot of guys.* Capisce?"

Juicy nodded, his mouth full of eggplant. *"I gotcha."*

A fat guy at the bottom of the screen, with his back to the camera, piped up. *"But what about the money Golden Boy owes us? That's a big piece of change. We s'posed to forget about that?"* Gibbons recognized the whiny, disgusted delivery. Frank Bartolo, Mistretta's hand-picked choice to run Sal's crew while Sal was acting boss. Very heavy into the construction unions, dipping into pension funds, paying off the right people to get bids, extorting payments to make sure people show up at work, that kind of stuff.

Sal pointed with a wine bottle. *"Hey, Frank, don't you listen? I already said I'm taking care of that. We're gonna get paid. Don't worry about it."*

"Yeah, but, Sal, that's not the way Sabatini set it up." Bartolo was gesturing with both hands. *"This whole thing . . . I don't know. It's not the kind of thing Sabatini goes for. He likes to get his bread when it's due, cut-and-dried, none of this fancy razzle-dazzle shit."*

Sal was chewing, his mouth full, pointing two fingers at Bartolo like a cannon, about to make a point as soon as he swallowed. But then his sister suddenly chimed in. *"I spoke to Mr. Mistretta the other day and I told him all about it, Frank. He's behind it one hundred percent. He loves the idea."*

Gibbons squinted at her face. What the hell does she have to do with it?

Bartolo held up his hands in surrender. *"That's all I want to know, Cil. If it's all right with Sabatini, fine. Because if it wasn't okay with him, I wouldn't want to know nothing about it. You know how he is—when Sabatini gets mad, he gets mad. You remember what happened to Tommy Ricks and his crew?"*

No one said a thing. They all looked down at their plates and ate. No one had to be told what had happened to Tommy Ricks and his crew. Not even Gibbons. Gaetano "Tommy Ricks" Ricciardi and six of his men had been ground up like hamburger and mixed in with a load of cement, then poured into the foundation of a high-rise on the corner of Sixty-eighth and Second Avenue. The word on the street was that Mistretta went nuts when he found out Tommy Ricks was doing cocaine deals behind his back with a couple of Colombians from Queens after he had warned Tommy twice not to do business with South Americans. The police had to get an injunction to stop work on the building so they could smash up the foundation and look for the bodies. The biggest chunk they'd found was about the size of a fifty-cent piece, but they couldn't find any teeth to make a positive ID on any of them. Everybody knew it was Mistretta who had ordered the hit, but they had nothing to take to court. The guys putting up the building threatened to sue the city so they could get back to work, so the cops had to give up. They ended up dumping fresh cement on the crime scene, put up thirty-two floors of overpriced condos, and Mistretta got away with it. Ruthless bastard.

Gibbons watched them all eating in silence. He noticed Sister Cil looking back and forth between Sal and Bartolo, nervouslike. She was the one who finally broke the silence. *"Mr. Mistretta was particularly happy that we'd finally have enough money to build the new facility for the Mary Magdalen Center. Out of Sal's cut, of course. Isn't that right, Sal?"*

Sal looked up and nodded, chewing. *"Yeah, Cil, don't worry about it. You'll get your new building. Just don't say anything to the archbishop yet."*

"Oh, I know, I know." She nodded up and down, the chandelier lights glinting in her glasses.

Something wasn't right about her, but Gibbons couldn't put his finger on it. She was more than just peculiar.

Gibbons didn't recognize the short little guy who spoke next. *"Hey, Sal."*

"Hey, what?"

"How're you gonna get Mr. Mad to go along with this? He don't look too cooperative from what I seen on TV."

A couple of guys laughed. The nun was staring hard at the little guy who asked the question.

Sal sipped his wine. *"Don't worry about him. He's not dumb, he knows how to add. He'll go for the money."*

"But what if he doesn't want to do it?"

A big grin opened up across Sal's face like a crack in a dinosaur egg. *"Don't worry about it. I'm a very persuasive guy."*

Everyone laughed, even the nun. Except she seemed to be forcing it. Maybe she thought it was expected of her.

Around the dinner table, the wiseguys kept making jokes about Sal's powers of persuasion, Juicy Vacarini saying that Sal might have to show Mr. Mad a few new moves. The men howled. Gibbons frowned. He didn't get it. The Golden Boy? Mr. Mad? People placing big bets in Las Vegas? None of this jibed with anything he'd read in the latest file on Sal Immordino. He looked at Dougherty who looked just as confused as he was.

Dougherty shook his head and shrugged. "This is all news to me."

"Who's Mr. Mad?"

Dougherty shrugged. "Beats the hell out of me."

Gibbons went back to the monitor. Watching them eat was making him hungry. He sipped his coffee and strained to make out what had degenerated into barely discernible hubbub. He wondered where the hell Dougherty had the mikes stashed.

Frank Bartolo asked someone to pass the grated cheese then, and he was told the bowl was empty. Sal picked up a cut-glass bowl and held it out toward one corner of the table. *"Joseph,"* he said, *"get some more cheese, will ya?"*

It was the first thing Sal had said to his brother since they'd sat down to eat, and Joseph was looking daggers at him now. *"What do I look like? A waiter? Go get your own fucking cheese."*

The room was instantly silent. Sal held out the empty bowl, staring at his brother. *"I said we need more cheese, Joseph. I asked you nice. Now go get it."* Sal's tone wasn't menacing. It didn't have to be.

Joseph's eyes darted around the table. They all stared back at him in silence, like buzzards. Even his sister. Finally he leaned across the table, snatched the bowl out of Sal's hand, and left the room in a huff. Cil looked at Sal and shook her head in disapproval, but Sal didn't acknowledge her. She folded her napkin and put it to next her plate, then got up and went after Joseph.

Dougherty quickly threw a couple of switches and turned a few dials. Another monitor came to life with Joseph leaning against a kitchen counter, a row of cabinets behind him, a big refrigerator by his side. Sister Cil was standing in front of the sink, clutching her elbows. *"Don't be mad at him, Joseph,"* she said. *"He's your brother."*

Gibbons caught Dougherty's Irish eyes. Who's he kidding? Gibbons thought. This sound is too good. He had to have gotten into the house and bugged the place silly. "Come on, Dougherty. Where are they?"

Dougherty waved him off, grinning. "Just listen."

"Sal is forbidden from being himself, and that's a terrible thing, Joseph. He may not show it all the time, but I know that he really does appreciate all that you do for him."

Joseph threw his hands up. *"Then why does he treat me like a flunky, huh? He isn't fair to me, Cil. I never get to do anything on my own. I just take orders. I'm a nobody, as far as those guys out there are concerned."*

Sister Cil smiled tolerantly and held up the gold crucifix hanging from her neck. *"You remember what Grandma always used to say?* 'Gesù Cristo vede e provvede.' *Jesus sees and provides. He'll take care of you when the time is right, Joseph."*

Joseph held the gold cross, leaned closer, and stared at it. *"Hey, what's wrong with Jesus' head?"*

"What?"

He was pointing at something on the cross with his pinkie. *"See? All these tiny holes in His head? That's your big-deal brother Sal for you. He buys you crap, that's what he does."*

Sister Cil tucked in her chin and inspected the cross herself.

"Look close at the back of His neck. You can see where it was welded. Gold, my foot. This is a cheap piece of—"

"Be quiet, Joseph. Don't say another word." She reached behind her neck to unfastened the chain. *"I can't believe this,"* she said as she fumbled with the clasp. *"It's a sin, a sacrilege. How could anyone do such a thing? To Jesus, for God's sake. Sal's gonna have a fit."* When she finally got the chain undone, she took down a glass from the cup-

board and filled it with water. Her hand was shaking. It looked like she was the one having the fit.

"Whattaya talking about, Cil? You're not making any sense."

"Be quiet, Joseph!"

She dropped the cross into the glass of water, and Gibbons's headphones let out a high-pitched squeal.

Dougherty ripped off his headphones. "Shit," he muttered. "She found it. The only goddamn bug I had in there, and she found it. Shit, fuck, piss."

Gibbons glanced over at Dougherty. His Irish eyes weren't smiling anymore. "I had a feeling that's where it was." He shook his head and smiled with his teeth. "Sticking a bug in the Lord's head. You're gonna burn in hell a long time for this one, Dougherty. A *long* time."

Dougherty scowled at him. "Yeah? Well, I won't be alone, Gib."

Gibbons poured himself some more coffee from the Thermos bottle. As he took a sip he looked up at the silent nun in sheep's clothing staring at the cross in the glass on the counter, chewing on her finger, ignoring whatever it was her stupid brother Joseph was saying to her. Gibbons lowered the cup to his lap and wondered what the hell her problem really was.

• 7 •

Gibbons sat by himself at a small round table in the cocktail lounge that was tucked around the side of the soaring escalators that led up to the lobby at Nashe Palace. He sipped the beer from his glass and made a face. He glared at the half-empty brown glass bottle with the frolicking country maiden on the label. Imported German piss was what it was, *expensive* imported German piss. Four fucking bucks a bottle. Waitress recommended it, said it was Russell Nashe's personal favorite. Just goes to show that money can't buy taste. Christ. Coulda bought a six-pack of Rolling Rock for what he was paying for this.

He looked down at his shoes and frowned at them too. They were white, to match his belt. All part of the costume: burgundy pants, yellow short-sleeved shirt, royal-blue polyester blazer. He'd been here two days and he'd worn this outfit the entire time, hoping to blend in with the thousands of senior citizens who were shuttled into Atlantic City every day by bus. He'd picked up Tozzi's trail last night, and he'd been trailing him ever since. The outfit must've worked, because Tozzi hadn't spotted him yet. Gibbons sort of wished Tozzi would've made him by now, though. He didn't think he looked *that* much like a senior citizen. He glared over at Tozzi sitting at the bar with his back to him. Asshole.

He watched Tozzi trying to make time with the blond bartender again. This was the third time he'd come back here in the past eighteen hours, and the German piss was the fifth different beer Gibbons had tried. He wished Tozzi would go somewhere else, somewhere where they served something other than Bud and imported shit. But the asshole apparently had the hots for this blonde, so he kept coming back here. A real piece of work, this guy.

The blonde was wearing a gray fedora, a man's hat. She'd worn it yesterday too. She wasn't a knockout in the looks department, but there was something very appealing about her. She was different, Gibbons could tell, and in that hat she was very sexy, not centerfold sexy, really sexy. He'd heard her giving Tozzi shit earlier today, making fun of his oily guinea charm. She was sharp, with a good sense of humor and, more importantly, a functioning brain. Gibbons liked her. In a way, she sort of reminded him of Lorraine—the way she used to be.

Gibbons watched the blonde in the hat move down to the end of the bar to take care of a customer. He picked up his glass, went over the bar, and took the stool next to Tozzi. *"Qué pasa, goombah?"*

Tozzi did a double take. He didn't seem happy to see his old partner. Suddenly his eyes were all over the place, looking for who knows what. Tozzi had always been a paranoid bastard, but never quite this obvious about it. Gibbons wondered whether Tozzi was afraid he was compromising his cover. Or was Ivers on the money with his suspicions about Tozzi going cuckoo? Tozzi did sort of have that unpleasantly surprised expression, like reality had just dropped by for a visit without calling first.

"What the hell you doin' here?"

Gibbons smiled with his teeth. "Shouldn't use that tone of voice with the customers," he said. In fact, Gibbons didn't like his tone of voice at all. He'd overheard Tozzi doing the wiseass routine with the blond bartender before. He realized Tozzi was trying to stay in character, but the Nicky Newark act was a little *too* good. Gibbons looked down at the rock glass in Tozzi's hand. Bourbon, no doubt. Wild Turkey. Either that or that peculiar rum he likes. But at one-thirty in the afternoon? Was that part of being in character too? Gibbons had a bad feeling.

"What the fuck you doing here?" Tozzi repeated. Again, a little too belligerent for Gibbons's liking.

Gibbons nodded at the blonde in the hat pouring tomato juice into a Bloody Mary. "You boppin' her too? What'sa matter? Can't get enough from the boss's wife?"

Gibbons was guessing, but from the hateful glint in Tozzi's eyes it looked like he'd guessed right. He'd seen Tozzi with Sydney Nashe in the parking garage last night, and even though they were in public there was something about the way she smiled at him and kept touching his sleeve that indicated a little more intimacy than there should've been. He'd followed them into the lobby, and when they got on the VIP elevator alone together, Gibbons caught a glimpse of her reaching up for Tozzi's face as the doors closed. Gibbons had assumed they were going up to the seventeenth floor where Sydney kept her own private suite. He knew about Sydney's playroom from a New Jersey State Police surveillance report that was on file with the Bureau. Tozzi had never mentioned it in any of his reports.

The lines around Tozzi's mouth were getting deep and mean now. Gibbons shook his head. It never fails. When it comes to women, he always leads with his dick. Of course, with this dish Sydney, Gibbons could hardly blame him. "So tell me it isn't true."

Tozzi glanced down the bar to make sure the blonde was out of earshot. "What do you think? Sydney's my best source. Also, my only source."

"So enlighten me. What has she told you that you haven't been telling us?"

Tozzi's nostrils flared when Gibbons said "us," and Gibbons wondered why. Was Tozzi storing up some kind of resentment against the Bureau? Or was he reacting to the fact that his old partner seemed to be putting himself on Ivers's side instead of where they usually were, out on the edge together? Tozzi looked back down the bar before he spoke. "She hasn't told me much. She doesn't give it away."

"So what *has* she told you?"

Tozzi leaned closer. "Nashe is in deep with the Mistrettas. Five years ago they sold him the land we're standing on to build this place. Now his note is overdue and they want their scratch, badly. Sal Immordino has been down to make the collection himself. But as far as I can tell, the balance is still outstanding because Immordino has been back a few times."

Gibbons unconsciously took a sip of the German piss and made a face. "So what's the big secret? You couldn't call this in?"

"I haven't been able to corroborate the stuff about the land yet."

"So what?"

Now Tozzi made a face. "What're you, crazy? I got this from the subject's wife. Wives don't have to testify against their husbands in court. That happens to be the law, if you remember. We could never use this to bring charges against Nashe. *That's* why I didn't call it in." Tozzi took a swig of his drink. "Besides, Ivers would go nuts if he found out I was—you know, with Nashe's wife."

"Yeah, I know." Gibbons swirled the beer in his glass and stared at Tozzi. This undercover had really brought out the guinea in him. The European-cut suit, the little Italian loafers, the styled hair. He had the look down perfect, low-echelon wiseguy with big ideas, the kind of punk who starts out as a driver or a bodyguard and works his way up in the family, hoping to be made a member some day.

Getting made in the mob was like making the varsity team for these kind of guys. It's what they live and breathe for.

Gibbons nodded to himself, thinking, still staring at his old partner. Tozzi's act was on the mark, but he hadn't flipped. No, Ivers was wrong about that. Gibbons knew in his gut that Tozzi was playing it straight, doing his job. He was just doing it his way, the asshole. It would never occur to Tozzi that he could report what he'd learned so that Ivers could dispatch another agent to do the legwork that could back up his information. No, that wasn't Tozzi's way. He had to fly solo, make it a big adventure, then bring it in on a silver platter all by himself. He was like a dumb cat who brings dead birds to your doorstep and sits there, pleased as shit with himself, waiting for praise. Fucking Tozzi. Never was much of a team player. Gibbons sighed and took a sip of the piss. Neither was he.

"So what's the story with the blonde?" Gibbons nodded toward the bartender.

Tozzi smiled. "Valerie. Valerie Raynor. She's nice. I really like her."

"Yeah, and she's got a good beat, easy to dance to."

"Fuck you! It's not like that." Tozzi was suddenly vicious.

Gibbons raised his eyebrows. Could this be love? "It must be something. You been buzzing around her like a fly around shit."

Tozzi stared down at the bar. "I told you. I like her. I mean, I *really* like her. You know what I'm talking about?"

Gibbons looked over at Valerie in her gangster hat, pouring shots, and thought about Lorraine, Lorraine the way she used to be. He knew what Tozzi was talking about. "She mixed in with all this? Nashe and his creditors, I mean."

"No, no, no . . . she just works here." He sounded frustrated, like things weren't working out the way he wanted with this Valerie.

"Then what's the problem? She's not interested in you?"

Tozzi shook his head slowly. "No, I'm getting all the right signals. All systems are go, as far as I can tell."

"But—"

"But how the hell can I put the moves on Valerie when Sydney's always popping out of the woodwork? I gotta be careful just coming here to the bar."

Gibbons frowned. I got news for you, pal. You're not that careful.

Tozzi took another sip. "Sydney's a weird little bitch. If she thought I was getting serious with someone else, she'd cut me right off. Probably have me fired. I've got to be at her beck and call all the time, or else I don't get any more info. When she's in the mood, I've got to drop everything for her. It's getting to be a real pain."

"You're breaking my fucking heart. Such a hardship, porking a babe like Sydney." Asshole.

"Suck my dick." Tozzi knocked back the rest of his drink.

Gibbons sipped his beer. Tozzi was moodier than usual. Either it was the strain of being undercover, or he really had it bad for this Valerie. Whatever it was, Gibbons didn't like his attitude. It wasn't what he said so much as how he said it. His voice had that cocky, wiseguy edge to it. He also seemed a little too quick-tempered. Was Tozzi that stressed out trying to keep his personalities straight? Gibbons reconsidered his original assessment. Maybe Tozzi was wavering on the edge, trying to figure out which Mike was the better one to be, Tozzi or Tomasso.

"Hey, listen, I'm glad you're here," Tozzi said then, a bit conciliatory but not a whole lot.

"Oh, yeah? Why?"

"This bodyguard gig is crazy. I'm supposed to be on a regular schedule, but Nashe is always changing his plans at the last minute and I end up having to put in a lot of overtime. So between guarding Nashe and playing spin the bottle with Sydney, I don't have time for anything. I've got a few leads I've been wanting to run down, but I just can't get away. Let me fill you in and you can do the legwork. First, go over to city hall and find out whose name is on the deed to this land, then—"

"Hold it, hold it, hold it. You know, you do this to me all the time. You make up your mind that you're gonna do things your way, then you drag me into it to hold your hand. Well, you can go fuck yourself this time—"

"Hey, don't yell. You're making a scene here." Tozzi scanned the lounge nervously. "I'm not asking you for a big favor. All I want you to do is go to city hall."

Gibbons rubbed his mouth and looked at the rows of bottles behind the bar. "The last time I did a favor for you, I wound up in the hospital. You remember that?"

Tozzi bit his bottom lip. "I have never in my life met a guy who can hold a grudge like you. We're supposed to be partners. At least we used to be. I'm just trying to make a case here. Why don't you want to help me?"

Gibbons growled under his breath. "Because for one thing your idea of making a case usually involves swinging from the chandeliers, jumping through windows, acting like a cowboy—"

Tozzi made a face. "Come on, will ya?"

"And for another thing, you don't have enough time to make a case like this. There's too much ground to cover, and so far you've got zilch."

"What do you mean, I don't have enough time?"

"Just what I said—you don't have enough time. Ivers is getting itchy. He's giving you till the end of next week to come up with something concrete on Nashe, or he's shutting you down. That gives you—what?—ten, eleven days? You and I both know that you can't make this kind of case in that much time."

"Bullshit. *We* can."

"No, don't give me this *we* shit. I don't want to hear it."

Tozzi clapped Gibbons's shoulder. "Come on. We should at least try."

Gibbons removed his hand. "Forget it."

Tozzi leaned over and whispered in his ear. "Gib, this is your last chance to score a big one before you get married. You know Lorraine's not gonna let you go out on the street once she becomes Mrs. Cuthbert Gibbons."

The muscles in Gibbons's jaw were working. Bastard. He hated it when people used his real name, and he hated it when Tozzi was right. Lorraine was already busting his balls about retiring or at least staying with a desk job at the field office. Fuck that.

Tozzi flashed his big baby browns. "Gib? Am I asking for a lot?"

Fucking snake-oil salesman. "Look, Tozzi, I told you—"

"Is this man harassing you, sir?" Valerie was suddenly standing behind the bar right in front of them. "I'll have him thrown out if he's causing trouble." She pointed her finger in Tozzi's face, looked him in the eye with a wry grin. "We have some very nasty security people here who are trained to take care of people like you."

"Hey, Val, I want you to meet my Uncle Bert. Uncle Bert, this is Valerie Raynor."

"Nice to meet you." She held out her hand.

Gibbons shook her hand and nodded, stomach acid creeping up his throat. Uncle Bert, huh? He hated it when Tozzi made cracks about his age. Fucking wiseass shit.

"What do you need?" she asked, pointing to Gibbons's glass. "Another one?"

"No thanks." Not the German piss.

"You?" she asked Tozzi. "As if you need it."

"No, I'm driving." Tozzi grinned up at her, staring into her eyes. He did have it bad for Valerie. Gooney bastard.

She laughed at him. "You know, you're not kidding anyone, pal. I know a lush when I see one."

"Val, you hurt my feelings."

The two of them went on like this for a while. Gibbons studied Valerie. She had a teardrop nose, sad eyes, and a husky voice. Her mouth favored one side more than the other, and she definitely wasn't a natural blonde. But it was all put together right, so that the whole was a lot better than the parts. She seemed to have a lot on the ball—even if she did like Tozzi—and she was good at putting him in his place. Gibbons just couldn't figure out why she reminded him so much of Lorraine. They looked nothing like each other. Maybe it had to do with having a lot on the ball. Lorraine did. Or at least she used to, before she started worrying about curtains and caterers and all that shit.

Gibbons let out a long sigh. Getting married didn't seem so inevitable sitting down here at the bar in Atlantic City. He couldn't back out now, though. It would destroy Lorraine. He just wished he could work up a little enthusiasm for this thing. But what with the way she'd been acting lately, his heart just wasn't in it. Maybe they'd end up making each other miserable. He looked over at Valerie in her gray fedora, sticking her tongue out at Tozzi. Maybe he should think about this.

Gibbons pulled a ten out of his wallet and laid it on the bar. "Say, Valerie, I changed my mind. How about a shot of VO and a glass of whatever you have on tap that tastes the least like piss?"

She smiled at him. "A man after my own heart. Beer and a bump, coming up." She grabbed a bottle of whiskey and a shot glass and poured him a drink, then moved down the bar to draw a draft from the tap.

Tozzi leaned toward him. "A little early in the day, isn't it?"

"Look who's talking." Gibbons turned the shot glass around on the bar, waiting for his beer.

"So what do you say? You gonna stay and help me out here?"

Gibbons glanced at him out of the corner of his eye. "Sure. Why not?" It'll be a nice break from your cousin the Curtain Queen, give me some time to think.

Valerie delivered the beer, picked up the ten, and went over to the cash register to ring it up. Gibbons hoisted the VO and threw it back in one gulp.

"I knew you'd change your mind, Gib. I know you like a book. You can't resist."

Gibbons took a slow, cool sip of beer, letting it trickle down his throat. He looked at Tozzi over the rim of his glass.

Tozzi was flashing his wiseguy grin. "You're a good guy, Gib. You really are. I owe you."

Gibbons put down his beer, laid his hand on his old partner's shoulder, leaned in close, and smiled warmly with eyes crinkling, just like ole Uncle Bert. "Lemme tell you something, Toz."

"What?"

"Eat shit."

Sal had his arm crooked behind his head against the headboard. He was scratching his balls under the sweaty sheet as he watched Sydney sitting up next to him, rubbing cuticle cream on her nails.

The woman ought to keep a dipstick up her twat, he thought, what with all the oils and creams and shit she uses. She gets all greased up before she goes to bed, and now she gets up and does it all over again. Jesus.

He reached over and started to rub her nipple between his thumb and index finger, mimicking the way she rubbed the cream into her nails. She gave him a sly little grin through the strands of hair falling over her face, but she didn't stop working on her nails. She needed a pair of heart-shaped sunglasses right now, he thought. Like Lolita. That's what she looked like now, sitting up in bed here. She was about as big as a kid in eighth grade, he figured, but she definitely had all the grown-up equipment. Half the time she had this real sweet, drop-dead gorgeous face, but if she caught you looking, it would change. She'd turn into a lusty bitch, like a horny milkmaid looking for a roll in the hay, something like that. Maybe that was why he couldn't stay away from her. Because she just looked like fun, like something you weren't supposed to have.

He grinned and circled the dark, pebbly skin around her nipple with his thumb, feeling the texture. She did have great tits. He wondered if they were real, though. Lots of rich broads get those implant things, Baggies full of silicone sewn up in there. He plucked the nipple like a guitar string.

"Easy." She shrugged away from him, the little sly grin behind the white-blond strands. She didn't want him to stop.

He reached over and gently played with her tit, feeling around for surgical scars. As he felt around, his mind wandered and he started thinking about that bug Cil found in the crucifix. Fucking cops. They must've paid off the jeweler. Juicy was gonna send one of his guys over to have a little talk with him today. Cops could've broken into the guy's shop, though, did the work on the cross without his knowing about it. Bastards. At least Cil hadn't been wearing the damn thing very long. He'd only given it to her that morning. If the bastards heard anything, it was when they were all eating. But what had they said, really? Not that much. Sal kept worrying Sydney's nipple, trying to remember if anyone had mentioned the fight directly. He couldn't remember. Shit. Maybe they ought to forget about this deal with Nashe.

Sydney stopped rubbing her nails. "You're gonna wear it out, Sal."

"Huh?" Then he realized she was talking about her tit, and he dropped his hand and scratched his balls through the sheet instead.

He sighed and looked around the purple room. No, excuse me—*lavender.* The whole room was lavender, just like the rest of this fucking boat. Inside and out, all the same color. The famous lavender yacht. Custom-built, twelve bedrooms, big ballroom glassed in on the deck—who knows how many fucking feet long?—big crew, wine cellar, the whole number. And everything lavender. Her favorite color. Sal looked at Sydney, lashes lowered on her cheeks, still concentrating on her nails. A little gift from Russ. *Madonn'!* What money these people must have.

Not just millionaires, *billionaires.* A billion dollars . . . one thousand million clams. And how many times over? Goddamn depressing. Nashe's got all that money to work with, and fucking cheap-shit Mistretta leaves me a lousy thirty mil to run the whole family. What the hell am I supposed to do with that? Son of a bitch, *I* should be dealing in billions now. The old guy's got a cheap-shit mentality. And when he gets out of jail it's gonna be the same old shit all over again. Playing it safe. Small risks and small rewards. Shoulda taken advantage when I had the chance. Shoulda done what I wanted to do. Pulled off some big scores when he first went in. Bought those cement factories. I could've done a lot. Too late now. Coulda, woulda, shoulda . . . At least I got this thing with Nashe. If I can trust the bastard. If he's really got the cash he says he does.

Sal looked at the fur comforter, ran his bare foot over it, and wondered about Nashe's assets. Rich people can be funny. They've got a lot of things, but they don't always have cash. No liquidity. That day at the construction site he said his money was all tied up. Is that what he's gonna tell me after the fight? What if I get Walker to throw it and Walker does, then Nashe stiffs him? Then what? Is Walker gonna run to the cops? Tell them the big bad mobster Sal Immordino made him do it? Fuck.

He looked over at her. "Your husband really as rich as they say he is?"

She shrugged. "I don't know. All I know is what I read in the papers." The sly little grin again.

Sal frowned. He needed real answers, not cute ones. "He can't be worth that much, c'mon."

"One point five billion. According to *New York* magazine."

"What do *you* think?"

Another shrug. "I've never had to wait for a check to clear."

Very funny. Did this broad ever get serious?

Sydney scratched more cream out of the little jar and went back to her nails. Sal's stomach rumbled. He hadn't eaten since lunch. There was a kitchen on this tug, but Sydney probably didn't know where it was. Those hands didn't do dishes. They could call the butler, or whatever the hell you call him on a boat, to bring some food, but Sal didn't want anyone else to know he was here. Bad enough that the bodyguard she's got watching the boat saw him coming aboard. And this wasn't the first time the guy's seen him here. Sydney says don't worry, he's okay, he works for her, not Russ. But who knows? Nashe is the kind of guy who'd drop a grand on a bodyguard now and then just to let him know what's going on with the wife. Yeah, he probably does that a lot, with all the help. That's money for you. Course Sydney doesn't seem to give a shit one way or another whether Russ finds out about them or not. And what the hell does he care who she's sleeping with? He doesn't sleep with her. Strange people. That's what too much money does to them, makes 'em strange.

Yeah, I should be so strange.

Sal sat up and opened the liquor cabinet built into the headboard. Maybe there was something to eat in there. He rummaged around behind the bottles of booze nobody drinks and found a can of smoked almonds. You could see from the picture on the can that they were the kind loaded with salt. Very bad for you. He kept feeling around behind the bottles until he found a big jar of macadamia nuts. These were good, but he knew he shouldn't have them. Lot of cholesterol in these things. Expensive too. Four, five bucks for just a little tiny jar. Sal unscrewed the cap and took a sniff. Fuck the cholesterol. You gotta live sometime. He poured out a handful and shot a few into his mouth.

They were good. He settled back against the headboard, popping macadamia nuts, staring at the lavender-dyed fur comforter hanging off the foot of the bed, wondering if it was mink or fox or what.

"You want a nut?" He held out the jar to her.

"No thanks." She shook her head, still concentrating on her goddamn nails.

"Go ahead, have one. Russ paid for them."

She shook her head, swishing all that great blond hair over her shoulders. He wished to hell he could think of some way to get her to talk about Russ's money without being too obvious about it, but he couldn't think of anything. Besides, when Sydney didn't want to talk, you could ask till you were blue in the face. She talked only when she wanted to talk.

Sal settled back down into the pillows and started thinking about the fight deal again, wondering whether he should pull out of it. If anything went wrong, Mistretta would go bullshit, might even do a Tommy Ricks number on him. It was possible. The old man was strict and losing money made him crazy. He could get that mad. But on the other hand, deals like this don't come along every day. When would he be able to make a score like this again? Maybe never.

He traced invisible figures on the sheet with his finger, multiplying in his head. If the odds are five to one at fight-time—five times thirty—we make one hundred fifty million. I get twenty percent . . . that's thirty mil. If they're six to one, we make one eighty and I get . . . thirty-six mil. I could buy two of the cement factories with that. Get something going with Frank Bartolo and the unions. Make sure we get a few contracts for some nice big buildings. It would be all right. Wouldn't make billions, but it would be all right. Could even buy a nice purple boat if I wanted one. Not a big stupid yacht like this thing, no. One of those speedboats. What do they call them? Cigarette boats. Nice. Sal popped another couple of macadamia nuts. Life is nice when you've got money, money like this. The cops couldn't have heard anything the other day. This fight scam is too good to give up. A once-in-a-lifetime opportunity. Hell, it would be stupid to back out now. Sal poured out another handful of nuts. He grinned and chewed, running his bare toes through the soft lavender fur. This was practically a sure thing. Just about a sure thing. Hey, what the hell—

"So are you going to tell me?" Sydney suddenly asked, still working on her cuticles.

"Huh? Tell you what?"

"What you and Russell are cooking up together?" She didn't lift her eyes from her work.

"What do you care?"

She looked at him. "I like to know these things. You know that."

Sal shrugged. "I don't know nothin'." He popped a few more macadamias and grinned at her. She's really something, this broad.

She turned on her side, reached over, and started twirling the hair on Sal's chest. "Why are you so suspicious of *me*? All I want is to save my marriage." She even said it with a straight face.

"Give me a break. You hate his guts."

"So? That doesn't mean I don't want to be Mrs. Russell Nashe anymore." She exposed one leg and ran her little toes through the lavender fur and up Sal's foot. "Face it, Sal, alimony could never match this. I wouldn't be poor if I divorced him, but all the excitement would be gone."

Sal shrugged again. "Money isn't exciting?"

"Not by itself, no. I like getting written up in the papers, getting invited to fabulous dinner parties, going places, meeting important people. *That's* exciting. My first husband had money—not nearly as much as Russell—but he had money. He was a farty vice president at Drexel Lambert, the classic Brooks Brothers type. When we were divorced, he was making something like a million a year with bonuses. We lived in a big house in Bedminster, threw boring dinner parties for boring people, *went* to boring dinner parties *thrown* by boring people. I mean, our big social event of the year was Malcolm Forbes's annual Christmas party. The last one I went to, Malcolm himself had the good sense not to show up. You can't imagine how dreadful that life was for me. I redecorated the house twice a year, and no matter what I did, the place always looked like a mausoleum. I had affairs, but that was boring, too, because my husband knew and he didn't care. All he cared about was his damn prostate. I felt like I'd died."

"So what's so great about being married to Nashe? He doesn't even sleep with you."

"Yes, he does. Once a year. Usually around Christmas. But that's not the point."

Sal poured out some more nuts. "So what is the point?"

She brought her face up close to his and opened her eyes wide. "The point is that being Mrs. Russell Nashe is a whole . . . lotta . . . fun."

Sal made a face. "Get outta here."

"It's true. Anybody can be rich, but not everybody can be celebrity-rich, superrich. I don't want to be locked up in some lonely mansion, staring at my bankbooks. I want to be where the action is. *Lifestyles of the Rich and Famous.* I want to *swim* in money."

"You're a wack, you know that? I don't know what the hell you're talking about."

Sydney sighed and fell back into her pillow. "Russell would love to divorce me, but I know too much about how he operates. Not always aboveboard." That sly little grin again. "He doesn't tell me anything about his business, but I find things out. And he knows I'm the type who'll kiss and tell. I think he's stuck with me."

Madonn', some Lolita. Sal shook his head and probed the back of his mouth with his tongue where a piece of macadamia nut was lodged in his molars. "You're a real wack."

She put her head on her shoulder and looked at him sideways. "How do you think I got this yacht?"

Sal thought about it. It's possible. Nashe supposedly

doesn't even like boats. She could've squeezed him for it. Rich people are all fucking nuts.

"So are you going to tell me what you and Russell are up to?" she repeated. "It has something to do with the fight, doesn't it?"

Sal had his finger in his mouth, trying to dislodge that piece of macadamia nut. "Who says we're doing anything with the fight?" Jesus, how the hell—?

"I have my sources." She grinned and moved the hair away from her face with her pinkie.

"So who told you?" He already had a pretty good idea. That bodyguard, the one who was feeling her up in the elevator . . . that tall fuck with the Dudley Do-right face, the one who looks like a cop. Tomasso. "Who told you I got a deal going with Russ? That's not true."

Sydney shrugged, then sat up and went back to her cuticle cream. Now she was gonna get cute.

"Who told you we got something going with the fight? That bodyguard your husband's got? The one who thinks he's such a hot shit? Tomassi, Tomasso, whatever his name is."

Sydney shrugged and kept rubbing her nails, still with the little grin.

"You fucking him too? He tells you what you want to hear in bed? Is that how it goes?"

"You sound jealous, Sal."

"Jealous? What are you, kiddin'? What do you think, you're my girlfriend?" Sal shoved his finger into the back of his mouth. He couldn't get that fucking macadamia nut loose. He wasn't jealous. She's a whore, for chrissake—what's there to be jealous? It was that fuck Tomasso. He knew there was something wrong with that guy the minute he saw him. He could be a cop, sure. He's sleeping with her, pumping her for information, same way she must do with everybody else. Tomasso could fuck everything up, depending on how much he knows. Shit. What if he knows about the fix? Oughta break his goddamn back, shut him up for good. Fucking Tomasso, he's gonna screw me up here. Bastard! If it is him who told Sydney, he's dead. Definitely.

"So what's the story with this guy Tomasso? He got a baseball bat in his pants or what?"

"Mike's a nice guy." Her eyelashes were on her cheeks again. She was gonna be shy and innocent now.

"Whattaya mean 'nice guy'? I'm not a nice guy?"

"Mike tells me little things."

"What little things?" He reached way back with his pinkie, but he couldn't get the nut out of his teeth. God-*damn* it.

Sydney grinned and kept her eyes on her nails, then she started to hum a little tune.

Sal rolled his eyes to the ceiling. Here we go with the singing. *Madonn'.* "This must be a new one. I don't recognize it."

"Sal . . ." She just looked at him. "It's the theme from *The Beverly Hillbillies."* She said it as if he was supposed to know.

She started humming again, and he knew she'd keep it up until he told her what she wanted to hear. She thinks she's clever when she pulls this crap with the TV songs. The last time it was the song from *Mr. Ed.* The time before that, *The Flintstones.* Yabba-dabba-doo, for chrissake. He hated it when she did this with the songs. But he had to know if it was Tomasso.

He waited, hoping she'd stop humming, but she didn't. He was going to have to play along with her, so he bit his bottom lip and rolled his eyes like Ralph Kramden. "All right, stop with the humming, will ya?"

She switched from humming to singing da-da-da, a little louder now.

"Shut up now, I'm asking you." Making like he was really getting mad.

She kept singing as she rubbed cream into her nails, the little grin turning into a smile.

"Come on, stop now." He put a little pleading into his voice.

She didn't stop.

"Hey, listen to me, listen to me. Your boyfriend Tomasso is right. Okay? You satisfied?"

She looked over at him, still singing, still rubbing her nails. She wanted more.

He clasped his hands together as if he were praying and looked up at the ceiling. "I swear to Christ, if this was my wife, I wouldn't divorce her, I'd kill her." This was what Sydney liked, the WASP version of an Italian. Guido in his guinea T-shirt, hanging out on the corner. Ha-ha-ha, very funny. Bitch.

She laughed and kept singing. *The Beverly Hillbillies.* Look at her. She's unbelievable. Superrich, my ass. Lee Iacocca's wife doesn't watch *The Beverly Hillbillies,* you can bet on that. Maybe when she was married to the other guy, she sat home all day watching television. She's weird enough. She's weird enough to keep this up all night and not tell him about Tomasso too.

"You know, it's no big deal," he said. "It's not what you're thinking. Yeah, yeah, Russ and I are doing business and it does involve the fight. Okay? You wanna know what it is? I'll tell you. It has to do with the unions."

She looked skeptical.

"Yeah, the unions. The janitors and the sanitation workers. Your husband wants to make sure the place is cleaned up right after the fight, *that night.* That means people will have to be working early Sunday morning and, by rights, they don't have to work then if they don't want to. That's why he came to me. For a price, I keep the unions in line so that the place gets cleaned up right away, no problem. There, that's the big deal we got going. You satisfied now? Now, who told you about it?"

That sly little grin. Very proud of herself. She reached over for the jar of macadamia nuts, took one, stuck it between her teeth, and crunched down loud enough for him to hear. She chewed a little, then started humming again.

Jesus Christ Almighty, this woman! He twisted his tongue and worked on that goddamn nut stuck in his teeth.

Tomasso told her. Had to be him, had to be. But how did *he* know? Sal contorted his tongue and finally got the piece of macadamia to come loose. He guided the tiny piece to the tip of his tongue and crushed it with his front teeth. "So what else did your friend Tomasso tell you?"

She screwed the cap on the small jar of cuticle cream and put it on the night table. "I didn't say it was Mike who told me. Besides, I never reveal my sources." She turned over on her side and started rubbing his crotch through the sheet.

"It was him. I know. It had to be." The son of a bitch. Thirty-six million. No one's gonna fuck me out of that. Cop or no cop. I want my own life-style of the rich and famous.

She started humming again as she got to her knees and dangled those tits of hers right in front of his face.

"Enough with the hillbillies! You're giving me a headache."

She threw back the sheet, clutched his stiff dick, straddled him, and used it on herself like a dildo. All greased and ready to go. Unbelievable.

"Ummm . . . 'black gold, Texas tea.'" Her eyes half closed, grinning.

He pulled her hands away, arched his back, and gave her the whole thing, right up to the hilt. She squirmed and twisted, but she wouldn't stop with the goddamn humming. "Hey, Sydney, do me a favor, will ya?"

"What would that be?"

"Just shut up and fuck."

She moaned and grinned—Lolita on a bucking bronco—but she didn't stop humming. He linked fingers with her and decided to give her a good ride. What a weird bitch. Weird and nosy. He wondered what the hell she sang for that bastard Tomasso.

9

Everybody was watching the action up in the ring, everybody except Tozzi and the other bodyguards. Tozzi was in position, standing a few feet behind Russell Nashe, his arms crossed over his chest as he stared across the crowded gym. He didn't like what he saw. The double doorway across the gym was open, bright with sunlight from outside. He could make out two silhouettes, one of them a huge figure, easily as big as the big man up in the ring, Charles Epps. Tozzi couldn't make out the faces, but the big guy was big enough to be Sal Immordino, Sal standing there with his brother Joseph. But what would they be doing here at Charles Epps's training camp with all these reporters and TV people? Much too much exposure for a slug like Immordino. Unless he was here for a reason, to make sure something was done maybe. To make sure a certain fed who was working undercover was taken care of? Tozzi stared at the silhouettes. He didn't like this. Suddenly *he* felt exposed. He squinted, trying to make out the faces, but it was no use. The sun was too bright.

Tozzi turned away from the doorway and glanced up at the ring. The harsh gymnasium lights were gleaming off Charles Epps's shaved head as he stalked his anonymous sparring partner, a black guy whose face was obscured by the headgear. The sparring partner bore more than a passing resemblance to "Pain" Walker in size, physique, and complexion. No coincidence. But Tozzi had gotten a good look at the guy's face before this demo bout started, and there was one big difference between him and the champ: he was a lot closer to Epps's age than to Walker's. The guy wasn't feeble, but he wasn't twenty-six either. Like Epps, he fought in bursts, on again, off again, pacing himself so he wouldn't run out of gas, punching in flurries, then backing off and circling to get a breather. Epps was doing that right now, circling backward with heavy loping steps that might've been mistaken for footwork once upon a time. He was still credible as a contender, though, because of his hard punch. Tozzi could tell from that keen homicidal look in his eye that he was looking to use it. It was the same look Sal had when he had his big paw around Tozzi's throat in the elevator the other day. Wonderful.

Epps circled back toward his opponent now and started throwing left-jab, right-cross combinations, still looking for that opening. Tozzi heard the hiss of tired lungs and saw sprays of sweat against the lights as Epps kept punching doggedly, hoping to get lucky. Then out of the blue he threw a freight-train right that just missed, grazing the sparring partner's headgear and whipping his head around as if it had really connected. The restless crowd woke up and took notice. Tozzi was surprised and impressed himself. Apparently so was the sparring partner because he wasted no time backpedaling out of range. By all indications, Epps's legendary killer right hadn't aged a bit.

The bell rang then and the fighters went to their corners. Tozzi looked back at the doorway, but he couldn't see the big silhouette anymore and that made him a little nervous. He wanted to know where the big guy had gone, wanted to know if it was really Sal.

The crowd started grumbling a little louder now, the reporters and photographers griping to each other, trading nasty opinions, looking over at the buffet table with hungry eyes, wondering when the hell this would get over with so they could eat. Nashe was smiling hard, scrutinizing the press, trying to read their collective feelings about the challenger. He'd invited them down here to Epps's training camp to build up some excitement for the fight, to prove to them that Epps wasn't the "shot" fighter they'd all been calling him, but this group didn't exactly seem thrilled to have made the trip out here to the middle of nowhere in the Jersey Pine Barrens.

Tozzi studied Nashe sitting on a folding chair next to the governor of New Jersey. Nashe was ignoring the reporters now. He wasn't going to let them bother him. He was smiling and yakking away now, having a grand old time with the gov. It was his party, after all. The governor didn't look very happy, though. He seldom did. The man always looked gray and constipated. Even the governor's bodyguards looked constipated. They were the usual Secret Service types—neat single-breasted suits, solid-color ties, Ray-Bans, little earplug receivers in their ears. One of these guys clearly thought Tozzi was an iffy character because he kept looking at him as if he expected Tozzi to suddenly erupt and do something crazy. This was almost funny. If the guy only knew. Tozzi suddenly looked over his shoulder and scanned the crowd. But does Sal know?

"Damn," Nashe said to the governor, loud enough for the whole gym to hear, "I hope we look as good as Charles when we get that old."

A few of the reporters snickered, but the governor didn't seem to get it. Epps did, though, and he glared down at Nashe from his corner. He was not amused.

The bell rang then, and Epps thundered out to the middle of the ring. Either Nashe's comment had gotten him riled or he'd decided to give the yawning scribes something to write about. Whatever the reason, Epps came out swinging. His sparring partner didn't like the look of this sudden burst of youthful energy, and after that last near miss he wasn't going to take any chances. He moved in close and hung on Epps's arms. The guy wasn't stupid. He knew he was supposed to be the sacrificial goat. He just didn't want to have to take the full wrath of that right just so Epps could get a little extra space in the papers. The guy must've figured he could take whatever the big man was throwing in close like this—long arms at short range get cramped, can't do as much damage. Theoretically at least.

Tozzi took a quick look around the room, then went back to watching the fighters. He put himself in the sparring partner's place, imagining what he'd do if he was in there with Epps. He certainly wouldn't box him, no way. Aikido, that was his thing. Never box a boxer, as his *sensei* always said. But as he watched these guys fight, the prospect of facing a boxer intrigued him. Offhand, he could think of a few techniques that might work nicely against a boxer's punch. A boxer might actually be great to practice with, since all aikido techniques are purely self-defensive, based on responding to an attack, never initiating one. In fact, the more aggressive the attacker is, the more the aikidoist can do. Since the boxer has to attack to score points, he might make the perfect *uke,* the perfect partner for aikido practice. Theoretically.

Watching the two fighters butting heads, trading sloppy uppercuts, Tozzi got a tremendous urge to go work out at his dojo again. He hadn't been to a class in over two months, not since he started this undercover assignment. Obviously, while he was Mike Tomasso, he couldn't do anything that might connect him to his real identity. He thought about trying to find a dojo around Atlantic City, but he usually put in long days guarding Nashe, and his work schedule was so unpredictable, he hadn't even bothered looking in the Yellow Pages. But watching these guys go at it now made him want to get back on the mat, do some big throws, get thrown, work on his falls, his *ukemi,* work on the techniques used against various kinds of attacks, put himself back into a martial frame of mind.

Yeah, but what do you do against a bullet?

Pray.

Tozzi sighed and scanned the room. Oh, where, oh, where is my little lost Sal?

The round continued without much excitement. Epps was working hard and getting nowhere. He was also doing a lot of grunting behind his mouthpiece—probably warning his sparring partner to wise up and take a good shot for the crowd if he wanted to get his paycheck this week. But the guy seemed reluctant to go along with this—maybe it was the way Epps was snorting like a bull—so he stayed where he was, in close, right in the man's face.

But then Epps managed to settle himself down and started making those uppercuts count, throwing them with rhythm, swinging down low and coming up with real force. Tozzi could hear that lung hiss with each blow and now it sounded like power, not age. These shots were landing, twisting the sparring partner's head violently with each punch. It didn't take more than a half dozen of these uppercuts before Epps had pried the man loose. The reporters were paying attention now, and Nashe was on the edge of his seat, overriding the hubbub, cheering Epps on.

Epps was putting on a real show now, jabbing effectively with his left while keeping the crowd in suspense by cocking his right and faking with it. The other guy had his hands up, but he wasn't doing much more than protecting his head. From where Tozzi was standing he couldn't tell if the guy was in a daze or just resigned to his fate. Epps was in full control now and he was playing it to the hilt, hanging back with the right, using it only to block, keeping it cocked for the knockout everybody wanted to see, making the crowd wonder when the hell he was going to let it fly. Finally someone from Epps's corner yelled out the time left in the round, and Epps nodded to himself. It was time to bring down the house. He kept jabbing and jabbing with the left until he had the man set up nice, right where he wanted him, then he paused half a second and launched it, let it fly like an ICBM straight to the chin. The punch hit so hard, the sparring partner fell back into the ropes, catapulted forward, and flopped back into the ring like a rag doll, hitting the canvas flat on his face.

Cameras flashed as Epps sauntered back to his corner, slow and deliberate. People rushed into the ring and surrounded him, thrusting microphones and small cassette recorders in his face. He ignored them all as his people wiped him down and untied his gloves.

Peering through the jungle of legs crowding the ring, Tozzi got a quick look at the sparring partner's face pressed against the canvas. The whites of his eyes stood out against the dark face trapped in leather headgear. Not pretty. Sal Immordino used to do worse to his opponents in the ring. He'd killed a fighter once. Tozzi turned around quick and looked for a big man towering over the crowd. There were butterflies in his stomach. Float like a butterfly . . . sting like a slug.

Epps climbed down out of the ring, and Nashe made a big deal out of introducing him to the governor. Barechested, skin shimmering with sweat, he stood between the two men, smiling his big gap-toothed smile for the cameras. Nashe, an old pro at smiling for the cameras, held up the fighter's taped hand like a referee declaring the victor. This was the picture Nashe wanted the papers to run—the big man sandwiched between a multibillionaire and a sitting governor, three winners all in a row. To get people to pay to see this fight, Nashe had to get the message across that Epps was a credible contender, that he actually could beat "Pain" Walker. If the papers ran this photo, Nashe didn't give a shit what the writers said about Epps. The photo always carries more punch that the print, Tozzi had once overheard Nashe saying. Your average fight fan just reads the box scores and looks at the pictures, according to Nashe.

The cameramen had all jammed in together to get that

shot of the "three winners." They were like a single giant organism, flashing and squirming and yelling and muttering. Tozzi didn't like this setup—the reporters were too close, too disorganized. It was bad, security-wise. In that chaotic mass of cameras and bodies, a gunman could get off a good shot or two before he was even noticed. Tozzi squinted against the camera flashes, getting spots in front of his eyes, his heart beating fast, waiting for the first gunshot, ready to hit the floor and go for his weapon.

Why the hell did I take this undercover? he thought. This is crazy. I'm gonna die!

The camera flashes kept firing and firing, then they trailed off and Epps put his arm down, the "three winners" dropping their pose. Nothing had happened. No hitman in the crowd. As the cameramen dispersed, Tozzi was left with nothing but the sound of his own heart pounding.

He took a deep breath and hoped he didn't look as rattled as he felt. Nashe and the governor were at the edge of the ring now, discussing something privately. Epps and his entourage were moving toward the locker room. The reporters and cameramen were stampeding the buffet table, getting what they had really come here for. Nashe had brought along a gang of people from the casino to serve free food and drink for the press. More than anything else, an open bar will win you a writer's good will—another Nashe-ism. Between the spots in front of his eyes, Tozzi thought he saw a gray hat behind the bar. He blinked and squinted, then smiled. It *was* her—white shirt, black vest, gray fedora and all. He didn't know she was supposed to be here. Val—

Oooww! Something stung the middle of his back. Instantly he dropped to a crouch and went for the gun in his ankle holster. Shit!

"Hey, Tomasso! What the hell you doin'?"

Tozzi looked up at the black suit standing over him. His heart was slamming. It was Lenny Mokowski. Tozzi rolled down his pant leg and stood up. "Don't do that, Lenny." He'd only slapped Tozzi on the back.

"What the hell's wrong with you, Tomasso? Who you s'posed to be guarding over here? A ghost? Mr. Nashe is way over there, behind you." Lenny's greasy pompadour was pointed right up in Tozzi's face.

"Yeah, I know. I'm watching him."

"The eff you are, Tomasso. You know, you're something else, I'm telling you. You woulda never made it as a cop. Never."

"Get off my case, will ya, Lenny?"

"No, I won't get off your case. Not until you shape up."

"I'm working on it, I'm working on it." Go away. I just want to go talk to Val. Before I have a heart attack.

"Listen to me now. We got a change in plans." Lenny took out a set of keys and dangled them between his stubby fingers. "Mr. Nashe is gonna ride up to Trenton with the governor in the governor's car now so they can talk. The 'copter's gonna pick him up there. Frank and me are staying with Mr. Nashe, Johnny the chauffeur's gonna drive the Rolls back, and I want you to drive our car back."

"Right." Tozzi took the keys and nodded, trying to look bored. He didn't want Lenny to pick up on the fact that he was overjoyed to be getting out of there sooner than he'd expected.

"Go ahead, go now. With the governor's men here, we're more than covered. I'll catch up with you later at the Plaza." Lenny turned and walked away.

Tozzi gave him a salute good-bye. It was amazing. From behind, in that black suit, the man looked even more like a bowling ball than he normally did.

Breathing easier, Tozzi pocketed the keys and pushed his way through the crush at the bar. Valerie saw him coming and she just looked at him with that sly half grin of hers.

She tipped her hat back and leaned on the bar. "What can I do you for, stranger?"

Tozzi grinned. About a week in bed.

"Excuse me, excuse me." A reporter elbowed his way in front of Tozzi, a tall, gangly preppy type with googly tortoise-shell glasses and suede patches on the elbows of his jacket. "I'd like a vodka on the rocks. Do you have Stolie back there? I'll take the Stolie."

"In a minute, pal," Tozzi said. "I got business here." He turned back to Valerie. "I'm driving our car back to the casino. Alone. You want a ride?"

Her smirk widened. "My mother warned me about boys like you."

"What'm I gonna do to you? I'll be driving."

"As if I haven't heard that one before."

"Finlandia. Have you got Finlandia? I'll take Finlandia."

Tozzi glared at the pushy asshole. He only *looked* like a mild-mannered academic. "She'll be with you in a minute. Just take it easy. You're not paying for it, for chrissake."

"When you leaving?" she asked.

"Whenever you're ready. No rush." God, she looked good.

She picked up a rock glass and flipped it from hand to hand. "This'll die down in a half hour, maybe less. I can take off then."

"Absolut. How about Absolut? Vodka? I'll take Absolut."

Tozzi grabbed the guy by his tweedy lapels. "Listen, my friend. Can't you see that I'm trying to put the moves on this lady? Can't you see that this is a critical juncture in our relationship and that you and your fucking drinking problem are putting my future happiness in jeopardy? Have any of these things occurred to you?"

The preppy rotated his head like a turtle trying to get back into his shell. "Let go of me."

"Has it occurred to you that I outweigh you by about fifty pounds? That I have markedly violent tendencies and that it's entirely possible that I'm carrying double-Y chromosomes? That people like me are just plain bad and should simply be avoided?"

"I said let go of me." He started bending and curving in the weirdest way, like he was going to change into something else. Val reached over and stroked Tozzi's cheek then. "What a man. How can a woman resist such masculine charm?"

"Let go of me!" The preppy was melting. He was made out of wax.

Tozzi tightened his grip and looked at Valerie. "I'll wait for you out in the parking lot. It's the black Mercury parked under the trees."

"I said let go of me!"

"And get this guy a vodka, will ya? Smirnoff's will do." He let go of the preppy's lapels, and Valerie fluttered her eyelashes, clutched her heart, and let out a deep sigh. My hero. Tozzi shook his head and laughed as he worked his way out of the crunch. She was something else.

He jingled the keys in his pocket as he walked through the noisy gym. He felt good, hopeful. He was getting out of that madhouse, but better than that he was finally going to be able to spend some time with Valerie without having to worry about Sydney showing up. Sydney had taken the lavender yacht up to Manhattan to throw a cocktail party or something. She wouldn't be back until tomorrow night. So if he and Valerie decided to take their friendship to—how would you put it? the next plateau? a higher plane? whatever—at least the night was all theirs. Tozzi couldn't help grinning to himself. As he passed the heavy bag on his way out, he balled his fists and gave it a few quick shots. *Pow-pow, pow!* He felt good.

Stepping out into the red-dirt parking lot, he shaded his eyes from the sun. It was hot for April and the birds were making a racket up in the pines. They seemed to be confused by the unseasonably warm weather. Why start building your nest early when it could snow again? Jersey weather was like that. Tozzi squinted up into the tree and spotted a couple of cardinals flittering around on a branch.

Oh, what the hell, go on, do it. Have a little faith.

He walked across the dusty lot, heading for the shade of the big pines over by the lodge where the Mercury was parked. The sun was glinting off the car hoods, and suddenly it felt more like mid-June than early April. Tozzi loosened his tie. Maybe they could get out to the beach this afternoon. As he approached the black Mercury he noticed that Nashe's white Rolls was already gone. Johnny the chauffeur had already left.

Under the shade of the trees there was a blond guy huddled over a camera, cursing to himself. He was wearing jeans, a tan corduroy sport jacket, and running shoes—photographer chic. "Excuse me," he said as Tozzi approached the Mercury. "Could you give me a hand over here? Film's jammed and I need an extra finger."

"Sure." Tozzi walked into the shade to see what he could do for the guy. "What do you need?"

The blond guy showed him the open back of a 35mm with an elaborate flash attachment. "Here. See right here?" He suddenly whipped the camera up and bashed Tozzi over the nose with it.

Instinctively Tozzi grabbed his face. Blind anger told him to rip the guy's throat out, but before he could make a move he felt something in his back. Hard and small, dead center on his spine. A hand from behind grabbed the material on his shoulder and yanked him back, digging the gun barrel deeper into his flesh. Tozzi glanced over his shoulder and saw the gunman. He was wearing a cheap herringbone-tweed jacket, still crisp and new from the store, and the kind of designer jeans that aren't quite the right color. The hand on his shoulder had a heavy gold bracelet and a big gaudy ring with two rows of diamonds on it. Tozzi caught the guy's reflection in the window of the car parked in front of him. The gunman's dark hair was slicked straight back. A greaser in sheep's clothing.

The blond guy's hair was shaved close around his ears, long and wavy on top. He kept scratching behind his ear, like a dog, as he paced back and forth in front of Tozzi. He kept clenching his jaw and showing his teeth. Must've had a nervous tic or something. Maybe rabies.

Tozzi glanced at him as the pain of the blow to his nose gathered around his eyes. His head and his heart started pounding in competition. The gunman must've felt the vibrations. Tozzi was waiting for Blondie to say it: *You're a fucking fed, and we're gonna blow your fucking head off.* That's what he's gonna say. Immordino did know. Oh, shit . . .

Blondie kept walking back and forth, back and forth, clenching his jaw and making all kinds of faces. Tozzi couldn't stand it anymore. "What do you want with me?"

"Don't . . . say . . . a word. You . . . just . . . listen." The blond guy enunciated every word, but he didn't stop pacing. The greaser jammed the gun into Tozzi's spine for emphasis, as if he needed it. "This is from Sal Immordino. Okay? He says you're not a good boy. He says you don't know how to mind your own . . . fucking . . . business."

Maybe they don't know, Tozzi thought. Maybe Sal's just jealous, because of Sydney. It's possible. Maybe this isn't a hit, maybe just a warning. They would've done it by now if this was a hit. Hit and run, that's how they usually do it. Gotta stay in character, then. "Yeah, well, fuck you and Sal Imm—"

Blondie swung the camera backhanded and smashed the side of Tozzi's head. Slivers of glass from the shattered flash fell into the dead pine needles on the ground. Tozzi shook his head. Fucking asshole. He wondered if he was bleeding.

"Now don't be such a wiseass, Tomasso." Blondie clenched his jaw again. "Just shut up and listen."

Tozzi wanted to kill the bastard, but with the greaser back there . . . His gun was in his ankle holster. No way he could get to that. He tried to get a better look at the greaser's face in the car window, wondering just how trigger-happy this guy might be. If he was a kid, maybe he was new to this kind of shit. Tozzi considered turning on him quickly and wrestling him for the gun. Of course, Blondie probably had a weapon of his own, besides the Nikon. Shit. He suddenly had a bad feeling then. Maybe Immordino did know. Maybe Blondie had been instructed to tell him something before they kill him. That's what was holding things up. Shit . . .

Then Tozzi suddenly remembered something, a move he'd practiced in aikido class a long time ago, what to do if someone is holding a pistol in your back. He didn't remember it exactly, and the hand on the shoulder was a variation they hadn't practiced. He tried to visualize how his *sensei* had done it. Roll to the gunhand side until you're shoulder-to-shoulder with the attacker. Grab the wrist of the gun-hand . . . Yeah, that sounds right. Bend the wrist back, point his fingers to the ground, and throw him down with a *kote gaeshi.* Yeah, that would work, but what about the hand on his shoulder? How do you start the technique with that other hand holding you in place? Well, what if you turn to the other side, away from the gunhand? Can't do *kote gaeshi* from that side, but how about a *kokyu nage,* a big throw? Yeah, but what about the gun? Gotta get control of the gun. Can't do anything before you take care of the gun. How the hell do you do that? Shit . . .

"What'sa matta?" Blondie said. He kept pacing up and down, three steps this way, three steps back, clenching his jaw with every turn. "This too much for you to figure out? It's not hard. We're gonna make it short and sweet for you, Tomasso."

Fucker. Next time he turns away I'm gonna try it, the *kote gaeshi.* The greaser's not holding on that tight now. I'll make it work. Go ahead, Blondie, turn around, turn away from me. I'll throw the greaser down on his back, take his gun, and put a hole in your stupid fucking head with it. Come on, Blondie, come on. Turn around, turn around . . . Good. *Now!*

But just as Tozzi started to make his move on the greaser, he glanced into that car window and saw the reflection of another head rising up behind the greaser, a head in a gray fedora. Holy shit! What the fuck was she trying to prove? He glanced quickly at Blondie, whose back was still turned. Just get out of the way, Val.

Tozzi was about to turn on the greaser when he caught

Valerie's reflection in the glass, slapping the greaser's ears with the palms of her hands. The greaser wailed as his eardrums burst, and as he went to grab his head, Valerie took the gun right out of his hand, just like that. She jammed the muzzle into the greaser's pimply neck and told him not to move or she'd blow his fucking head off.

Well, fuck me. Tozzi couldn't believe this.

"The other one," Val shouted then, nodding toward the open parking lot.

Blondie was making tracks, hightailing it across the lot. Tozzi got down on one knee, pulled the .22 out of his ankle holster, and took off after him. He was just about to yell, *Stop! FBI!* when he caught himself. "Get back here, you fuck!"

He caught up with Blondie just as he was about to jump into his car, but the guy was wiry and he turned on Tozzi unexpectedly, shouldering him in the gut. They both hit the dirt, Blondie trying to strangle Tozzi's gunhand like a snake, beating it on the ground. Tozzi punched him in the kidney—once, twice, once more—but the guy didn't let up. He slapped his free hand over Blondie's nose and hooked his thumb on the pressure point where the jaw met the ear. Tozzi pressed, then kept pressing, searching for the right spot, but he wasn't hitting it because the guy didn't seem to be affected. Fucking wiseguys aren't even human.

Tozzi noticed the tire of Blondie's car right in front of his face. Who knows? Maybe it'll do something. Tozzi struggled to bend his wrist and aim, then he fired a shot into the tire, closing his eyes as he pulled the trigger. He felt the whoosh of escaping air and flying dirt in his face.

Blondie groaned and rolled away, rubbing his eyes. "Shit! There's shit in my eyes!"

"There's shit in your head." Tozzi hauled him up by the lapels and slammed him against the car. He frisked him, then dragged him back across the lot to Val and the greaser. "Watch this one," he said to Val as he frisked the greaser and found a small automatic in the pocket of his jacket. Tozzi heaved it into the woods, then took the greaser's 9mm from Val and threw that into the woods too. He grabbed the greaser by the shirtfront and threw him down on the ground, then pushed his buddy, who was still complaining about his eyes, on top of him. "Get on your bellies with your hands behind your heads. Now!"

The greaser complied right away. Blondie took his time about it, bitching about his eyes the whole time.

"Hey, Blondie, make sure you tell your boss he can go fuck himself. You got that?"

He turned to Val. "Come on, let's go." He gave her the car keys and kept his gun on them. She got into the Mercury and started the engine as he went around to the passenger side, keeping his gun on them over the roof of the car. "Let's go," he said as he got in. "Fast." She kicked up dirt as he slammed his door closed. He got on his knees on the seat and peered out the back window at the two wiseguys on the ground.

"You okay?" he asked her.

"Fine."

She did seem fine. She drove fast but in control. She took the big car out to the county road and maintained a nice steady speed. When she tipped her fedora back and showed some forehead, Tozzi thought of Gibbons. He always did the exact same thing with his hat in these situations.

"Who were your friends back there?" she asked.

"No friends of mine. Not even acquaintances."

"Didn't think so." She braked at a stop sign, then pulled out onto a two-lane highway. She picked up speed and cruised at sixty-five, fast but not too fast. She was a good driver.

Tozzi rolled up his pant leg and put his gun back in the holster. "Where'd you learn how to do that?"

"Do what?"

"Burst that guy's eardrums like that."

"I took a self-defense course once. You know, one of

those courses for women who're scared shitless of being raped."

"Where'd you learn how to handle a gun?"

She looked over at him and grinned. "I've never held a gun in my life."

"Bullshit."

"Swear to God. I used to take acting lessons, though."

"You're full of it, Val."

"No, just centered."

"Huh?"

"Centered. Calm for the fight. I practice this Chinese martial art called t'ai chi. It's something we work on." She kept her eye on the road.

"T'ai chi, huh?" *Chi* in Chinese is the same as *ki* in Japanese. As in ai*ki*do. They called it being "centered" in his martial art too. Calm for the fight? Same thing in aikido. Tozzi stared at her holding the wheel. He was trying very hard not to be steamed because she'd stolen his thunder back there.

They drove in silence for a while. She turned on the radio and played with the dial until she picked up one of the Philly stations. Bruce was singing about the tunnel of love.

"So," she finally said, "am I taking *you* to the casbah, or are you taking me?" She looked over at him with that little lopsided grin of hers, waiting for an answer.

Tozzi shook his head and laughed. She was great. He couldn't stay mad at her even when he wanted to.

There was just one thing that bothered him. Would Sal Immordino let him live long enough to find out just how great she was? The smile turned brittle on his face.

• 10 •

The air was clear and cold, and the moon was bright enough to read by. Joseph's face looked a little purple in the moonlight—lavender actually. Sal wished the hell his brother'd loosen up. Joseph stood there by the door with his hands jammed into the pockets of that big overcoat of his, collar up, hat brim pulled down. William Powell as the Thin Man. Except Joseph wasn't thin.

Sal touched his elbow. "You know what to say?"

"Of course I know what to say. Hey, look, Sal, I'm not stupid."

"I don't need the attitude, Joseph. I know you think this is stupid, but let's just do it the way we planned, okay?"

Joseph shook his head. "I don't know why you don't want to go directly to Walker. That makes more sense to me. But you're the boss, Sal. I'm just a *jooch.* I don't know nothin'."

Sal held his tongue. You know pork chops, you jackass, that's what you know. "Just trust me, Joseph. I know how these guys are."

Joseph shrugged. "Yeah, sure, whatever you say."

Sal bit his bottom lip. Always the attitude with this guy. If it wasn't for Cil's insistence that he take care of his brother, he'd send the bum back to that goddamn butcher shop in Sea Girt where he belongs. For the life of him, Sal didn't know why the hell he listened to his sister half the time. Just because she's a nun she don't know everything. But you gotta take care of Joseph, she says, he's your only brother. Family, huh? Bullshit. Sometimes they were more fucking trouble than they were worth. Both of them.

Sal pushed through the door and stepped into the gym, and instantly the memories started coming back. The place was the same, exactly the way he remembered it from when he trained here—when was it? '72, '73?—for the Lawson fight. A square of moonlight slanted in through a window and cut across the heavy bag. Sal remembered working that bag for hours on end. Henry Gonsalves would hang on to the backside of the bag like he was humping it, yelling instructions at him, "Uppercut! Cross! Right! Right! Left! Jab it! Cross! Lower! Work the body! Lower! Lower!" For hours they would do that. Probably did the same thing with Walker.

But maybe Henry had better methods now. After all, he'd brought "Pain" Walker through the ranks and taken him all the way. When Henry was Sal's trainer they never even got close to a title shot. He was the stepping stone other guys used to get into contender position. Everybody wanted to fight him on their way up—he was a good draw because he was so big and such a hard puncher—but he'd lost more than he'd won, a lot more. Sal realized, of course, that he was a very different kind of fighter from "Pain" Walker. He didn't have Walker's footwork, for one thing. Or his physique. He didn't have Walker's dumb fearlessness either, leading with his head, leaving himself open to bait his opponent, that kind of stupid shit. In his heart of hearts Sal always thought he could've had a shot at the title, but he was no "Pain" Walker. He was a different kind of fighter altogether. Anyway, that was a long time ago and it just wasn't meant to be. Sal wasn't bitter. No.

Joseph was looking all over the place. "Where is he? I don't see him," he whispered. "If he was here, there'd be lights on."

"Shuddup, will you please?" *Abbott and Costello Meet the Mummy.* Jesus, he acts like a jerk sometimes.

Sal scanned the old gym. He looked at the rectangle of moonlight laid out on the canvas of the old ring, the old worn leather corners. Sugar Ray Robinson had trained in that ring. So did Sonny Liston. Henry always used to say he liked this place because it had magic. Sal looked up at the rafters. Magic for some guys.

"So where the hell is he?"

Sal glared at his brother. I'm gonna kill this *stunade—*

"Hey! Who's over there?"

A figure came out of the shadows in the ring. Stocky, snow-white hair, electric-blue satin jacket, a pretty big gut now. Sal watched his old trainer step into a patch of moonlight. Henry had aged. He wasn't an old man, but he'd gotten old. Everybody does. Eventually.

"Who's over there? Dwayne? That you?"

Sal nudged Joseph. "Go ahead."

Joseph looked at Sal, the attitude plastered across his face as he called out. "It's an old friend, Henry. He wants to see you."

"Wha'?"

Sal bunched his shoulders and walked his palooka walk toward the ring. "It's me, Henry. Your old boy Sal. 'Member?"

"Sal who?"

The overhead lights sputtered on and stomped out the sweet moonlight. "Sal Immordino," Joseph said, his hand on the wall switch.

Henry squinted and shaded his eyes, standing at the edge of the ring with the stumpy cigar in the middle of his mouth, like the captain of a ship.

Sal kept walking the walk, smiling his dopey smile at his

old trainer. "It's me, Henry." Sal climbed into the ring and threw his arms around the man. "How ya doin,' Henry? How ya doin'?" Henry smelled of cigar, always had. He wasn't exactly returning the embrace. Sal figured he was gonna be this way.

Joseph looked up at Gonsalves from the floor. "We were in the area, and Sal said he wanted to come say hello, wish you luck. I hope you don't mind."

Henry looked suspicious, hostile almost. He knew what Sal's line of work was—there was no question about that—but that was okay. Sal wanted to see those little flashes of fear in his eyes, the ones Henry didn't think he was showing. Fear was good. It would save everybody a lot of time and aggravation. Sal stood there grinning, shoulders rounded, his head swaying, moving his feet, feigning vague punches at the old guy who just stood there with his hand glued to the ropes. This was good. Okay, Joseph, you can talk now. Give 'im the rap.

"My brother thinks the world of you, Mr. Gonsalves," Joseph started. "He talks about you all the time, even tells his doctors about you. That's why we came here to see you." Joseph hauled himself up to the ring, then leaned over the ropes and whispered to Henry. "His doctor said it might do him some good, make him happy. Sal's been very depressed these past few years."

Henry shrugged. "So whattaya want from me? I ain't no doctor." He was trying to be tough, but his eyes were giving him away. What he knew about Sal now was probably what he'd read in the papers, and the papers always gave the FBI version, that Sal was faking it, that there was nothing wrong with him. Henry had known him when he was an ambitious kid trying to get ranked. The FBI said he was a dangerous criminal, an underworld boss. The only thing Henry could be sure of, though, was Sal's fists—*they* were dangerous. Henry kept looking at Sal but avoiding eye contact. Poor Henry didn't know what to think.

Joseph leaned over the ropes again. "Just play along with him. I'm asking you, please, Mr. Gonsalves. My brother thinks he's a nobody. He doesn't want to live. All he talks about is you and fighting. That's it. Just do us this one favor. Please. Act like you're training him for a big fight. Just for five minutes. It would mean a lot to him."

Henry took the cigar out of his mouth and gestured helplessly. "I mean, what can—? Hey, how the hell did you know I'd be here in the gym? What'd you guys, follow me, for chrissake?"

Joseph shook his head. "Sal knew you'd be here. He said you always hung around the gym on Sunday nights when you were training for a big fight. Sunday night was your worry night. That's what he said you told him. His memories of you are very, very clear."

Sal nodded, grinning like a dope. "That's just what I told him, Henry, yeah. Sunday is *worry* night. You always throw me out of the gym on Sunday night. You like to be alone so you can worry." Sal kept nodding, punching air. Joseph was doing all right. He could be very ingenuous when he wanted to be, very convincing. A perfect front man when he wants to cooperate.

"So why'd you guys sneak up on me like this? Huh?" Suspicious bastard.

Joseph looked properly embarrassed. "You may not be aware of this, Mr. Gonsalves, but there are certain law-enforcement agencies—the FBI, for one—that have it in their heads that my brother is in the *Mafia.* For some reason they think he's some kind of kingpin, a boss, whatever they call it." Joseph switched back to whispering. "I mean, look at him, Mr. Gonsalves. Sal's not . . . capable."

"But why'd you have to sneak in here? That's acting pretty shady, if you ask me." Henry took the dead cigar out of his mouth, then put it back in and sucked on it a little.

"We came here like this to save you and the champ a lot of embarrassment. We're being persecuted unfairly. There's no reason why you and the champ should suffer by association. If we'd called you up first, came during the day, you'd have cops questioning you and all kinds of crap you don't need. And if the papers got wind of it, oh, man . . ." Joseph shook his head sorrowfully. "It just wouldn't be fair to the champ."

Henry chomped on the cigar as he stared at Sal. He was trying to look tough, but his eyes told the tale. Sal kept grinning and bobbing, boxing the air, acting like he hadn't heard a thing his brother said. Joseph did all right. Now it was his turn.

Sal shuffled around the trainer with a clumsy sidestep, throwing cramped little punches at nothing. "Let's put the gloves on, Henry. Gotta work on my timing. My timing is shit. You told me that. C'mon, Henry. Let's get the gloves."

"We'd really appreciate it, Mr. Gonsalves. Just five minutes." Very nice, Joseph. That face is beautiful. Sincerity like that you can take to the bank.

"Well, I—"

"C'mon, Henry. My timing's bad, real bad."

The trainer raised his bushy eyebrows and shrugged. "I guess . . . I dunno. Five minutes?"

"That's all," Joseph said.

"All right, sure, I guess. There's some gloves over there." He nodded to one of the corners where a few beat-up pairs of gym gloves were hanging from the turnbuckle.

Joseph picked out two pairs and handed one to Gonsalves.

The old trainer pulled the cigar out of his mouth. "Hang on. Gotta get rid of this." He ducked under the ropes and climbed down to go put it someplace. When he came back Joseph helped him with his gloves. "I used to do this for Sal when we were kids," he told Henry as he carefully pulled the laces tight and tied them with double knots.

Joseph went over to help Sal with his gloves then. Sal grinned as his brother tied bows in his laces.

Joseph moved out of the way when he was finished, and Sal started toward Gonsalves in an exaggerated crouch, dragging his feet. "Okay, Henry. Here I come now, here I come." He threw a few weak punches at Gonsalves's gloves. The trainer looked confused and a little embarrassed by the whole business. He still didn't know what to make of it. "Tell me not to drop my right, Henry. I always drop my right. That's what you told me."

"Yeah . . . that's right. Don't drop your right." Gonsalves moved away from Sal, cautious. He remembered Sal's right.

Sal kept coming at him, throwing weak, sloppy punches. "C'mon, Henry. Tell me what I'm doing wrong. Tell me what to *do.* You tell the champ what to do, don'tcha?"

"Yeah, sure, Sal . . . I tell the champ what to do." He kept moving away.

Sal moved in and cuffed Gonsalves's ear with a soft left. "He's a good guy, the champ, isn't he? He listens to what you say, right? Even if he's the champ, he's gotta listen to you. Right, Henry?"

"Yeah, Sal, he listens to me."

Sal cuffed the ear again, a little harder. "Yeah, Walker's a good kid. He listens to everything you tell him. Everything. You're like his father, right?"

"Walker's a good kid, yeah."

Sal smacked that ear with a sharp pop. "When I was up at the hospital—you know, the hospital?—I heard that guy on TV with the funny hair say that you're the only one the champ listens to, Henry. They all say you're the only one he listens to." Another pop to the ear. "He's like your dog."

"No, Sal, he's not—"

Another hook to that ear. Harder. "They say if you told him to jump off the Empire State Building, he'd do it, Henry."

"No—"

Whap! A little harder.

"They say if Henry Gonsalves told 'Pain' Walker to throw a fight, he'd do it."

"No—"

Whap! Harder. Gonsalves winced and covered up.

"That's what I heard, Henry." Sal broke up the cover-up with a right uppercut. "That's what I heard."

"That's not—"

Whap! Whap! Two quick rights, half strength.

"I bet he'd do it if you told him to, Henry." *Whap!* "That boy loves you. Like a father, Henry." *Whap! Whap!*

Gonsalves bent over and tucked himself in like an armadillo. Sal unleashed a deep uppercut and blew the old man open.

"Okay, okay, enough! That's five minutes—" *Whap-whap!*

"How 'bout if *I* told you the champ should throw the fight, Henry? How 'bout it if I made you a very good offer to let Epps take it in the third? An offer good enough for you *and* the champ. Would you tell him to do it?"

"No, Sal—"

POW! Right uppercut to the gut, full power. Henry doubled over, hanging on Sal's arm.

"I'm gonna ask you again, Henry." Sal untied the bow on his right glove with his teeth. "What would you say, Henry? For three mil, say." He shook off the glove.

"Enough, Sal—"

"Hey, take it easy, Sal." Joseph yelling from outside the ropes. "You're gonna kill 'im."

Shut the fuck up, Joseph.

Sal balled his fist and threw a right cross. Gonsalves's head whipped around, blood flowing from his nose, smearing his upper lip.

"I'm asking you, Henry. Will you tell him to do it? Huh?"

Oooph!

Sal lifted him off his feet with an uppercut to the stomach. He untied the left glove and threw it off, then started on that ear again. "I don't hear you, Henry." *Whap!* "I don't hear you."

Gonsalves was gasping for breath. "I—I can't—"

"Easy, Sal, easy."

Shut up, you little fuck, you!

Sal was thinking about Henry taking Walker to the championship and all the shitty little two-bit fights he'd made Sal fight, fights that made other guys look good, punks like Walker. He clenched his jaw, moved in, and—*WHAM!*—a straight right square on Gonsalves's chin, the killer right, the right that took care of Lawson, that could've decked Ali. A shock of white hair stood on end as Gonsalves's head flew back, then his knees buckled, and he collapsed in a heap. Out cold.

"Jesus Christ Almighty, you killed 'im, Sal. What the hell good is he now? Whatta we gonna do, Sal? There goes the fight, that's for sure. I toldja we shoulda went straight to Walker with this."

"Shut your fucking mouth!" Sal yelled. He crouched down and looked at the old guy. Jesus, *did* he kill him? Sal started to panic. Shit, if Henry dies, they might have to back out of this fight deal. Fuck. "Go get some water," Sal shouted. "Hurry up!"

Sal stuck his finger under the trainer's nose. He thought he could feel him breathing. Sal was relieved but, in a way, disappointed too. Sal muttered under his breath, "You *should* die for what you did to me, you old fuck, you."

"What's taking you so long, Jo—" Just then the front door banged open.

"Hey, Gonz, what the fuck're you doing in here with all them lights on, man—?"

It was "Pain" Walker, with this black chick on his arm. The champ sensed that something wasn't right. He froze where he stood, staring up at Sal. Then he spotted his trainer laid out on the stained canvas.

"Gonz? Gonz, dat you?" There was panic in his voice. He shrugged the girl off and ran for the ring. "Gonz! What'd you do to Gonz, man?" Walker threw off his leather jacket and leapt up into the ring. He stopped and stared down at Gonsalves lying on the canvas, just stood there and stared. Then he started shaking. He raised his head and looked Sal in the eye. "Motherfuckin'—" The champ lunged like a panther and cracked Sal across the jaw with *his* killer right. It hit like a freight train. Sal stumbled back, dazed. Then Walker got him by the shirtfront and started whaling into his face. *"What the fuck you do this for, motherfuckah, huh? What'choo hurt Gonz for? Why?"*

Walker was crying as he punched, crying and screaming and punching.

Sal swung at him, but he couldn't get a good shot in, not with the way Walker had him bent back over the ropes, so he tried to block the onslaught, but there was no getting away from Walker. He was all over him. Sal took a good one on the nose then, and time stopped. Then he felt it, that old familiar pain, brain-damage pain, like a spider-web crack spreading through his whole face, slowly shattering the skull underneath. Panic grabbed Sal by the balls. This fucking mental case was the heavyweight champion of the world, and he was pulling a nut on him, pulling a nut *bare-fisted.* This boy was gonna hurt him, hurt him bad.

Walker pounded Sal's ear. "Why you do this, motherfuckah? Why?"

Sal covered up to protect his head. "Joseph! Jo—!"

A gunshot cracked through the hollow gym.

Walker stopped short, fist cocked in the air. He stared across the gym.

"Cool it, brother, or your honey here's gonna be looking for a good plastic surgeon."

Sal blinked and refocused his eyes. Joseph was looking up at them from the edge of the ring, holding his big 9mm to the girlfriend's cheek, pressing the muzzle right in there. He had her arm twisted up behind her. She had that kind of straight hair black chicks have that doesn't move. Like a Supreme. Her eyes were wide, white, and scared. Sal looked up at Walker who stood there like a dummy, trying to figure it all out. Sal pushed him off, straightened up, and smiled. Buckwheat and Farina. Thank you, Joseph. I take it back. You're not a total waste.

"What'choo *do*in' this for, man?" Walker's voice was high and strained. Too high for a guy his size.

Joseph took on that reasonable tone again. "We were trying to make Mr. Gonsalves a proposition, something that would be very good for you, champ. But he wasn't listening to us, so my brother had to press our point."

"You talkin' shit, man. I don't know what'choo—"

"It's very simple, champ," Joseph continued. "You throw the fight with Epps, and you'll end up with more money in your pocket than if you'd won."

"Bullshit! Can't—"

"Three million, champ. All for you. Just stop and think, now. How much of that seventeen mil will you see if you win it? How much? You know how it works, champ. I don't have to tell you. Uncle Sam takes his big piece, the state gets their piece, the casino gets some, the promoter takes a lot, Henry gets some, then there's all the fees, and this guy's gotta get paid and that guy and the other guy's cousin, and when it's all over, what's left for you? Not too much, right? You take our deal and no one will know about it. Put it in a bank in the Islands. Nobody knows nothing. All for you. What do you think, champ?"

"Dwayne!" The girlfriend squealed, pleading.

Walker glared at her, hate in his eyes. This was a little too much for his limited capacity. You could see he was trying hard to sort it all out, but he had a slow processor and he didn't like being pressured by the babe. He didn't give a shit about her. That was for sure. What was probably making him mad, Sal figured, was that somewhere deep in the back of his head he was already making up his mind about throwing the fight, and now he was just pissed that she'd heard about the three mil.

"Dwayne! He's hurting me, Dwayne!"

"What you want me to do? He got the gun. Tell him."

Sal had to laugh. He pulled out a handkerchief and dabbed at his nose. He was surprised it wasn't bleeding. He grinned to himself. Always could take a punch.

"So whattaya say, champ?" Joseph said. "It's a good deal."

"I, I . . ." Walker couldn't get the words out. He stared down at Gonsalves on the canvas. "I don't know."

Sal folded the handkerchief and put it back in his pocket. "Listen to me, champ."

"Whattaya doin', Sal? Don't be stupid. Let me talk." Joseph looked hurt again. He was too sensitive.

"It's okay, Joseph. I want to make the champ understand a few things."

Joseph shrugged, disgusted. He didn't like it when Sal stopped playing dumb without warning. He liked being the mouthpiece. It made him think he was really in charge.

Sal turned to Walker. "You know, champ, you have to understand that this isn't *Wheel of Fortune* we're playing here. It's not a take-it-or-leave-it situation. We want you to throw the fight, and if you don't want to cooperate, you better start thinking about being a janitor or a doorman or something suited to your abilities, because if you don't do it, you're finished in boxing."

"Fuck you, man. You don't know nothin'."

"Oh, no? Well, chew on this, brother. You don't throw this fight, I find a convicted drug dealer who'll swear on a stack of Bibles that he sold you steroids, coke, crack, heroin, you name it. I'll get *two* fucking drug dealers."

"That's bullshit, man. I don't take no steroids."

Sal shrugged. "So what? The accusation alone will be enough to get the Boxing Commission on your ass, and everybody knows how they feel about you. Those old guys are dying to make an example out of you, Walker. Guilty or innocent doesn't matter. As soon as you're connected with drugs, there's no way they're gonna sanction a title fight with *your* name on the bill. Forget about it. They'll strip you of your title. And who the hell's gonna want to fight you if you're not ranked? That'll be it for you, pal."

Come on, Walker. You're gonna do it. You *wanna* do it.

The champ was speechless. Comatose was more like it. He stood there, his chin on his chest, staring down at Gonsalves, waiting for him to rise from the dead and tell him what to do. He got down on one knee, touched the trainer's neck, his chest, his face. He didn't know what the hell he was doing. He just wanted Gonsalves to get up and handle this, be his daddy and take care of the tough decisions. Hell, he was just supposed to fight—Henry was supposed to take care of the rest. Henry had a way of making his fighters dependent on him like that. That's why he and Sal had never really hit it off. Sal had other obligations.

"You gotta think for yourself, champ," Sal said. "Henry means well, but he's a little old-fashioned, if you know what I mean. Sure, you can whup Epps. Everybody knows that. But in the long run that's not gonna put the cash in your pocket. Don't be stupid. Always go for the money, champ. You can't go on forever. Everybody gets old. It's a fact of life. You gotta think of your future. The smart guy always goes for the big money, champ. Be the smart guy."

"Dwayne!" Joseph was squeezing the black chick again. It was more *braciòl'* than he'd squeezed in a long time. "Dwayne, he's hurting me!"

"Shut the fuck up, bitch!" Walker looked like he wanted to punch her lights out. He turned back to Sal and whispered. "Three million dollars, you said?"

Sal nodded.

"And nobody can touch it but me?"

"You throw it before the fourth round, and the money'll be waiting for you in a bank in the Cayman Islands. All for you. Nobody else."

Walker started nodding like he was in a trance. He was mumbling something.

"Whatcha say, champ?"

Walker kept mumbling under his breath, bobbing his head up and down, staring at Gonsalves. What the hell was this? Voodoo?

"Champ, I'm talking to you."

Walker didn't seem to hear him. He wanted Gonsalves to get up and make the decision for him. Fucking Henry. He turned his fighters into babies. They couldn't shit without his okay. That's why he'd stopped pushing for Sal way back when. Sal wouldn't be his baby. Fucking Henry. Sal felt like stomping on his sleeping face.

"Look, champ, let me explain something to you. Henry's a good guy, but do you really think he's got your best interests at heart? What the hell's he got you fighting this has-been Epps for? You fight has-beens, pretty soon people start calling you a has-been. You should be knocking down all those guys coming up the ranks, taking fights that're gonna keep you on top. Listen to me now. Take this deal, pocket the three mil, and you'll be free to take any fight you want. You won't have to be tempted by jerk-offs like Nashe waving big-money purses in your face, big money that you never even get to see. Am I making sense or what, champ? Am I?"

Walker was looking at him, eyes narrowed, face all scrunched up like a prune. He mumbled something.

"I don't understand what you're saying, champ. Speak up."

Walker looked down at the floor, shoulders bunched, back rounded. "I said, all right, all right, I'll do it . . . I'll do it."

Sal clapped his hands. "You're a smart guy, champ. You made the right decision." Sal ducked under the ropes and climbed down out of the ring.

Joseph let the girl go, reluctantly. He kept the gun out and started backing toward the door, like George Raft. *Jooch.*

Sal stood at the edge of the ring, eye level with Walker who was kneeling over Gonsalves now. "Hey, champ, listen up. This is important. You make sure you get Henry to Our Lady of Mercy Hospital over in Reading. Our Lady of Mercy. It's about forty-five minutes from here. You register him under the name of—" Sal shrugged and frowned—"Hector Diaz. Yeah, Hector Diaz. You got that? They'll take care of him. No questions asked."

He turned to his brother. "Remember to call Dr. Steve and arrange it."

Joseph nodded once, his eye on the ring.

Sal turned and headed for the door, Joseph walking backward with the gun trained on the champ. "Put that fucking thing away before you shoot yourself in the foot." Fucking nitwit. Lou Costello.

He looked back at the ring then. The black chick was hanging on the champ's back, looking for a little consoling, but Walker was only worried about his trainer. His daddy. "Hey, champ," Sal called out, "don't think this over too hard. Just do what you promised. You think about it too much, you might get second thoughts, and second thoughts are no good for anyone. Especially you, kid."

The girl looked up and stared at Sal, tears pouring out of her eyes. If Walker wasn't listening, she'd remind him. She'd remind him about the three mil too. You could bet on that.

Sal turned away and took a deep breath. He felt nice. He felt warm inside. It was all gonna work out. It really was. "C'mon," he said to his brother. "Let's go."

• 11 •

Gibbons couldn't get over it. He stared across the long marble floor at the short little fat guy in the black raincoat standing in front of the big dinosaur skeleton. He'd been following the guy around Manhattan for the past three days—coffee shops, department stores, museums, Central Park, all over the place—and he just couldn't get over it. It wasn't just his face, the sourpuss with the lopsided mouth. It was the way he walked, the way he snapped at people and glared at them behind their backs, the way he was always straightening his tie clip, his cuffs, his lapels, the way he shook out his handkerchief and blew his nose like a fog horn. Gibbons just couldn't get over it. Sabatini Mistretta was a dead ringer for J. Edgar Hoover.

Gibbons tipped back his hat and looked at his watch. It was almost three. If Mistretta followed his usual pattern, he'd start heading for a coffee shop soon. Coffee, light with Sweet 'n Low, and a piece of pie. Yesterday it had been peach pie. The day before, coconut custard. Gibbons had been thinking about coconut custard pie ever since. Lorraine told him he shouldn't eat things like coconut custard pie anymore. His cholesterol was too high. She had the doctor do a work-up on his cholesterol when they went for the blood test. It was over two twenty, whatever the hell that meant. She said she'd buy him frozen yogurt pies from now on, and that's what she did, that very night. He took his hat off and put it back on. Yogurt is not coconut custard. Not by a long shot. Holy Matrimony. Can't fucking wait.

Gibbons strolled through the dinosaur hall, stopping at the information plaques, keeping his eye on Mistretta. He and Lorraine used to make it up here to the Museum of Natural History at least once a year. This place and the Metropolitan Museum of Art were their favorites. She really liked the room at the Met with the armor and the swords and the lances. It wasn't her period, but the sight of all those knights tilting forward on their armored chargers gave her a thrill. Plate armor is early Renaissance, not medieval. He'd learned that from her the first time they went there together. In the Middle Ages they wore chain mail. He used to like to bait her with his bias for the ancient Romans, telling her that in the days of the Caesars, an imperial legion could've beaten the shit out of any army from the Middle Ages, Christian or barbarian. As proof, he'd take her to the case where the Roman short swords were kept. Faster, lighter, more compact. They were like Uzis compared to the heavy broadswords the French and the English had used in the late Middle Ages. But then Lorraine would always point out that the long bow was the product of the late Middle Ages, and he'd say that projectile weapons marked the beginning of pussy-shit fighting. Toe-to-toe, man-to-man the way the Romans did it—*that* was fighting.

Gibbons sighed. He and Lorraine didn't seem to do stuff like that anymore. Now they went to malls and looked at curtains. He stared at Mistretta and wondered if his wife made him pick out curtains. No, Mistretta probably didn't give a shit about curtains. Probably thought replacing perfectly good curtains that only needed a good washing was a waste of money. He was supposed to be a cheap son of a bitch. But it *was* a waste of money.

He walked over to the other side of the big dinosaur skeleton that Mistretta was looking at and watched him through the dark copper-colored rib bones. Gibbons had to laugh. It looked like the boss was back in prison. That's where he should be, the little shit.

Mistretta looked up from the information plaque in front of him and stared Gibbons in the eye. Gibbons looked away. Mistretta probably just assumed he was being followed. The parole board had had someone on his tail from the minute he arrived at the halfway house here. That's why he spent his days on the I-Love-NY tour, religiously avoiding all contact with his mob boys.

According to Mistretta's watchdog, that guy Saperstein, Mistretta hasn't seen anybody since he's been back, except for Immordino's sister, the nun. That was last Friday, two days before the big powwow at Immordino's house. According to what he and Dougherty had overheard from the surveillance van, Mistretta has given his blessings to whatever scam Immordino's got going, the one that has something to do with Vegas, Golden Boy, and Mr. Mad—whoever the hell they were. But somehow this didn't jibe with Mistretta's profile. He was a hands-on boss, and his family had been unusually quiet while he'd been in prison. Why would he let his people start something now, so close to his release? If in four years he hadn't trusted Sal Immordino to be anything but a caretaker, why trust him now? It didn't make sense.

Unless Immordino was making an end-run play on his own. One big score before he has to surrender the reins? Behind Mistretta's back? If it has something to do with Las Vegas, it has to involve big money; and if Gibbons had learned anything in his career as a special agent in the Organized Crime Unit of the Manhattan field office, it was that when big money is concerned *anything* is possible.

Gibbons made like he was examining the bones, keeping

Mistretta in his peripheral vision. He wasn't sure whether Mistretta had made him yet, but the way the guy was staring at him through the bones now seemed to indicate some kind of recognition. But maybe Mistretta was just naturally hostile toward everyone who crossed his path. The Director was like that. Or maybe Mistretta was so cautious that he was constantly on guard, perpetually on the defensive. You don't get to be *capo di capi* of the second-largest crime family in New York by being careless.

"You want something?" Mistretta's gravelly tones echoed through the long hall.

Gibbons tilted his head back and stared at him for a few moments. "You offering anything?"

Mistretta's eyes narrowed. "You been following me all day. Yesterday too. What do you want with me?"

Gibbons sauntered around the iron railing encircling the dinosaur, passed under the long neck, and walked up to Mistretta. He reached into his inside pocket and pulled out his ID.

Mistretta raised an eyebrow as he glanced at Gibbons's ID. "I'm impressed." J. Edgar used to raise one eyebrow in contempt the same way.

Gibbons scanned the bones, following the dinosaur's long long neck way up to the little head. "Tell me something, Mistretta. How's Sal?"

"Sal who?"

"Immordino."

Mistretta shrugged. "Don't know him."

Gibbons smiled. "You were seen saying your prayers with his sister last week."

"I know his sister. I don't know him."

Gibbons pinched his nostrils. "Seems funny that you'd leave a guy you don't even know in charge of your family."

"I don't know what you're talking about. My kids are all grown. My wife takes care of herself."

"I'm sure she does." Women do.

"What's that supposed to mean?"

Gibbons shrugged and smiled with his teeth like a crocodile. "What do you know about Seaview Properties, Incorporated?"

"Never heard of it."

"Really? You're on the board of directors."

Mistretta didn't answer.

"Seaview Properties holds the title to the land that Nashe Plaza Hotel and Casino is built on in Atlantic City. That's what it says in the tax records down there."

"So what?"

"Sal Immordino has been spending a lot of time down in Atlantic City. Having meetings with Russell Nashe."

"Who's he?"

Gibbons showed his teeth again. "Now, why would the acting head of your family—your *other* family—be having meetings with the man who built his casino on your land?"

"Sal Immordino doesn't have an acting head. He's a functional idiot. A very unfortunate person."

"I thought you didn't know him."

"That's what his sister told me."

Gibbons nodded and stared down the length of the dinosaur's tail. Supposed to have had a second brain in the tail. About as big as a walnut. "I'm gonna take a wild guess, Mistretta, but I'll bet Nashe owes you money on that land and Sal's down there doing the collecting for you."

Mistretta looked up at the dino head. The flesh on the lopsided side of his mouth was all wrinkled and knobby, just like the Director's.

"According to what's on file at the Atlantic City Municipal Tax Board, Russell Nashe signed a ninety-nine-year lease for that land five years ago. Five years and twenty-six days ago."

Mistretta shrugged, still looking up at the head.

"Five years is a nice neat period of time. I'm thinking maybe Nashe was supposed to make some big payment on the fifth anniversary of the lease. Maybe he didn't make that payment. Maybe Sal Immordino's trying to find out why, trying to help him along with his delinquent payment." But what's this got to do with Vegas? Nashe doesn't have any casinos in Vegas.

Mistretta fussed with his tie clip until it was perfectly horizontal. He ruffled the lapels of his raincoat, then rubbed his nose and sniffed.

Gibbons stared at him for a minute, waiting for him to say something. A couple of little old ladies in L. L. Bean mountain parkas walked into the room, took a gander at all the bones, and turned right around. Not their cup of tea. "Does any of this sound plausible to you, Mistretta?"

He raised that contemptuous eyebrow again, then let it down slowly and relaxed his face. "You see this big dinosaur here? They used to call it the brontosaurus, but then they found out that there was no such thing as a brontosaurus, because this guy who thought he made a big new discovery really only found pieces of the same kind of dinosaur he'd found a couple years earlier. See, what he thought was a completely new thing was just a plain old—" Mistretta looked down at the plaque and scanned it with his finger—"an old *a-pat-osaurus.* An apatosaurus." He shrugged and raised his eyebrows. "For years everybody said it was a brontosaurus, but all the while it was just another stupid apatosaurus. See, that's like circumstantial evidence you guys use. People—experts—they think something is one way. They go to court and swear on the Bible that that's the way it is, absolutely, couldn't have been any other way. Juries hear this shit and convict innocent people, ruin their lives. Then, years later, these big experts come back and say they made a mistake. It wasn't the way they'd said, after all. Turns out it wasn't a brontosaurus. Just an old apatosaurus." Mistretta nodded. "Happens all the time that way."

Gibbons rolled his eyes. Mistretta was gonna be cute now. "Very edifying. Know anything about any bones buried under Nashe Plaza?"

Mistretta glowered at him with the bulldog face. Pure J. Edgar. Incredible.

Gibbons leaned on the railing. "You believe in reincarnation?"

Mistretta narrowed his puffy eyes and scowled. "Wha'?"

"Never mind." Gibbons focused on the dinosaur's disproportionately big feet. Had to be big to hold up that much weight. "What's new in Vegas these days?"

"What the fuck do I know about Vegas? I been in prison. In Pennsylvania."

"Juicy Vacarini. You know Juicy? He's one of your boys. I hear Juicy's got a lot of close friends out in Vegas. Friends he can trust to make bets for him. Big bets, fifty grand apiece. So what's the game? Maybe I wanna get a piece of that action."

The eyes bulged, and the mouth took a nosedive on the droopy side. For just a moment Mistretta seemed genuinely rattled. Was this news to him? Hell of a way to find out what your people are doing, from an FBI agent. The bulldog snapped then, "I dunno what you're talking about."

Gibbons pursed his lips and nodded. "You don't know what I'm talking about?"

"No."

Mistretta seemed impatient now. It wasn't real obvious, but it was there, Gibbons could sense it. Maybe he was reading in because Mistretta reminded him so much of the Director. Hoover always had that barely perceptible edge of impatience, like he had to get away, be someplace else, see to something more important than what was in front of him. But why so jumpy all of a sudden? Special agents don't make big mob bosses jumpy. In three days of touring the city Mistretta hadn't seemed jumpy. Maybe he'd hit a nerve. Maybe Mistretta didn't know what was going on in his own family. Maybe he knew less than he and Tozzi knew. Great. Three days of tailing this guy and all for nothing.

Mistretta checked his watch, a big gold Rolex. He wore it loose on the underside of his wrist. "Hey, look, I'm going for a coffee. You don't mind if I leave you now?" Very sarcastic.

Gibbons shook his head. They both knew he'd be following along. Mistretta started to head for the elevators. Gibbons was feeling antsy, though. He wanted to accomplish something for his efforts. Well, if he couldn't find out what was brewing, at least he could stir up the pot.

"Hey, Mistretta?"

Mistretta stopped and glared at him. "Whattaya want from me?"

"Is it true that you're retiring, that you're gonna make Sal the permanent boss?"

Mistretta glared at him. "I dunno what you're talking about," he snapped. Very angry.

"You don't have to answer that, Mistretta. It's pretty obvious from the way Sal's been wheeling and dealing lately. It's very admirable of you, stepping down and letting a younger man take over. Very admirable."

Mistretta turned his back on Gibbons and walked away. Gibbons followed, smiling with his teeth.

"Hey, Mistretta. One more thing."

"What?" He kept walking, sounded annoyed.

"You gonna have pie with your coffee today?"

The old boss stopped and looked over his shoulder. "Why? Is that a crime too?"

"Only if it's coconut custard."

Mistretta's scowl went south again. "How about pecan? Is pecan pie okay with you?"

Gibbons nodded. "Sure. Whatever makes you happy."

Mistretta's steps echoed through the dinosaur hall. Gibbons watched him for a moment, then glanced over at another skeleton, a meateater who stood on his hind legs, a million sharp teeth in his deadly grin. Pecan pie, he thought. He loved pecan pie. But that was another one on Lorraine's hit list. Too much sugar, plus cholesterol in the nuts. Gibbons headed for the elevators to catch up with Mistretta so he could watch him have his coffee and pie, see if he made any phone calls, see how agitated the boss got. If Mistretta didn't know what Sal was up to, maybe he'd really stirred up the pot. If . . .

Gibbons glanced up one last time at the skull looming over him and thought about pecan pie again. He suddenly realized that if Lorraine had her way, he could die without ever having coconut custard or pecan pie again. He took off his hat and put it on again. Fuck that. If that little shit Mistretta was gonna have pie, so was he. Lorraine doesn't have to know everything.

• 12 •

Tozzi unlocked the door and went into his tiny two-room apartment at the Plaza. He stopped short, with his hand over the light switch. He thought he'd kicked something, something that wasn't supposed to be there. He reached out with his foot, but there was nothing there now. His eyes adjusted to the dark room and then he saw them, all over the floor. Balloons. He grinned. This had to be Valerie's work. But when he turned on the lights, he saw that they were all the same color. Sort of a thin milky white. He shook his head. Naughty girl.

"Val?"

He walked through the living room with the kitchenette along the right-hand wall, kicking these white "balloons," then turned the corner into the bedroom.

"Val?" He was grinning, thinking she was here already. He hit the wall switch in the dark bedroom.

The first thing Tozzi saw was the gun. Then he saw who was holding it—Sal Immordino stretched out on his bed,

Sal Immordino holding a 9mm automatic fitted with a silencer, that long, evil-looking barrel pointed right at him. Tozzi suddenly felt very cold, cramps snaking through his stomach. He didn't move.

His box of condoms was open on the bed next to Sal, torn tinfoil wrappers all over the place, more milky-white "balloons" in this room than the other. Tozzi couldn't believe it. There must've been two dozen in this room alone. For chrissake, how the hell long had Immordino been here blowing up his rubbers? This guy *is* bats.

Sal propped himself up on his elbow, the gun still leveled. "You must be a very hopeful guy, Tomasso. You keep more rubbers here than a fucking drugstore."

You need 'em with Sydney. "What do you care?"

"Oh, Mr. Attitude here." Sal shook his head disapprovingly. "Sit down, Tomasso. Take a load off." He pointed with his gun to the armchair opposite the bed.

Tozzi took a seat as Sal unrolled another condom and started blowing it up, the gun in his hand pointed at the ceiling. When he finished, he realized he couldn't tie off the end while holding the gun, so he just let it go. It sputtered and farted, looped over the bed, crashed, and died on the rug.

Sal smiled at Tozzi. "So how you doin', Tomasso? You feeling all right?"

"Oh, I'm just great." Shit.

"Good." Sal squinted and aimed at a balloon. The 9mm went *pfitt,* real soft, and a balloon popped and disappeared. The others around it skittered away in fear. Tozzi noticed a small entry hole in the bottom drawer of the bureau. The sweater drawer. Son of a bitch.

"So tell me the truth, Tomasso. What are you? A cop? A fed? What?" Sal squinted down the barrel at another balloon.

Tozzi waited for him to fire, but he didn't shoot.

"I'm talking to you, Tomasso. I asked you a question."

"Whattaya want from me? I'm a bodyguard."

Pfitt! Another balloon disappeared. "Uh-huh." *Pfitt!* He missed this time, but he plugged the sweater drawer again.

Sal set the pistol down on his big belly. He was daring Tozzi to try something. Tozzi was sitting on the edge of the armchair with his elbows on his knees, trying to breathe evenly, wishing he didn't feel so jittery. He was thinking about the little .22 in the holster strapped to his left ankle. Sal had fired three shots; a 9mm like that could hold seventeen bullets in the clip. Tozzi thought about going for his gun, but even if Sal was slow as shit, he'd still get to his gun before Tozzi could get his pant leg up. Fuck.

"You didn't answer my question, Tomasso. *What the hell are you?*"

"You know what the hell I am. I'm one of Nashe's bodyguards."

"Uh-huh." Tozzi expected Sal to grab the gun and put a few more holes in his sweaters, but he didn't. Instead he took in a deep breath and let it out slow. The automatic slowly rose on his big belly, then sank with the exhale. "What'd you do to my boys at the Epps camp? I want to hear your side of it."

"What do you mean?"

"Let's not be modest, huh? You must've messed them up pretty good 'cause they came back like two mamelukes with their tails between their legs. I take it they gave you my message, but apparently it didn't make much of an impression."

Sal yawned and stretched his arms, rapping his knuckles on the headboard. Tozzi was tempted to go for his gun, but he hesitated and lost the moment. Sal laid his paw back on the 9mm before he shut his mouth.

Tozzi tried not to stare at the gun. "I heard what your guy had to say."

"But it didn't make an impression on you." Sal scratched his cheek with his free hand.

Tozzi didn't answer right away. "What do you want with me?"

Sal scratched under his chin. "Who was the other guy?"

"What other guy?"

Sal laughed out loud. "You're real funny, you know that? They said there was another guy with you. He was dressed like one of the bartenders, had one of those Al Capone hats. Pete says his ears are still ringing from what he did to him. He's your partner, I assume."

"Just a friend." Shit.

Sal shook his head. "You guys . . ." He kept shaking his head. "Admit it, why don't you? You and the guy with the hat are both cops, and you're working together."

"If you say so." Tozzi held his breath; the cramps were getting worse. Valerie was supposed to meet him here any minute. He'd given her a key this morning in case he was going to be late. He didn't want her walking into this. Especially wearing that hat.

"I suppose he's a 'bodyguard' too, your friend?"

Tozzi studied Sal's face, trying to figure out how much he really knew. Those two torpedoes he sent probably didn't get a good look at Valerie. She'd had her hair tied back that day. Between the bartender uniform and the hat, they must have thought she was a guy. Thank God for dumb bastards. "Hey, Sal, what do you want from me? If you got something to say to me, just say it. Okay?"

Pfitt-pfitt! Pfitt!

Holy shit! Tozzi felt his balls go numb. There were three neat bullet holes in the oatmeal upholstery at the base of the chair. Right between his legs.

"You have quite an attitude, Tomasso." Sal scolded him with the barrel of the gun. "I'll bet your parents didn't believe in spanking."

Something suddenly occurred to Tozzi. Sal was speaking like a human being. He wasn't doing the rope-a-dope, wasn't bothering with the dummy routine. A big hand clenched Tozzi's gut and started to squeeze. Sal never lets his guard down in public. He always plays the mental case. The fact that he was acting natural now meant one thing: Sal was gonna kill him.

Tozzi felt a little woozy. His left leg was like a lead

weight, he was so aware of it. The gun, he had to get to his gun somehow. He wished he was wearing a wire or that the room was bugged and that Gibbons was down the hall listening to all this. Sal's lucid conversation, the implied threats, firing the gun—altogether this could be enough to haul him back into court on all those old charges he'd walked on by pleading mental incompetency. They'd have it all down on tape—better, videotape. Then Gibbons and maybe a few other agents would come crashing through the door. Sal'd get all shook up, look away, give Tozzi time to go for his gun. Drop it, Sal! FBI! Then Gibbons and the other guys would pile in, fan out around the bed, guns drawn on that big fat belly. Yeah, that's the way it should be going down . . . yeah . . . but Gibbons wasn't down the hall . . . nobody was hearing any of this. All Tozzi had was the gun in his ankle holster and no way to get to it fast enough. Oh, Jesus . . .

"You know, Tomasso, I really don't care who the other guy is. At this point it really doesn't matter." Sal was aiming at the balloons again. "What I'm *really* curious about is you and Nashe's wife."

Tozzi wasn't listening. He was thinking about how fast Sal could put three holes in his chest, just the way he did to the chair. *Pfitt-pfitt-pfitt!*

"You been fucking Nashe's wife, haven't you?"

"What?" Tozzi was thinking about three holes in his chest, bowling-ball holes.

"You don't have to play stupid with me, Tomasso. I got eyes, I can see. You been screwing Sydney behind Nashe's back." Sal was smiling, like he was happy about it. "Yeah, she's something, isn't she?"

Tozzi just looked at him. No . . .

"I wish the fuck I had a camera. The look on your face is one in a million, Tomasso. What is it? You jealous? You in love with her?"

"Sydney? No."

"Then what is it?"

"Nothing."

Sal pinched his nose, laughing like a leaky radiator. "Yeah, sure. You don't love the bitch."

Tozzi stared at the big slob lying on his bed, all those inflated rubbers floating around him. He was thinking about bowling-ball holes with blood coming out of them. He felt a little queasy way back behind his molars. No . . . not with Sydney . . . not *him.* Oh, man.

Sal put his free arm behind his head. "It's nice doing it with her, isn't it? It's like stealing from that asshole husband of hers."

Tozzi stared at the balloons. *Pfitt!* Another one over by the window disappeared.

"Pay attention, Tomasso. I'm talking to you. You're falling apart here. I thought a guy like you'd be—you know—Mr. Cool. I mean, Jesus Christ, it takes some balls for a two-bit bodyguard to put the moves on the boss's wife. Especially when the boss is Russell Nashe. Didn't you think Nashe'd do anything if he found out? Or you thought you'd never get caught? Or maybe you just didn't think that far ahead? Or maybe it's"—Sal narrowed his eyes and snapped his fingers a few times, trying to remember—"unbridled passion? Yeah. Isn't that what they call it? Is that what your problem is, Tomasso? Unbridled passion?"

Tozzi shifted in his seat, straightened his leg and bent it again to loosen the material a little so he could get to the gun easier. If he got the chance. "Look, Sal, I—"

Pfitt!

Tozzi felt the slug hit wood under his seat. He looked down and saw a fourth hole in the chair.

"Sit back, Tomasso. All the way back." Sal wasn't smiling now.

Tozzi settled down, nice and slow, wondering if he should just be cool or if he should force the issue, go for his gun and take his chances. He could feel the cold sweat creeping down his back. Immordino was a killer, no doubt about that. But if Immordino really believed he was a fed, would he risk killing him? That would be stupid. But then again he has to, now. Sal had talked to him, showed that there's nothing wrong with him. Cold sweat trickled over Tozzi's skin. He knew he was fucked.

"So you gonna talk to me or what, Tomasso?" Sal was looking mean now. Tozzi remembered a picture he'd seen of Immordino from his boxing days. The Lawson fight. Sweat spraying out from Lawson's Afro. Immordino's right mashing Lawson's face. Sal looking real mean, like he was really enjoying it. That was the fight where he'd killed the guy.

Sal rested the butt of his gun on the bedspread by his side, leveled at Tozzi. All he'd have to do was squeeze the trigger, nice and easy, one two three. Tozzi forced himself to look at Sal, not the gun. His shirt was soaked now. Sal stared him in the eye. He wasn't smiling. It was quiet except for the blown-up condoms making little squeaky noises as they drifted into each other. Tozzi held his breath.

But just then they heard something, both of them together. Sal sat up, glaring. The key in the front door. Val. Oh, shit.

"Who's that?" Sal hissed.

Tozzi shrugged. If Sal thought she was the "other guy," he'd plug her as soon as she came around the corner.

"Hey, Mike!" she called out.

Sal glared at him.

"Mi-ike! Are you here? What is it? My birthday?" She was laughing. Probably thought *he* had blown up all the rubbers. He looked at Sal's gun, thought about going for his, but then he heard her coming. Shit, stay out there.

Sal threw his legs over the side of the bed and dropped his gunhand down to his side where she couldn't see it.

Tozzi sat forward, elbows on his knees again, and she appeared in the doorway. "Hey, Val." She wasn't wearing her hat. Thank God. Probably took it off and threw it on the couch when she came in. He looked at Sal, who was hauling himself up to his feet, mumbling to himself, doing his numskull bit. Tozzi was impressed. Wiseguy code of honor. Sal wasn't going to kill her just because he wanted

Tomasso. Colombians pull shit like that, but Mafia guys don't like to waste people who don't deserve it. Bad for the image. Tozzi was impressed. And grateful.

Valerie looked confused, disappointed, a little miffed. "You guys having a party in here?" A little testy. Not much, but he could hear it in her voice.

"No," Sal mumbled, "no party over here." He sniffed and shuffled his feet a little, all hunched over now.

Tozzi stood up. He could see where Sal was holding the gun, down behind his thigh. "Val, I want you to meet an old friend of mine. Just ran into him on the way up." He caught Sal's eye. "Val, this is, ah, Clyde. Clyde Immordino." Tozzi looked at her and shrugged as if to say, Look at the poor bastard. What could I do?

"Hi," she said. Miffed, but she wasn't gonna say anything in front of company.

Sal muttered something, looking down at the floor. "Gotta go," he said then and sort of shuffled off toward the door.

Tozzi followed him out, with Valerie bringing up the rear. He saw Sal sneak the gun back into his pants under his jacket. Tozzi let out a long breath.

"You be a good boy, Tomasso," Sal grumbled under his breath, scowling up from under his brows.

Tozzi opened the front door. "I'm always good."

"Yeah." Sal nodded, too many times. "See ya 'round, Tomasso." He shuffled out then.

After Tozzi closed the door he looked over at Val who was in the kitchenette, running a glass of water for herself. "Who's he?" Still a little frosty.

"Some guy I know." What'd she think? They were gay? Jesus.

Tozzi went over to the cupboard and pulled down a bottle of Saint James. He held up the bottle to show her. "Rum. You want one?"

"Why not? On the rocks."

He took down two glasses, grabbed some ice from the freezer, and poured, hoping he didn't look as rattled as he felt. He handed her a glass, clinked, and drank down about half of what he'd poured for himself. The fireball of paranoia he'd felt a few minutes ago was passing. Now all he had to worry about was the fallout. Sal Immordino, the head of the Mistretta crime family, was on to him. Sal knew he wasn't Tomasso, and he'd figured out that he was some kind of cop. Sal knew he was screwing Sydney, who he was screwing too. Worst of all, Sal had let Tozzi know that he wasn't a mental defective, that he was certainly competent to stand trial in a court of law. How many more reasons did Sal need to kill him?

Tozzi took another long swig. He was a dead man.

He looked over at Valerie sipping her drink and he noticed her hat on the counter. She reached over and stroked his cheek with the back of her finger, smiling apologetically, giving him the big cow-eyes. He worked up a smile for her and finished his drink.

God help me.

• 13 •

"What's that?" Gibbons stared at the thing in the middle of the table. It looked like white Jell-O in the shape of a dead fish. Gibbons didn't even want to think about what it could be.

Lorraine yelled from the kitchen, "It's a fish mousse. I got it from the caterer. She suggested it for the reception. Try it. It's pretty good."

Gibbons sat there holding the edge of the table, frowning at the fish. Not on your life.

Lorraine whisked in from the kitchen then, carrying a platter in each hand. She set them down on the table on either side of the fish, and Gibbons nearly threw up. He looked up at her, and she actually looked pleased with herself. It was that same home-sweet-home, Betty Crocker look she had whenever she showed him a page in a catalog that had curtains she liked.

"What's *that*?" he asked.

"These are chicken breasts in Mornay sauce."

"I don't see any chicken."

She laughed that stupid little titter-laugh. "It's under the sauce."

"That's loaded with cream. What about my cholesterol?"

"I told you. This caterer does a modified nouvelle cuisine. She makes the sauce with skim milk."

He kept looking at it, thinking maybe it really wasn't that bad, but it didn't get any better. It was all gloppy sauce and no chicken. Sorta like hot tapioca pudding spread out on a plate. He leaned over and took a whiff. *Oooofff*—it even smelled like puke. He checked out the other platter. It was all brown and mushy. He didn't even want to get close to that one.

He looked up at Lorraine, pleased as punch with this atrocity. "That," she said, pointing to the brown stuff, "is a carrot-prune compote."

Gibbons's eyes narrowed. "Isn't that what you're supposed to put in flowerbeds?"

"That's *compost,* not compote."

He nodded at it, frowning. Same thing. "Carrot-prune compost." He kept nodding. "You sure you don't put this around the tomato plants?"

She just tittered again. Goddammit. He was getting sick and tired of this relentless good nature of hers. Why didn't she just tell him to shut up and eat it or go hungry?

He breathed through his mouth so he wouldn't have to smell it. "You know, I keep telling you. Your relatives won't eat this kind of stuff. Baked ziti and sausage, veal parmigian', spaghetti and meatballs—that's what they want." That's what *I* want.

"It's not their wedding. If they don't like the food, that's their problem."

She was spreading fish mousse on a cracker, very slow and careful about it. He watched her hands, the way they moved. He'd always liked watching her hands. They were beautiful. He looked at her face as she concentrated on that cracker, her eyes lowered, her hair loose, her mouth serious. A Neapolitan *contessa.* She really was beautiful, *really* beautiful.

"Why don't we just elope?"

Her eyes sprang open. "You're not serious?" A flash of pain and anguish in her face, as if he'd just said he wanted to shoot her dog or something.

"It was just a thought. We wouldn't have to worry about what to feed these people. We wouldn't have to bother with *any* of this wedding shit." Which is just making you stupid, Lorraine.

"There's nothing to worry about," she said. "It'll be fine. The relatives will fend for themselves. And the people from Princeton will definitely appreciate this kind of food." She waved her hand over the chicken puke.

His stomach grumbled. Oh, yes, the professors. A real fun bunch. Shit, they'll eat anything if it's free. Even the compost. He looked down at the brown mess, then he thought of something. "You know, your cousin won't eat this. Tozzi's a fussy bastard when it comes to food." For Tozzi, she'll change the menu. She loves him like a little brother. She'll change it now. Watch.

She wrinkled her brow. "Why do you think he won't like—"

The phone rang then. She started to go for it, but Gibbons leapt up and headed for the kitchen. "I'll get it," he said. Anything to get away from the table.

He snatched it off the wall in the middle of the second ring. "Hello?"

"Hey, Gib." It was Tozzi.

"Speak of the devil. How's it going?" Gibbons knew better than to mention his name on the phone.

"I'm calling from a pay phone. I got trouble down here."

"What wrong?"

"I had a visitor about an hour ago. Sal Immordino. He knows I'm not kosher. If Valerie hadn't walked in on us when she did, I don't think I'd be talking to you now. You know what I mean?"

Tozzi sounded tense. Gibbons didn't like this. Tozzi had

a way of getting crazy when he felt threatened. "I'll call the office. Tell me where you'll be, and I'll have some guys go down and meet you—"

"No, no, wait. I don't think it's that bad yet."

"Sal Immordino shows up to kill you, and you don't think it's that bad yet?"

"I've put a lot of time into this assignment—*too* much time, considering that I've come up with absolutely nothing to show for it. If I hightail it out of here in a panic, it'll be a good long time before Ivers lets me back out again."

Gibbons rubbed his face. Here we go with the Tozzi logic. "Whattaya got, shit for brains? I told you, Ivers is gonna pull the plug on you if you still don't have anything on Nashe by the end of the week. That's this Friday. This is Monday. What are you gonna know on Friday that you don't know today, genius? Shut it down now and save me a funeral."

"Listen to me, listen to me. I can take care of myself. I know I can."

"Give me a fucking break—"

"No, listen. Something's not right with all this. Why did Sal come to kill me himself? He's the acting head of the family, for chrissake. Why didn't he send one of his flunkies to get me?"

Gibbons exhaled into the phone. Here comes the theory. "I don't know why he came by himself, but I got a feeling you're gonna tell me."

"Because he's doing something behind Mistretta's back, and he thinks I know about it. He feels he has to get me out of the picture, but he can't just order a hit. It would get around in the family, and they'd start wondering why Sal's having this guy whacked. Sal doesn't want people asking him questions he doesn't want to answer. It's the only explanation. You told me yourself Mistretta looked all shook up at the museum when you hinted around that Sal was putting deals together on his own. I'm telling you. Whatever Sal's doing, he's doing it without Mistretta's okay, and he thinks I know what it is."

"That doesn't make any sense."

"Him personally coming to kill me doesn't make any sense. I gotta stay and find out what he's doing. He's not sending his people out after me, so all I have to worry about is him and maybe his brother, that's all. I can stay out of their way for four days. Shit, what's that?"

Tozzi talked a good game, but Gibbons knew him better than that. Tozzi was trying to convince himself. "No. I don't like it. You've been threatened, you come in. Now."

"No, not yet. I'm gonna see this through. Now, whether you want to help me or not is your business."

Gibbons squeezed his eyes shut. "I knew this was coming. You never can fuck up alone. You always need me."

"Yes, I need you, you big fucking asshole. You're my partner, aren't you?"

"Lucky me."

"Go ahead, be sarcastic. That's always very helpful."

Gibbons spotted the dirty Tupperware containers the shit from the caterer came in. They were sitting in the sink. "So what is it you want me to do? I can't wait to hear."

"No, forget about it. You don't want to help."

An oily brown residue coated one of the Tupperware pieces. The compost. "I wanna help! Whattaya want me to do, beg?"

"All right. Go find Immordino's sister the nun at the Mary Magdalen Center in Jersey City. Just go talk to her. You know, show her your ID, ask her about Sal and the family, that kind of stuff. That should shake things up nice. If I'm right about Sal, when it gets back to him that an FBI agent was questioning his sister, he'll go nuts. If we get lucky, he'll get sloppy and do something stupid."

"Get sloppy, my ass. You're in fairyland. This man is a career criminal. You don't think his sister hasn't been questioned a million times before?"

"Of course she has. But Sal's hiding something from Mistretta now, so this time it'll bother him."

Gibbons looked through the doorway. Lorraine was

loading up a plate for him. Oh, shit . . . "All right, I'll go see Sister Cil first thing in the morning."

"Great—"

"Hold on, my friend. You better fucking keep me informed, or I'll go down there and do the job *for* Immordino. *Capisce, paesan'?* I want to hear from you. Tomorrow. All right?"

"Of course. What do you think? We're partners, aren't we?"

Gibbons didn't answer right away. "Yeah."

"Okay, so I'll call you at the office in the afternoon sometime. Around two."

Gibbons was watching Lorraine. She was spreading that fish-mousse stuff on another cracker. "Tell me. How's that girlfriend of yours? The bartender, Valerie."

"Fine." Tozzi sounded puzzled.

"You said she walked in on you and Immordino?"

"Yeah, but nothing happened."

"I hope you're not treating her like that slut Sydney. She seems like a good kid. She doesn't deserve that kind of shit."

"What kind of shit? What're you talking about?"

"Just remember, she's not part of all this."

"I know that. What do you think I am, stupid?"

"You want me to answer that?"

"I'll talk to you tomorrow. And don't hit the nun or anything, will ya?"

"Can I genuflect on her foot?"

"Good-bye." Tozzi hung up.

Gibbons leaned against the refrigerator with the phone in his hand. He looked through the doorway and watched Lorraine eating that brown stuff, the compost. She wasn't just eating it, she was *enjoying* it. Gibbons let out a long sigh. Valerie would never bring crap like that into the house. Lorraine wouldn't either—not the old Lorraine.

The phone started to blare with that obnoxious hurry-up-and-hang-up-the-phone noise.

"It's getting cold," she called from the dining room. She must've heard the phone blaring.

"Yeah, I'm coming." He hung up the receiver. Shit.

Gibbons parted the lace curtains and looked out the bay window to see if his car was still there. The Mary Magdalen Center was in that kind of neighborhood—lot of misguided youths hanging out and looking guilty, lot of little crack vials in the gutters, lot of slick dudes in old Caddies cruising the streets. It was the kind of neighborhood where cop cars come by only when they have to. He spotted his car and, by some miracle, no one was yanking the radio out—yet. He sat back down on the worn rose-colored brocade sofa and waited for Sister Cil to come back.

A little kid with long dark bangs down to his eyes was on the floor next to his foot, digging his grubby fingers into a hunk of flesh-pink Play-Doh. Gibbons assumed that was the color you get when you mix them all together. The kid was really ripping into it, using his fingers like claws. Maybe he thought it was real flesh. Gibbons studied his mean little face. Future perp, sure as shit. You could see it already. The kid kept edging closer to Gibbons's foot, and Gibbons had a feeling the kid was eyeing the toe of his wingtips, thinking about smushing Play-Doh into all the little holes. Gibbons watched and waited. He had his handcuffs in his pocket. If the little bastard tried it, he'd cuff him to the radiator.

Gibbons looked through the doorway that Sister Cil had gone through a few minutes ago, wondering where the hell she was. Maybe she was calling Sal to tell him the FBI was on her case. So far she'd been pretty cool, not quite answering what he asked her but very polite and agreeable. He decided he'd press her a little harder when she came back, just to make sure it all got back to Sal.

Gibbons glanced down at the kid who had worked his way a little closer to his wingtip. The room was hot and sticky, ripe with the smell of kids. There were overhead ice-cube-tray fluorescent lights stuck to the ceiling that lit the place like an operating room and clashed like hell with the scrollwork moldings that edged the tops of the walls in the brownstone's old parlor. Gibbons spotted one of those juice boxes lying on its side on the hardwood floor, and he shifted in his seat, wondering what he might be sitting on.

"I'm sorry, Mr. Gibbons." Sister Cil whisked back into the room, her headpiece flying behind her, a wailing baby in her arms now. "A small crisis," she said with an apologetic smile, showing him the infant. As she sat back down in the shabby armchair across from him, the fluorescent lights glared off her big eyeglasses. She settled down with the cranky, flailing baby and stuck a bottle in its mouth. It calmed right down.

Gibbons smirked. How fucking transparent. She thinks she's clever. She went out to get a prop. Bring in a baby, and the big bad fed will melt right down and ease up on her. Yeah, just watch.

"Colicky," Sister Cil said, looking down at the baby. "Can't blame you, can we, sweetheart?" She looked at Gibbons over her glasses. "Her mother was a crack addict."

"Was?" Probably croaked.

Sister Cil smiled proudly. "Wanda's mommy has come a long way since she's been with us. Hasn't she, sweetheart?" She jiggled the baby in her arms.

Gibbons nodded. Keep that up and the kid's gonna throw up all over you.

"Mr. Gibbons?" She held the baby out toward him. "You wouldn't like to—"

"No, I wouldn't."

"Oh . . ."

Gibbons glanced down at the kid on the floor. He was gouging out chunks from the Play-Doh blob with a Popsicle stick. Serial killer—you watch.

"Now, what was it we were talking about, Mr. Gibbons?"

"Well, Sister, you were assuring me that your brother Sal isn't the acting boss of the Mistretta crime family and that he couldn't possibly have anything to do with the real estate tycoon Russell Nashe." Gibbons smiled like a crocodile.

Sister Cil nodded, and her glasses glimmered. "Yes, that's true." He wished he could see her eyes behind those glasses. He couldn't figure out if she was lying for Sal or if she really believed this crap.

"And you contend that your brother actually does suffer from irreversible brain damage?"

She paused to let out a big sigh before answering. "It's a terrible burden my brother has to bear. He was a very bright young man at one time, but he loved his boxing and . . . well, the human head can just take so much. It was the boxing that did it. As a result, his mental capacity is . . . Well, what can I say? In most aspects he's about on the level of a normal seven-year-old." She looked down at the Play-Doh killer and sighed again. "But such is God's will."

How many times has she given this little sermon?

"Tell me something, Sister. I'm not of the Catholic faith myself, and frankly I'm a little curious about something." He bit the inside of his cheeks to keep from grinning. "Why would God choose to turn a healthy, athletic man like your brother into a walking dummy, Frankenstein with a weak battery? Why would He do that?" You wanna bust balls with the baby and the holy of holies? I'll show you how to bust balls.

She looked down at the baby and smiled serenely. "Mr. Gibbons, it is simply beyond our humble understanding. Our job here on earth is to praise and obey the Lord. It isn't our place to question His intentions. If God has decided that Sal should be a walking dummy, as you put it, then it's part of a greater plan that we could never hope to understand." The light flashed off her glasses. "Or as my grandmother told us so often when we were growing up, *'Gesù Cristo vede e provvede.'* Jesus sees and provides, Mr. Gibbons."

"Uh-huh . . ." Gibbons nodded. She was something. Calm and even-tempered the whole way. She knew the family drill and nothing was gonna upset that. Ma Barker was the same way, supposedly. Well, rattling the nun wasn't the important thing here. Just as long as the message got back to Sal that the FBI had been there asking questions about him. That's all that was necessary.

He stood up then. "Well, Sister, thank you for your time."

"Not at all, Mr. Gibbons. I hope I've shed some light on your understanding of my brother."

Gibbons smiled with his teeth. "When you see him next, give him our best."

He looked out the window and saw that his car was still there, then he glanced down at the floor. The kid was gone, but the toe of his right shoe was smeared with flesh-pink Play-Doh.

Fucking little sneak! That kid's picture will be in the post office someday. Little son of a bitch!

The nun was busy feeding the baby, busy not noticing his shoe. Gibbons didn't bother asking for a Kleenex. Didn't want to give her the satisfaction. He just picked up his hat from the sofa and walked out with the Play-Doh on his toe and his hand in his pocket on the cuffs.

Little bastard.

14

Joseph kept blotting his forehead with his handkerchief, the nice silk one that matched his silver tie. He kept standing up and sitting down, first pacing the sidewalk, then dropping down on the park bench to wipe his face again. Sister Cil stared across the street at the row of old brownstones, pressing her forearm into her aching stomach. She regretted ever telling Joseph about Mr. Gibbons. It had been a mistake, she hadn't been thinking. Joseph is a baby. He's no help at all.

"You *sure* he was FBI, Cil?"

"I've already told you a hundred times, Joseph. He showed me his identification. Who else would he be if he wasn't a real FBI agent?"

"I don't know. Maybe he was from one of the other families. A spy, like."

Cil pressed her stomach harder and fingered the wooden rosary beads in her lap. This didn't even deserve a response. No wonder Sal got so fed up with him. Joseph could be so useless sometimes. Why did she ever tell him?

She'd panicked, that's why. That was stupid. She wasn't thinking straight when she called him. Stupid.

Joseph nervously twisted that nice handkerchief around his fingers, ruining it. "We gotta tell Sal, Cil. He's gonna wanna know about this."

"No!"

Joseph got up again and started pacing. "You keep saying no, Cil. I don't understand why. Why, Cil?"

Cil wasn't listening. She was staring at their shabby brownstone squeezed in among all the other shabby brownstones, the Center, their too-small brownstone, thinking that if they tell Sal about this and he gets cold feet and abandons the plan to have the champ throw the fight, then it'll be God only knows how long before they get their new building . . . if they ever get it at all. The agencies keep calling with referrals—pregnant girls, young girls with babies, babies who need a home—and she has to keep turning them away because they just don't have the room. She gripped the wooden crucifix in her fingers. This wasn't right. She was being forced to turn away so many. It made her feel like the innkeeper who had turned Joseph and Mary away on Christmas Eve.

Joseph dropped back down on the bench. "Say something, Cil. You're just sitting there. We gotta do something here."

Cil adjusted her veil, pulled it forward a little at the hairline. Her stomach was in turmoil. Maybe Sal *should* abandon the plan. Maybe she *should* confess to him that Mr. Mistretta didn't want him to bet family money on this boxing match, that he'd been definite about that, that she'd lied about that. Maybe it's not too late. But she couldn't stop staring at the Center. What if it all worked out and Sal did make all that money, what could Mr. Mistretta say then? Give it back? Of course not. The boxing match was just a few days away. So close. It's not as if she were being selfish—the money wasn't for her. It's for the new building, for the girls, the *babies.* It's for something very important, something that's desperately needed. It's money for an act of charity that should excuse the lie she had told Sal. If the new facility is built, God will forgive her. And if He forgives her, so will Sal and Mr. Mistretta.

"Cil, you're not helping things here." Joseph blotted his brow and stood up again. "How about this, Cil? How about we go to Mr. Mistretta with this? Ask him if—"

"*No!* Absolutely not." Dear God, no . . .

"But, Cil, if the FBI is gonna put the screws to the fight deal, we gotta protect ourselves. We got *thirty million dollars* tied up in this thing."

"I said no. Now, sit down and stop panicking. You can't go over Sal's head. That wouldn't be right."

"What do you mean, it wouldn't be right? You don't wanna tell Sal, you don't wanna tell Mistretta—whatta we do? Just sit around and wait for everything to go wrong?"

The pain in her stomach flared like the flames of hell. "Will you please sit down and calm yourself, Joseph. You're getting all worked up over nothing. When we were kids you were always the nervous one."

Joseph sat down and glared at her. "Whattaya talking about, when we were kids? I was eleven years old when you were born. What do you know what I did when I was a kid?"

She looked at him and pushed her glasses up her nose. "Sal told me."

"Fu—The hell with Sal. You think Sal's Mr. Wonderful, and I'm just some *jooch* you happen to be related to. That's what you think. I know." Joseph was on his feet again.

"Joseph, you're not thinking straight. That FBI agent doesn't know anything about the fight. If he did, he would've—"

Suddenly something rustled in the overgrown forsythia bushes behind them, and they both turned quickly. A homeless man sprawled out on a sheet of cardboard under the bushes sat up and stared at them. He had wild red hair and a wild red beard, wide pale blue eyes. Cil's heart was pounding. Was he another one, another FBI agent, one of Mr. Gibbons's associates?

But as she stared into the man's face, something occurred to her, something profound. This man's appearance, this was the way she always pictured Barabbas, the way she remembered him from a *Hallmark Hall of Fame* Easter special about Jesus that she'd seen on television a long, long time ago, before she'd entered the convent. She put her hand on her chest and pressed against the thumping. This man wasn't an FBI agent. No. He was a sign. A *sign.*

Joseph was as white as a ghost, staring at the poor, unfortunate man. "Calm down, Joseph. You're not thinking clearly. You're not seeing the whole picture. You're only thinking of yourself."

"Whattaya mean, I'm only thinking of myself? Why shouldn't I think of myself? Nobody ever thinks of me. I *gotta* worry about myself 'cause nobody else does."

"Just calm down, Joseph." Calling him down here had been a mistake. Telling him about Mr. Gibbons had been a mistake. If she could just reassure him so he would keep quiet, everything would be all right, everything.

He slid over close to her and whispered in her face. "Listen to me, Cil. I gotta worry about myself. This deal blows apart, I'm left with nothing. I'm supposed to run those cement factories Sal wants to buy with the money we make on the fight. We don't get the money, I don't get the job, simple as that. Mistretta gets out of jail soon, Sal goes back to being a captain. Where's that leave me? Nowhere, that's where. I'll be the gofer, the guy they send out for coffee, taking crap from every bum in his crew. Well, shit on that. I'd rather go back to cutting meat. Even if I have to work for someone else." He hung his head and looked down at the bluestone sidewalk. "Can't afford to buy a shop of my own again. And I'll be damned if I'll ask Sal for the money . . ." He shook his head. "Man, this, this . . . this stinks, Cil."

She drew in a deep breath. Tell him everything will be

all right, pacify him enough to keep him quiet at least until after the boxing match. He's a child. Treat him like a child. "Joseph," she said, speaking to him calmly but firmly, "there is nothing to worry about. The FBI is harassing me as a way of harassing Sal. This is just a new strategy in something that has been going on for years. Now, the boxing match is this Saturday. Logically, what could they do to stop it?"

"Hey, these guys are the government. They do whatever the hell they want." He was twisting that silk handkerchief again. It was ruined now.

"You're not being logical, Joseph. Think. If the FBI knew that Sal was involved with the boxing match, why would they bother to send an agent to see me? Wouldn't they go directly to Sal or to Mr. Nashe or to Mr. Walker and Mr. Epps?"

"Yeah, but what about the bug we found in your gold cross?"

She pressed her lips together and shook her head. Just reassure him. "Joseph, how many times did we go over what was discussed at the house after he gave me that crucifix? Whatever they heard meant nothing to them. *They don't know anything.*"

"Maybe someone squealed, got nervous and ran to the feds."

"Who would do that?"

"I dunno—maybe Nashe. Maybe he's cutting a deal with them, giving them Sal in exchange for reduced charges on something else they caught him at. Like tax evasion. Guys like that are always going up for tax evasion. The feds get Nashe in a corner, and he cuts a deal with them to save his own hide. You don't think that kind of stuff happens all the time?"

The man with the red beard, who'd been staring at them in a daze until now, flopped back down on his cardboard and turned over on his belly.

Her heart was pounding again. Tell Joseph anything.

Make him calm down. "Joseph, you have so little faith. Don't you think Sal has taken precautions?"

He suddenly turned on her. "Sal, Sal, Sal! Everything is Sal with you."

She glared at him over her glasses. "Joseph, he has been in this business considerably longer than you have. I think he knows how to handle these things."

Joseph turned away in a snit. "Yeah, he knows how to handle things. That's why the FBI is crawling all over the place."

A child! Jealous of his brother, just like a child. "I'm sure Sal is doing something to make sure this investment is protected. Don't you think?"

Joseph hung his head again, disgusted. "Sal doesn't tell me nothing. I'm just a dummy."

"This jealousy of yours, Joseph—I just don't understand it. You know that Sal has everything under control. You just don't want to say so because you're jealous of him. You ought to be ashamed."

Joseph snapped back like a mad dog. "*I* ought to be ashamed! You wanna know how your dear brother has everything under control? Huh? You wanna know what he's doing to keep tabs on Nashe so he doesn't screw us? You really wanna know? He's screwing Nashe's wife, that's what he's doing. Real smart, huh? I sleep real good at night, knowing that Sal's getting it on with Sydney Nashe. I bet you feel better now too, huh?"

Her face was suddenly burning. She could feel her hair tingling at the roots under her veil. She was mortified, ashamed, furious with Joseph. He'd only said this to hurt her, to get back at her, just like a child. But Joseph had never lied to her before, and that's what hurt more. How could Sal do such a thing? Adultery is a sin—he knows that —but that wasn't half as bad as the fact that he was doing it with that . . . that woman, that peculiar, ostentatious woman. Mrs. Nashe? How could he? *Why* would he? She was so . . . so cheap. Why with her, of all people? What could Sal possibly see in her?

"What'sa matter, Cil? You got nothing to say all of sudden?" The sarcasm was like poison in his voice. "Aren't you impressed by how clever Sal is? Sleeping with Nashe's wife—a real stroke of genius. She must know everything her husband's doing, right? She sees Sal, she must tell him everything. Right? He's so smart, my brother. You know, I *admire* him. I really do."

Cil looked at that homeless man sleeping on the ground. All she could see were his legs—dusty brown pants, filthy gray wool socks worn through at the soles, no shoes. She tried to put it out of her mind, but she couldn't stop trying to imagine Sal in bed with that woman, her dyed blond hair, her painted fingernails all over his skin. She felt nauseated, and she stayed very still. How could Sal succumb to such animal lusts with that horrible woman? How could he? Joseph was right about that: It served no purpose. Lust, it was just lust. That's all it was.

Then it gripped her. Jesus saw him in bed with that woman, acting like an animal with her. Jesus *saw* him. *Gesù Cristo vede e provvede.*

She looked over at the brownstone and her face felt like stone. Sal was no better than those men who seduced her girls, who made them promises just to have sex with them, then left them pregnant. The girls. The girls. What about them? The more she thought about all this, the worse she felt. Lying to Sal, lying about Mr. Mistretta's orders, Sal sinning with that Nashe woman, Joseph running around like a chicken without a head—it was all so confusing. She clenched the rosary beads in her fist, the wooden crucifix digging into her flesh. Her stomach was a mess. It was almost as if God were testing her. Yes, she decided, that's exactly what it was. God was testing her. The road to good is not straight and it's not well lit. God was putting obstacles and distractions in her way to test her faith. What she must do is stay on the road, no wavering, no detours, no matter what. She must achieve her original goal. The girls must have their new building. That is the goal. Her brothers' weaknesses and failings cannot divert her from that goal.

She was suddenly startled when Joseph put his hand on top of hers. "You see what I'm saying, Cil? It's *not* all right. Sal doesn't have a handle on this thing. We've got some problems here." His tone was conciliatory, softer, more rational than he'd ever been. He was just trying to confuse her.

"There's no problem, Joseph." She tried to put him out of her mind so she could think. She hadn't told anyone about Mr. Mistretta's objections to betting on the boxing match. It was no time to say anything about that now. Sal was as weak as Joseph. He'd panic if she told him, cancel the whole thing. Then when it was all over, he'd just shrug and say, Someday, Cil. Don't worry. You'll get your new building someday.

No. No more somedays. Now.

"Cil, say something. You're making me nervous. Do we tell Sal about the FBI guy or not?"

She ignored her brother and stared straight ahead at the Center across the street, willing her stomach to settle down. Then it occurred to her. Perhaps Joseph wasn't the only one being selfish. Perhaps she'd been selfish too, seeing this whole thing only from her own perspective instead of recognizing that she was just one small piece in God's larger plan. They were all small pieces—her, Sal, Joseph, Mr. Nashe, even Mr. Mistretta. Naturally none of them could ever understand the scope of God's plan. No one can. She'd been thinking too much, thinking as if she were God, as if she had control over the situation. Good Lord, forgive me.

It was obvious now what she should do. Nothing, do nothing. Stop trying to outwit God. We are the pieces, He is the player. He has set all this in motion. Mortal beings have no control over it. Just let it happen, let it play itself out the way He had planned it, the way it *will* happen. Yes. This was all preordained. It will all happen as He had planned it at the beginning of time. No matter what. Cil started to breathe easier. Her stomach felt a little better.

"Cil, you're too quiet. You're making me nervous. I gotta know what you think we should do here. Do you wanna tell Sal about the FBI guy or not?"

She shook her head. "Don't tell him. It's too close to the fight. There's no reason to upset him now. It was nothing. Just more harassment, I'm sure of it. If we mention it to Sal, he'll get upset and he might do something foolish. His mind should be on the boxing match right now, nothing else."

Joseph nodded, smiled a little. He obviously liked being in on something that didn't include Sal. For once it was Sal who was being kept in the dark for his own good, and it made Joseph feel important. She shook her head. He was such a child. But that was how God wanted it.

"You really don't think we should tell him about it?" Joseph was still unsure of himself.

She shook her head.

"You sure, Cil?"

"Yes, I'm sure."

"I dunno, Cil. If we don't tell him, don't you think we should at least do something, like—?"

"Pray."

"Pray?"

"This is the time for prayer. It's all we can do." She stood up from the bench and looked down at him. "And it's the *best* we can do." She turned and walked to the curb, waiting for a break in the traffic so she could cross.

"But, Cil—"

"Pray, Joseph. Have faith." She stepped off the curb and headed for the Center. "Good-bye, Joseph," she called over her shoulder. He sat there on the park bench, dumbfounded.

She crossed the street and stood on the bottom step of the old brownstone, looking up at the windows. There wasn't a single one that wasn't cracked, and all the shades were torn and yellowed. The condition of this building was shameful. She pressed her lips together and shook her head. Mrs. Nashe would never live in a building like this.

• 15 •

"You know, I had a feeling you guys were going to ask me about Nashe." David Holman paused to take a sip from a big white coffee mug with the company name on it—Pope Sedgewick Samms, one of the "Big Eight" accounting firms.

Tozzi watched the moon-faced accountant's eyes behind the round tortoise-shell glasses. *Gleeful* was the word he'd use for them, gleeful eyes. Very strange. The first thing that struck Tozzi about Holman was that he didn't react the way most people do when the FBI shows up. Most people get scared. Right away they think they're the ones in trouble. Holman seemed glad to see them, almost from the moment he and Gibbons had walked into his office and shown their ID. When Gibbons had given him the standard line about him not being the target of this investigation, Holman just smiled and said, "I know." Funny guy.

Tozzi sipped coffee from an identical white mug and decided to let Gibbons do the talking. He didn't want to be here in the first place. You don't need two agents to question an accountant, for chrissake. What was he, dangerous? Tozzi wanted to be back down in Atlantic City, with Valerie. Today was his day off and she didn't start work until three. They could've been doing something together, but no, Gibbons insisted that he shouldn't be hanging around the boardwalk, not after Sal Immordino's visit the other night. Actually, Gibbons was probably right—as long as he was guarding Russell Nashe, he was safe, but off duty, wandering around on his own, he was fair game. The night Sal came gunning for him at his apartment, they had gone over to Valerie's and spent the night there—a very nice night there—but since then he'd been sleeping alone, moving around from one cheap motel to another. If Sal or one of his goons came back, he didn't want Valerie to be there. Yeah, Gibbons was probably right about his not hanging around. Dammit.

The phone on Holman's desk beeped once, no ring. "Excuse me for just one minute." He flashed a pleasant smile and picked up the receiver.

Tozzi looked at Gibbons sitting next to him in the cramped little office, their knees almost touching on the other side of Holman's desk. Gibbons glanced at him, then stared up at the ceiling. Gibbons had picked him up at the Lucky Seven Motel on Tennessee Avenue just after six this morning, and they'd had it out in the car coming up here. It took almost four fucking hours to get to White Plains because Gibbons had decided to cross the GW right at rush hour. Perfect timing. They're stuck in traffic in the middle of the bridge and he says something like, Shit, this is useless, and all of a sudden Gibbons goes ape-shit, starts yelling at him, giving him this rap about how it's their duty to stay with the investigation, even if Ivers is shutting it down tomorrow, even if there's no way in hell they could come up with something substantial on Nashe by then. Gibbons starts getting real hot about it, jabbing his finger, getting red in the face. Do or die, right to the end. Mr. Hard Ass. Who the hell does he think he's kidding? He just wants to keep this thing going so he won't have to go back to his desk job at the office. Asshole.

Tozzi set down his mug on the edge of the desk and crossed his arms over his chest. This *was* useless. Holman was stroking his pale yellow print tie, leaning back in his chair, the phone caddy propped on his shoulder, while he was discussing something about an internal audit that had to be redone in San Francisco. It sounded like it was going to be a hassle, but he didn't seem very upset about it. Strange guy.

Holman was a senior auditor here and he looked the part. The shirt was white enough to make you snow-blind, and his yellow suspenders matched the tie. Six months ago he'd been working for Russell Nashe in the casino's accounting department. Tozzi wondered whether he'd been this happy when he was working for Nashe. Nashe likes everybody around him to be happy, but not as happy as him. Holman might've been too happy. Maybe that was why he'd been fired.

He looked over at Gibbons again, but now his partner was squinting at Holman's diplomas on the wall. Stubborn bastard. Had to do everything by the book. But even if Holman did know about all kinds of skeletons in Nashe's closet, there wasn't enough time to follow up on any allegations he might make. Holman would have to give them gold for Ivers to keep this undercover going, and when did a subject ever give a special agent gold on the first interview? Never, that's when.

Naturally, he'd love to have something he could pin on Nashe so that the U.S. attorney would sit on the billionaire's big head and plea-bargain him into giving them something good on Immordino. He'd love to see Sal's ass in the fire more than anything. But it wasn't going to happen. There just wasn't enough time. They weren't going to find out anything new today and he was gonna go to work tomorrow as Mike Tomasso and then, after his shift, that would be it. Tomasso would disappear, and Nashe and

Immordino would keep doing whatever the hell they were doing together.

In a few weeks he'd give Valerie a call, explain as much as he could about who he really was so he could reestablish some contact with her, they'd have another date or two, he'd avoid the difficult questions as best he could, she'd come up to his place in Hoboken maybe once, then they'd find out it wasn't working because of the distance and the fact that their hours were both pretty weird and it was too difficult to get together, and then that would be it too. Hopeless. It was hopeless. Tozzi picked up his mug and drained it.

Holman hung up the phone then. "Sorry. I'll let my machine pick up for a while." He sat up straight and linked his fingers on top of his desk. "So what is it you want to know about old Russ?"

Gibbons uncrossed his legs, ready for business. "You worked for Russell Nashe in Atlantic City. Is that correct, Mr. Holman?"

"Uh-huh. I was one of the head accountants at the Plaza. I ran the department that took care of the hotel side. The casino had a bigger department all to itself. The two had to be treated as separate businesses. Gaming Commission rules."

Gibbons nodded, encouraging him, easing him along. Why bother? Holman didn't need much encouraging. He looked like he was champing at the bit to tell them anything they wanted to know. Come on, Gib, cut to the chase. This guy doesn't need the foreplay.

"And is it true that you were fired from that position, Mr. Holman?"

"That's right." Holman didn't seem bitter or ashamed about it. Maybe he took drugs, a discreet snort in the bathroom at coffee break, the executive high.

"Why were you fired?" Gibbons sounded like a funeral director, very somber.

Holman leaned back in his chair and rocked a little.

"Why was I fired? That's a hard one to answer. You'd have to understand how Russell Nashe operates."

Gibbons glanced at Tozzi and shrugged. "I've got time. Educate me."

Oh, Christ. Real clever, Gib. Now it's gonna be *The Story of My Life* by David Holman. He'll have us here past lunch, for chrissake. Tozzi looked at his watch. By the time he got back to Atlantic City, Val would be at work. Goddammit!

"Well—" Holman started, then paused to look out into the distance. "No. Let me put it this way. Russell Nashe is a very insecure person. I was going to say he was crazy, but that's only part of it."

"What do you mean by 'insecure'?"

"Russell Nashe has this pathological need to be the biggest wheeler-dealer on the block. Whenever he finds out somebody is putting together a big deal on something, he has to put together a bigger deal. There are a few people who drive him up a wall, he's so jealous of them, but most often it's Donald Trump who gets his goat. Obviously. Trump started work on the Taj Mahal, Russ had to go up against him with the Paradise. Trump promotes fights at his casino, Russ has to put together this big fight deal with Walker this week. Insane."

"Why do you say it's insane?" Gibbons's eyes did not waver from Holman.

"Because between you and me, I don't think he has the money to pay that humongous purse." Holman turned the corners of his mouth down and shook his head. "Seventeen million for Walker? The figures just don't work out, not the way I see it. Walker will be taking Russ to court to collect his money. I predict it."

"Do you know this for a fact, that Nashe won't have the money to cover the purse?"

Holman wrinkled his brow. All of a sudden he didn't look happy. "Well, no . . . not really. I was gone by the time this fight deal came together."

"Then how do you know Nashe won't have the money?"

Holman sat forward again, hands joined on the blotter. "I know how Russ operates, and I know how much the Plaza takes in. The Gaming Commission keeps close tabs on the casino money, so Russ can't fool around with that. But the hotel money is another thing. He was always dipping into the till for one thing or another, wheeling and dealing like crazy but never paying the bills for basic operations. We were *constantly* negotiating with creditors, placating them, giving them free weekends at the hotel, comping them to the ceiling just to put them off a little while longer."

"You mean Nashe takes from Peter to pay Paul? That kind of thing?"

"No, it's more like he takes from Peter *and* Paul and then screws them both."

"How does he get away with it?"

The glee returned to Holman's eyes. "Promises."

"Promises?" Gibbons looked skeptical.

"Sure. Say he's got a . . . a bakery, say, that's delivering —I don't know—say, fifty dozen croissants to the Plaza every day. At some point Nashe tells me don't pay them, ignore the invoices. The bills pile up, the bakery starts calling, we make excuses, tell them we love their product, maybe even increase the regular order a little to get their hopes up, but we still don't pay the bills. Then after a couple of months of getting nowhere, the bakery gets mad and starts demanding their money. Russ says tell them anything, but don't pay. The bakery gets a lawyer then, threatens to sue. That's when Russ steps in with the bullshit.

"He gets in the limo and takes a ride down to the bakery. Shows up unannounced and says he wants to talk to the boss. The boss comes out, and Russ tells the guy he's beautiful, he's wonderful, he makes the best croissants in the whole world, better than they make in Paris, croissants worthy of his hotel. The baker knows he's full of shit, and Russ knows the baker knows he's full of shit, but Russ has that way about him. It's this very special kind of charm he's got. Totally calculated on his part, but it always seems to work for him. You think you see right through him, but that's what he wants you to think because it makes you feel smarter than him. The baker says to himself, Hey, I'm standing here with this big-deal billionaire who gets on TV and in the papers all the time and he thinks he's pulling one over on me, but he's not because I can see right through him.

"So what Russ does then is he gets this baker feeling real good about himself, thinking he's real smart. That's when Russ moves in and makes 'the promise.' He confides in the man, tells him about his plans for the Paradise, his big dream, the biggest hotel casino in the world, two and half times bigger than the Taj. He throws figures around like he's talking to the Secretary of the Treasury, complains about the high cost of labor and construction, then tells the guy he must have the same kinds of problems in the bakery business, puts the guy on his level, which of course makes the guy feel even more important.

"Then he tells the poor schmuck about the temporary cash-flow problem he's having because of the Paradise construction and that this is why he hasn't been paying his bills for the croissants these past few months. *But* if the baker will be gracious enough to float him just a little while longer, he'll have Russ's solemn promise on his mother's grave that every croissant that is ever served in the Paradise will come from this bakery and no other. Scout's honor. Then Russ gives the man the bullshit grin, like he may be full of shit or he may not. But by now the guy feels that he and Russ are equals, fellow entrepreneurs. The guy feels that he can deal with Russ, that his business is gonna triple, that he's gonna be the Famous Amos of croissants if he just hangs in there with Russ. And so he goes along with it because a contract like that you can take to the bank. Right? The guy's dreaming about custom-built houses, a big black Mercedes, sending his kids to Harvard, a boat, European vacations, all that stuff, and in the meantime Russ is getting a million croissants on time at no interest."

Holman shook his head. "I've seen him do this to I don't know how many people. Works every time. He's incredible."

Gibbons nodded. "That's very interesting."

Tozzi picked up his mug, then frowned down into it. He forgot he'd already finished the coffee. So Gib thinks this is "interesting." Interesting but not indictable. Bullshitting people is not a crime. We're wasting our time here, Gib. This is stupid.

Gibbons stopped nodding and stared Holman in the eye. "So why were you fired?"

Holman sipped his coffee, eyes sparkling behind the glasses. "You know, after all this time, I'm still not sure." He shrugged. "Maybe he couldn't afford me anymore. I had been with him for almost four years. Maybe he figured he could hire a younger guy, a little less experienced, save twenty, thirty thousand in salary."

"Doesn't sound like much of a savings for a billionaire." Gibbons sipped from his mug.

Tozzi rubbed his chin. The guy's dodging the question, Gib. Can't you see that?

Holman narrowed his eyes as he wagged his finger at Gibbons. "That's the thing about Russ. He's a billionaire, yes. But on paper. A very very small portion of those assets are liquid."

"Why's that?"

"Because Russell Nashe is a deal junkie. Each deal has to be bigger and more complicated than the last. I told you, it's pathological with him. He can't control himself. He owes everybody money and he's leveraged to the eyeballs. At this point he *has* to keep making deals to keep his debts from catching up with him."

Gibbons squinted at him. "Doesn't make any sense. Sooner or later creditors get pissed, and they sue."

"Except that he's promised everybody in the world a piece of the Paradise. You see, it all rides on the Paradise now. It's been the source of all Russ's promises since he first dreamed it up. I'm glad he fired me. Once that monstrosity is finally built and all his buddies start calling in their markers, the shit's gonna hit . . . the . . . fan." Holman enunciated each word.

But as far as Tozzi was concerned it was bullshit that was hitting the fan. Holman's bullshit because he still hadn't said why he'd been fired, and Gibbons wasn't doing much to get it out of him, except looking soulfully into his gleeful little blues.

Tozzi was about to ask the question himself when Gibbons beat him to the punch. "When you worked for Nashe, did he have you keep two sets of books?"

Holman laughed out loud, too loud. "Two! Try fifty-two. I'm not kidding. I had people on my staff who just cooked the books based on these wild scenarios Russ would come up with. I mean totally off-the-wall stuff, like the hotel being booked eighty percent on all five weekdays, like the big room selling out without a big act, that kind of stuff. Insane. I asked him once why he wanted us to cook up books that showed more profit than we actually made. I always thought you were supposed to do it the other way, in case the IRS calls for an audit. He told me these books weren't for the IRS. He said he just wanted to see what it would look like on paper." Holman shook his head, eyes sparkling. "That's what he said, I swear. I think Russ really loved it, going over these totally outrageous books that made him look like—I don't know—like Donald Trump. No, better than Trump. He actually told me once that he loved to curl up with these stupid books in bed, said it was like reading a really good thriller that had him as the hero." Holman shrugged, eyes still twinkling.

Tozzi was getting sick of this shit. Fuck Gibbons. He'd put it to Twinkle Eyes himself. "But why did—?"

"Excuse me," Gibbons said, giving Tozzi the hairy eyeball. "I don't want to lose my train of thought."

Eat your fucking train of thought.

"This business about creating bogus records, not paying creditors, and so on—who else had knowledge of these practices?"

"Well, there were the people on my staff . . . I can't think of anyone else, though."

"Any partners?"

Holman shook his head. "Russ is the sole owner of the Plaza."

"How about his wife? She know anything about all this?"

Holman paused. His eyes weren't so bright. "Sydney." He pounded his chin with his fist a few times. "Sydney." Another pause. "If you think he's weird, you ought to meet Sydney."

I have. Tozzi watched his eyes.

"Weird in what way?" Gibbons asked.

"Theirs is the most fucked-up relationship I've ever seen."

"How so?"

Holman paused again, staring into the space. "Well," he finally started, "it's not based on love, that's for sure. They can barely stand the sight of each other."

"So why don't they get divorced?"

Holman shrugged. "They're very weird. See, they play this strange game where he doesn't tell her a thing about his business, nothing, and she plays spy, trying to figure out what he's up to. When she finds out something good—you know, the kind of stuff that could embarrass him—she blackmails him with it. Basically she blackmails him into staying married. It's all a very elaborate game they play. Very sick."

"And how does she get her information?"

Another pause, then a weak grin. The eyes weren't even remotely gleeful now. "She sleeps around. She must be pretty good at worming things out of men in bed. Very sexy woman—if you've ever met her."

"How do you know that she—"

"You know, another thing about her." Holman cut Gibbons off. "I heard a rumor once that when she gets a really good piece of information—something she can't blackmail Russ with but something she knows he'd love to know—she sells it to him. You know that lavender yacht she has? A payoff from Russ for some really good piece of information." Holman shook his head again. "She must be a real Mata Hari in bed."

Tozzi felt the blood draining out of his face. That bitch. He didn't want to believe it. All this time he thinks he's getting info out of her, she's running back to Nashe, telling him about their afternoon delights, probably telling him what kind of nosy questions he's been asking. Shit. Nashe must've figured out a long time ago that he's some kind of agent working undercover. And if Nashe suspected him, he'd keep him at arm's length, make sure he didn't go anyplace where he might hear anything . . .

And what had he heard in the last eight weeks?

Shit . . .

Tozzi's stomach rumbled. But how did Sal know he was a fed? Did Nashe tell him? Why? Is whatever they're doing together that big that they'd risk killing a fed? It would have to be pretty big for that. But what was it? Tozzi felt itchy. He wanted to know what the hell was going on. He was also pissed as hell at Sydney, that bitch. He didn't like being manipulated.

"Gentlemen, I'd love to help you any way I can, but I am pretty busy and if there aren't any more questions . . ."

Tozzi's face was hot. "Just one thing, Mr. Holman, and I'd like a straight answer this time. You've been avoiding this since we got here. Why *did* Russell Nashe fire you?"

Holman wouldn't look at him. He was pounding his chin with his fist.

"Well?"

"Before I answer, I want to know if I can be forced to testify to anything I say here. I don't want my wife to know anything about this." He looked more like a nervous little accountant now.

Gibbons assured him, "Mr. Holman, I told you. You're not the target—"

"Just answer the question, please." Jesus Christ, Gib.

Holman stared at Tozzi, looking helpless. "He fired me because . . . because I was . . . carrying on with his wife. I told her a few things about how the hotel was doing that I suppose Russ didn't want her to know, and she must've thrown it up in his face." Holman was quiet for a few seconds. "He said I was disloyal, that I couldn't be trusted . . . Look, my wife was pregnant at the time and . . . and Sydney is a very attractive woman. Not the kind of woman the average guy gets the opportunity to be with. If you know what I mean."

Tozzi could feel Gibbons grinning at him. Smug fucking asshole. Tozzi didn't want to look at him, didn't want to give him the satisfaction. Hey, this was Holman's version of things. He knew Sydney. She wouldn't go down for an accountant, for chrissake. This guy was dreaming. A squeeze in the elevator maybe, a kiss in the broom closet, something like that. Christ, he's making like they were Antony and Cleopatra.

Holman muttered into his fist then, *"Car 54, Where Are You?"*

"Excuse me."

He looked up at Tozzi. "I was just remembering. Sydney used to sing these songs from old TV sitcoms when we were in bed. *Car 54* was the one she sang most often." Holman exhaled a bittersweet laugh. "Toody and Muldoon." He shook his head. "Weird lady."

Tozzi wanted to break something. He wanted to get up and move. He looked at his watch. It wasn't even eleven yet. There was still time. They could still dig up something to bring down the whole fucking bunch of them: Nashe, Immordino, Sydney—

"We finished here?"

"Huh?"

Gibbons with the hairy eyeball again. "You got anything else you want to ask Mr. Holman?"

"No."

Gibbons turned to the accountant. "Thanks for your cooperation. We'll be in touch if we need you."

"My wife won't find out about this, will she?" The little shit was pathetic.

"Don't sweat it," Tozzi said, "We won't tell your wife you were porking some other bitch while she was in labor. Come on, Gib. Let's go." He got up to leave but Gibbons just sat there, looking at him as if he were from the moon.

"You have to excuse my partner," he said to Holman. "He's Italian."

Tozzi shoved the chair out of his way and walked out. Asshole.

16

Tozzi lay on his back in bed, his arm crooked behind his head, staring out the big triangular picture window at the gulls soaring through a solid blue sky. He'd been up since six, tried to go back to sleep, but there was too much on his mind now. He looked over at Valerie sleeping next to him, the sheet pulled up over her face, tousled blond hair all over the pillow. Tozzi sighed. She was nice—too nice to lose.

He reached over her and took her fedora off the brass bedpost, put it on his chest and ran his finger along the silky band. It's a good thing he'd found her last night, a good thing Lenny Mokowski had let him have the keys to this place. No telling what he might've done when he'd gotten back from White Plains yesterday afternoon.

He and Gibbons had started arguing as soon as they got into the car. He'd wanted to get back to the Plaza right away, see if he could chat up one of the accountants who used to work with Holman, see if he could pick up anything substantial enough to justify keeping the undercover going. Gibbons, of course, gave him his usual rap about being cautious, taking it slow, being methodical, all the old Bureau platitudes. Gibbons told him he was gonna get his ass shot off if he went back there like a mad dog. If Nashe and Immordino know who he is, Gibbons had reasoned, he should just lay low, stay away until he was scheduled to go to work, and worry about protecting his ass because nobody was gonna break this case in the next thirty-six hours. Just be a good Do-Bee and wait it out. Yeah, bullshit.

Gibbons had left him off at his apartment in Hoboken, thinking he'd spend the night there, but he had no intention of doing that. As soon as Gibbons was gone he called Avis and rented a car, took a cab out to Newark Airport where he picked it up, and headed straight down the Garden State Parkway for Atlantic City. Even if he couldn't get what he wanted on Nashe and Immordino, he was determined to have a little talk with Sydney, the bitch.

But Sydney hadn't been around when he got to Nashe Plaza, and it just so happened that when he stepped out of the elevator coming down from her private suite, he ran into Lenny Mokowski who yelled at him for hanging around here on his day off. What the eff you doing here, Tomasso? he says. Get outta here, go rest. Here. And he pulls out a set of keys from his pocket and tells him he can use Nashe's beach house tonight, his place on Long Beach Island that favored employees get to use when they're good.

Tozzi settled back into his pillow and scanned the row of picture windows that overlooked the ocean. Some beach house. Eight big bedrooms, two Jacuzzis—one inside, one out on the deck—sauna, gym, private screening room . . .

He ran his finger up and down the satin band on Valerie's hat, staring out the triangular window. He wished she'd wake up.

It was almost seven o'clock when Lenny had given him the keys and told him to get lost. The accounting people were gone by then. He'd considered talking to Nashe directly, but that seemed like a stupid idea—Nashe wasn't going to admit to anything—and Sal Immordino he could do without. He really wanted to do something, but there was nothing he could do, so he wandered over to the bar by the escalators to see Valerie. She poured him a Saint James on the rocks with a wedge of lime, just the way he liked it, and told him he didn't look happy, saying it with this sly smile, like she knew what would make him happy if he wanted to. It was good seeing her—sad but good. He knew he had to be with her at least one more time before the clock struck twelve and he turned back into a pumpkin. He told her he had the keys to the beach house for the night. She told him to pick her up when she got off at eleven-thirty.

Valerie sighed in her sleep then and Tozzi suddenly felt empty inside. She was really beautiful, the first woman he'd ever known who could make love and wisecracks at the same time. They're both coming and she's making him laugh so much he keeps slipping out of her and she's yelling for him to stick it back in, quick, making more jokes so that he's practically paralyzed, he's laughing so hard. He looked at her now, eyes closed, sheet pulled up to her chin. She was great. They were great together. He sighed and thought of Brant Ivers peering over his half glasses. This was his last day as Mike Tomasso. He tried to be hopeful, and a part of him was. He and Valerie could keep it going, depending on how she took it when he told her he wasn't really Mike Tomasso. It was possible. It wouldn't be easy, but it was possible. He didn't want to get his hopes up, though.

He sat up a little, bunching the pillow behind him, and put her hat on, pulling the brim down over one eye like Michael Jackson. He wished the hell she'd get up. He was getting antsy, he wanted to do something. Maybe they should just spend the whole day in bed, forget about going to work today, wind down the undercover right here, under the covers. It wasn't such a bad idea. He wasn't going to accomplish anything for the government today. Might as well just fuck off and have a good time with Valerie. Enjoy her company—while he still had it.

He looked down at her, sleeping so nice, lips parted a little, eyelids so relaxed, and he peeled the sheet away. He stroked the end of her nose with his finger, very lightly. She frowned and turned her face to the pillow. He moved the hair away from her ear and started playing with her earlobe.

"Sto-op," she moaned.

He kept it up, circling around the whole ear.

She hunched her shoulders. "Nooo."

He grinned. "This is your wake-up call, Ms. Raynor."

She opened one eye. "What time is it? It's too early."

"It's quarter after seven."

She pulled the covers over her shoulder. "Go back to sleep."

"I can't sleep. I've got too much energy."

She grunted. "You're not one of those, are you? You *like* to get up early?"

Tozzi shrugged. "If there's something to get up for."

"Nothing's worth getting up for at seven o'clock." She burrowed into the pillows.

"Come on, let's go take a walk on the beach."

"Get bent."

"Come on, we'll do it on the beach, in the dunes."

She turned over. "You go start. I'll catch up with you later."

Tozzi threw off the sheet and stood up in bed, naked. He straddled her, standing over her with her hat on his head. "Come on." He started bouncing on the bed, wagging his dong at her. "Let's go for a dip. Cold water is very purifying. Japanese monks do it all the time."

She opened her eyes a little and looked up at his swinging dick. She couldn't hold back the grin. "Screw the Japanese monks."

"I don't think they screw. You have to make do with me." He stepped down off the bed and sat on the edge on her side.

She closed her eyes, still grinning. "I'll make a deal with you. Give me another half hour and I'll be your love slave for the rest of the day, okay?"

"And what am I supposed to do for a half hour?"

"I dunno, go make coffee, watch cartoons. Go take your walk. You figure it out." She turned over and shrugged the covers up.

He stood up on the floor, scrunched his mouth to one side, and thought about trying out the Jacuzzi in the bathroom. He wandered over to the triangular picture window and looked out at the ocean. The sun was bright and the fog was burning off the beach. The water was calm, slate-blue right below him, silvery in the distance. A couple of hundred yards offshore there was a fishing boat, just one, all by itself, bobbing on the waves. To hell with the Jacuzzi, he was too antsy to wait for it to heat up. Makes too much noise anyway, all that burbling. She wants to sleep. "I'm gonna go take a walk," he said.

Valerie didn't move. She'd already fallen back to sleep.

There he was. Sal could see him. Standing in front of that big triangle window with nothing on but a hat. Fucking Tomasso. Mokowski said he'd get him here. Sal stood under the overhang in the back of the fishing boat and fiddled with the focus on the binoculars to get a better look at him. The hat was pulled down low over the asshole's eyes, like he was some kind of tough guy. Bullshit.

Tomasso moved away from the window then. Sal set down the binoculars and leaned against the galley door so the captain up there in the driver's seat couldn't see. He took the gun out of the gym bag he'd brought and stuck it in his pants, then pulled the baggy gray sweatshirt over it and left the plaid wool shirt unbuttoned.

Sal came out from under the overhang, shading his eyes as he yelled up to the bridge. "Yo, Captain. I want you to take her in as far as you can. Over near that big gray monstrosity, the one with the triangle windows. See it?"

The captain squinted over toward Nashe's place, looked

at it for a while, then scratched his head. Sal figured the guy was about his age, close-cropped red hair, wavy on top, light eyebrows and lashes, wrinkles and freckles. The kind of guy always named Brian or Kevin, something like that. Kind of guy Sal couldn't relate to at all. Sal waited for the guy to say something but he didn't, just scratched his head and squinted at the house.

"Something wrong with that, Captain?" Better not be anything wrong with that. I'm paying you enough.

The guy laid his hands on the rail. Rough, red hands, like lobster claws. "Wellll," he said, dragging it out, "I'll take her in as far as I can and drop anchor for you. Pretty calm today. You shouldn't get too wet." He was saying one thing, but his tone was saying something else.

"What's wrong? You sound like something's wrong?"

"Wellll . . . I'll tell you. Can't park in there too long. Coast Guard choppers patrol the whole shore, looking for drug smugglers and whatnot. Not s'posed to go in that close to a swimming beach. Chopper comes by, he'll chase my tail back out to sea just like that."

"Yeah, so what're you saying here? You're not gonna do it? We had a deal."

The captain kept squinting at the house. "Nooo . . . I'll do it. I'm just saying whatever you gotta do over there, make it quick. Else I might not be there when you come out. Don't stick around for no birthday cake or nothing."

"Yeah, fine." Sal had told him he was doing this as a birthday surprise for a good friend of his. A kind of a beach assault.

The captain went back to the wheel and turned the boat around. Sal sat in the fishing chair and started pulling on the black rubber hip waders he'd bought last night at a Herman's in some mall in Toms River, the kind of waders that go right up under your armpits. They were new and they didn't go on easy. Reminded him of his grandmother getting into her girdle. The ones that came in those cardboard tubes and smelled to high heaven. These hip waders stunk of new rubber but nothing like that sharp, powdery smell he remembered from his grandma's new girdles.

Thinking of his grandmother reminded him of Cil because she was always talking about her. Two of a kind, both religious nuts. Only problem with religion was that people like her make such a fucking religion out of it. Yeah, but Cil was a nun, for chrissake—she was supposed to be a religious nut.

Sal got the waders on up to his thighs, then stood up to pull them up the rest of the way. Fucking Tomasso, the supposed bodyguard. Mokowski thought there was something wrong with him too. Said he wouldn't be surprised if the guy was a fed. Sal wasn't surprised. He figured the Bureau was on his case again. Putting the bug in Cil's crucifix was their kind of thing. But the way Sal figured it, if the FBI knew anything at all, it wasn't from that bug. No, it had to be from Tomasso. Mokowski said it wouldn't have been that hard for him to get into Nashe's office. He probably found some papers on the land under the Plaza. That had to be it. If they tried to make a case against him, one of those bullshit RICO charges, Tomasso—or whatever his real name was—would be the one who'd have to testify in court.

So it was simple: Tomasso had to go. Nip it in the bud before they get down to business with the warrants and the subpoenas and all that shit. Tomasso's still around working undercover, so the investigation's still underway—meaning he hasn't sat down with the legal guys yet. Without him, they can't build a case against anybody. Best to nip it in the bud right now. Tomasso dies and that'll be the end of it.

Sal pulled the straps over his shoulders and nudged the gun around under all the layers until it was comfortable. He pictured Tomasso's face—cocky bastard in that Dick Tracy hat. He knew there was something wrong about the guy the minute he saw him. Little bastard. Tomasso thinks he's hot shit, fucking Sydney. We'll see. That's why Sal didn't want to let anybody else take care of this. He wanted to do it himself, to see how cocky the bastard's face would be this time. You fuck with me, *you* get fucked.

Sal looked out over the water at the big modern gray house, the boat's engine rumbling low under his feet. He nudged the gun again, put his hand on it. He took a big breath, smelled the salt air. This was good. He was taking care of business. He was a little anxious, what with the fight and all, but right now he felt good.

Tozzi picked up a piece of driftwood and flung it into the waves. A bunch of gulls screamed and swooped down around it, thinking it was something to eat. Old Barney, the lighthouse over in Barnegat Light, was in front of him, two miles at least in the distance. He considered walking to it, just for something to do. Valerie wanted to sleep. They'd been up late last night and— If she wanted to sleep, let her sleep.

Tozzi trudged through the sand in his bare feet. The wet sand down by the water was cold, so he moved up to the dry sand, but that was harder to walk in. It was a trade-off. So was this undercover, he thought. He loses Valerie probably, but at least he gets out before Sal Immordino blows his head off. That's a fair trade-off. Except he wasn't very satisfied with it.

He wanted everything. He wanted to nail Nashe and Immordino for whatever they were doing. He wanted Sydney to get hers, the manipulating little witch. He wanted his efforts on this assignment to be a resounding success so that Ivers would stop treating him like the problem child. He wanted Valerie.

He glanced over his shoulder at the big gray beach house, the triangular picture windows on the third floor. Nobody gets everything. He stopped and stared up at those windows where she was sleeping. He thought about going back, waking her up, having his last few hours with her. Like the condemned man's last meal.

Then he turned around and headed for Old Barney. Let

her sleep, he thought. She's really tired. She won't disappear at sundown. This isn't the end of the world.

A real brain, this Tomasso. Leaves the sliding glass doors unlocked. Regular people do stuff like that. Feds are supposed to be smarter, more security-minded.

Sal stepped inside and scanned the big room. Enormous. Sunken living room with a free-standing fireplace at one end, sofas and easy chairs everywhere, long black lacquer table and chairs in the dining area, floor-to-ceiling windows with those big vertical blinds all around. And lavender wall-to-wall carpeting. Sydney's touch. This was kind of the way he imagined the Playboy mansion, the kind of place where Hef used to have those wild parties. Just like that TV show he used to have. Hef in his bathrobe, the bunnies with the incredible tits all around him. This was that kind of room. All except for the lavender carpet. Hef would go for red.

Sal slowly slid the glass panel closed except for a few inches. The sound of the ocean was muffled and suddenly he heard music, faint and far away. He stood there, listening. It was coming from upstairs. Bebop sax, Charlie Parker, it sounded like. He slid the straps off his shoulders and reached down into the layers of clothing for the 9mm. He finally got it out and released the safety. Leading with the gun, he slowly followed the sound of the sax to the blond wood staircase on the other side of the room. The rubber feet of the waders on the plush lavender carpeting didn't make a sound. Sal liked that.

Tozzi stared out at the ocean, trying to spot a shark fin or a whale's tail, waiting with hope and dread and terrible anticipation the same way he'd done when he was a kid, thinking that if he wished hard enough, the Creature from Twenty Thousand Leagues would suddenly come crashing out of the water, whipping his ugly head back, screaming and roaring and royally pissed off, ready to start ravaging the land. Tozzi kept looking, but he didn't see anything.

She must be special, he thought. Even Gibbons likes her.

He dug his toes into the dry, warm sand and thought about some of the disastrous relationships he'd had with women in the past. His ex-wife, the chandelier heiress from Rhode Island. The Mafia princess in sheep's clothing. The half-English redhead who ran the nanny agency. The NYPD detective from the Sex Crimes Unit. The married woman . . . These were just the featured players; there were minor characters, going all the way back to high school, more than he wanted to think about. None of them had been like Valerie, though. Not even close.

The wind blowing off the ocean whistled in his ears. If he suddenly disappeared, then called her in a month or so, out of the blue, what was she gonna think? That he's an asshole, that's what. He could just hear the sarcastic remarks. An FBI agent? Yeah, sure, she'd say. It would be better if he told her today, before he disappeared. At least there'd be a chance for them to pick up where they'd left off. Only one problem with that: Telling her his real identity while the undercover was still under way would be a direct violation of Bureau rules, the kind of infraction Ivers could use to hang his ass up for good.

He wiggled his toes and moved his feet, probing for warmer sand. He looked out at the waves. The ocean was still blank, no monsters. Fuck the rules. She was worth the risk. Anyway, she wouldn't tell if he asked her not to, she's a stand-up chick. That's why she's so great. That's why she's worth it.

Tozzi stared at the ocean, the wind blowing around his head. He was gonna do it. He was gonna tell her. Valerie was too good to lose. He turned his back on Old Barney and started back toward the house.

Leave it to fucking Beaver. Da-dump, da-da-da, da-da, dada . . . all night long. Even though Charlie Parker was getting louder as he climbed the stairs to the third floor, Sal couldn't get that stupid Beaver song out of his head. It was what Sydney sang that whole night when she brought him here. She's coming, for chrissake, but she's still singing the damn song. What a fucking wack. She must've taken Tomasso here too. Same bedroom and everything, the one with the lavender Jacuzzi in the bathroom. Probably sang him the *Leave It to Beaver* song too. Crazy bitch.

Sal's rubber feet squeaked on the hardwood floor in the hallway, but the stereo was blasting in there, so he didn't think anyone could hear. He peered into the bedroom through the doorway. Sheets messed up on the bed. Tomasso's suit hanging on a chair. Bra and panties on the floor. Hey, maybe Sydney was in the Jacuzzi with him. He could shoot 'em both. Nice idea, but he knew that Sydney had been in New York all week on her lavender tug. Tomasso must've brought some bimbo up here to keep him company while he hid out. Too bad. She'd have to go too.

He racked the slide on the automatic and entered the room, walking softly across the rug that looked like someone had spilled a gallon of paint on it. He stopped short when the song on the stereo suddenly ended. Just the sound of bubbling water from the Jacuzzi. He waited for the next song to start up and make some noise. He leveled the gun at the doorway to the bathroom, just in case someone walked out. The music started up again. Sal knew this one. He had the record. "Nights in Tunisia."

He stepped closer to the doorway and peered in. The bebop horns reverberated off the lavender tile walls. Water bubbled and whooshed. He couldn't make out a body under the foamy water. All he could see was the top of that fucking gray hat on Tomasso's head propped against the side of the lavender Jacuzzi. Stupid asshole. Wears the damn hat in the Jacuzzi. For what? To impress the girl? Sal glanced back into the bedroom. Where was the girl? He shrugged. Who cares? Long as Tomasso gets it.

He aimed the gun down at the Dick Tracy hat. "Hey, Tomasso." He had to repeat it louder to be heard over the music. "Tomasso! Wake up!"

The head turned, and suddenly he saw the face under

the hat. Shit. It wasn't Tomasso. It was that blonde, from the other night at Tomasso's apartment. Shit.

"What the hell're you—" Then she spotted the gun. Her eyes jumped back and forth between the gun and his face.

Sal shouted, "Turn around!"

But she didn't turn around. She just kept staring at the gun, frozen. Then she stared up at him, and he could tell from her eyes that she recognized him, that she remembered him. And then he remembered that Tomasso had introduced them, told her his name was Clyde, Clyde Immordino. *"Turn around, I said!"*

She didn't do it, though, and that's when the gun sort of went off by itself because he didn't think about it. He just did it because he knew it had to be done, and the shot sounded like a goddamn cannon with all the tile in the room. The girl jerked forward, went under face first, and now she was coming back up, her bare back rising like an island of white skin in a boiling sea. He spotted the entry wound right away, between her neck and shoulder, close to the spine. Two more cannon shots, without thinking. Her body twitched, twisted as it went under a little, then came back up, floating, in slow motion. It was the part with trumpet solo. "Nights in Tunisia." Dizzy Gillespie with his bent horn.

Tomasso. Where the fuck was he? Sal spun around, went back into the bedroom, gun ready, expecting Tomasso to come bounding into the room. But he didn't. Where the fuck—

Then he heard it, another horn, not Dizzy Gillespie, a horn outside, like a fog horn—*blap! blap! blap!* Hurry up, hurry up, hurry up. He looked out the triangle window opposite the foot of the bed. *Blap! blap! blap!* Hurry up. He saw the boat. Then he saw the helicopter. About two, three hundred yards up the beach, coming this way. Coast Guard helicopter. Coming to chase the boat away from the beach. Or stop it for drug smuggling. Shit. Where the fuck is Tomasso, that little chickenshit?

Sal ran out of the bedroom, his rubber feet squeaking on

the hardwood floor, rushing down the stairs, wishing Tomasso would show his fucking face so he could blow it off. He couldn't hear Dizzy Gillespie or Charlie Parker or anything else now. Just the horn on the boat outside. *Blap! blap! blap!* Hurry up!

The beach house was still a football field away when the chopper came up from behind and roared over Tozzi's head. He shaded his eyes and followed it as he walked in the soft sand, watched it stop and hover over a small fishing boat. The boat was in pretty close to the beach. Tozzi wondered if it was in trouble.

He looked at the house and realized that the boat and the helicopter were right by the house. Gonna wake Valerie up, he thought. Then he spotted this guy in hip waders running into the waves, a big guy, galloping like a horse through the water, heading out to the boat. Another guy in the boat helped the big guy with the hip waders get in. Tozzi could hear the loudspeaker on the chopper, but he couldn't make out what they were saying to the guys in the boat. Coast Guard probably giving them hell for being so close to the beach. Valerie must be staring out the window, wondering what the hell—

Galloping like a horse, a big guy . . . Tozzi's heart started to pound. Fucking Immordino. Val! He started to run, feeling the dread like sludge in his stomach. Val! His legs dug into the sand, but it sucked at the soles of his feet and slowed him down. He wanted to be there—*now*—but he couldn't run fast enough, and he started to blame himself before he even knew anything was wrong. Val!

He kept trying to run, but the sand didn't want him to. He moved down to the wet sand and picked up speed, but by the time he reached the house, the chopper was gone and the boat was way out there. He ran in through the sliding glass door, wide open, not the way he'd left it.

"Val!"

He ran up the stairs, turning on the landing, more stairs, second floor, more stairs, another landing, taking the stairs two, three at a time, third floor, pounding barefoot on the wood floor. The jazz sax, the bubbling water.

"Val, answer me!"

Rushing into the bathroom, he slipped on the wet floor and banged his knee on the tile. It hurt like a bastard. He squeezed his eyes closed and clutched it, pressed it to his chest. But then he opened his eyes and he saw her. He didn't feel the pain anymore. She was half out of the water, flat on her belly, like a beached dolphin in one of those dolphin shows. Thin lines of blood squiggling down her wet back, trickling over her ribs. Val!

He crawled over to her, felt her wet hair, probed for a pulse in her neck, put his ear to her back at the same time and heard the faint, shallow breathing.

He jumped up and slid again, scrambled for the phone in the bedroom. He punched out 911, looking into the bathroom, wanting to go to her. One ring, two rings. Come on, come on. Hurry it up, goddamn you.

"Long Beach Island emergency services." A woman's voice. Too goddamn calm.

"I need an ambulance right now. Seventy-fourth Street on the ocean side. Russell Nashe's house. A woman has been shot. Do you have that? Seventy-fourth on the ocean side, the great big gray place all by itself. On the top floor, in the bathroom. You understand me?"

"Yes, sir. They're on their way now." Too damn calm.

"Hurry, you gotta hurry. She's hurt *bad*!" This woman is too fucking calm. She doesn't realize how serious this is. "Please, hurry!"

"Sir, are you hurt also?"

"Me?" He realized he was rubbing his knee and he stopped. "No, no, I'm not hurt."

"Then you should go down to the street and be there when the ambulance arrives to direct them to the injured person."

"Right, yes. I know that."

Tozzi dropped the phone on the floor. He ripped a blanket off the bed and brought it into the bathroom to cover

Valerie. He felt for the pulse again. He didn't want to leave her. He stroked her hair, put his cheek to the floor, and looked into her glassy eyes.

"They're coming, Val. They're coming."

He heard the sirens then and he jumped up, about to run downstairs, but he stopped to shut off that goddamn music, too loud, too loud. He twisted the volume dial on the unit built into the wall and happened to glance out the bathroom window. That little fishing boat was almost a speck on the ocean.

Fucking Immordino. I swear to Christ I'm gonna kill that bastard. I don't give a shit. I'll fucking crucify him.

The doorbell suddenly jolted him, made him jump. Like a big fishhook speared through the chest. He pushed off the wall and ran down to let the ambulance guys in.

They're here, Val. They're here. They're here. Hang on. Please!

17

"... *In other news, police arrested seven Jamaican immigrants in a predawn raid in the Crown Heights section of Brooklyn. The seven men are accused of belonging to a notoriously violent drug posse specializing in the sale and distribution of marijuana. A police spokesman reported that half a ton of marijuana was found in an apartment where the suspects were in the process of dividing and packaging the drug for street sale . . .*"

On the screen seven handcuffed black guys were being marched into a police station one by one, all greasy dreadlocks and drop-dead eyes. The picture switched to the grungy apartment, cops showing off the cache. Two burlap bales, the sides slit open to show the grass. Hundreds of neat plastic Baggies, rolled tight and taped shut, ready for sale. A plastic laundry basket full of cash. A sawed-off shotgun, an AK-47, three 9mm automatics, a .357 Magnum. The camera panned by the arsenal quickly, but Gibbons was almost certain the .357 was a Colt Python, the one with the six-inch barrel. A real Wild West item. Nice bunch, these guys.

The picture switched to one of the arresting officers, an undercover cop sitting in a darkened office, his head just a shadow in order to maintain his anonymity. An off-camera reporter asked him how the arrest had been executed.

"The suspects had been under surveillance for several weeks prior to this morning's arrest. Three of the men were observed picking up a major shipment yesterday at—"

"Did I tell you that Brant Ivers's wife RSVPed today?" Lorraine said. "She said she was very sorry, but they won't be able to make the wedding."

Gibbons looked over at her sitting on the other end of the couch, flipping through a magazine. A stupid magazine. He looked back at the TV, but the undercover cop was gone. Goddammit. He wanted to hear where the Jamaicans were bringing in their weed.

"Mrs. Ivers was very apologetic in her note, but they're already committed to parents' weekend at Groton. That's where Brant, Jr., goes. Her husband went there too, apparently. He's very active with the alumni association."

"Too bad." Gibbons stared at the magazine in her lap, one of those oversized magazines with a lot of pictures of girls in their early twenties wearing clothes for women in their late forties, the kind of pictures that make women crazy because even after they buy the clothes, they still don't look like the models and they refuse to believe that it isn't the clothes that's the problem. It's the years. Gibbons turned back to the news.

A still photo of Richie Varga appeared over the anchorman's shoulder. Gibbons sat forward.

"Lawyers for convicted mobster Richie Varga appealed his 1987 murder conviction, citing improper procedure by the Federal Bureau of Investigation in making his arrest. Varga, who is currently serving a life sentence at the Ray Brook Federal Correctional Institution in upstate New York, was convicted of running a renegade La Cosa Nostra *faction while he was living under the protection of the*

government's Witness Security Program. In seeking to overturn the murder conviction, Varga's lawyers hope to have their client moved from a maximum-security facility to a medium-security prison. In filing their appeal, Varga's attorney's charge the FBI with illegal use of—"

"Is there a buttonhole in the lapel of your new suit?"

"Wait!"

"—which led to Varga's eventual capture. In other news . . ."

Goddammit! What the hell's wrong with her?

Lorraine paused and looked at the television. "You and Michael were on that case, weren't you? You're the ones who caught him."

"Yes."

"Do you think they'll overturn the conviction?"

"Beats me."

"You worked so hard on that case. You nearly got killed. Thank God Michael found that warehouse where they were keeping you."

Yeah . . . lucky me.

The commercial came on then, a commercial for Maalox. Gibbons was biting his tongue, dying to say something. But where the hell do you begin? How do you tell the woman you love she's turned into an idiot and she better snap out of it?

"So does it?" she said.

"Huh? What're you talking about?"

"Does your new suit have a buttonhole for a boutonniere?"

Gibbons was sitting on a volcano, about to explode. "I don't know. Does it matter?"

"Well, yes. You can't wear a flower in your lapel if you don't have a buttonhole."

"If you don't have a hole, you use a pin." Nitwit.

"That's true. I hadn't thought of that." She folded over the magazine and extended it to him. "I was thinking you should wear a yellow tulip to offset the gray suit. See the girl in this picture? On the bottom of the page. Don't the tulips look nice with her—"

"Do you think you can hold on to this crucial information until after the news?" Before I throw you out a fucking window.

"Oh . . . I'm sorry."

A cornflakes commercial was just ending, and the anchorman came back on. *"And now, Lou Moses with sports . . ."*

The camera switched to Lou Moses, the worst hairpiece in broadcasting. Looked like something dead on the side of the road. The guy'd been on TV for ten years, probably made four, five hundred grand a year, and he couldn't get himself a better rug? One of the mysteries of the universe. Just like women.

Lou started going over the baseball scores. Gibbons glanced over at Lorraine. She was all jammed up in the corner of the couch, like she was trying to make herself small. She had the whipped-puppy look, something new for her. Christ Almighty, he wished he could figure out what in the hell was wrong with her. They had to talk. As soon as the news is over.

"—and there's been a mysterious development in the War Down the Shore, the heavyweight-championship bout between reigning champ Dwayne 'Pain' Walker and former champ Charles Epps scheduled for this Saturday night in Atlantic City. It seems that 'Pain' Walker's longtime trainer was secretly hospitalized earlier this week in Reading, Pennsylvania. Reporter Craig Wood at our sister station in Philadelphia is at Our Lady of Mercy Hospital in Reading—"

"I'm sorry I interrupted—"

"Not now, not now!"

A heavy-set guy in a plaid jacket held a microphone in one hand, a clipboard in the other. He was standing outside a hospital emergency-room entrance. *"Lou, Henry Gonsalves, the champ's trainer—and, some say, the only man the erratic young fighter trusts—was admitted to Our*

Lady of Mercy Hospital here late Sunday night under the name Hector Diaz. A nurse, who would not give me her name, told me today that Gonsalves, who remains in critical condition, was unconscious from the time he was brought in until late Monday afternoon and that he had facial lacerations, a broken jaw, and two fractured ribs. He was later diagnosed as having sustained a severe concussion, and some degree of brain damage is feared. The nurse told me that Henry Gonsalves's injuries seem to indicate that he'd been beaten up very badly.

"The Walker camp had no comment when I called today, and they refused to even acknowledge that the champ's trainer was in the hospital. Officially the hospital is also refusing to comment, saying only that it's their policy to respect the privacy of all patients under their care. However, 'Pain' Walker's former wife, model Bonnie Kilmer, did tell me today that the champ's temper is very unpredictable and that he's capable of lashing out at anyone, including those he supposedly loves. While she expressed doubt that her ex-husband would ever turn on Gonsalves, who she feels is responsible for their breakup, she would not rule out the possibility.

"A very bizarre development coming on the eve of the big fight. We hope to bring you more information on Henry Gonsalves's condition at eleven. Reporting from Our Lady of Mercy Hospital in Reading, Pennsylvania, this is Craig Wood. Back to you, Lou."

Our Lady of Mercy, Our Lady of Mercy . . . Why did that sound so familiar? Our Lady of Mercy . . .

"Lorraine, do you remember a—" He looked over at her. She was scrunched up in the corner of the couch, crying. Oh, for chrissake.

"What's the matter?"

She blew her nose into a Kleenex. "Go to hell."

"What's wrong?"

"Nothing." She was sobbing.

"Tell me. What's wrong?"

She blew her nose again. "Just don't talk to me."

Her Kleenex was a wet little ball, but she was still trying to use it. He took the handkerchief out of his back pocket and offered it to her.

"Go to hell." She opened up the shredded Kleenex, looking for a usable spot.

"Are you going to tell me what your problem is or not? You know, I've had it up to here with this crap."

She spun around, eyes flashing. "*You've* had it up to here! *I've* had it up to here!" Shrill. A madwoman.

Gibbons was speechless. He couldn't believe it. It was the old Lorraine.

"I was going to get us tickets to the closed-circuit broadcast of the fight, to surprise you, but you can go to hell now." She turned back to her raggy Kleenex and muttered to it. "Selfish son of a bitch."

"What're you, kidding? You hate boxing."

"Well, I was going to do it for you, but forget it. I'm tired of bending over backward, trying to make things nice for you."

"Why? Why do you have to make things nice for me? They were nice before. We decide to get married and suddenly everything is different. I don't understand."

She flashed those psycho eyes at him. "I wanted to make everything perfect for you so that you'd be comfortable with the idea of getting married. I knew you still had doubts."

Gibbons saw red. "What do you mean 'comfortable'? What the hell's that supposed to mean? Why don't you just be honest and say it? You're afraid I'll back out of this. Right? That's what you're afraid of. That's why you've been acting so stupid."

"I act stupid? Just asking you a simple question is acting stupid?"

"It is when I'm trying to watch the news." He pointed at the TV. "Some of this stuff happens to pertain to my job." The weatherman was pointing at the map.

"I only asked a simple question and you jumped down my throat."

"It wasn't *one* simple question. I'm listening to a story and you're telling me that Brant Ivers can't come to the wedding because he's going to his class reunion or some such shit. What the hell do I care where Ivers is going—"

Then it dawned on him. Ivers. He was the one who'd told him about Our Lady of Mercy Hospital. In Reading, Pennsylvania. That was where Sal Immordino had supposedly been treated for Pugilistic Brain syndrome, where his bogus headshrinker was affiliated. Our Lady of Mercy. The doctor who'd testified that Sal was mentally incompetent, poured on all the medical bullshit, lied through his teeth. But Walker's camp is down around Philly—why didn't they take him to a hospital there? How the hell did he end up in Reading? A coincidence? No way. Immordino's recommendation? But how does Gonsalves know Immordino? How does *anyone* at Walker's camp know Immordino? Unless Immordino arranged to have Gonsalves taken to his hospital, to hush things up. Because he beat the shit out of Gonsalves himself? The way he did to that guy Lawson back when he was a pug? Why? He glanced at the TV, stared at the computerized weather map, green blobs moving over the Midwest. Because Gonsalves has a lot of influence over the champ, that's what the ex-wife said. Immordino wanted Gonsalves to get the champ to do something, he refused, and Sal pounded his head in . . .

Jesus. Gibbons couldn't believe it. It was so fucking obvious. Immordino is fixing the fight. The mob pretty much gave up on fight-fixing thirty, forty years ago. That's why he didn't think of it until now. But so what if they haven't fixed a big fight since the fifties? No crime like an old crime. Right? He looked at the screen. A smiling sun. It was going to be nice tomorrow. He jumped up from the couch and headed for the kitchen.

"Where are you going?" The fishwife.

He stopped and looked at her. She looked like she was gonna bite him. "I gotta talk to Tozzi."

"He's not home. I tried him a little while ago."

He went to the closet and got Excalibur out of the shoe

box on the top shelf, clipped the holster onto his belt. They used to fix fights back when he'd bought this gun, 1955. Thirty-eight Colt Cobra. Didn't make these anymore. He threw his suit jacket on and grabbed his hat.

"Where the hell are you going?" she yelled from the couch. "You're not going to leave this unfinished. Come back here and talk to me."

She-demon. Fantastic. It was great to have her back. "I'm sorry. I gotta go find Tozzi. This is important. We'll talk later."

"Oh, wonderful! And this isn't important?"

"Don't put words in my mouth." He had his hand on the doorknob. "That's not what I said."

"You don't have to say it. It's obvious how you feel."

He took his hand off the doorknob, walked back to the couch, and kissed her on the cheek. "I love you. We'll finish this fight later. But I have to find Tozzi now." He headed back to the door.

"If you walk out that door, Gibbons, the wedding is off."

Facing the door, Gibbons rolled his eyes to the ceiling and showed his teeth. Jesus Christ Almighty. She finally shapes up and now she doesn't want to get married.

"I'm not kidding. You leave me here and I'm calling the whole thing off."

He turned the knob but held the door closed for a second.

"I'm serious."

Medea. The Gorgon. Screaming Mimi.

"I gotta find Tozzi." He opened the door, stepped out into the hallway, and looked back in at her.

She was shaking her head, waving her arms like an umpire calling the man safe. "That's it, that's it. I'm serious."

"Later, Lorraine. Later."

He closed the door, but he could still hear her saying she was serious, that was it.

He put on his hat and headed for the stairs. Fucking women. When you want them, they don't want you. When they want you, then they don't look so good.

Gibbons hurried down the worn marble apartment steps. At least this proved she wasn't permanently brain-damaged by the wedding shit. That was good. He turned the landing and looked back up at the apartment door. She's not serious. She's just mad. That's all. I hope.

Gibbons remembered this dingy little lobby as soon as he opened the door. He walked over to the open doorway that led to the practice space and saw a group of people wearing those white martial-arts pajama outfits, running around like nuts out on the blue mats. He spotted Tozzi right away. He had a feeling Tozzi would be here. He went to the pay phone on the wall then, dropped a quarter in, and dialed the 800 number. Pulling up one of the orange plastic stacking chairs, Gibbons propped his foot up and stretched the cord as far as it would go so he could look through the doorway into the dojo. It rang three times before someone picked up.

"Federal Bureau of Investigation."

"Yeah, this is Gibbons, four-seven-oh-nine. Who's the night clerk on tonight?"

"Moran."

"Put me through to him."

"Hold on."

Gibbons watched the nuts out on the mat. Tozzi was standing in line with the others, waiting to get his ass kicked by one of the guys with the baggy black pants, one of the black belts. When it was his turn Tozzi ran up and grabbed the black belt's wrists. The guy whipped Tozzi back like it was nothing, then whipped him forward again and threw him over, countergrabbing Tozzi's wrist so that he hit the ground hard—real hard—right on his side. Gibbons winced, but Tozzi jumped right up and ran back to the end of the line, ready to get pulverized again. Gibbons shook his head. These people were fucking crazy. Tozzi said aikido was supposed to be a soft martial art, supposed to make you calm. Bullshit.

A tired voice came through the line then. "What do you want, Gibbons?"

"What'sa matter, Moran? I wake you up?" Moran was always so happy when he had to do night duty.

"I wish. Now what do you want?"

"Tell me something. Did Tozzi call in today?"

Moran snorted a laugh into the phone. "No, Tozzi didn't call in. But we got a shitload of calls about him."

"Why? What happened?"

"Let's see." The sound of shuffling papers, Moran going through the log. "Well, it seems that Tozzi discovered an attempted homicide this morning. A woman named—where is it? where is it? here—Raynor, Valerie Raynor."

Oh, Christ. "What happened?"

"The details are pretty sketchy. Most of what we have came from the local cops down there. Apparently this Raynor woman was shot twice in the back. One bullet punctured a lung. Tozzi got the rescue squad right away, and they rushed her to the hospital. She's stable now. The hospital says she'll recover."

Gibbons pinched his nose and pressed his lips together. Immordino again? But he was supposed to be out gunning for "Tomasso." Why'd he shoot her? "And what was Tozzi doing while all this was going on?"

"Making a big pain in the ass out of himself."

"In what way?"

Moran snorted that laugh again. "Well, he was apparently out of control when he got to the hospital, running around, acting crazy, demanded that he be allowed to see the woman. The staff ended up calling the cops on him, and Tozzi tried to throw his weight around, told them he was a special agent, showed them his ID and all. They told him they'd have to confirm it before they'd believe it, and they insisted that he surrender his gun until his story was confirmed. You can just imagine how that went down."

Gibbons shut his eyes. He was glad he hadn't been there.

"We confirmed that he was who he said he was, and the police returned his weapon, but they suggested he go out and get a coffee because the nurses were getting sick and tired of having him around. He wouldn't budge, though, even after they assured him that this Raynor woman was out of surgery and she was okay. He said he *had* to see her and, of course, the hospital people said no, not until tomorrow. So what does Tozzi do then? He bribes a nurses' aide to go into the recovery room and give this Raynor woman a message. He wanted her to know that he was there and that he wanted to see her, that he loved her and all that shit. The nurses' aide apparently came out two minutes later, all shook up. She'd delivered Tozzi's message, but the Raynor woman wasn't too happy to get it. From what I gather, she told the nurses' aide to tell Tozzi that he could go fuck himself, that she didn't want to see him—not now, not ever. Apparently she was still pretty weak from the surgery at this point, and her monitors started beeping and bleeping like crazy. The doctor on duty ran in on a Code Blue—or whatever color it is when your monitors go off like that—and he gave her a sedative to calm her down. After that, the cops came back and *insisted* that Tozzi go out and get himself a coffee and not come back for a while. This happened about three-thirty this afternoon."

Gibbons could imagine Tozzi wandering out of the hospital, going outside for the first time since that morning and being disoriented by the afternoon sun, not knowing where to go, what to do with himself, then realizing that Sal Immordino was out there someplace looking for him, probably mad as hell and determined to whack "Tomasso" once and for all, after having botched it twice. Tozzi had probably driven up the parkway, back to his apartment in Hoboken, then got paranoid, wondering whether Immordino had figured out that he wasn't Tomasso the bodyguard, that he was really Tozzi the fed. Tozzi had a way of working himself into a froth—"spiraling," the shrinks call it. He'd probably started thinking that Immordino had him followed all the way up from the shore, that they were watching him, waiting for the right moment to make their move on him. That's when he'd probably decided he didn't want to be alone, and coming over here to play with his aikido buddies was the logical choice. Tozzi had told him that he always liked to come over here to practice whenever he was feeling crappy. Said the worse you felt when you got on the mat, the better your practice would be. Well, he must be having one hell of a practice now because he must feel like a bag of shit after all that had happened today. Poor bastard.

Gibbons looked through the doorway, and Tozzi hit the mat again with another booming thud that made Gibbons wince. He got right to his feet and went back to the end of the line. He must be feeling awful.

"You still there, Gibbons?"

"I'm here."

"Tozzi should be home now," Moran said. "You want me to relay a message?"

"No, that's okay."

"He's a real piece of work, that partner of yours."

"So are you, Moran."

"You're tying up the line, Gibbons. Is there anything else I can do for you?"

"Yeah."

"What?"

"Go back to sleep."

"Eat it, Gibbons."

Moran hung up and Gibbons put the receiver back on the hook. On the mat Tozzi was at the head of the line again, but this time he bowed to the black belt and took the guy's place in the middle of the mat. It was his turn to do the throwing. He stood there with his wrists out for the taking, waiting for the next nut in line to come grab him so he could start slamming bods the way he'd been slammed. Gibbons noticed that he was wearing an orange belt now. Tozzi had said something about earning a new belt, but Gibbons usually tuned him out whenever he started preaching about the wonders of aikido. He did look pretty good out there, as far as Gibbons could tell. Nothing like the guy with the baggy pants but better than the other orange belts. He moved pretty smoothly, and his attackers made a nice *thunk* when they hit the mat. Only thing was, it all looked fake. Not just when Tozzi did it, all of them. It always looked like the guy being thrown was helping. Tozzi agreed that it looked fake, but he swore it was all real if you did it right. Gibbons couldn't figure it out, though, the passion Tozzi had developed for this aikido stuff. Tozzi was crazy, of course, but what about all these other people? What was their excuse?

The teacher, one of the other guys wearing those baggy black pants, yelled out something, and the whole class stopped abusing each other and they all bowed, very polite. Then the teacher called out *"Kokyu Dosa,"* and they all paired off and sat on their knees facing each other. One person held out his hands while the other person held him by the wrists, then they pushed. Yeah, Tozzi had told him about this one. It wasn't a contest, like arm-wrestling or anything. It was supposed to be a way of testing yourself, getting centered and finding your "one-point," the spot below your belly button where all your energy is supposed to come from. That's what Tozzi said anyway. Gibbons was skeptical. Sounded like a lot of crap to him, but it did do something for Tozzi. At least that's what he said. Gibbons glanced at his watch. It was nine-thirty. After a day like Tozzi had, he needed a good "one-point." Either that or a bottle of something with a good proof.

After a few minutes of these people pushing each other over—first to the left, then to the right—the teacher called for the end of class. They all lined up in front of him, sitting on their knees; then they bowed to the front of the room where three Japanese characters were hanging in a frame on the wall; then the teacher spun around and he bowed to the class as they bowed back to him yelling, "Thank you, *sensei.*" He got up and walked to the edge of the mat, then told them to thank their last partners, which they did. Awfully polite for people who like to beat the shit out of each other.

He watched Tozzi walk to the edge of the mat, bow to

those Japanese characters on the wall again, and put on his sandals. Gibbons caught his eye then. Tozzi didn't seem very surprised to see him. Not very happy either.

Tozzi wiped his brow with his sleeves as he came over. "Valerie's in the hospital—"

"I already heard. They say she's gonna be all right."

Tozzi raised his eyebrows and shrugged. "Yeah . . . that's what they said."

"I heard about her telling you to get lost too. She didn't mean it. She must've been all drugged up with the anesthesia and the painkillers and all. She didn't mean it."

Tozzi just looked at him. He didn't believe it. Gibbons put his hat on. He felt for the guy, but he wasn't about to play "Dear Abby" for him. He had his own problems in that department. "Come on, get dressed," he said. "We gotta go see somebody. About the fight."

"The fight? What're you talking about?"

"Just hurry up and get dressed. I'll tell you in the car."

Tozzi rotated his head and let out a long sigh. "The Nashe investigation is over, Gib. Ivers shut me down as of today, you remember?"

Gibbons frowned and shrugged. "So what?"

Tozzi looked curious all of a sudden. "So what've you got?"

"Just get dressed, will ya?"

"What'd you find out? Just tell me."

Gibbons rolled his eyes to the ceiling. "Hurry up and get dressed, then I'll tell you."

Tozzi didn't look so sad now. "All right, all right." He headed for the locker room, walking backward. "You don't want to give me a little hint?"

"No."

"Come on, Gib."

"Get dressed."

"Okay, okay." He kept walking backward. "Just tell me one thing. How'd you know I'd be here?"

Gibbons smiled with his teeth. "I'm a freaking G-man. I

track down assholes like you every day of the week. Now get moving. We've got some driving to do."

Tozzi was grinning as he went into the men's locker room.

He'd be all right.

• 18 •

"You know, Gib, I can't even smell it anymore."

Gibbons looked over at Tozzi sprawled out on the beige plastic couch, his feet up on the arm, his leather jacket bunched up under his head. "Smell what?"

"That hospital smell. I can't smell it anymore. All day yesterday in the hospital down the shore with Val, all night here waiting to get the go-ahead to see Gonsalves. I can't smell it anymore. My nose is dead."

Gibbons didn't move. His feet were on the coffee table, his cheek on his fist. He was slouched down in a waiting-room armchair. Four hours in the car with Tozzi yapping nonstop about how much he loves Valerie and how much he hates Sal Immordino and how his one-point is fucked up because he loves Valerie so much he'd like to put a bullet through Immordino's brain for what he did to her. Christ Almighty, the guy's a walking loony tune.

But having to put up with Tozzi wasn't bad enough. They finally get here to Our Lady of Mercy, way out in the middle of nowhere in Pennsylvania, and the night-shift nurses on Gonsalves's floor are like some commando unit left over from Vietnam, a real bitch-team, and they get it into their heads that *no one* gets in to see *their* patient at *this* hour of the night, no matter *what* the reason. He and Tozzi show them their IDs, threaten them with the obstruction-of-justice jazz, do the whole big-bad-fed routine, and these women just cross their big arms over their big chests, dig their heels in, and literally block the hallway to Gonsalves's room. No way, they say. Gotta get the patient's doctor's okay. It's like they're defending the fucking Maginot Line, for chrissake.

Then Tozzi starts getting huffy, starts screaming at them, and he has to put the crazy bastard on a leash, send him down the hall to cool off before he makes things worse. Gibbons tries to be nice about it then, goes over and asks the head ballbuster, real nice, to please call the doctor at home because this is very important. But she comes up with a new one this time and says to him, You got a warrant? Must've picked this up from some TV show, no doubt. She says unless we have a warrant or something that looks legal, she's not about to disturb a doctor in the middle of the night so that the health of a patient can be jeopardized. Then she threatens to call the cops, and now he has no choice but to back down because he knows how local cops are. They'd be on the horn to the nearest Bureau field office in no time, and that field office would have to call the New York field office to verify and explain the presence of two agents from the Manhattan office in their jurisdiction, and first thing in the morning it would all get back to Ivers, who didn't need to know anything about anything right now.

So that's why they'd spent the wee hours trying, in vain, to get some sleep in this overlit waiting room with the beige plastic furniture and the Holiday Inn landscapes on the walls, waiting for the goddamn doctor to show up at eight so they could ask him if they could talk to Henry Gonsalves for just five fucking minutes.

"I'm gonna sue these damn hospitals," Tozzi said, staring up at the ceiling. "They killed my nose. I have no sense of smell anymore. I'm handicapped."

Gibbons closed his eyes. "Tozzi, I don't give two shits about your nose."

"What is it you gentlemen want here?" A woman's voice, and not a nice woman's voice either.

Gibbons opened his eyes and sat up. Tozzi took his feet off the couch. She was standing on the other side of the coffee table, no more than five feet even, brunette, hair tied back, bangs, glasses. She was wearing a lab coat, stethoscope draped around her neck.

"I'm Dr. Conover," she said. "I understand you want to talk to one of my patients."

Tozzi stood up and unfurled his leather jacket. "Yes. We'd like to ask Henry Gonsalves a few questions."

The doctor just stared at him, looking stern and annoyed. Now Gibbons understood why the night Valkyries had given them such a hard time. The doctor in question was one of them. It all made sense now. She kept staring at Tozzi with this brutally sour, pissed-off face. She had the hots for him. It was obvious.

"Mr. Diaz—if that's who you're referring to—is in no condition for visitors. He shouldn't be upset."

Tozzi had that punk-biker posture—knees locked, head tilted back and to the side, jacket hooked over his shoulder. "We have no intention of upsetting him. We only want to ask him a few questions."

She kept staring at him, real grim. The doctor was kind of cute. Gibbons liked women with glasses . . . some women. Dr. Conover was one of those women who looked sexy in glasses. So did Lorraine when she wore hers. Oh, boy . . . Lorraine. He'd forgotten to call her last night. He didn't even want to think about that now.

The sweet voice of one of the killer nightingales warbled through the PA system and interrupted the standoff between Tozzi and the doctor. *"Dr. Conover, a call on three-two. Dr. Conover, a call on three-two."*

"Excuse me." She turned and left the waiting room.

Gibbons stood up. "Go follow her. Use your guinea charms on her."

Tozzi curled his upper lip like Elvis. "Wha'?"

"She's got the hots for you. Go make time with her. Buy her a coffee, take her into the supply closet, use your imagination. Just tie her up for five minutes so I can talk to Gonsalves."

"What're you, crazy? Women like that don't have the hots for anyone. Believe me."

"Wrong again, Tozzi. It's women like that who have the kind of hots guys like you are always looking for. Believe *me* . . ."

Tozzi looked pissed. "What the hell's wrong with you? I poured my heart out to you last night. Valerie's lying in a hospital with two holes in her, and you want me to go play up to this munchkin MD. I can't do that, Gib. It wouldn't feel right."

"I don't give a shit how you *feel,* Tozzi. This is work. You're not supposed to *feel* like doing any of it. You just do it. Now hurry up. Go."

"Gib, I can't—"

"Look, you're the one who told me you wanted to nail Immordino's balls to the wall. You wait around till it *feels* right, it won't happen. You understand? Figure out your priorities, *goombah,* and make it fast."

Tozzi's face didn't change, but he started nodding. "All right, all right, you're right."

"Go to the nurses' station and wait for the doctor. Keep her busy for a while. I'll take care of the rest. Now hurry up."

Tozzi shrugged. "Whatever you want."

They walked out into the hallway together, and Gibbons noticed that the commando unit from last night was off duty. The nurses' station was empty except for one nurse, who was busy doing paperwork. She glanced up at them, but there was no turn-to-stone, death-ray glare. Maybe the night girls hadn't told her about them.

Gibbons pushed the elevator button and told Tozzi he'd see him later. Tozzi leaned against the counter at the nurses' station and waited. The busy nurse stood up and asked Tozzi if she could help him. The elevator arrived then and Gibbons got on. As the doors closed Tozzi started explaining that he was waiting here for Dr. Conover to continue the conversation they'd started. This one was probably getting wet panties for Tozzi too. Gibbons shook his head as he rode the elevator down to the lobby. He'd never understand what women saw in Tozzi. He stayed on the elevator and rode back up to the sixth floor, where he'd gotten on. The doors opened and Tozzi was still leaning on the counter. He didn't see the nurse. Tozzi looked at him and nodded once. All clear. Gibbons walked out, turned left, and headed straight for Henry Gonsalves's room.

There were numbered doors on both sides of the hallway, some closed, some open. Shit. Gibbons didn't want it to look like he didn't know where he was going. He poked his head into the first open door. Some guy with his leg in traction watching cartoons on TV. A bunch of little blue people with squeaky voices running around in the woods. The guy hit the remote control and shut it right off, probably embarrassed to have been caught watching cartoons.

He moved on to the next room, a closed door, and glanced up and down the hall before he twisted the knob. A woman with dark bags under her eyes and long stringy hair was sitting up in bed. The room reeked of cigarette smoke. There was an open paperback in her lap, one of those *Gone with the Wind* kind of books. Gibbons noticed that both wrists were bandaged with gauze. "You here to see me?" she said.

"Nope." He closed the door and moved on.

The next door was open. Gibbons poked his head in and saw somebody's big fat can sticking out of the sheets, a skinny gray-haired nurse standing over it. She was holding a hypodermic needle. "Can I help you, sir?" She sounded just like she looked, an old battle-ax. Shit.

"Ah . . . yes. Yes, you can," Gibbons said.

The battle-ax seemed annoyed by his mere existence in her world. The ass didn't flinch.

"I'm looking for Henry Gonsalves's room. Or Hector Diaz, if that's the name he's registered under."

"You should not be on this floor without authoriza—"

"I'm from Blue Cross/Blue Shield, Claims Investigation. My name is Baker. I'm here for an on-site identification of the patient and confirmation of treatment."

"I wasn't told—"

"We don't make a practice of announcing on-site inspections."

"I've never heard of anything like this."

Gibbons shrugged. "If you don't want me to see him, I won't see him. But all payments for treatment will be withheld until the claim is investigated to our satisfaction." He took out his notepad and pen. "I'll just need to have your name for my report."

"Oh . . ."

Gibbons bit the insides of his cheeks to hold back the grin. Blue Cross/Blue Shield was like the IRS—you just don't fuck with them. And the battle-ax knew that.

The fat can spoke up then. "I'm getting cold, nurse."

The battle-ax frowned down at the big wrinkly thing hanging out of the sheets, then looked at Gibbons. "Our Mr. Diaz is across the hall in 618."

"Thank you." He put his pen and notebook away.

He crossed the hall to 618 and opened the door. He didn't like what he saw. Gibbons knew what Henry Gonsalves was supposed to look like—square-shouldered, fireplug build, perpetual tan, full head of thick salt-and-pepper hair. The man laid out on the bed had no color in his face at all, the flesh under his chin hung loose, and his hair was greasy, flat to his skull. There was a tube up his nose, IV drip in his arm, a green wire going down the neck of his hospital gown, and two yellow wires taped to his temples. Two monitors bolted to the wall over his head bleeped out his vital signs. Gibbons didn't know what the squirmy green lines on the monitors were supposed to look like, but they didn't seem very lively, just little bumps and dips that seemed like they could flat-line at any moment.

Gibbons stepped over to the side of the bed and wondered how the hell close to death this guy really was. He wondered if Valerie was in a similar situation at her hospital down the shore. Poor kid. He felt cold all of a sudden. He was afraid to go near the guy, afraid Gonsalves would croak if he touched him. He stared at the poor bastard, wondering if the guy was as delicate as he looked. This wasn't going to be easy. Where the hell do you start?

"Hey, Gonsalves. Wake up." Gibbons touched the man's hand. It was colder than his. Shit.

"Come on, Gonsalves. Wake up." Gibbons shook his shoulder a little. It was like feeling Jell-O in a plastic bag. Gibbons drew his hand away, thinking the guy was starting to rot before he'd finished dying. He looked around for a more solid spot, then finally went back to his hand. "Wake up, Gonsalves. You hear me? I gotta ask you about Sal Immordino."

The trainer's eyes fluttered and he moaned.

"Yeah, Sal Immordino. You know him. Let's talk about Sal."

Gonsalves moaned a little louder. One of the monitors bleeped a little louder. Gibbons assumed these things were connected to the nurses' station. Shit.

"Calm down, Gonsalves. I'm not Immordino. I just want to talk to you *about* him. Come on now, wake up."

His eyes fluttered again, then slowly opened. They were glassy and unfocused; the whites were yellow. He moaned again, seemed to be trying to say something.

"Come on, come on, come on. Wake up now, wake up." Gibbons slapped his cheek as hard as he dared, which wasn't very hard. "Do you hear what I'm saying, Gonsalves?"

Gonsalves's head slumped to the side. "No, no," he moaned. "Don' do tha'."

Gibbons slapped him a little harder. "Gonsalves, tell me. Did Sal Immordino do this to you? Is he paying off your man Walker to throw the fight with Epps? Did he do this to you because you tried to interfere with his scam?"

"Noooo . . . Don' . . . Stop . . ."

"Gonsalves, pay attention. Is 'Pain' Walker going to throw the fight?"

"No, Clyde . . . Stop . . . You're gonna kill him . . ."

Clyde? Spikes started appearing in the green line on one of the monitors. Gibbons felt terrible doing this, but this was important. Valerie had taken two slugs she didn't deserve and wound up in the same condition. Immordino's work. Then he remembered something. Clyde was Immordino's nickname from his fight days, back when Gonsalves was his manager. Gibbons looked at the monitor, then looked at the door. He wanted to lock it, but hospital doors don't have locks. "What're you talking about, Gonsalves? You're not making any sense. Tell me about Immordino, tell me about Clyde." And make it fast.

The trainer started rolling his head on the pillow, his eyes open but still glassy. "No, Clyde . . . You're gonna *kill* him."

"Who? Kill who?"

"Stop now . . . You're gonna kill Lawson . . ."

Lawson. Earl Lawson. Gibbons remembered that fight very well. Somewhere in Florida—not Miami, maybe Tampa—1970, '71 maybe. They'd played clips from that fight on the news for weeks afterward. It was a nothing fight, a middle-of-the-card bout, both fighters on their way down, so there was nothing at stake for either of them. They were both pathetic, but Lawson still had a little style, some footwork, so he was outscoring Immordino. Then late in the fight something happened. Immordino went crazy. The bell rings to start the round, and all of a sudden, Sal shoots out of his corner and starts beating the shit out of Lawson, gets him on the ropes, and starts roundhousing Lawson's head like he wants to punch it off. The tapes showed the whole thing, nearly three straight minutes of Immordino hammering Lawson's head, no let-up, no mercy. The crowd's going wild, Gonsalves is screaming at

Immordino from the corner to back off, just let the guy fall, but Immordino's not listening. And the ref is just standing there, letting it happen. On the tape you can see the ring doctor yelling for the ref to stop it, but the ref is ignoring him, making like he can't hear. The bell rings to end the round, but Sal doesn't stop. Guys have to run into the ring to help pull him off Lawson. Must've taken seven, eight guys to hold Immordino back.

Lawson ended up dying on the way to the hospital, brain hemorrhage. The ref was brought up on charges, but Sal wasn't indicted. At the time the rumor going around was that Immordino had paid off the ref to let him do his thing on Lawson, but the DA couldn't prove it because there was no evidence of any heavy betting on the fight. It was pure malice. Apparently he'd just wanted to see if he could do it. That's how Gibbons saw it.

"Noooo . . . Stop . . ." Gonsalves's face was contorted in agony now. The green line on that one monitor was getting real spiky. Gibbons looked at the door. He felt awful doing this, but when was the FBI gonna get this close to Immordino again? If Immordino did do this to Gonsalves, wouldn't *he* want them to get Immordino, bring him to justice? *If* Immordino was the one. Gibbons was just assuming that part.

Gonsalves's breathing was wet and ragged. His head kept writhing into the pillows in anguish. Gibbons glanced up at the spiky line, then looked around for a chair to prop against the door but realized the floor was too slick. He went over to check the metal doorframe. Sure, it might work. He scooped all the change out of his pocket and picked out all the pennies. He hated fucking pennies, hardly worth carrying anymore, but now he was glad he had a lot of them. He made a short stack and carefully wedged them into the space between the closed door and the frame. He used his key ring to force the last one in. That would hold them off for a while.

He went back to the bed and grabbed Gonsalves's face, held it still. Jell-O in a bag. "Listen to me, Gonsalves. Is Sal

Immordino fixing the fight? Is Immordino paying Walker to throw the fight?"

"No, Clyde . . . Stop . . . No more!" Gonsalves's eyes still weren't focused, but he was speaking a little clearer now.

Gibbons gripped his face tighter, felt bone, and raised his voice. "Is Sal Immordino fixing the fight?"

"No, Clyde, no! My guys don't do dirty."

"Is Sal Immordino fixing—"

The doorknob turned, back and forth, back and forth, impatient, then there was pounding on the door. "Open this door! Open this door right now!" He recognized Dr. Conover's voice.

Gonsalves coughed, wet and harsh. "I tol' you"—he was gasping for air—"I tol' you. My guys don't do dirty, don't throw no fights, Clyde. Forget it."

More pounding. Big hubbub out in the hallway. He could hear Tozzi out there with them. Big pounding. What the hell was he doing, helping them?

"Just tell me," he said in the trainer's face. "Is Sal Immordino attempting to fix the Walker–Epps fight? Just nod, Gonsalves. Just nod."

"Stop, Clyde. You wanna kill me like Lawson? Stop it now. My guy don't throw no fights. We don't do that. Don't . . . No way, no . . ."

Gibbons heard the door squeal. Someone was prying it. It flew open with a boom, pennies hitting the floor and rolling all over the place. Dr. Conover rushed in followed by a couple of nurses, Tozzi and an orderly bringing up the rear. The monitors were squealing, green spikes on one, flat line on the other.

The little doctor shouldered him aside. "Get out of the way!" she shouted. "What the hell did you do to this man?" She put her stethoscope in her ears and didn't wait for an answer.

"Get out! All of you! Get out!" The skinny, gray-haired nurse pushed Tozzi out into the hall, then grabbed Gibbons by the jacket and shoved him out too. A guy in scrubs pushing a crash cart nearly ran them over trying to get in.

Tozzi's eyes were wide. "I thought you knew how to be subtle. What did you do to him?"

Gibbons straightened his jacket. "Just asked him a couple of questions."

"He tell you anything?"

"Sort of."

"What do you mean, sort of?"

He looked in to see the monitors over the bed as he took Tozzi by the elbow. They were still going crazy. He felt bad. "Come on, let's get out of here."

They walked briskly to the elevators, not saying a word. No use hanging around here unless you want to spend the rest of the day answering questions you don't want to answer. Tozzi pressed the Down button to get an elevator. Gibbons glanced at the big wall clock over the nurses' station. Twenty of nine, Saturday morning. An elevator opened up, empty. They got on and Tozzi hit "1." Gibbons stared up at the numbers over the doors, watching them light up in descending order as they went down. The fight was scheduled for ten o'clock tonight, which meant it wouldn't start till ten-thirty at the earliest. They had less than fourteen hours. Probably not enough time to stop it. At least not legally.

• 19 •

Tozzi was buttoning the double-breasted as he came out of his apartment at Nashe Plaza. He locked the door and headed for the elevators, not wanting to be late for work. Had to look good today, had to blend in with the rest of the gorillas on Nashe's goon squad. Had to watch himself too. Had to get into Nashe's office somehow and see what he could find. Had to find something good enough to placate Ivers because he was gonna be pissed as shit when he found out Tozzi was still down here working the undercover. It had to be something good enough to give a judge reason to issue a restraining order to stop the fight, something on paper that would link Nashe with Immordino in a dirty deal so juicy that Sal would be wishing he really was nuts.

Tozzi was determined as he stepped briskly along the money-green carpet, but then he turned the corner to get to the elevators and as soon as he saw them, he knew he was fucked.

"What the eff are you doing here, Tomasso?" Lenny Mokowski, with two of the bigger gorillas, Frank and Jerry. "I knew you were stupid, Tomasso, but not this stupid."

Instinctively Tozzi backed away from them, made some space for himself in case he had to get to the .22 in his ankle holster. He backed away—one, two steps—then backed right into somebody. Two somebodies. Two big somebodies. He looked over his shoulder. Vinnie and Tootsy, also from the primate pen. They grabbed his arms before he could do anything, pinned them back, and escorted him over to Lenny.

"In there." Lenny jerked his head and pointed with his greasy pompadour. The gorillas shoved him through the stairwell door.

"Hey, come on, will ya? What is this?" Tozzi tried to act surprised and put-out, but the sinking feeling in his gut told him these guys were here for something more than a fraternity hazing. The stairwell had that cold-cement feel, just like a city morgue.

Lenny pointed a stubby finger in Tozzi's face. "Don't kick or it'll be worse." Then he looked at Frank. "Go 'head."

Frank swept up Tozzi's left leg in his big paw and rolled up his pant leg. He ripped the Velcro straps on the holster, removed the .22, and dropped the leg. Tozzi felt his one-point floating up into his belly and playing with the butterflies. He was fucked.

Lenny stared at him. Frank too. Tootsy was grinning. Vinnie looked blank. Tozzi's brain was spinning, thinking of options. Maybe come clean, identify himself as an FBI agent, warn them of the consequences of assaulting a federal agent. He looked at Tootsy again. Forget it. These guys don't know from consequences.

He kept trying to think of something he could say, something he could do, and suddenly he remembered the times he'd seen aikido black belts taking on a *randori* attack, five guys at once. It was beautiful to watch, the black belt like the calm center at the eye of the storm, throwing guys out right and left. But he was fucked already. You're supposed to act before you get grabbed. Vinnie and Tootsy had his arms pinned way back. Almost impossible to get out of that. Impossible for him anyway. Shit. He was fucked.

"Hey, Lenny, you gonna tell me what this is all about or what?" He tried to smile, be a wiseguy about it, talk his way out.

Lenny ignored him. He looked at Jerry and Frank instead. "Go 'head."

Jerry balled his fist and sent an uppercut into Tozzi's gut that would've lifted him off the ground if the other two hadn't been holding him. Tozzi bent forward, thought he was gonna throw up. Vinnie and Tootsy yanked him back upright and Jerry did it again, to the breastbone this time. A ringing pain vibrated through Tozzi's body, like banging a tuning fork on the edge of a table.

"Lemme," Frank said, shouldering Jerry out of the way. He slapped Tozzi's ear with the flat of his hand, and a spike went through his brain. The head bodyguard curled his fist and threw a roundhouse into Tozzi's face, snapping his head back.

Tozzi could feel the cheek getting hot and numb. He heard one of them snickering. Then Frank threw another right into his face, same spot. Then there was another punch, right on top of his nose. He squeezed his eyes shut with the pain, but he didn't see stars. He saw worms—curly, neon-green worms. Someone grabbed a fistful of hair and yanked him back, and he got it in the gut again. Except for the initial impact he hardly felt any pain this time. He was worried about the neon worms behind his eyelids, though. They looked sort of like those microscopic pictures of chromosomes. Tozzi was worried that they were brain cells, ghosts of all the brain cells these guys were bashing to death.

He looked up, but the glare of a naked light bulb on the wall blinded him. All he saw were dark gorilla shapes outlined in blinding light. Then someone gave him a shot in the gut again, and he doubled over.

He heard Lenny's voice. "Save your hands," he said. Then it smashed into his forehead, hard, bone on bone, and Tozzi was sure his skull was cracked. A knee—Frank or Jerry, somebody had thrown a knee right into his forehead. The neon-green worms floated and flashed. More dead brain cells.

The goons let him go and he fell to the floor, flopped down on the glossy painted concrete like a bag of flesh with no bones to hold him up, like a body bag. He tried to open his eyes, but he couldn't. The glare was overwhelming.

The last thing he remembered was the cold floor on his hot cheek and the neon worms floating up to heaven behind his eyelids.

Things were starting to come back into focus—the lamp, the windows, the desk—but Tozzi was still too dizzy to move. He closed his eyes, afraid to sit up, afraid he'd puke if he tried. He hadn't passed out—at least he didn't think so, not really. He remembered Lenny and the gorillas hauling him down the stairwell, how the lights got softer and the air didn't have that concrete chill when they'd dragged him back into the hallway and dumped him on this green velvet couch. He might've passed out on the couch for a while—he couldn't be sure. His head started to throb now and it hurt to keep his eyes open, so he just sat there very still, waiting for everything to settle down. He felt like shit, but at least the neon worms were gone. That was good, he thought.

It was either five minutes or an hour later when he opened his eyes again. He couldn't tell. Someone was sitting at the desk now, telephone cord stretched around the side of the big leather chair, elbow on the armrest, hand twiddling a pen. Tozzi noticed a big painting on the wall, a portrait of the Nashes, Russ in a dark blue suit hovering over Sydney in a low-cut lavender gown, the skirt spread out all around her, like Scarlett O'Hara. Beside the desk there was an easel. The War Dcwn the Shore poster was on it. Walker and Epps facing off, looking mean. Tozzi's head started to pound again. He closed his eyes.

"How's the head, Tomasso?"

Tozzi opened his eyes. Russell Nashe was sitting behind the desk, facing him. A background of dark green leather with brass studs along the edges framed his smiling face. He looked happy.

"I don't have to call you Tomasso anymore, do I? The jig's up, right?"

Tozzi ignored the question. He stared at the rug and rubbed his temples. The fucker knew. Shit.

Nashe picked up something from his desk and held it up between his fingers, a T-shirt. Printed on the front was a silkscreen of the same picture of Walker and Epps that was on the poster. Same printing across the top: THE WAR DOWN THE SHORE. On the bottom it said Nashe Plaza, Atlantic City, May 12.

Nashe admired the shirt, smiling with his bunny teeth. "Nice, huh?"

Tozzi sat up and stared at all the junk on his desk. It was cluttered with all kinds of shit: coffee mugs, bright red kiddie boxing gloves, dolls, videocassettes, programs, bracelets, pins, buttons, money clips, cuff links. Next to the easel there was an inflatable punching bag with Walker's picture on one side, Epps's on the other. Nashe loomed over all this crap, smiling, the master of all he surveyed.

"This is where the real money is," Nashe said, giving him a wink. "Merchandising."

Tozzi rotated his head, carefully. "Oh, yeah?"

"That's right. The fight itself—forget about it. Too many hands out afterward for anyone to make a real profit, too many people waiting for their piece of the pie. But the merchandising is another story because *I* control that." Nashe pointed a finger into his own chest. "It's all mine, minus a nominal royalty to each of the fighters. Now I can see from your face that you think this stuff is all crap. Who the hell wants it, right? But come tomorrow night, people get all worked up waiting for the fight to start—they get crazy—and then this crap doesn't look so cheesy. Not just here on-site, no, everywhere, everywhere they're showing the fight, all the closed-circuit outlets, eight hundred sixty-three of them across the country.

"See, fans want to take part in an event like this, hold on to it for a while, bring it home to the kids, and buying a T-shirt or a coffee mug or a doll does that for them, makes them part of the event. If it's a good fight—and I'm certainly expecting that it will be—more people will buy even more of this stuff on their way *out* so that they can remember the fight, prolong it in their minds, keep it with them. You see what I'm saying? It sounds ridiculous, I know, but that's how it happens." Nashe shook his head and picked up the T-shirt again. "Twenty bucks for a two-dollar T-shirt. It's almost robbery. Don't you think?"

Tozzi frowned. "I wouldn't know."

"No?" Nashe picked up the bright red kiddie boxing gloves and started to squeeze his hands into them. "You know, people like you, people living on a fixed salary, you don't understand how money works. You have no idea how to make money. Real money, I mean."

"Apparently not." Tozzi was looking at the oil painting, Sydney's lavish gown.

"Money has to keep moving to be useful. It's like a shell game." Nashe pushed imaginary shells around with the boxing gloves. "I move it here, I move it there, but the important thing is that *I'm* the guy doing the moving. That way I'm always the one who knows where it is, and in the end I always win. Except with me, it's not a matter of cheating. It's simply a matter of control."

Tozzi touched his nose. It was tender, crusty blood around the nostrils, maybe broken. "What're you telling me all this for?"

Nashe laughed. "Why am I telling you all this? You know why. Because I know who you are, Mike."

"So who am I?" So who told you, your lovely wife?

Nashe rolled his chair over to the inflatable punching bag and started jabbing at it. "Your real name I don't know, but that doesn't matter. What I do know is that you're somebody's little spy. An IRS agent, I assume. Maybe the SEC. Possibly Alcohol, Tobacco, and Firearms. I mean, but don't feel bad about it, Mike. It's not like you're the first one. There's always some brand-new eager beaver in some office down in Washington who gets the bright idea that he can sneak a man into my organization and get the goods on me." Nashe shook his head, smiling. "Sending a guy to be my bodyguard—now that's a new one. Usually they send accountants so they can get into my books."

Tozzi just stared at him. "I don't know what the hell you're talking about." It was Sydney. Sydney told you I was asking too many questions.

"You don't have to pretend anymore, Mike. Come on, I know." He punched the punching bag a few times, making the head dip down and hit the rug. "You guys, so goddamn loyal. I wish I could find people like you to work for me. All right, fine. You wanna be Mike Tomasso, be Mike Tomasso. I don't care. Whatever dirt you think you've got on me, my lawyers will take care of it."

Tozzi didn't say anything. Haven't got shit on you, Russ. That's the problem.

"You look skeptical, Mike. Trust me. If I'm in trouble, my lawyers will get me off the hook. And do you know why they'll get me off the hook? Not because they're the best lawyers money can buy—even though they are. No, it's because every so often the government has to be reminded just how much goddamn cash I fork over to them every year." The punching bag took it on the chin. "So what if I cut corners and find loopholes and bend the rules sometimes? So what? I'm worth more to them in the taxes I *do* pay than just about anybody else they've got on their books. Even if you say I'm a crook—even if you can *prove* it—I'm a very valuable crook. When you come right down to it, the government would rather collect whatever taxes I decide to give them than not have me at all. The *big* guys in the government, the guys who *really* count, they know that if they knock me out of the box, they stand to lose a good chunk of income. They'll also create a hell of a lot of unemployment. And maybe worst of all, they'll be losing the best fucking cheerleader this country ever had for free enterprise and the good old capitalist way." Nashe kicked the punching bag and sent the thing flying across the room.

Tozzi's gut was burning. He wished to hell he could bust this arrogant son of a bitch right now. But he didn't have the evidence, and now that Nashe was on to him, it wasn't very likely that he was going to get it. There had to be a way, though, there had to be. He tried to make connections, find angles, a thread of a legitimate excuse for making an arrest here and now, but there was nothing. Just Sydney's inadmissible pillowtalk, the opinions of a disgruntled ex-employee, which any good defense lawyer could tear to shreads, and the highly questionable mumblings of an incoherent Henry Gonsalves. It was bullshit. It was nothing.

Nashe rolled his chair back behind his desk and pulled off the boxing gloves. "So what *do* you know, Mike? What're you after? Why not just ask me directly? Maybe we can work something out." He tossed the gloves down on the desk. "You ever been to the Cayman Islands, Mike? Beautiful place. I've got a resort down there. You know, we've been looking for a good security consultant for that place. If you're interested in something like that, I could help you set up your own business. I have a lawyer in Panama who can set you up. It'd be nice for you. You bill the resort, they pay your company direct deposit, you don't even have to be there to sign the checks. No one has to know what you make. You do whatever you want with it. But, ah"—Nashe smiled and wagged his finger at Tozzi—"don't forget to pay your taxes on it."

Tozzi wished he were wearing a wire. Panama. There must be a hundred sleaze-bag lawyers down there who just set up dummy companies for the purpose of receiving hot money. The Cayman Islands. Nice place to do your banking if you don't want any questions asked. Then Tozzi thought about Nashe's high-priced lawyers here in the U.S. Even if he had Nashe's bribe offer down on tape, it could be construed as a job offer, career advancement, a leg up for a good employee. Goddammit, he's a clever bastard. Just play stupid, Tozzi told himself. Maybe he'll say something to hang himself. Maybe.

"I don't follow you, Mr. Nashe."

Nashe just smiled and shrugged. He had a big mouth, but he knew when to stop talking. "You know, you look awful, Mike. Go look in the mirror. Your face is all swollen on one side. Your nose too. You got blood all over your shirt, and that suit—you might as well just throw it out. God, you're a mess. You ought to take care of yourself. Why don't you take some time off, give yourself a good rest, walk along the beach and be alone with your thoughts. When you're feeling better, come back and see me if you still want to work for me. I'm sure we can work something out."

Walk along the beach. Like when Valerie got shot? "Yeah, sure, Mr. Nashe. I'll let you know." Bastard.

Tozzi hauled himself to his feet. He tottered there for a moment, afraid that his knees would give way. He moved his feet a little and the knees seemed to firm up. If only his head would stop reeling.

Tozzi looked up at the oil painting—Sydney's demure smile, the perfect hair, the plunging neckline on the gown. Did she really tell Nashe that he was a fed? Saw that he was nosy and made a lucky guess? Maybe she sleeps with all the agents they send over to check up on Russ. FBI, IRS, SEC, AFT . . . all those guys. Maybe by now she can smell 'em.

Tozzi moved toward the door, then stopped and looked back at Nashe. He had to know. He nodded toward the painting. "She the one who told you I was an undercover agent?"

Nashe shook his head. "She must've liked having you around. Didn't tell me a thing. You must be something, Mike. I guess it's true what they say about you Italian guys, huh?"

"Yeah . . . we're something. So who told you?" Sal told you.

Nashe smiled like a bunny and shrugged. "Somebody."

Sal Immordino told you. Had to be. Sal got suspicious and made a good guess. That's why Lenny just happened to be there with the keys to the beach house. It was a fucking setup. Russ and Sal. The bastards. Tozzi's head was throbbing. He turned toward the door.

"Oh, Mike, by the way, I meant to tell you. I'm very sorry about your girlfriend. Valerie? Is that her name? Look, whatever her insurance doesn't pay for, I'll take care of it. You let her know, okay?"

Tozzi glared at him sitting there with that big stupid smile on his face and all his merchandising crap all over the desk. He was about to tell the bastard to drop dead, but he didn't. Why bother? He just turned away to leave.

A big grandfather clock stood by the door—he'd just noticed it. It had a decisive *tock,* like the pounding in his head. Tozzi stared at the face, the classy roman numerals. It was twenty-five after noon. The fight was nine and a half hours away, and basically he didn't know much more than he knew ten weeks ago when he started this goddamn assignment. Crap . . .

• 20 •

Tozzi lifted the dark glasses off his sore nose and scanned the room until he spotted Gibbons sitting at one of those little Formica fast-food tables where the seat is attached to the table and the whole thing is bolted to the floor. He'd told Gibbons to meet him here at the huge food gallery on the third floor of Ocean One, the mall they'd built on the old Million Dollar Pier, which he thought was the one where people used to come to see the horse jump off the end and land in the water. It was either this one or the Steel Pier, he couldn't remember. He winced and rubbed his sore shoulder. He felt like a goddamn horse had landed on him.

The place was jammed, every table taken. This was where the slot players came to eat because it was cheaper here than in the casinos. As he made his way through the crowd, Tozzi noticed that Gibbons had a big greasy Philly cheesesteak and a cup of coffee in front of him. Gibbons was ripping a big bite out of the sandwich just as Tozzi sat down across from him.

"Lorraine'd take a shit if she saw you eating this. Pure cholesterol."

Gibbons looked up at him and chewed. "Mind your own business."

Tozzi shrugged. "Hey, I'm not gonna tell her."

Gibbons sipped his coffee. "I don't give a shit if you do or not. I'm hungry."

"So eat." Tozzi tugged on the brim of the Yankees cap he was wearing.

Gibbons looked him over then. "What's with the outfit? You look like a jerk."

Tozzi gave him the finger. He had gone back to his apartment and changed his clothes after he left Nashe's office. Now he was wearing khakis, a black T-shirt, and a blue satin baseball jacket with "Mets" embroidered in orange on the back. The Yankees cap was part of the disguise so he could blend in with the boardwalk crowd. The sunglasses were meant to cover the shiner.

Gibbons ripped off another hunk of cheesesteak. "So what's the deal? Why aren't you with Nashe?"

Tozzi scratched some melted cheese off Gibbons's paper plate. "They made me."

Gibbons chewed and thought it over. "Sal was on to you a long time ago. He must've told Nashe."

"Yup." Tozzi pictured the oil painting in Nashe's office. Sydney as Scarlett O'Hara.

"So where do we stand?"

"Nowhere." Tozzi touched the bridge of his nose. It didn't hurt so much now, but it felt swollen. "They're right on course, and we're sitting here with our dicks in our hands."

"You wanna call Ivers, see if he can get a judge to issue a restraining order to stop the fight?"

Tozzi shook his head in disgust. "Even if we could convince Ivers to do it—which is a longshot to begin with—no judge is gonna fuck around with a guy like Russell Nashe, not without a very, very good reason."

Gibbons took another bite and nodded. "You're right."

"Maybe we ought to go straight to Walker and tell him we're on to their scam. Tell him point-blank—you throw the fight, you're in deep shit."

"Great idea, genius. Then he can hit us with a harassment suit, get our asses booted out of the Bureau for good. Even if you could bring him up on charges *after* the fact, how do you prove that a guy threw a fight? All he's gonna say is he had a bad night and he lost. Talking to Walker now won't do anything. Whatever his take is, he's already got it spent. Anyway, from what I hear, he doesn't relate to white people very well."

Tozzi sighed and spun the plastic saltshaker on the table. "You're right." Goddammit.

They didn't talk for a while. Gibbons ate and Tozzi thought about Valerie. He'd called the hospital when he went to change his clothes. They said her condition was stable. He asked if he could talk to her, but they said no, she was in no condition to accept calls. He felt awful. He wanted to talk to her, make her understand that he wanted to make it up to her, do something to show her that he really cared about her. He kept spinning the saltshaker around and around. What he really wanted to do was put a hollow-point bullet through Sal Immordino's eye so that he could watch the back of his head blow open and make modern art on the wall. That's what he really wanted to do.

Tozzi broke the silence. "You got another gun with you?"

Gibbons shook his head and wiped his mouth with a paper napkin. "Just Excalibur. Why? Where's yours?"

Tozzi sneered. "My fellow workers relieved me of it."

Gibbons stopped eating and looked at him for a moment. "Your face looks a little puffy. You okay?"

"Yeah, I'm fine. They just wanted to scare me." He was sore all over, but it was his nose that was worrying him. "Lemme have the other half. I didn't have breakfast this morning." He started to reach over for the other half of Gibbons's cheesesteak, but Gibbons pushed his hand away.

"Get your own."

"Come on. Give me half. Won't be so much cholesterol for you."

"Go fuck yourself." Gibbons moved the paper plate out of his reach.

"My partner, real nice guy. Thanks a lot." I just got my ass kicked, and you won't even give me half of your cheesesteak.

"The place is right over there." Gibbons pointed to the Philly Cheesesteak concession. "Get your own."

"No, I don't want it now." He went back to playing with the saltshaker.

Gibbons raised the coffee to his lips. "You gonna sulk now? Big fucking baby. Here. Take it." He pushed the paper plate in front of Tozzi.

"I don't want it."

"Go 'head, take it now. You wanted it."

"No, you eat it."

"No, I don't want it. You're gonna tell Lorraine, and I'm gonna end up getting the cholesterol lecture again from Miss Mazola Margarine, the goodness of corn and all that shit."

Tozzi looked down at the melted cheese oozing over the mess of meat and fried onions. Wasn't really good for him either. But they did taste good. He picked up the sandwich. Just one bite. "You know what the problem is, Gib?" He took a bite, chewed a little, then wiped his mouth. "Everything's going their way. It's working like clockwork for them. At this point they can't go wrong. We gotta make something happen. That's what we have to do. Fuck up their plans a little so somebody slips up and gives us a chance."

Gibbons put down his coffee and scowled. "Here we go. So how should we disregard the Bill of Rights this time, *goombah*?"

"No, seriously. Nashe and Immordino think they're home free. We gotta shake them up, make them think—"

Gibbons was shaking his head no when Tozzi suddenly spotted them over Gibbons's shoulder. They were leaning on one of those stand-up counters, coffees steaming in front of them, both of them trying not to be obvious about it, but they were looking right at him. It took a minute for Tozzi to be sure, but he remembered the blond guy's hair, how it was shaved around the ears and wavy on top like a Hitler *Jugend.* And the other guy, the greaser, he was still wearing that herringbone jacket, the sleeves too long. That was them, the two torpedoes Immordino had sent to ambush him in the parking lot at the Epps camp. They were hunched over, talking, taking turns looking at him. Tozzi rubbed his ankles together, wishing he had his weapon. Shit. Crowded room, lots of confusion. They were here to make a hit. Finish the job they'd screwed up two weeks ago, the job Immordino fucked up the other day. Shit.

Tozzi kept his eye on the torpedoes. "Come on, Gib. Let's go."

"I haven't finished my lunch—"

"Fuck lunch. Let's go. Now!"

Gibbons wiped his fingers, serious now. "Who is it?"

"Two of them. A blond German-looking guy in a tan suit, and a greaser—herringbone sport jacket, designer jeans, black dress shoes—you know the look, guinea collegiate. Immordino's guys."

"Too many people here. Take it outside." Gibbons stood up, picked up what was left of his lunch, and carried it to the trash, nice and easy.

Tozzi walked ahead, wondering whether they should take the escalator or the stairs. Either way was bad. Too many people. He turned to face Gibbons, glanced back at the torpedoes. They were taking their last sips and dumping their coffees. "They're coming."

"Take the escalator down," Gibbons said. "Turn left when we get out on the boardwalk. Go to the first stairway down to the beach. Take it there."

They got on the escalator and started to glide down. A giant banner was suspended from the ceiling, swaying gently over the moving stairs: THE WAR DOWN THE SHORE—NASHE PLAZA. Walker and Epps, twenty feet tall, glaring at each other. Tozzi leaned against the rail, put his foot up on the higher step, and caught a glimpse of Blondie and the greaser getting on up top. A bunch of giggly Chinese kids and a lot of retirees were between them. He glanced up as they passed under the giant boxers, followed them with his eyes. Fee-fi-fo-fum . . .

They stepped off the escalator on the ground floor and headed for the front doors, walking through the mall fast but not too fast, weaving through the strolling crowds, keeping track of each other, Gibbons lagging behind a little, jacket unbuttoned, ready to go for Excalibur if he had to. They passed a salt-water taffy shop. The warm, sugary smell reminded Tozzi of when he was a kid and he used to watch them make taffy on the boardwalk in Asbury Park. Ladies in white aprons and hairnets twisting these giant wads of taffy—like an elephant's foot on one end, tapering down to a pencil point on the other—feeding it into a clacking machine that cut off pinkie-sized pieces and wrapped them in waxed paper. He glanced into the store's window, but there was no one working a big wad inside. In the reflection off the glass he could see Blondie behind him, closer than he thought. He walked faster. Gibbons followed.

"I don't like this," Tozzi said, looking straight ahead.

"Why?"

"Because I don't have a gun, that's why."

"I do."

Tozzi rolled his eyes toward Gibbons. "And who're you, Rambo? Forget it. The odds stink."

"So what do you wanna do? Split up?"

"Yeah. They want me, not you. How about if I go down to the beach alone, see if they follow me? You know those columns in front of Convention Hall? Get there ahead of us. You can get the drop on them from up there, pick 'em off easy if they don't want to surrender."

Gibbons scowled at him. "Get the drop on them? What're you, the Cisco Kid?"

"You got any better ideas?"

"Not really."

"Then?"

"All right, go ahead. Do it."

They pushed through the front doors simultaneously. Gibbons dodged in front of boardwalk strollers, getting lost in the crowd. Tozzi sprinted for the stairs that led down to the beach. As he ran down the wooden steps, he could see them coming, Blondie and the greaser, knocking people down left and right to get to him. Great.

Tozzi hit the sand and started running up the beach. His shoes sank into the dry sand, slowed him up, reminded him of yesterday, running back to the beach house, to Valerie. He couldn't run fast enough. He glanced back over his shoulder. The greaser already had his gun out, holding it out in front of him as he ran. Good. Gibbons would have good cause to plug the stupid fuck without bothering too much with the formalities.

He looked up at the boardwalk as he ran. He could hear people up there yelling and screaming, probably the ones who saw the greaser waving the pistol. By now Blondie probably had his weapon out too. Tozzi glanced at the people up there, the crowd whizzing by. He hoped to hell Gibbons could run. Then he remembered the cheesesteak, the cholesterol. Fuck. Why the hell couldn't he have had a salad instead? Why doesn't Gibbons ever listen—

A spurt of sand appeared a few feet in front of him, then he heard the crack of the shot behind him. He glanced back at them. Blondie did have his gun out. Goddamn them. Tozzi scanned the beach for innocent bystanders. It was mostly deserted, except for a couple of sunbathers willing to brave the stiff spring winds. Someone up on the boardwalk actually stood a better chance of taking a stray bullet. Wonderful. Tozzi was panting, breathing through his mouth. His legs felt like lead, but he forced himself to keep pumping. His head was throbbing again, and he was beginning to wheeze. He was angry with himself for punking out so soon. He blinked back the grit in his eyes and ran, forcing himself to focus on what was up ahead. You better fucking be there, Gibbons.

That's when he spotted them. In front of the columns. Kids. Girls in matching pink bathing suits and white sneakers—nine, ten years old. Skinny little girls with batons. And a woman in sweats, the instructor. Baton twirlers. Right in front of the columns. Of course.

"Get down!" he yelled. "Get down!" Wheezing for air. Head pounding.

Another shot hit the sand, the report following. Then two more shots, one right after the other.

"Get down!"

They just stood there, gawking at him. What the hell's wrong with that woman? Make those kids get down flat, for chrissake. Stupid girls. Where's Gibbons?

They were thirty feet in front of him, just standing there like a bunch of stupids, gawking at him, just like everybody else up there. Tozzi looked up, spotted Gibbons in front of one of the gray stone columns. He was shaking his head.

Yeah, right, genius. I know that! Can't fucking shoot with a bunch of stupid little girls hanging around, can we? Goddamn idiot instructor. *She* ought to be shot.

Tozzi considered taking a sharp left and heading for the waves, but then changed his mind and ducked under the boardwalk. Dark and cool under there, herringbone pattern of light beaming through the planks overhead, thundering herds above, the gambling hordes pounding the boards. Easier on the legs under here, the sand not so dry. But these mossy black timbers—you had to dodge around them like a Porsche on a goddamn road test.

He stopped behind a timber to let his eyes adjust to the dim light so he could see where they were. He squinted out toward the bright sand on the beach, and—*zing!*—a bullet tore a chunk out of the timber just above his head.

He dropped to his knees, covered up, scrambled to the next timber. He peered out at the rows of black uprights, whalebones seen from the inside. A dark silhouette breathing hard clung to one of them. Where was the other son of a bitch? Shit. Tozzi turned and ran—legs aching, head splitting—wondering where the other guy was, where the hell Gibbons was. It got darker, colder. What the hell was down here? Couldn't see shit. He felt trapped all of a sudden—no weapon, no escape, couldn't outrun them much longer—

But then he saw it, a light. A cheapskate twenty-five-watt bulb over some kind of entranceway, a stairway, it looked like. Concrete steps. He zigzagged toward the light bulb. He didn't have much choice.

It was cold in the concrete stairway, but the cold didn't help his pounding head. He leapt up the steps, three at a time, his chest about to explode. At the top of the stairs he could see there was a door, a warped wooden door, the laminate split and curling at the edges, a rusty padlock in the hasp. Shit. Tozzi didn't stop, he just kept going, shoulder first, and *crash!* He bent over, gripping his shoulder. The pain was incredible. It felt like he'd been hit with an electrified ax. Then he heard their voices, remembered Blondie's nasal whine from the parking lot that last time. Tozzi stood up and kicked the door, kept kicking it again and again, splintering wood until there was a crack right up the center. The torpedoes were at the bottom of the stairs, he could hear them. He rammed the ruined door with his back—once, twice—then fell through, losing his balance, shocked that the door had given up without more of a fight. He was on his back, on a concrete floor. He rolled over and got to his feet, ran on without thinking, clutching his shoulder, down a dark corridor, green-painted cinder-block walls, dim light bulbs on the ceiling in little red cages, a few closed doors on either side. The shoulder was hot with pain. He squeezed it as he ran up to a metal staircase at the end of the hall. There was another door at the top, but this one wasn't locked. He could see a sliver of light beaming through, more than a sliver. Thank God for small favors. Tozzi pounded up the metal steps, struggling for breath, stumbled through, closed the door behind him. A brick wall was on his left, a curtain—plum-colored velvet—on the right. Folding chairs, a big standing fan, and a flock of music stands were blocking his way in front. He stopped and tried to listen for Blondie and the greaser over his own rough breathing, see if they were coming up the metal stairs after him. But what he heard was coming from somewhere else. The other side of the curtain.

Tozzi dropped to his knees and looked under. It didn't make any sense at first. Rowdy crowd of people in the audience, lot of cameras flashing, couple guys onstage with no shirts on, lot of other people crowding around them. Somebody yelling at somebody else, some black guy. Then he saw the scale and he knew what this was. It was the weigh-in for the fight, Walker and Epps stripped down to their trunks, getting weighed, last chance to scream at each other and make the news. Of course. He was backstage inside Convention Hall. Son of a bitch.

He shut his mouth and forced himself to breathe through his nose to get his wind back. He took off the Yankee cap, wiped his brow with his sleeve, put the hat back on, then bent over with his hands on his knees and took deep breaths. Then he heard them—felt them first—the vibration of feet pounding up the metal stairs on the other side of that door. Abbott and Costello.

Without thinking, Tozzi ducked under the curtain and stumbled out onstage into the bright lights. He froze for a second, squinting to see past the lights, but then realized that no one was paying any attention to him. There were a lot of people onstage, a lot of hubbub. "Pain" Walker was up on the scale, muttered and cussing like a soup-kitchen psychotic. Epps was off to the side, pointing at him and snickering. Tozzi moved toward the crowd gathered around the fighters, worried that Blondie and the greaseball might start shooting through the curtain.

He peered into the audience, looking past Walker's well-defined back, wondering if Gibbons was out there. Then it came back to him, what he was telling Gibbons before he'd spotted Immordino's torpedoes in the food gallery. The only way they could nail Immordino and Nashe now was to shake things up, upset their plans, make *them* do the scrambling. It was the only way.

Dizziness suddenly overcame Tozzi and he had to stop for a moment and close his eyes. Charles Epps's baritone laugh suddenly boomed through the PA system, and Tozzi's splitting headache was back. He opened his eyes, blinked, and started shouldering through the crowd, determined to shake things up royally. Despite his head.

"Yo, Walker!" he shouted.

No one heard him. He pushed his way to the front, right up to the champ standing on the scale.

"Hey, Walker, you ugly mother, I'm talking to you!"

Cameras flashed. Walker looked down at him, scowling. He *was* ugly. Tozzi closed his eyes, dizzy again.

Somebody took Tozzi's arm. "Come on, pal. Let's go."

Tozzi snapped his arm away. This was their only chance to make something happen. He wasn't running on all cylinders, but he knew what he had to do.

"You're a chump, Walker. That's all you ever were, a chump. Never fought a decent fighter in your life. Charles is gonna show you. You watch. He's gonna knock you right on your ass. You watch."

Walker's lip curled back. "Who da fuck're you?"

Tozzi gave him the bird. "You suck. You're finished. Why not just give Charles the belt now, save yourself the pain, 'Pain'?"

Walker looked to his men. "Get him outta my face." Two big black guys moved fast and pinned Tozzi's arms back before he knew what was happening.

Shit. Couldn't shake the dizziness. Tozzi bent his elbows, bent his knees, made himself heavy, unmovable, but this aikido technique wasn't working. He couldn't focus, and he'd lost the moment. They had him and they were dragging him offstage. Well, fuck it. It was now or never.

"What is this shit, man?" he shouted back at the champ. "Can't fight your own battles, Walker? Need your homeboys to do your work for you? Hey, forget about Epps. You couldn't even beat *me* up, chump."

That's when things started to happen—fast. Other guys crowded around him—big guys. Someone said something about getting this away from the TV cameras, but then Walker was right in front of him, bare chest, ugly face. He muttered something that ended in "motherfuckah," then Tozzi felt it before he realized what had happened. It was like a spike driven between his eyes, the sunglasses digging into his flesh. He'd gotten it in the nose again. Walker had punched him, right in the face. Tozzi dropped down to a squat. They hauled him right back up, curled in a ball, holding him up as he tried to cover up and clutch his face. His head felt like it was going to explode. He couldn't open his eyes. He was afraid to breathe. The goddamn nose again. Shit!

" 'Pologize! 'Pologize! Talk!"

Tozzi could hear Walker's voice, but the words didn't register.

"Say it, man," somebody else said. "Apologize to the champ. Say it or he hit you 'gain."

Tozzi opened his eyes and it was like being underwater. Underwater with a shark staring him in the face.

Another voice: "Do 'gain, do 'gain. C'mon, do 'gain."

They hauled him up, and Tozzi could see the shark coming through the water, the mean ugly face, the shining pecs, the fist cocked.

"No more," he groaned and squeezed his eyes shut, bracing for the next shot. "Le' go—"

"Will you look at this, ladies and gentlemen?"

The booming voice of God from on high in the form of Charles Epps.

Walker forgot about Tozzi and lunged over him to get at Epps. "Shut up your fat mouth, ol' man."

Charles Epps was standing at the edge of the stage, the microphone in his hand, his big, mocking laugh thundering through the hall. The reverberating sound made Tozzi wince with pain.

"That man is right, Dwayne. You are a chump. Lookit you. Supposed to be the world champeen, and you need all your homeboys to hold the man down so you can mug him. Sheeeet. You can't bring those boys in the ring when you fight me. You know that, don't you? You are a dee-scrace to the title. I'm gonna have to take it away from you just to rescue its good name. Beating up a poor defenseless white man like that. You oughta be ashamed." The booming laugh thundered. The great and powerful Oz.

Walker sputtered, looked at Epps, then looked at Tozzi, his face twitching. He wanted to say something to Epps but he wasn't finished with the white man who'd sassed him."Let 'im go, let 'im go. Do it! Now!"

They let go of Tozzi's arms.

"C'mon now, motherfuckah. I be fair wit' you. I want you to hit me. Gimme yo' best shot. C'mon, mother." Walker's voice was low and calmer now. Much scarier.

Tozzi touched his nose and stared at Walker. Thinks he's a clever bastard. He wants to make it look like he was attacked, so he can justify the mugging, after the fact. No way.

Walker moved in close and breathed in his face, his big fist balled against Tozzi's gut. "C'mon, motherfuckah, I telling you now. Hit me or I put this roundhouse upside yo' head, yo' ear be coming out the other side. I telling you now."

Tozzi looked him in the eye, amazed and grateful. Thanks for the tip, champ.

The great and powerful Epps: *"What you doing over there, chump? Making love to that man?"*

Walker's teeth clenched, the eyes were wild. "I do it. I swear. Make yo' brains mush."

Tozzi stepped back, made some room, dying for Walker to do it. He smiled in the champ's face. "Suck my dick, asshole."

Walker's face was like a comic-strip character on a wad

of Silly Putty being pulled in two directions. He was breathing hard out his nose, pissed as shit. "I tol' you!" he growled. Tozzi was ready.

Walker threw the roundhouse, true to his word, threw it hard. Tozzi slid in fast to beat the punch, caught the crook of Walker's elbow with one hand, the side of his face with the other, and—*wham!*—threw the champ down flat on his back, hard.

Tozzi grinned. *Tsuki kokyu nage.* Too bad his *sensei* wasn't here, he thought. Ought to be able to jump a rank for this.

"Whooooweeee!" Epps was impressed.

Cameras flashed. Pandemonium in the aisles, chaos onstage. The homeboys jumped Tozzi from behind.

"The chump is down for the count!" The great and powerful Epps was howling. The reporters were howling.

Tozzi curled into a ball again, worried about his nose but happy with himself. *Whooooweeeee,* indeed. The press boys would have plenty to report now.

Tozzi covered up as the homeboys started to drag him offstage again. "You dead now, sucker. You dead now." Tozzi tried to make himself heavy, but one of them had him by the collar and the satiny material of the Mets jacket slid easily on the polished wooden floor. He struggled to break free, grabbing at their clothes to haul himself up, but they kicked him with their knees and one caught him on the side of the head. He stopped struggling, suddenly dizzy again, sick to his stomach. Head spinning and pounding—a little guy with a jackhammer trying to break his way out of Tozzi's skull, right through the middle of his forehead. Tozzi covered his face, but touching his nose was like putting ice water on a tooth with an exposed nerve. He was stiff with pain.

The noise of the crowd was fading. The space around him seemed smaller. They'd gotten him into the wings, out of the crowd's sight. Oh, shit . . .

"Get 'im down the hall, down that way. We show him. He one dead fucker now."

"Stop right where you are and release that man immediately. He's under arrest."

Tozzi opened one eye and peered up at the familiar voice. Gibbons waving his ID, jacket open so they could see his holster, pushing the homeboys out of the way. "Come on, get away. Move it. He's mine."

"Who you, man? You don't look like nobody to me."

Gibbons drew Excalibur, barrel pointed up. "Am I somebody now, asshole?"

The homeboys made room, lots of it, backed away grumbling, returning to the stage.

Gibbons took Tozzi's arm, helped him up, breathed in his face. "I ought to arrest you for that stunt. What the hell do you think you're doing?"

Tozzi blinked his eyes, tried to focus. "I'm making things happen."

Gibbons started to lead him down the hall. "Yeah, that accomplished a whole lot. You're a real piece of work, Tozzi."

"No, think about it. If you were Walker, would you throw the fight now? After some guy comes out of nowhere and humiliates you in front of a million reporters, I mean."

Gibbons's face changed. He was considering the possibility. "Who knows? It's no secret that Walker's got a chip on his shoulder. He may have something to prove now. He could change his mind."

"That's what I'm figuring." Tozzi was able to walk on his own now. They came to the stage-door entrance, and there was a War Down the Shore poster taped to the door. Tozzi remembered the easel in Russell Nashe's office, their little chat.

"Walker gave you a pretty good shot there. I saw it. Let's go find a hospital, have a doctor look at you."

"No, I'm okay." The little guy with the jackhammer was still working on his breakout. "Really. I'm fine."

"You look like shit. You sure?"

"I'm fine." He pushed through the door with the poster

on it and winced as the bright sunlight assaulted his eyes. "What time is it?"

"Almost two."

Eight hours to fighttime. Tozzi nodded to himself, wondering where she might be now. "I gotta go see someone."

"Who?"

He shaded his eyes and looked straight up at the big white building next door, Nashe Plaza. "I've got an urgent rumor to plant." On the seventeenth floor.

Gibbons made a face. "What're you talking about?"

Tozzi didn't answer. He was focusing on the windows on the seventeenth floor.

• 21 •

Cil had her wrist crooked around Sal's elbow. Sal patted her hand and smiled at her, glad that she'd decided to come to the fight. People in the crowd made believe they weren't looking at her—a nun at a prizefight wasn't something you saw very often—but Sal didn't give a shit about the attention she drew. It was the kind of attention he didn't mind having. He knew there'd be cops and feds around—a big event like this, they're always around. Tomasso and his friends. So let them take all the pictures they want. He liked it when the papers printed those kind of pictures, him with Cil, the poor numbskull palooka being led around like a little kid. It was just what he wanted everybody to believe.

He looked at Joseph sitting on his other side and wished to hell Cil had been a boy. Cil had smarts, Joseph was a *jooch.* Look at him with that suit. Sharkskin, for chrissake. Who the hell wears sharkskin anymore? No brains this guy has. I tell him don't get the real good seats, just close enough so we can see something. We gotta blend in with the crowd, Joseph. So what does he do? He gets seats ten rows from ringside and he wears his glow-in-the-dark Guido suit. Shit for brains, that's what he's got. What's the use? Can't say anything to him here. Someone might see.

The card girls climbed into the ring then, and the catcalls started. A blonde and a black chick, spike heels and bathing suits, like the Miss America contest. They walked around the ring for no particular reason, just giving everybody something to see while they were waiting for the fight to start. The black chick grabbed the ropes and started doing bouncing squats, like she was warming up for a fight herself. From where they were sitting, they had a good view of her ass coming down on her black heels, real *Penthouse* stuff. Cil was frowning. She didn't approve of this kind of thing, women looking nice like this.

Sal leaned over to her. "How you doing, Cil?"

"Fine." The bright lights were bouncing off her glasses. Death rays, turning the bimbos into piles of salt, just like in the Bible.

Joseph leaned over from the other side, sticking his big nose in. "How you like it so far, Cil? You never thought it'd be like this, did you?"

Cil didn't answer. She was looking at something, not the bimbos in the ring, something over there in the seats to the left. She still wasn't smiling.

"What'sa matter?" Joseph said.

"Mr. Mistretta is here." She nodded toward the seats where she'd been looking. "At the back of the section, third or fourth row in. Frank Bartolo is with him. I think he sees us."

Sal looked. She was right. It was Mistretta, looking right at them. Way in the back, big sourpuss right in the middle of the row, Bartolo with that cue-ball head of his sitting next to him.

"Oh, yeah, I see him," Joseph said, real happy.

"Don't wave, Joseph," Cil said, grabbing her brother's arm before he lifted it.

"Yeah, but he's the boss, Cil. We should go over and say hello, how you doin'."

"Not here. He'll get mad."

Sal didn't want to stare at Mistretta. Feds love to take pictures, then make up stories with them afterward. He looked back at the black chick's bouncing ass, wondering why Mistretta hadn't gotten in touch with him as soon as he got out. Not even a call. Maybe something's wrong. Why didn't he call, though? And what's he doing with Frank?

There was a big commotion on the other side of the ring then, lot of cheering, some booing too. One of the fighters was coming out. Epps. Red satin robe, hood covering his bald head. He climbed up and ducked under the ropes, strutted around the ring like a king. Stopped by the black chick then, patted her ass with his glove, big smile, big reaction from the crowd. Cil coughed into her fist. My man, Sal thought. But he was still thinking about Mistretta.

Lot of boos now, cheering too, about fifty-fifty. Walker and his entourage swept into the ring like a gang of street punks, the champ leaping over the ropes, his black robe open, black satin flying behind him like Batman. He looked pissed as usual. Started pacing, throwing punches, rolling his head, his new trainer—Henry Gonsalves's last-minute replacement—massaging his shoulders. From the other side of the ring Epps watched the champ. He looked amused. Sal glanced up at Mistretta. Walker better not fuck around. He does and he'll die with the title.

"Hi, Sal."

Sal looked up. It was Sydney Nashe, standing in the aisle. Shit. What does she want? They were taking pictures, for chrissake. *Damn!*

Sal started nodding and mumbling. "Hey, how ya doin'? How ya doin'?"

Cil was staring at her, big frown, same way she stared at the bimbos, the sequins on Sydney's dress sparkling in her glasses. Long-sleeved dress with big shoulders—lilac, of course—hemline above the knee. Real low-cut too. Those tits practically hanging out. Jesus.

"I've got something to tell you, Sal." Sydney rolled her eyes and sidled her tight little bod into the row, leaning against the seat back of the guy in front of Cil, ignoring Cil like she wasn't even there.

Sal felt hot. She wants to play games, this one, always with the games. "Later," he muttered and started rocking in his seat.

"You won't want to know later." Lolita with the bedroom eyes. Thanks a lot, Sydney.

Now Joseph's hanging on his arm. "What's she want, Sal?"

"Nothin'." Mind your own business, *jooch.*

Sydney leaned forward then, that white-blond hair of hers all over his shoulder as she whispered in his ear. "The fix is off."

"What?" He stopped rocking.

She stood up again, nodding with that smug little smile on her face. "That's what I heard."

"From who?"

"Mike. You know, Russ's bodyguard?"

Fuck. *That* bastard. Why the fuck is this guy always in my face? Bastard. "He don't know shit."

Sydney shrugged. "Sounded like he knew a lot when I talked to him. He told me Russ changed his mind." She whispered in his ear again. "He said Russ promised the champ a little bonus for *not* throwing the fight."

"That's bullshit. Don't make no sense." Unless the feds got to him, made him a deal. No . . .

She shrugged again, lifting the tucked-under ends of her hair on her naked shoulders. "According to what I heard, Russ did some refiguring. Decided he could make more money on merchandising if the champ won since people know him better than Epps. You know, the T-shirts and the toys and the coffee mugs and all that. I asked him about it, but you know Russ, he never tells me anything."

Why'd she look so happy about it? She liked this kind of

shit, being in the middle of things. She thinks this is great. But maybe Russ sent her over. Maybe the feds are pulling the strings here, using the Nashes to set some kind of trap. She said she likes being Mrs. Nashe. Maybe she is working with them, protecting her position.

"What's going on, Sal? What's wrong?"

"Just shut up, Joseph. Nothing's wrong." I'm gonna kill this asshole, I swear.

"Sal, be quiet," Cil said. "You're talking too much." Cil was looking daggers at Sydney.

"It's not true," he whispered up at her. "Tomasso doesn't know what the hell he's talking about." Unless the fucking feds got to Nashe and made him a deal. They do shit like that. Nashe calls it off, they don't prosecute. But what else? They must want to know about me too. I'm the one they want. The big bad wolf from the mob. Sure, Nashe hands me over to save his own ass. That's how the feds do it. Make one guy rat on the other. Son of a fucking bitch!

"Did you hear about what happened at the weigh-in today?" Sydney said, sweet as pie, la-di-da. Bitch.

"Yeah, some wiseass picked a fight with Walker and pushed him down. What about it?"

"From what I heard, it was more like he knocked the champ right on his *bee*-hind. Mike told me the odds changed real fast after that. You know, the unofficial ones? Out in Las Vegas? Walker was the favorite, five to one, but he's dropped now, a lot." She whispered in his ear again. "I guess Russ was betting a lot on the other guy. You know him—he likes to bet on longshots. I don't know. Maybe he figured he wouldn't make as much money with these new odds, so he decided to take a loss on his bets and make it up on selling the fight junk, the merchandising." She shrugged and stood up. "You know Russ. He always goes for the biggest profit. For him, that is."

Sal grabbed her wrist to keep her from leaving. "Whattaya telling me this for, huh?"

Sydney opened her eyes wide, the sly little grin. "Because I knew you'd want to know. I mean, I couldn't very well *not* tell you"—she glanced down at Cil and Joseph—"you and your yubba-dubba family."

Sal squeezed her wrist, felt like breaking it, the little lying bitch, but Cil was prying his fingers loose.

"Stop it, Sal," she hissed. "People are looking."

When Sydney got her wrist back, she looked over her shoulder, cool as could be, that hair swishing so nice and pretty over her delicate little shoulders—shoulders he could snap in two like nothing.

"The fight's starting," she said. "See you 'round, Sal."

The sly grin and the eyes. Little bitch. She sidled past Cil and stepped lightly down the aisle, showing some nice leg through the slit in that short dress, heading back to Russ and their ringside seats on the other side of the ring. Fucking little bitch. I'll break both those legs, see how nice they'll be then.

"Sal." Joseph's face was all sweaty. He was getting nervous. What the hell was *he* getting nervous about? I'm the one who should be nervous. "I heard what she said, Sal. What does she mean? The nigger's not gonna do it? Is that what she's saying? Jesus Christ, Sal, this is bad."

"Just shut up, Joseph. Don't say anything—will you please?—before I break your fucking neck. *Capisce?"* Sal looked up at Mistretta. The ringside announcer was introducing the fighters, reading their stats. Mistretta was staring down at the ring. Shit. Thirty mil down the tubes. Holy Christmas, Mistretta's gonna go nuts. Look at him up there with Bartolo, that kiss-ass bastard, like teacher's pet. *I'll take care of Sal for you, Mr. Mistretta. No problem, Mr. Mistretta. I'll take care of it.* Bastard. Shoulda put up a stink when Mistretta decided to give him my crew. Shit. And fucking Nashe. I oughta go down there and scare the shit out of him, make him choke on his fucking bunny teeth if he doesn't get to Walker and refix it.

Sal started to stand up. "Lemme out, Cil."

Cil gripped his arm. "Where are you going?"

"I gotta go talk to Nashe. Lemme through."

"You can't do that. People are watching. You're supposed to look mentally disturbed, Sal. Did you forget?"

"Don't worry about it, Cil. I'm just gonna go talk to him. It won't look like anything. Now lemme through."

"But Mr. Mistretta is up there. He'll see you."

What the hell's with her now? "So what if he sees me?"

She let out a long, melancholy sigh and looked up at him over her glasses. "Sit down, Sal. I'm afraid I have something to confess to you."

"Hurry up. What?" He sat down.

"Sal, when I told you that Mr. Mistretta approved of you betting all that money on the fight? When he was at the halfway house in New York? Well, it wasn't quite like that. The truth is, he didn't want you to bet that money. He disapproved very strongly."

"What?"

"I'm sorry, Sal. I lied to you. I thought my prayers would make everything work out for the best—you'd win the money, you and Joseph would get those concrete factories, my girls would have a new facility—but apparently God thought differently. It wasn't part of His plan. I shouldn't have lied to you. Now God is punishing me. I should've remembered what Grandma always said: *'Gesù Cristo vede e provvede.'* I'm sorry, Sal."

Sal saw himself in her glasses, two of him. Punishing *you*? I can't fucking believe this. God's punishing her? And what the fuck is Mistretta gonna do to me? He's gonna fucking crucify me, that's what he's gonna do. "Come on, get out of the way, Cil. I gotta go see Nashe. Now move."

"No!" She wouldn't let go of his hand. "Be still. You're just going to make things worse."

"Sal! Sal!" Joseph was hanging on his other arm. "I heard what she said. This is bad, Sal. Jeez, this is real bad. I'll go talk to Nashe. Okay?"

"No! You sit down. *I* have to talk to him." But they were both hanging on him, keeping him down.

The bell rang then, and a brief hush came over the crowd as the fighters came out of their corners. Sal watched, flexing his fist as if he had his rubber ball, the boxers circling and stalking, Walker doing a lot of moving, Epps slower, more deliberate. Walker was impatient, coming in fast for a few quick jabs. Epps countered with a left hook to his ear. Good! Good! Sal started to smile, but then Walker delivered a straight right to Epps's face, scoring points with that one. Cheers and whistling. Epps backed away, backed toward the ropes. Sal's stomach sank.

"Get outta the way, Cil! Lemme out!"

"Sit still, I said." She was gritting her teeth, eyeglasses flashing. "They'll take you back to court, Sal. They'll say there's nothing wrong with you, they'll send you to jail. Is that what you want?"

"If Walker wins, I'm gonna wish I was in jail. Don't you realize that? Don't you understand what you did?"

Her face was like stone, no compunction at all. "I did what I thought was right. I made a mistake and I'm sorry. But now you're panicking and you're going to make things worse. Joseph."

He leaned over Sal's lap. "What is it, Cil?"

"Joseph, I want you to go talk to Mr. Nashe. You remind him that he and Sal had an arrangement, and we expect him to honor that arrangement—"

"Get away." Sal pushed Joseph back into his seat. "He doesn't know how to talk to a guy like Nashe. 'Arrangement.' What's that? That's lawyer talk. I gotta lean on this guy. He's gotta know how badly I can fuck him up—"

"Salvatore! Your language!"

"Forget about that, Cil. Now get outta the way. You're aggravating me."

"You're aggravating *me.* Joseph, go do what I told you."

"Where is he, Cil? Nashe, where is he?"

Cil pointed. "Right down there. On the other side, directly across from us. You see the front-row seats? The whole section that's roped off? He's with his wife and two other couples. Do you see him?"

"Yeah, I see him." He stood up but Sal wouldn't let him pass.

"No, Cil—"

"Let him by, Sal. Do you *want* to go to jail? Have a little faith in your brother for a change. He is older than you, you know."

Joseph pushed his way through and stepped on Sal's foot getting out. "Don't worry, Sal. I'll take care of this." He started down the aisle.

Oh, shit! Look at him. Mr. Big Deal. He's a functional idiot, for chrissake. He's gonna make it worse than it already is.

Sal looked all around, trying to figure out where the hell the cameras were. Maybe the feds aren't here. Maybe they forgot to come. Then he spotted the gang of photographers down at ringside. Shit. Any one of them. Maybe all of them.

Sal wiped the sweat off his face with his hand and looked at what was going on in the ring. What he saw gave him instant *acido.* Walker was right in Epps's face, in close, cutting the ring. For such a dumb shit, he was fighting smart. Epps had a four-inch-reach advantage, but with Walker in this close it was useless, actually worked against him. He kept throwing hooks and uppercuts at Walker, but they had no power at this range. Walker had no fucking brains, so he didn't give a shit about taking shots like this to the head. He just kept his head down and pounded away on Epps's body. He was fighting his fight, goddammit, fighting too goddamn smart. He wasn't supposed to be that smart without Gonsalves in his corner. Epps couldn't take more than three, four rounds of that kind of punishment. Not at his age. Oh, man! This can't be happening.

The bell rang, ending round one. The fighters returned to their corners, Walker bouncing on his toes, Epps walking. Sal didn't like the way Epps looked. End of round one and he already looked tired. Not good, not good at all. He looked through the ropes at the bimbos parading around the ring with the round cards and saw his brother standing in the aisle in that roped-off section where Nashe was sitting, waving his hands like some old greenhorn from the other side, yelling over Sydney's blond head. Nashe was just sitting there with that big fucking smile of his. He don't give a shit. He made his deal with the feds, he don't care. He's not listening to Joseph, he's laughing at him. Joseph's a *jooch.* He's a butcher for chrissake. Why should anybody listen to him? Oh, Christ!

He stood up, nerves jangling in his hands and forearms. "Move, Cil. Lemme out!"

"No!" She stood up and stuck her face in his. "You don't trust Joseph, that's obvious, and you're determined to get caught. If you don't sit down and behave right this minute, something *will* happen. You'll go to jail. This is *my* fault. *I'll* go talk to Mr. Nashe. He'll listen to me. Now you stay here."

Before he could say anything, she was rushing down the aisle, her veil flapping behind her. She had a point. He'd done time before. He didn't want to go back. But he didn't want to end up in the foundation of some building either. He swiped his face again, he was sweating buckets. He watched her working her way around the ring, saw her glaring at the two bimbos with the round cards. He felt pains in his chest, little pains, but they were in his chest. Jesus Christ, is this how it starts, a heart attack? He was breathing hard and he hadn't done anything since they'd come in, just sat here. He watched her moving through the pack of cameramen, calling to Joseph through the bodyguards, Nashe nodding, letting her into his private section. He glanced over to his left then, toward Mistretta. The old sourpuss was pointing at her, leaning over and telling Frank Bartolo something. He spotted Cil—Christ, you'd have to be blind not to see her with that habit on. There she was, standing next to Joseph, giving Nashe her two cents' worth, Nashe not giving a good goddamn about either one of them. And Mistretta's watching. Oh, shit! He put his hand over his heart. I'm gonna die. Right here. I'm gonna die.

Sal jumped when the bell rang to start round two. Walker leapt up out of his corner, bounced into the middle of the ring. Epps hauled himself up off his stool, flat-footed. The crowd yelled. Sal sat down, his heart thumping in his chest like it was trapped in there.

Gesù, Gesù! I'm gonna die!

• 22 •

Tozzi was hunkered down at the edge of the ring, holding a 35mm camera, looking across the canvas through the fighters' legs at Gibbons, who was leaning on the skirt on the other side, holding up a camera of his own, shoulder to shoulder with all the real photographers. He wondered how convincing Gibbons really looked, wearing a green nylon windbreaker over his white shirt and suit pants. Gibbons was a good agent, the best man the Bureau had, as far as Tozzi was concerned, but he was from the old school, Hoover's school. No matter how you dressed him up, he looked like a fed. Tozzi hoped nobody was picking up on that.

He looked up at Walker and Epps in the ring. Walker was making Epps look bad, real bad. Lot of red leather smacking Epps's midsection again and again and again. Lot of sweat flying, shining like starbursts in the overhead lights. Lot of lung power hissing out of their noses with each punch—more from the champ than the challenger, though. If the champ intended to throw this one, it sure didn't look like it. As Gibbons had predicted, it looked like Walker had something to prove. Still, Tozzi wouldn't mind seeing Epps get in a few good shots, maybe tag him one on the nose with that legendary right of his, make Walker see some of those neon-green worms. Tozzi squeezed the swollen bridge of his nose and winced. It hurt like a bastard, had to be broken. He also had one of those little nagging headaches that just wouldn't go away, right behind his eyeballs.

The Nashes were on the other side of the ring where Gibbons was. Tozzi could see Sydney sitting there in the third row in Nashe's private section, sparkling like a little purple star, unruffled by Sal's brother Joseph and his sister the nun sitting next to her, jabbering over her head, pleading their case with smiling Russ, big black bow tie under his chin, butterfly collar, satin lapels on the tux. Russ was smooth, but the smile was for show. The Immordinos were beginning to draw attention, but he couldn't sic his gorillas on them, not on a nun, not here. Sydney, on the other hand, seemed to be getting a real kick out of seeing Joseph and Sister Cil in such a state. That sly little grin, just eating it all up. Tozzi hoped he'd read her right and that she delivered the gossip the way he'd given it to her. He glanced back at Sal Immordino sitting all by himself, rocking back and forth, looking very upset. All three Immordinos seemed pretty shook up about something, and Sydney had been over there whispering in Sal's ear. Seems like she did tell him, but with Sydney you could never be sure. She had her own agenda. He sniffed his shirt. He could still smell her perfume on his clothes. Sydney, Sydney, Sydney . . .

Gibbons was looking at him now, giving him the eye. He nodded toward the seats on Tozzi's side, and Tozzi followed his gaze to Sal Immordino coming down the aisle now. Tozzi moved fast, rushing into the aisle and blocking Sal's path. He could tell right away from Sal's face just how glad he was to see him.

Immordino didn't slow down as he came up to Tozzi, just threw an arm out, intending to push past him. Tozzi settled in, got his one-point, and extended his arms, laying his palms on Sal's big fleshy chest. No muscle, just *ki.* Sal was thrown back, startled. Tozzi kept pushing, wouldn't let him get his balance, pushing the big man back until they were secluded on the exit ramp.

"Get outta my face, Tomasso!" Sal was huffing and puffing, gonna blow your house in.

Tozzi moved closer. "How's it going, Sal?"

"Move, Tomasso!" Sal grabbed Tozzi's forearms, Tozzi grabbed his. The big man tried to toss Tozzi aside, but Tozzi held on.

"Get out of my fucking way, you little bastard!"

Tozzi didn't say anything, just held on while Sal tried to shake him loose.

"I'm gonna fucking kill you, Tomasso. I don't give a shit who you are." Sal suddenly wrenched his right arm loose and punched Tozzi in the chest. Tozzi held his breath. It wasn't much of a punch, but after the beatings he'd taken from Nashe's gorilla squad and then "Pain" Walker, just the residual vibrations of the punch's impact made the rest of him hurt. Tozzi held his breath, grabbed Sal's lapels, and hung on tight, intent on staying very close. Sal's punches won't have any power this close. He hoped.

"So what's the big hurry, Sal? Aren't you enjoying the fight?" Tomasso the wiseass talking. Had to goad him.

"You're dead, you little shit. Let go of me!"

Tozzi let his body go slack and just hung on Sal. "Come on, Sal, let's go back to your seat and watch the fight. C'mon, we gotta hurry up. It's not gonna last long. Look at your boy Epps. He looks older than you, for chrissake. Next round—you wanna bet? Ten bucks. Walker's gonna knock him out in the next round. Wanna bet?"

"Fuck you!" Sal tried to shake Tozzi off, wrestle him down to the floor, but Tozzi just held on for the ride. "I'm gonna punch your fucking heart out, Tomasso. You think I can't? You think I can't?"

Tozzi shook his head and his nose brushed against Immordino's. A sharp pain shot up to his forehead. "No, Sal," he said, holding his breath, "I don't think you can do shit."

"No?" Sal was still struggling. "You ever hear of a coon named Lawson, a pug? I did him that way. I'll do you too."

"What're you, Fred Flintstone? That's ancient history. Anyway, don't flatter yourself, Sal. That was just a freak accident."

"Bull*shit* it was!"

Tozzi yanked on his lapels. "No, *you're* bullshit. Big mob guy everybody's supposed to be afraid of, so tough. Tough, my ass. You sent your guys after me twice, they couldn't do shit. You try it yourself a couple of times, and you fuck up worse than them, end up shooting a fucking woman. What'sa matter, Sal? You don't know girls from boys? Huh?" Tozzi yanked again. "Huh, Sal? Huh?"

Sal swung his hands up from underneath, slammed down on Tozzi's forearms, and broke Tozzi's grip on his lapels. But Tozzi locked on to Sal's forearms again and held fast. Sal wrestled with him, pushing him this way and that, but Tozzi wasn't letting go. "I whacked tougher mothers than you, Tomasso. With my fists."

"Whacking guys with your fists—you expect me to believe this? What're you, Bruce Lee now, back from the dead?"

"Fuck you!" Sal squeezed harder on Tozzi's forearms.

Tozzi's fingers were getting numb.

The crowd roared then and Tozzi saw Sal staring at the ring. He glanced over his shoulder to see what was going on. Epps was down on one knee. The referee was counting. Three, four, five . . . Epps got up. The ref held the challenger's face and checked his eyes. He nodded and let the fight go on.

"Get the fuck away from me!" Sal screamed. His eyes were wild, his face shaking.

"You're full of shit, Sal. You don't scare me. You slap your brother around, that's about it. Yeah, and you beat up old men like Henry Gonsalves, guys collecting Social Security.

That's what you do. Whattaya think you're gonna do to me, huh? I'll tell you what you're gonna do. Nothing, that's what."

Sal snapped one hand up and grabbed Tozzi's throat. "I'll do worse than I did to Gonsalves. I'll make you wish you were him. At least he lived."

Bingo!

Tozzi tensed his neck and smiled in the man's face as he reached into his pocket and brought out his ID. He flipped it open, waved the shield in the big dummy's face. "You're under arrest, Sal."

"Big fucking deal."

Tozzi stuck his ID back in his shirt pocket, then unbuttoned the top two buttons and showed Sal the wire taped to his chest. There was a tiny microphone, the size of a pencil eraser, in Tozzi's chest hair. It was connected to a microrecorder taped to the small of his back. Sal's eyes became hubcaps. He was rewinding the tape in his mind, trying to remember what he'd said, trying to convince himself that he hadn't really admitted to the attempted murder of Henry Gonsalves or the murder of Earl Lawson, or that this tape could be used to prove mental competency, which would mean that he would have to face all those old charges he'd walked on a few years ago. Tozzi smiled. Bingo.

Tozzi removed Sal's limp hand from his neck and turned him around as he took the handcuffs he'd borrowed from Gibbons out of his back pocket.

"Hey, wait a minute now."

"Shut up and spread your legs. Wider. Wider! Put your right hand behind your head. Hurry up!"

"Tomasso, let's talk about this—"

"Do it, asshole!"

Sal sighed and put his left hand behind his head. "C'mon let's be reasonable here, Tomasso."

"Shut up!" Tozzi bent Sal's right arm up behind him and held the wrist one-handed while he cuffed the hand behind Sal's head. "You have the right to remain silent, Sal, which you should've been doing all along if you were smart, you big fucking dummy. You have the right to legal counsel. If you cannot afford—"

The hall exploded then, people jumping out of their seats, screaming and yelling. Sal arched his head back to see what was going on in the ring.

Don't look, Tozzi told himself.

"Shit," Sal muttered. "I'm fucking dead."

The crowd was going crazy. Whatever was going on down there, it must've been good. But don't look, he kept telling himself, not until he's cuffed. But Tozzi could hear people in the crowd counting, counting with the referee . . . three, four, five . . . Could Epps have done it? Was Walker down for the count?

Tozzi turned and looked. He couldn't help it. Epps was the one on the canvas, Walker was standing—

"Hey!"

Sal broke loose from the hold. Tozzi tried to tie up his right arm again, but Sal snapped it away, then hammered his elbow back, right into Tozzi's face, right into his nose.

Tozzi clutched his face. The pain shot through his head like there was a Sidewinder missile sunk into his face. He dropped to his knees. Colors flew by, Steven Spielberg special effects flew by, eight million miles an hour, speeding through space. Noise and space banshees whizzing past him. His head exploding, one long, continuous, mounting explosion. It wasn't stopping. Tozzi stopped breathing, couldn't relax his face, couldn't open his eyes. All he could do was brace himself like this and not move until it stopped —if it stopped.

Finally it started to calm down. He was breathing. It hurt like hell and his head was throbbing, but the spaceship ride was over. Just the neon-green worms behind his eyelids again. Those good ol' green worms. Oh, shit . . .

When he could finally unclench his face, he pried his eyes open, but it was all a blur. Brain damage, he thought. And an ugly fucking nose. Worse than Sal's. No woman will ever want him with a nose like that. Then the blur became double vision and gradually the images merged together. He got to his feet. In the ring Walker and Epps were in their corners, getting sponged and massaged. The round was over. Sal was gone. He looked past the ropes. Sal was over with his brother and sister, yelling over Sydney's head at Russ, jabbing his finger at the smiling billionaire, the handcuffs dangling from his wrist. He looked for Gibbons, but he couldn't see him.

The room started to spin then, and Tozzi had to sit down.

• 23 •

"Don't tell me you don't know what I'm talking about, Nashe, because you do."

Gibbons watched Sal jammed into that row, his brother right behind him trying to look useful, his sister the nun hanging on his arm trying in vain to pull him away. He was on his feet now, his face like a Jersey tomato as he yelled at his friend Nashe, pointing two fingers at the billionaire, the blond wife sitting between them, apparently enjoying it from the catty look on her face. "She told me you changed your mind, you went to Walker on your own." Sal was pointing down at Sydney's blond head. "Isn't that what you just told me?"

The wife just shrugged, bare shoulders and a Mona Lisa smile.

Nashe fingered his bow tie. "I *don't* know what you're talking about. I'm not sure I even know who you are, sir."

The billionaire looked calm—a good act. He was clever, though. Besides the two got-rocks couples in the row behind them, there must have been at least a hundred people within earshot, the way Immordino was yelling. Nashe wasn't about to acknowledge the fix or that he even knew Immordino, not where someone could hear. Particularly someone like a special agent from the FBI posing as a photographer. Gibbons stood at the back of the pack of photographers crowding around the edge of the ring so he could eavesdrop on the activity in Nashe's private section. He peered through the viewfinder on his camera and shot off pictures at random to make it look like he was paying attention to the fight. There were at least five bodyguards that Gibbons had noticed—one guy standing next to Joseph, another one on the other end of that row, one at the top of each flanking aisle, and a floater, an older guy with a build like a fireplug who was keeping tabs on the others. This must be the Polack Tozzi told him about. Gibbons pegged him right away for an ex-cop. The little pirogi was sharp, the kind who'd notice a photographer not taking enough pictures. Gibbons scanned the other side of the ring through the camera lens. Tozzi was probably staying out of sight because he knew the Polack would spot him. He was still wondering, though, what the hell had happened over there with Immordino. He hoped Tozzi was all right.

"Don't fuck with me, Nashe! I'm telling you! Don't fuck with me!"

The nun yanked on his arm, but it was like trying to move an elephant. "Come sit down, Sal. You're being stupid. Come *on*!"

"Lemme talk to him, Sal. Lemme talk." The greaseball brother was tapping Sal on the back. "Go 'head, Sal. Go sit down."

Sal ignored them both, but something else seemed to be bothering him because he kept looking up into the crowd in that side section over there. At first he thought Sal was looking for Tozzi, but now he didn't think so. Gibbons scanned the section, but he couldn't figure out what the hell Sal was looking at.

Up in the ring Walker was cutting the ring nicely, jamming Epps into the corners, pounding the man's body. Epps was throwing punches, but they all seemed weak. The man looked beat.

Sal was having a conniption fit. "Send one of your flunkies to Walker's corner and give him the message. Put the nigger in reverse. You hear me? Now, you fucking bastard! Do it now!" He was out of his mind.

The nun was straining to move him. "Stop, Sal. Will you listen?"

The wife reached up then and ran her hand along Sal's cheek. The nun's mouth dropped open. She looked like she was gonna blow a gasket. Sydney didn't give a shit about Sister Cil. Look at her rolling those big green eyes, the sly little pout. She was like a sexy little rich-bitch cat in a cartoon. "Listen to your sister, Sal," she said. "Be a good boy and go sit down now."

The nun slapped the little cat's arm away. "You leave my brother alone. Don't touch him!"

The bodyguards jumped, and Gibbons was about to move in when Nashe waved them off. The Polack confirmed the order, signaling the goons to back off. The two couples in the back looked very put out.

Sal shrugged his sister off his arm, told his brother to get the fuck away from him, then he glared down at Nashe again. "Hurry up now. I'm not kidding here, Nashe. You know I'm not. Send one of your boys over there right now. Hurry up!"

Nashe ignored him and looked at the nun. "Sister, we're all here to enjoy the fight, but your brother is interfering with some people's enjoyment. Now I don't want to be unpleasant about it, but if you can't get him under control, I'm going to be forced to have him escorted out. Okay?"

Light flashed in the nun's glasses. "Don't threaten me. You can't throw my brother out."

Sydney piped up then. "Oh, yes, he can. And there's no law that says you can't have a nun ejected for disorderly conduct as well." Mona Lisa smirk, real cool.

The nun's frown was like a horseshoe hanging under her nose.

Suddenly the crowd was on its feet, screaming like crazy. Gibbons looked up into the ring and saw Walker slamming uppercuts into Epps's gut, one right after another, Epps just taking it, arms practically at his side, serious pain in his face. People from way back in the cheap seats were flooding down the aisles to get a better look at the onslaught. Gibbons was suddenly pressed up against the photographers in front of him, and it was a struggle just to turn around and see what was going on with the family feud. In the middle of all the commotion the bodyguards were doing their best to block the rows and keep the invaders out of Nashe's private section. Brother Joseph was getting huffy now, shouldering big Sal out of the way. Gibbons could see that they were yelling at each other, but he couldn't hear over all the jerks yelling in his ears. Then he saw it, just a glimpse, but he definitely saw it coming out of the sharkskin jacket. Joseph had a gun.

Gibbons dropped the camera and started shoving bodies out of his way, palming faces like basketballs. He was only about fifteen feet away . . . with about sixty bodies between them. Shit. He tried to muscle through with his shoulders, but the photographers around him were leaping at him like salmon swimming upstream, lunging for a shot of the action in the ring.

Through the bodies Gibbons could see Sal and his brother fighting for the gun. Sal suddenly threw Joseph's arm in the air, and Gibbons saw that the gun was a fucking cannon, a stainless-steel 9mm automatic. When the rich people in the row behind saw the cannon, they leapt over their seats like deer and took cover, fancy clothes and all. Sal twisted Joseph's wrist—gun and handcuffs glinting over the waves of jostling heads—twisted until Joseph let go, then he took it away from him, easy as pie. Joseph looked hurt, but Sal didn't notice. He was crazy mad. He leaned over Sydney and grabbed Nashe by his pleated shirtfront, hauled him up out of his seat, and jammed the pistol into the billionaire's gut. Nashe was white, looking all over the place for his bodyguards, but they were so busy dealing with the riffraff, they didn't notice what was going on with Sal and their boss.

"Turn around, you assholes!" Gibbons yelled to the bodyguards. "Your boss is in trouble!" But it was no use yelling. There was too much noise. No one could hear him.

Gibbons didn't like the look on Sal's face now, mean but satisfied. Gibbons knew that look. Sal was resigned. He was gonna do it. Jesus. Gibbons pushed heads out of the way, threw his elbow right and left, battling his way through the crush.

"Drop it, Sal," he yelled. "FBI!"

Nobody heard him, still too much noise.

Then he saw it in a flash. That hard, sweet look of satisfaction passing over Sal's face as he was about to pull the trigger, then surprise and annoyance as Sister Cil suddenly yanked on his arm just as the gun went off. Gibbons saw the muzzle flash. A faint crack through the uproar confirmed it. That and Sydney jolting back into her seat, a fright wig of white-blond hair, her head whipping back, bobbling, finally coming to rest, slightly askew on those delicate, bare shoulders. The bodyguards heard the shot, but they were confused, couldn't figure out what had happened. The rich people heard it too because they were climbing over seats, climbing over people, fighting like hell to get out of there. Sal was backing away, trying to get out too, but there was nowhere to go. He was hemmed in, bodies everywhere, bodies who had no idea they were in the middle of a murder scene.

In the middle of Sydney's white chest, there was a neat little entry wound rimmed in black. No blood for a second, then the gush. It gurgled out in a rush and poured down into her cleavage, soaking through the sequins. A big splotch of deep purple started spreading down the front of her sparkling lavender dress. Gibbons's first thought was that a woman that small couldn't possibly have so much blood. The gush died down to a thick flow then. She wasn't moving. Screams, cheers, arms flailing, open mouths, intense eyes all around . . . but she wasn't moving. The killing had hardly been noticed in all the craziness. Most everybody else was watching the killing in the ring.

Gibbons finally made it to the end of the row where the Immordinos were all jammed in together. The Polack and one of Nashe's goons were blocking them in so they wouldn't escape. The Polack had his heels dug in with his back up against Joseph's. Any paying customer who got too close, the Polack shoved back into the crush. Gibbons moved in and stuck his ID in the guy's face. The Polack shoved him back like all the rest, the little son of a bitch. Gibbons got his footing, grabbed the guy's ugly tie, and made him look at the ID.

"Wake up, asshole. FBI."

"Le'go of me—who the eff're you?"

Gibbons recoiled from the guy's greasy head. It stunk of sweat and hair oil. "Special Agent C. Gibbons, Federal Bureau of Investigation, and I don't want any more lip outta you. You understand me?"

The Polack sneered at him. "You got no jurisdiction here."

Gibbons wrapped the tie around his fist and hung him high. "Listen up, my friend. I'm a fed. I got jurisdiction everywhere. Now you get your guys to clear this aisle right here *immediately,* or I make sure you get named as an accessory to murder."

"Get the eff' outta—"

Gibbons yanked him up higher. "You think I'm joking? Huh? I know a lot of judges who don't look kindly on ex-cops who get involved with the wrong element. Aiding and abetting, obstruction of justice—all kinds of nice things they can hang ex-cops with. I'll bet you know of a few judges like that too. Huh, Kowalski?"

They just glared at each other, the tie digging a line into the tough little Polack's jowls. The guy didn't say anything, but he was thinking hard. He knew the score. Gibbons let go of the tie.

"Now get your guys to clear that aisle. I'm deputizing you."

Mokowski gave him a dirty look, but he did what he was told, ordering the two nearest goons to clear a space. Gibbons had to remember to have him picked up later. The guy was dirty, sure as shit. Cops never cooperate with feds, not even ex-cops. He'd given in too easy. For the time being, though, he'd let the guy think he was getting away with something. Gibbons figured he might need him if Tozzi didn't show up soon. And where in the hell was Tozzi, goddammit?

Gibbons drew Excalibur. He got into the empty row behind the Immordinos and moved in fast. He extended his arm and stuck the muzzle of his gun behind Sal's ear. "Gimme your weapon. Two fingers." He dug the .38 into Sal's flesh. Sal didn't say a word. He just switched the big automatic to his other hand and held it out upside down by the grip. Gibbons took it with his left hand, felt for the safety to make sure it was off, then pointed it at Joseph. "Put your hands on your heads. All three of you."

The nun looked at him, shocked.

"That's right—you too, Sister."

Joseph was reluctant. Gibbons stuck the automatic in his face, shining metal to sweaty flesh, and Joseph started to cooperate. Real tough guy. "Now face me, all of you, and move out into the aisle. Keep some space between you. Go on, move."

Gibbons shifted his gaze between Sal and Joseph, back and forth, as they moved into the aisle with their sister in the middle. Sal was probably too smart to try something stupid, but Gibbons wasn't going to count on anything, not now. Joseph was a jerk-off, but he was dumb enough to try something he might've seen in a movie. "Turn around slowly and face me. And keep those hands where I can see them."

The crowd was going nuts. He could just imagine what was going on up there. Sal tried to stare straight ahead and look blank, but his eyes kept darting up to the ring. Joseph was staring at the fight. He looked like he was in severe pain. The nun's mouth was a flat line, her eyes hidden behind the glasses. Then the three Immordinos winced as camera flashes blanched their faces. The photographers must've picked up on the arrest, figured they could get a few quick shots in before Walker sent Epps to bed for the night.

Gibbons heard someone yell "Hey!" in his ear, and when he turned his head a flash went off in his face. Asshole photographer. He was blinded, big spots in front of his eyes. "Down on the floor," he barked at the Immordinos, making like nothing had happened and he could see perfectly. "On your bellies, legs apart, hands over your heads. Right now. All three of you."

"I will not," the nun said.

"You heard him! Do it! Now!"

Gibbons recognized that maniac scream. Who else? His eyes started to clear and he could see Tozzi muscling his way through the photographers. Gibbons blinked. Tozzi looked awful. His face was gray, one eye almost closed, it was so swollen. What the hell did he do, cut through the ring between Walker and Epps to get here?

"Here, take this." Gibbons gave him the automatic. "You take the brother. I got Sal."

Gibbons hunkered down and put one knee in the middle of Sal's back as he nestled Excalibur's barrel in the hair at the back of Sal's neck. Sal's right hand was already cuffed. How convenient. Gibbons gripped the open cuff for control. "Put your left hand behind you," he ordered. Sal complied. "Now your right." When the hands were together, Gibbons cuffed the other wrist, then proceeded to pat Sal down.

When he was finished, he looked over at the victim and her husband. They hadn't moved, Nashe sitting there with his mouth open, pulling on his bottom lip, staring at his wife, the beautiful hair and all that blood. It was hard to read the expression on Nashe's face. It was somewhere between disbelief and revulsion. It wasn't love or compassion, that's for sure.

Gibbons got up off Sal's back, grabbed his elbow, and helped the big man to his feet. Tozzi was just finishing up his pat-down on Joseph, ordering him to stay right where he was on the floor. He moved on to the nun, who had actually assumed the position, spread-eagled on the floor. Gibbons noticed that Tozzi kept pausing to shake his head. As he started to frisk Sister Cil, he suddenly stopped and nearly keeled over on top of her. He had to brace himself with his hand on the floor, he was so punchy. He continued the body search then, running his hand down the nun's side under her arm, and Gibbons was just about to say something, tell him to just keep her still and wait until a female officer got there, when a camera flash distracted him, a lot of camera flashes. A dozen Nikons were all pointed down at Tozzi feeling up the nun. "Tozzi!" he yelled. "Hold up!" But he didn't hear him.

The crowd surged like a tidal wave then, and Gibbons looked up at the ring. Walker was poised in the follow-through of a right cross, Epps reeling back into the ropes, head flung back, the side of his face smeared with blood. The challenger rebounded off the ropes, stumbled forward, and walked into a right-uppercut, left-hook combination. Epps's knees buckled and he fell straight down on them. Gibbons winced. Epps wavered there on his knees for a few seconds, the ref holding Walker back, Walker crazy to finish the man off, as if he hadn't already. Finally Epps fell over like a tree, bloody cheek and swollen eye pressed flat against the canvas. Poor bastard looked almost as bad as Tozzi.

The ref started to count. "One . . . two . . . three . . . four . . ."

Gibbons looked up at Sal. "Good fight."

". . . eight . . . nine . . . ten!"

Screams, cheers, total craziness.

Sal grunted. "Fuck." He shook his head, then looked over to that side section where he'd been looking before.

Gibbons followed his eyes and spotted an island of stillness in the agitated sea of fight fans. Sabatini Mistretta glaring down at them, glaring at Sal. He looked like a little pissed-off bulldog. Just like old J. Edgar. Gibbons smiled like a crocodile.

Sister Cil and Joseph were standing up now with their fingers linked over their heads. Tozzi looked like he was about to pass out, swaying on his feet, the automatic limp in his hand, his eyes going in and out of focus.

"Sit down, Tozzi. I can handle it from here."

Tozzi nodded and let him take the big automatic, then he fell into the nearest seat, cradling his face in his fingers. He looked awful. Camera flashes started exploding again and Gibbons turned his head away. Bastards. He stuck the automatic in his belt.

Up in the ring the ref was calling the winner, raising Walker's arm into the air.

Sal shook his head and smirked. "Shit . . ." He glared at Nashe who was still sitting there pulling on his lip and staring at his dead wife. "Son of a bitch."

Joseph was shaking. He was ready to shit his pants. "Sal, Sal, what do we do now, Sal? That was my gun, Sal. I mean, what's gonna happen now, Sal?"

"Shut your goddamn mouth, and don't talk to me." Sal was mean.

"Salvatore, shush." Sister Cil had her finger over her lips. "Don't you talk anymore, Sal. Listen to me for a change," she whispered. "Everything will be all right. Don't worry about Mr. You-Know-Who. I'm sure he'll understand about the money. *I'll* take the blame. Don't worry. I'll talk to him. He likes me."

Walker was prancing around the ring, waving the championship belt over his head. It was the first time Gibbons had ever seen the guy smile.

Sister Cil watched Walker for a moment, then she looked over at Sydney's lifeless body. The nun's contempt for the dead woman was all over her face. She shook her head, staring at Sydney. "You see, Sal. This is what happens. It's just the way Grandma always told us: *Gesù Cristo vede e provvede.* He sees and provides, Sal. He will provide for us, Sal. He will. I know it. Believe me."

Sal sneered at her. "Just shut the fuck up, will ya, Cil?"

Her mouth fell open. Camera flashes glinted off her glasses. Uniformed cops were pushing through the crowd, coming down the aisles with weapons drawn.

Gibbons smirked at the cavalry, annoyed. It's about time, he thought.

Tozzi was moaning into his hands.

Sal sniffed and grunted, like a hog on a chain.

Joseph was trying not to cry.

Nashe was pale, still pulling on his lip.

Sydney was dead.

The nun's mouth was still open when Gibbons looked at her again. She was crossing herself now, crossing herself over and over again.

Gibbons just shook his head. Amen.

• 24 •

The fancy brass clock on Brant Ivers's desk said it was nine-twenty. So where the hell was he? Special Agent in Charge is supposed to be Mr. Punctual. He said he wanted to see Gibbons first thing Monday morning, and Gibbons had been here at nine sharp. What the hell, Ivers have too many bran muffins for breakfast? Jesus. Gibbons crossed his legs and laid a hand on his ankle, looking around the SAC's office to see what else was new.

Next to the brass clock there were two picture frames. One displayed a formal sit-down portrait of the three Ivers boys, the other one had a picture of the lovely Mrs. Ivers. Gibbons reached over and turned it a little so he could see what she looked like. Ivers always kept it facing him, so Gibbons had never really gotten a good look at the wife. She might've been all right–looking at one time, but she was a real whipped poodle of a suburban matron now. Tired-looking, long-suffering, put-upon. Sort of a nothing blonde. Eyebrows sloping away, like she was always fretting about something. In a way, she kind of reminded him of the actress who played the wife on the old *Dick Van Dyke Show.* What the hell's her name?

Gibbons put the frame back where it had been and looked at the pictures on the wall instead, but he kept coming back to Mrs. Ivers. He was thinking about Lorraine, wondering whether she was heading down the same road as Mrs. Ivers. He suddenly remembered Tozzi's friend Valerie and her Dick Tracy hat. He thought about Lorraine wearing that hat. She'd look good in it, mysterious. He kept staring at Ivers's wife, thinking about the blond bartender in the gray fedora. Lorraine the way she was, Lorraine the way she will be? He let out a long sigh, wondering whether he'd end up with one of these pathetic pictures on his desk. Maybe they should forget about it. Can the wedding. Just live together, put things back the way they used to be.

The way they used to be . . . Fat chance. Last time he saw her, she swore she'd call it off if he walked out the door. When he'd finally gotten back to his place on Sunday, she was gone, no note, nothing. He must've called her place down near Princeton at least twenty times, but all he got was the answering machine. Guess he didn't have to worry about getting stuck with dopey wife pictures on his desk. Shit . . .

The door opened then. Gibbons looked over his shoulder, expecting Ivers. It was Tozzi.

"What in the hell are you supposed to be?" Gibbons said. "Spiderman?"

Tozzi shut the door. There was a metal brace over his nose, white tape crisscrossing his face to hold it in place. Two nice shiners, one still a little puffy. He went over and took the chair next to Gibbons, across from Ivers's desk. He looked like hell.

Tozzi nodded at the SAC's empty chair. "So where is he?"

Gibbons shrugged. "He's late. What're you doing here? I thought you were gonna stay home and rest."

"What the hell am I gonna do at home? Take painkillers and jerk off?" Tozzi's voice was low, subdued. It was hard to read his face with the bandages and the black eyes.

"Oh . . . I thought you were hurting."

Tozzi just shrugged and stared out the window.

They didn't say anything for a while. The phone rang and one of the buttons flashed on Ivers's console. It stopped in the middle of the second ring. The secretary must've picked up at her desk outside.

Gibbons turned in his seat to face Tozzi. "You hear from Valerie?"

Tozzi started nodding, still staring out the window, more like he was thinking than saying yes. "I saw her yesterday. At the hospital. I'm getting sick of hospitals."

"You talk to her?"

"Yeah."

"So how is she?"

"She's over the hump, she'll be okay."

"And?"

"And what?"

"And what about the two of you? She still mad?"

Tozzi nodded again. "Yeah . . . kind of."

"At least she's talking to you. That's something."

"Yeah . . ." Tozzi started feeling his face. "I think she was happy to see me like this. Like we were even now."

"Yeah, but at least she's talking to you."

Tozzi nodded, but he didn't seem to be listening. Maybe she'd told him to fuck off and he just didn't want to talk about it.

It got very quiet. You could just make out the faint sound of Ivers's secretary's printer zipping through a letter behind the door. Gibbons waited for Tozzi to say something. Must be the painkillers. He's never this quiet. "What'd they give you for the pain?"

"Percodan."

"Makes you dopey, huh?"

"I didn't take any this morning." Tozzi looked at him. "I drove in."

"Ah . . ." Gibbons pressed his lips together and nodded. Depressed. Valerie must have given him his walking papers. He doesn't want to talk about it. Poor bastard.

"So where the hell is he?" Tozzi said. "I figured Ivers'd have his guns loaded for me, ready to chew my ass out."

"For what?"

"Whattaya mean, for what? For screwing up the undercover." Tozzi's eyes were wet and shimmering under the discolored flesh. "Nine weeks with Nashe and I didn't get a thing. We just got lucky at the end, that's all. Which is just what he's gonna say. He's gonna take me off the street, you watch. Sure as shit."

"Not necessarily." Gibbons wanted to be hopeful even though he knew Tozzi was probably right.

The phone rang again. Only one ring this time.

"You know, Gib," Tozzi said. "I got my ass kicked three times in one day. I'm a special agent, I'm supposed to know how to take care of myself. I practice aikido two, three times a week. But what did it all do for me? I still got my ass kicked."

Bad-mouthing aikido, a bad sign. He must really be depressed. He used to think aikido was the be-all and end-all. "Listen, Toz, you had five of Nashe's bodyguards gang up on you the first time. The second time Walker's guys were holding your arms while the heavyweight champion of the world worked you over. And shit, with Immordino at the fight, you were hurt, you were punchy, for chrissake. What did you expect?"

"Yeah, but I've seen guys who know aikido take care of five attackers at the same time. Easy."

"Black belts, yeah. What're you? Only an orange belt. What's that? It takes years to really learn that martial-arts stuff so you can kick ass. You've got a long way to go, right?"

Tozzi just looked at him. "How do you know?"

"I know because, unbelievable as it may seem, I pay attention when you bore the shit out of me with your aikido stories." You're supposed to smile, Tozzi. I'm trying to make you feel better. Why don't you cooperate for once in your life?

The door opened then and Brant Ivers whisked into the room.

"Good morning," he said to the rug. He dropped his morning papers on the desk and sat down in the high-backed swivel chair. Court was in session.

"What're you doing here, Tozzi? You look terrible. Why aren't you home?" Lot of compassion. Asshole.

"It looks worse than it feels. I'm okay."

Ivers adjusted his suit jacket. Black pinstripe, two-tone gray rep tie. The man meant business today. He stared at Tozzi's face, assessing the damage, then shook his head gravely. One of his practiced gestures. "Well, if you say you're all right . . . Actually I'm glad you're here, Tozzi. I want to get a few things straight about the events in Atlantic City this weekend. Some matters of procedure." The SAC was wearing that tight-assed headmaster look of his, the I'll-hear-your-side-of-it-then-I'm-gonna-bust-your-balls-because-I've-already-made-up-my-mind look.

Gibbons decided to head the asshole off at the pass. "I think Tozzi did a hell of a job down there. That tape he got of Immordino threatening him and admitting to murder and all? There's no way he can peddle that mental-incompetency bullshit anymore. Only bad thing is that with all the previous charges Immordino's gonna have to face on top of all the new charges, he'll end up spending more time in court than in prison."

Ivers linked his fingers on the blotter. "Perhaps."

Keep going, don't stop. "I talked to a guy I know at the U.S. Attorney's office last night. Immordino's lawyers were scrambling all day yesterday. Damage control. They know there's nothing they can do about the old charges, but they're very eager to deal on the current stuff. Since Nashe is gonna face charges for attempting to fix the fight and illegal gambling, they've offered to let Sal testify against him in exchange for immunity from prosecution on the same charges."

Tozzi coughed up a sarcastic laugh. "What good will that do him? He could get life for killing Sydney."

"That's still up in the air," Headmaster Ivers said. "What *I* hear from the U.S. Attorney is that there's been some back-and-forth as to what the charge will be on Mrs. Nashe's death. At the very least Sal will face a manslaughter charge, but some of the boys over there feel they can kick it up to second-degree murder, based on Immordino's vengeful intentions against both Mr. and Mrs. Nashe when he pulled the trigger."

"And what about Sister Cil?" Tozzi asked.

Ivers made a steeple with his fingers and touched his upper lip with it. "Now that's a very interesting question. They can charge Sister Cil as an accessory, but if they do, they'll have a very hard time selling second-degree murder for Sal. They could charge them both with manslaughter, but my guess is that they'll go after Sal on murder two and leave her alone."

Gibbons frowned. "They're just being chickenshit about it because she's a nun. She hated Sydney as much as Sal did, and anyway, Sal was gunning for Russ, not the wife. The nun's guilty as sin, if you ask me. They ought to charge them both with murder two."

Ivers tilted his head back and looked at him through half-closed lids. William F. Buckley now. "We don't prosecute them, Bert. We just arrest them."

Gibbons bristled when he heard Ivers call him Bert. A real sarcastic prick today. "I also heard that Henry Gonsalves has offered to testify against Immordino."

"Oh, yeah? How's he doing?" Tozzi asked.

Gibbons shrugged and raised his eyebrows. "Supposedly he's made a lot of progress, but he's never gonna be the same again. He has a hard time remembering things."

"The perfect witness." The sarcastic headmaster again. Ivers paused and just stared at the two of them, the eyes half closed. Gibbons could hear the printer running on the other side of the door.

Gibbons looked up at the ceiling and exhaled loudly. All right. Come on, say it.

Ivers's chair creaked as he leaned back. "Why is it that I feel we've been here before, that we've gone over this territory many, many times in the past? You're both competent agents, you get results, but can you tell me why you always have to undercut your successes by continually disobeying direct orders, stubbornly insisting on doing things your way, and ignoring well-established procedure? There's a big knot in my stomach right now from all the negative feelings I have stored up against you two. I really want to yell at you two, really lace into you, chew your asses out royally. But what good does that ever do? You don't listen. You don't improve. Why should I waste my breath? Why should I even waste my time with you?" Ivers grit his teeth. *"Why the hell shouldn't I have you two fuck-ups dismissed right here and now? Hmmm?"*

"Hold it right there." Gibbons was gritting his teeth too, but he waited for the blinding flash of rage to pass before he spoke. "There's gonna be some big convictions as a result of the arrests we made down there. But let's put all this into perspective. This was not some slap-dash shakedown. Tozzi collected more than enough evidence to put Sal Immordino away. Now I admit that we've been known to misinterpret instructions—yes, even disregard direct orders—but we have never ignored procedure. Never. No one's rights were trampled on down there, and no one was abused during those arrests, despite the fact that it was a very difficult situation. Everyone was mirandized. We did it by the book."

Ivers didn't say a word. His face was red, his jaw set, as he unfolded the two newspapers on his desk and laid them out so Gibbons and Tozzi could read the headlines. The *Daily News* had a big picture of Sister Cil and Joseph Immordino lying flat on the floor, hands over their heads as Tozzi was handcuffing Joseph. The picture on the front page of the *Post* was juicier: Tozzi hunkered down over the nun with his hand under her armpit as he was frisking her.

One headline said FBI BUSTS NUN. The other was FBI TO NUN: SPREAD 'EM, SISTER!

Gibbons let out a long, slow breath.

Tozzi coughed into his fist. "This is very misleading."

"You couldn't have waited until a female police officer arrived? There were cameras all around you, for God's sake. Don't you have any sense, Tozzi? Look at this." Ivers pointed to the frisking picture. "You look like some kind of thug from a Salvadoran death squad."

"Wait a minute, wait a minute, wait a minute." The knot was in Gibbons's stomach now. "That woman was in possession of a deadly weapon. There were people all over the place, innocent citizens. Nun or not, she could've been packing another weapon. Don't tell me about procedure. Common sense tells you she had to be checked. Christ, she could've had a rocket launcher under that habit. No, I don't want to hear any more about this nun bullshit. Tozzi did the right thing." Gibbons's knot got tighter. He'd told Tozzi to lay off the nun. Stupid shit.

"Would you like to know why I was late getting in here this morning? I was late because I had breakfast with the cardinal. He was very upset, Gibbons. *Very* upset. He gave me a real earful, and I had to sit there and take it. Nothing I said could calm him down. He told me he was going to call the Director in Washington this morning. And the President."

"He can call the fucking Pope, for all I care. We nailed a top mobster, a fucking murderer, for chrissake. We also nailed a billionaire crook who's got God knows how many scams going. And in the process we managed to deplete the Mistretta family's war chest by about thirty mil. All by ourselves. How can you weigh all that against this trivial bullshit you're giving us here? Frisking a nun. This is bullshit!"

The phone rang again. Tozzi was rubbing his temples. "Hey, Gib, don't yell. My head."

Ivers sucked in his breath, pointed his finger at Gibbons,

and was about to start screaming when the intercom buzzed. Ivers stabbed the button. "What is it?"

The secretary's voice came out of the intercom. *"The Director on line two, sir."*

Ivers's face was like a fistful of raw meat. His eyes were a little crossed too. Gibbons had never actually seen that, except in a comic strip. "Get out, both of you." The headmaster was shouting.

"Shall we reschedule this?" Gibbons was trying not to grin, but he wasn't trying very hard.

"Just get out! Now!"

Gibbons looked at Tozzi. "Come on, let's go. The man's got work to do." They got up and went to the door. Gibbons looked back at Ivers with his hand over the mouthpiece of the phone, waiting for them to leave. "Give 'im my regards." He followed Tozzi out and shut the door behind him.

The printer was zipping away on the secretary's desk. She was making herself look busy, scribbling something on a yellow legal pad. Nice-looking girl, in her thirties. The nervous type, though. Look at her. Oh, me! Oh, my! The Director's on the phone! Calm down, honey. It's not your ass that's gonna get reamed. Gibbons smiled and waved to her as they went out the door into the hallway.

Tozzi was over at the water fountain, getting a drink. He was wincing a lot. Maybe it hurt for him to bend over like that. Poor bastard.

"Why don't you go home, Toz? Give yourself a break."

"Actually I was thinking of taking off to go to the hospital."

"You in pain? I'll take you."

"No, not for me. The hospital down the shore. To see Valerie."

"I thought she gave you your walking papers."

Tozzi shook his head. "I never said that."

"Oh . . ."

"Yeah, I thought I'd go down for visiting hours, ask her if

she'll come to the wedding with me. I think she'll be on her feet by then. It's June ninth, right?"

"What?"

"Your wedding, *stunade.* Did you forget?" Tozzi was grinning under his bandages.

"No. I didn't forget."

"You better not. I'll tell Lorraine you forgot. She'll hit you over the head with a frying pan."

Ha-ha-ha, a frying pan. Real funny. "I didn't forget. Why don't you just get the fuck outta here before you cause any more trouble?"

Tozzi started walking backward down the hall. "So is it the ninth or not?"

"Yeah, it's the ninth."

"That's what I thought." Tozzi waved. "See you tomorrow." He disappeared around the corner.

The ninth. Less than a month away. Gibbons looked down at his shoes, the black wingtips, the ones he'd bought for the wedding. Tozzi's inviting Valerie. Nice girl. A lot like Lorraine . . . in some ways. He kept looking at the shoes. No, not really. Only Lorraine's like Lorraine. He stuck his head in the water fountain built into the wall and took a drink. The water was icy cold.

He stood up, wiped his mouth with the back of his hand, looked down at his wingtips, then headed for the Organized Crime Unit's section where his cubicle was.

When he got to his desk, he picked up the phone and dialed her number again. It rang four times, and he knew from the static on the line that it was gonna be the goddamn machine again.

"I'm sorry, but I can't come to the phone right now. If you'll leave your name, number, and a short message after the beep, I'll get back to you as soon as I can."

Beeeep.

Gibbons bit his upper lip. His face was hot. The tape was hissing, waiting for a message. Shit.

"Hey, listen, Lorraine. If you think I'm gonna apologize and tell you how I feel about you on this goddamn ma-